Between
Men

Between Men

Original Fiction by Today's
Best Gay Writers

edited by
Richard Canning

CARROLL & GRAF PUBLISHERS
NEW YORK

BETWEEN MEN
Original Fiction by Today's Best Gay Writers

Carroll & Graf Publishers
An Imprint of Avalon Publishing Group, Inc.
245 West 17th Street, 11th Floor
New York, NY 10011

AVALON
publishing group incorporated

Contents

Introduction

First, a recap. I was nine, and not beginning to figure out my sexuality —I didn't *have* one—when, in 1977, Seymour Kleinberg's *The Other Persuasion* was published. The demographic was emerging; the literature was there: ergo—or now it seems—an anthology of gay fiction. Unlike most subsequent collections, *The Other Persuasion* mixed male and female contributors. Marcel Proust and Jane Rule improbably rubbed shoulders. In another corner, D. H. Lawrence was buttonholing Forster, who was avoiding Radclyffe Hall, who was being ridiculed by Gore Vidal. Gertrude Stein was explaining something about a rose to Christopher Isherwood, who keened away, looking over his shoulder—longingly?—at a disengaged Paul Bowles. Ernest Hemingway and Graham Greene surveyed the rest, fixed observers, adding occasional wisecracks. They overlooked a Young Turk inspecting his fingernails, Edmund White (the sole link between Kleinberg's volume and this book).

I didn't see *The Other Persuasion* for almost a decade, but even then, it was very confusing. Thankfully I didn't come across Jeffrey Meyers's wretchedly unsympathetic *Homosexuality and Literature, 1890–1930* (1977), just about all that passed for literary criticism on the topic then. By the time I went to college in 1986, Kleinberg's groundbreaking gay collection had been joined by a number of others—all American in origin, even if they came out in England. Most worthwhile were two books sourced from the magazine *Christopher Street*. The first was *Aphrodisiac*

(1984), improbably edited by nobody. It featured a number of fine writers still prolific today, including two contributors to *Between Men,* White and Andrew Holleran. Christopher Bram made his debut, too, providing the title story. The second, *First Love/Last Love* (1985), edited by Michael Denneny, Charles Ortleb, and Tom Steele (three editors from none?), introduced more excellent writing from stalwarts like Holleran and Felice Picano, alongside other important new voices like David Leavitt and Ethan Mordden and—poignantly—someone who had swum so far beyond the tide of literary fashion in the thirty years he'd already notched up in print, James Purdy. (Fifteen years on, I would be especially fortunate in having all three agree to an in-depth literary conversation for my first book, *Gay Fiction Speaks* [2000], with Holleran, Picano, White, and six more.)

In 1986, an awkward, jejune eighteen-year-old, I'd been "persuaded" by these "others," sexually speaking—though only, thus far, in theory. I was stunningly ignorant in . . . well, everything. My future tutors sent a reading list the summer before I "went up," which I presented to staff at the main library in my hometown, Birmingham, then a postindustrial mess tottering on governmental economic life support. Did the library staff know of a poet called Arnold? Was it something Arnold, or Arnold something? I didn't know. I remember looking up Tennyson in a set of stained index cards under *L* for Lord. Nothing. The staff traced a few Brownings, but didn't have copies. I avoided asking about Carlyle's *Sartor Resartus,* fearing it was in Latin.

I traipsed despairingly to the city bookshop, where a big, bright window display confronted me: two dozen copies of a single paperback. A cocky, lustrous teenager in a blue singlet gazed out leftward. The way it was arranged, he was staring at himself, mostly. And himself. And himself. Who wouldn't? Only the left-hand column of "hims" gazed through the pane and over my shoulder—at a mass of cheap concrete, discount stores, and rain.

He couldn't have looked less like I felt. I can't remember if I got hold of any prescribed reading that afternoon. But I definitely bought the boy—oh, and the novel that came with him, in what the jacket trumpeted was its "First British Publication." (This was innovative, since "paperback originals"—novels first appearing in softcover—did not then exist.) It was Edmund White's *A Boy's Own Story.*

The real-life tale of boy-and-jacket is worth reading in itself. (White recounts it in *Gay Fiction Speaks.*) But what it did to my *own* story, needless to say, is what has stuck, and it's largely why I am writing this. I would later learn that gay fiction—especially in America, seemingly light-years ahead of Britain at that time—had had numerous "birth years" already. For example, I'd entirely missed—like most ten-year-olds, it's true—the so-called Stonewall literature of liberation; in particular, its annus mirabilis, 1978, which saw key novels by White, Holleran, Picano, Larry Kramer, and Armistead Maupin.

The narration of *A Boy's Own Story* marked a semantic shift in gay characterization. It wasn't, however, because White avoided making him a freak. He *was* a freak—in spades! But he was his *own* freak somehow: unadjustably, irreconcilably, often winningly freakish—and, for the record, aware of how freakishness worked; of the uses you might one day put freakishness to, if it didn't crush you. Unlike too many of his fictional forebears, White's "boy" wasn't endlessly denying his sexuality or explaining it away. He worried at it, yet *practiced* it, too. He consulted family members, shrinks, and the like—but their inadequate responses to his importunateness led the boy to a decisive break with their example and instruction; catalyst for the journey undertaken in the book's sequel, *The Beautiful Room Is Empty* (1988). I was so desperate to read that novel immediately, as a cash-strapped undergraduate, that it remained, for many years, the only hardback on my shelf.

Gay fiction today, naturally enough, aspires to do more than offer still more variations on the theme of "coming out." White's later foreword to his *Faber Book of Gay Short Fiction* (1991), however, succinctly described how coming to terms with one's homosexuality will always inform how the gay individual—in fiction and life—reacts to everything else:

> Since no one is brought up to be gay, the moment he recognizes the difference, he must account for it. Such accounts are a kind of primitive gay fiction, the oral narrations told and retold as pillow talk or in pubs or on the psychoanalytic couch. Every gay man has polished his story through repetition, and much gay fiction is a version of this first tale. . . . Acknowledging homosexual desires and integrating them into a larger notion of the self is the first bold action of gay fiction, whether written or whispered.

However much society has changed—particularly in the arena of sexual ethics—this cogent summary strikes me as enduringly true.

White's name led me to *The Other Persuasion* and the *Christopher Street* books; these to Holleran's *Dancer from the Dance* (1978), another obvious staging post; the defining gay novel of its decade, and the finest. I won't adumbrate its many virtues here; you'll probably know them. Still, as I'm reviewing here the trajectory of gay fiction anthologies, I should point out that Holleran's novel gave rise, inadvertently, to a sort of "watershed moment" in their history, some sixteen years after its publication.

David Leavitt's introduction to *The Penguin Book of Gay Short Stories* (1994; the volume was coedited by Mark Mitchell) took *Dancer from the Dance* to task for a number of things, among them a perceived "voyeuristic fixation with beauty that powers the novel." Leavitt felt this fixation "compels younger gay men who don't know better to wonder if that's all there is to the business of being gay." In consequence, "*Dancer from the Dance* romanticized—even exalted—what is to many of us the dreariest aspect of gay experience."

I've never found beauty—or the search for it—dreary; but so much comes down to taste. Yet Leavitt's argument is more complex than this quotation suggests. (He returns to it in the interview in *Gay Fiction Speaks*.) In any case—and not since I'm on decent terms with both authors—there's a more interesting way of responding to this claim than simple opposition. What struck me as odd was Leavitt appearing to criticize Holleran for failing to take account of *Dancer*'s effect on an ignorant reader. This might not necessarily be the young Leavitt himself, though he does discuss it at length precisely because it was the second gay novel he discovered. (A footnote added to a second edition of Leavitt/Mitchell's book in 2003 notes that "[t]oday, *Dancer from the Dance* is no longer the first gay book most young American gay men read; nor can any one book be said to play that role.")

Yet the very profileration of gay novels around and after *Dancer*, which Leavitt generally applauds—including a contrasting account of the sexual subculture, Kramer's *Faggots*—surely answers the complaint. The breadth and diversity of the lives being written up in gay fiction—and all gay literature—lessened the power any single rendering of gay life might acquire. For countless years, gay male readers had twisted their sense of sexual selfhood by way of the distorting prisms of Baron de Charlus, Querelle, or—much later!—Maurice.

White gives a neat variation on this dark notion in the *Faber* foreword, describing his oscillations as a teenage reader "between grim psychiatric case studies and the outrageous Anthony Blanche scenes in Evelyn Waugh's *Brideshead Revisited*." From 1978 on, the number of characterizations exploded ad infinitum—if not always for the better, then always toward diversity.

Leavitt may have regretted the "damage" done by *Dancer*. But he accidentally caught one of its key innovations, the reason why it remains so much more pertinent than most seventies gay fiction today. As he concedes, *Dancer* introduced characters no longer bound by the crippling "double life" of the closet. Yet the consequent temptation to advertise a gay, urban Shangri-la—certainly indulged in by some—is entirely resisted. *Dancer* is a nuanced, ambivalent study of its zeitgeist, with a near-exhausted "wait-and-see" quality attending the letters that frame the novel's exhaustive inventory of the subculture. Its pendant—to borrow a term from art—is thus Edmund White's nonfictional *States of Desire,* from a year before. Leavitt pinpoints the fact that Holleran fights shy of conveying any sense of liberation, since the very people who had left the closet "were made to suffer much more by each other than by heterosexual agents of oppression." Awkward and unpalatable as that fictional verdict may feel, it had—and has—the ring of truth. The new freedoms may have seemed ideal, but Holleran did not confuse this with idealizing the protagonists who were experiencing them.

The other "watershed moment" here is my sense that Leavitt's own work also answered the very objections he raises. His early fiction especially—*Family Dancing* (1984) and *The Lost Language of Cranes* (1986)—contributed strongly to the reimagining of what gay fiction could be about. Harold Bloom and George Steiner have both long promoted the idea that literature "answers" literature; that creative writers do, and should, react to their forebears. There may be—to adopt Bloom's term—anxiety in this influence, but it is a creative and vital anxiety. Still, in then arguing that "contrary to gay opinion, most gay men *do* want more from their lives than a few decades spent panting after unattainable perfection; indeed most want relationships based on spiritual as well as physical attraction, which grow more solid as the years go on," Leavitt's introduction risked providing yet another prescription for gay fiction. Auden memorably wrote in his poem on Yeats: "Poetry makes nothing happen." I find myself longing for someone to make the same high claim for fiction.

Nevertheless it's correct that, as White put it in the *Faber* volume, "If gays tell each other—or the hostile world around them—the stories of their lives, they're not just reporting the past but also shaping the future, forging an identity as much as revealing it." That's never to suggest that gay fiction could provide readers with an imprimatur, a code of conduct. Most of the protagonists in *Between Men*, I'm thrilled to say, behave badly, argue unconvincingly, backtrack constantly, misdescribe, misappropriate, and misbehave. They have little enough in common even in their own stories, and could not fall out of one author's vision into that of another. As Diana puts it in Patrick Ryan's "Pretend I'm Here": "There's no end to the sickness and depravity of the human spirit. . . . Maybe that's the good news." Or, to quote Daddy in Ethan Mordden's "The Ballad of Jimmy Pie:" "Tempt me, Satan, you win again!" (Bloom fans will appreciate the Miltonic reference.)

Leavitt and Mitchell's Penguin anthology—strongly and scrupulously edited—arrived at, or just after, the moment when the idea of *one* "gay fiction" became insupportable. It was either shattering or containing multitudes or both, depending on one's view. The book entered a much more crowded marketplace, vying for your attention alongside the *Men on Men* series (of which, more soon), Ethan Mordden's excellent gay anthology *Waves* (Vintage, 1994), and White's *Faber* collection of 1991, in which both Holleran and Leavitt rightly found a place.

The rest is history, usefully defined by one of Alan Bennett's "History Boys" as "one fucking thing after another." The 1980s and early '90s saw a number of extraordinary bifurcations in gay culture. On one hand, as the History Boy announced, the consolidation of gay lifestyle/spending power propelled more and more of . . . everything, if increasingly in niche markets; women and men would rarely share a stage. For a while, there was "one fucking [book] after another." At the same time, "crossover" works on gay themes—novels, plays, films with broad appeal—were notably rare. Often, whatever their virtues, such stories self-consciously acted as primers to gay lives and thoughts, turning us back into homogeneity just as most of our literature was freeing us from the same. Reader, beware the "universal"; it's *very* particular.

For a moment (almost), any gay man could publish a novel. It's bad form to loiter on the talentless, so I'll not name books that meant nothing to me, didn't convince, or clunked along without the benefit of drama, character, purpose—or proofreading. There were many—perhaps for you, too? A legacy of this tranche, and the admittedly ongoing trickle of inferior work, is that anyone researching gay fiction will be asked weekly: "But there aren't really any *good* books, are there?"

My "coming out" year, 1986, saw the launch of George Stambolian's essential gay fiction series, *Men on Men,* from Plume (later so ably stewarded by David Bergman). Stambolian steered a bright course, paying due attention to the established voices, which largely stemmed from the East Coast. (Maupin's *Tales of the City* was, naturally, far from the only gay fiction emerging from the West, but it was, in the late '70s and early '80s, just about the only material penetrating nationally.) In the first *Men on Men* volume, however, Stambolian broadened our understanding of American gay fiction decisively. Almost half the contributors hailed from the West Coast. Of these, three—Dennis Cooper, Robert Glück, and Kevin Killian—remain among the most innovative and imaginative gay authors two decades on.

Something still more decisive was happening of its own accord. If the spread of the gay literary diaspora in *Men on Men* was conspicuous, the number of contributors dead by the time it went to press was remarkable: Sam D'Allesandro, Robert Ferro, Michael Grumley, Richard Umans. Bruce Boone, John Fox, Richard Hall, and Stambolian himself followed. AIDS claimed the lives of eight of the nineteen contributors to the first *Men on Men.*

After the "rare cancer's" first appearance in the summer of 1981, gay writers were somewhat slow in tracking it in creative work. By 1986, the number of novels, films, and plays concerned with AIDS was still only a handful. The deluge would come. In 1991, Edmund White—in the *Faber* foreword—could write that "[t]he enormous body of fiction that has sprung up . . . about AIDS in the last few years reveals that literature is still the gay community's strongest response to crisis." In the early to mid-'80s, however, most people had other things to do. There was your own health, certainly—but also your lover's, friends', peer group's. There was worry, prejudice to counter, care to fight for: new circumstances to adjust to. The earth gave way. Holleran's collected AIDS journalism was called *Ground Zero*.

Nowadays, it may be tempting to consider that the arrival of the HIV/AIDS epidemic, and early literary responses to it, have become historical. AIDS-related fiction might likewise seem just one of many "waves" of gay self-expression which followed Stonewall. (Ethan Mordden's gay fiction anthology was entitled *Waves*.) There are apparently useful chronological and cultural lines of demarcation. Drug treatments have offered many in the West—though far from all—an extended, often near-normal experience of life. For some, it's a happy tale, if subject, like so much else, to the "for now" formulation. But it isn't, and cannot be, the only story. Gay men now, more than ever, have our ghosts to remember as people, and to reanimate as writers.

Holleran's latest novel, *Grief* (2006), pulls few punches in grounding us in the foundations of contemporary gay life. Its narrator moves between the Scylla of the temptation to forget his burdensome "lost" and the Charybdis of the all-too-human, only intermittently silence-able desires of his animate, sentient body. This oscillation is brilliantly summed up in two scenes. In one, the narrator tells his friend Frank that you should never get over grief: "It's the only thing left of that person. Your love for, your missing, them." Just as the reader may suspect Holleran of idealization, his narrator adds the critical, credible note of self-interest: "And as long as you have that, you're not alone— you have them."

In the second scene, he accompanies his landlord to an improbably cruisey Quaker meeting. The landlord articulates just the sort of simplified, truncated "AIDS survivor" story that the zeitgeist demands— and which Holleran here deftly ironizes:

"That one's so hot," my landlord whispered as he nodded at a man two pews away from us. "His lover died two years ago and left him a lot of money, which he spent on travel and drugs. Then he got sick, and looked really awful, but the cocktail brought him back, and now he's gorgeous again!"

In *Between Men*, John Weir's "Neorealism at the Infiniplex" reminds us that, in ever speedier circumstances, the AIDS dead are especially subject to the same simplifying and truncating handling. A rabbi instructs the narrator moments before the memorial service: "Quick, tell me about your friend. Say what he was like. Say three things. I don't need more than three. Add some color, make it personal, and make it fast." The less said, the better.

Holleran's *Grief* and Weir's equally extraordinary *What I Did Wrong* both contribute to a recent resurgence in AIDS fiction, after a hiatus— precipitated perhaps by uncertainty as to how to accommodate the new "treatment" culture in narrative. Still, British writer Adam Mars-Jones had argued back in 1992's introduction to *Monopolies of Loss* that the short story form afforded possibilities for writing about AIDS which were unique. That claim is borne out in a number of memorable pieces here. Mack Friedman's "A Joint and a Nice Piece of Ass" has all the virtues of his novel *Setting the Lawn on Fire* (2005) in miniature. Knowing, opinionated, poignant, and vulnerable by turns, Friedman's narrator—a health advisor—tells us of

the boys, always the boys, drinking and smoking and losing their teeth to crystal, wearing insouciance like cologne. "Cool, I'm not positive yet," they'd say. Or, "Oh well, guess I should see a doctor now?" I cried for them

> when they left because they could not cry for themselves,
> and the girl who was raped returned for results and gave
> me a trembling, feathery hug.

His summary of the Central Region AIDS Project dinners—"parodies of function, marked as they were by inedible catering, incoherent speakers, and the absurd resurfacing of volunteers who hadn't done anything for the place in years"—is devastating; angry as well as sad; then, unexpectedly, funny, too (if darkly so):

> This annual commingling always made me think of parties
> thrown by high-ranking Nazis to honor the rank and file,
> but maybe I'd just talked to one too many menopausal
> "buddies" who loved their collies, hated their husbands,
> and aspired to appear philanthropic with their time.

Weir's comparable black humor returns us to 1994 and the demise of his friend, novelist David Feinberg. His prose typically concentrates a bewildering series of experiences that only begin at the surreal experience of his friend's body melting as they wait for a last-minute rabbi: "I said, 'Dead guy on ice,' which sounds like a hard-core band." The surreal gives way to the absurd, the unpalatable, and, finally, the incredible. Kurt Vonnegut chorused "So it goes" every time the narrative of his *Slaughterhouse-five* stumbled upon death. Weir offers a comparably self-aware tiredness: "I'm through with stuff that really happens, like, people die and you don't. Or, they die and you don't feel bad in the way that you want." The image of his narrator "avoiding them [Feinberg's parents], crouched under coat hooks" crying is among the most moving, and truest, here.

AIDS is an important presence in other pieces, such as Dale Peck's "The Piers," Vestal McIntyre's "A Good Squeeze," and Robert Glück's "Bisexual Pussy Boy." It permeates, too, the opening and closing stories, by Andrew Holleran and Edmund White, respectively. Alan Hollinghurst's *The Swimming-Pool Library* (1988) was set in the summer of 1983, "the last summer of its kind there was ever to be." Britain's AIDS-related angst began then; America's began two years earlier; hence the poignant sense of decay around Holleran's San Martin idyll. "Hello, Young Lovers," set in "the winter of 1981," says nothing overt about the epidemic. But in focusing on the moment before it, Holleran conjures up a remarkable foreshadowing: "This was a place people came to collapse," his narrator notes. There's the funereal stage manager, who feels "people . . . look at you and see only one thing—old age and death!" There's Dennis, ready to dispatch his lover with this line: "I mean one is simply aware that there are magic moments in life that do not last—if you get my drift." Knowing what we do, it is just as shocking to read some lines of euphoria here, too, like Dennis's "He has a body that would *sink ships* . . . I'd *kill* for his stomach. And chest. And shoulders." It's still more startling to recognize this as gay argot *now,* as then.

"Hello, Young Lovers," like a gentleman caller, pays attention—no more—to the stories of Tennessee Williams, with more than a nod, too, to the torrid, unfocused play *Suddenly Last Summer.* It not only transcends but outshines such sources. (As a Brit, incidentally, I have a lot of affection for Kent and his winning, toxic volatility: "Let's get stinko! Let's get something started! It's all too dull!")

White's "The Painted Boy" features some of his finest prose. Fortunately for us, the author himself will never hear what his narrator, Stephen Crane, is told by his friend Garland: "These are the best pages you've ever written and if you don't tear them up, every last word, you'll never have a career." It would be easy, and too little, to state that many stories in *Between Men*, including "The Painted Boy," transcend gay themes. I was more struck by the fact that so many of the eighteen pieces offer accounts of gay life somehow "authored" by those outside it. White, typically, trailblazes, with the account of the heterosexual Crane's affection for Elliott, a "queer little boy tart" with syphilis:

> Standing in the doorway was a slight youth with a thin face and dark violet eyes set close together and nearly crossed. He couldn't have been more than fifteen but he already had circles under his eyes. He smiled and revealed small, bad teeth, each sculpted by decay into something individual. He stepped towards us and naturally we thought he was begging but then I saw his face was painted——carmined lips and kohled eyes (the dark circles I'd noticed were just mascara smudged by the snow).

The boundaries of his feeling for Elliott are yet unclear to Crane, and he looks to his friend, the "womanizer" critic James Huneker, to figure them out, since "Huneker also had a quasiscientific interest in inversion. Usually he'd scorn it. He condemned *Leaves of Grass* as the 'Bible of the third sex.'"

White's brilliant description of fin de siècle New York illustrates how much more there must be to human relations, empathy, and identification than sexuality. But it is, startlingly, in their mortality that Crane and the youth find one another:

> I had to convince him that he needed to take care or he'd be dead by thirty. Though that threat frightened him no

more than it did me. I expected to be dead by thirty or thirty-two—maybe that was why I was so fearless in battle.

Beyond this, Crane the storyteller recognizes in his counterpart an ideal subject for fiction—something just as rare for the novelist, perhaps, as spotting one's life partner should be for a gay man: "He counted for something and his story as well. I sensed that he'd guessed his young life might make a good story but he hadn't told it yet."

Sometimes anthologies like this are criticized for what they lack. The question of "representativeness" haunted Stambolian in 1986; it's surprising if we haven't got over it. As James McCourt's scribe S. D. J. phrases it in "Thermopylae": "Many things said to have happened never did." Stambolian noted how the book tours of early success stories in gay fiction publishing brought criticism alongside the adrenaline rush of new opportunity: "Writers were attacked for supposedly favoring one lifestyle over another or for offering images of gay life that were not representative of the majority of gay men and women." He countered this by saluting the "growing pluralism of gay literature," according to which "no one can view any single work as representing the entire gay world."

Stambolian was reacting to the emerging boom time I've already described. *Between Men* enters the game at a different juncture. The mid- to late '90s saw the tightening of corporate budgets in bigger publishing houses. Niche fiction, including gay fiction, with its reliable but unremarkable sales base, stopped being in vogue. Especially unmarketable were novels that had too much of gay men's beyond-the-rainbow realities: illness, death, loss. As T. S. Eliot wrote, "Humankind cannot stand very much reality." Many of the best gay writers found themselves removed from high-profile lists, even as they wrote the best books of their lives.

Still, "reality is something you rise above," said Liza Minnelli, and she *knows*. The present for gay fiction publishing arguably isn't all bleak, despite jeremiads. A few years ago, Karl Woelz wrote an epitaph for gay literary fiction in the afterword to *M2M: New Literary Fiction* (2003). Given the apparently steep demise in gay men and women's consumption of serious fiction, in five years, Woelz wrote, "there's a real chance that reading literary fiction may no longer be an option." This means that, by now, there's simply no audience for *Between Men*. With respect, dear reader, you do not exist.

The sentiment was understandable. Woelz had the demise of *Men on Men*, Little, Brown's *Best American Gay Fiction*, and Faber & Faber's *His* series to lament, and added: "Nor are gay publishers rushing in to fill the void." Meantime, however, many intrepid smaller presses—not exclusively gay by any means—have entered the breach; Serpent's Tail, I suppose, being the pioneer. (Any list that houses Juan Goytisolo deserves mention.) Soft Skull, Suspect Thoughts, Clear Cut, Terrace Books (from the University of Wisconsin Press), and Carroll & Graf: from these five lists, you could conjure up a roster of exceptional talent, and reading lists to endure. Most material submitted for *Between Men* came from authors published by smaller houses, and all but five or so of the eighteen featured are in the same camp. It may make living a struggle—hand-to-mouth—for gay writers, but being published and read by engaged editors and readers is feasible. There *is* a gay literary community.

❖ ❖ ❖

Without straying too far in the direction of "representativeness," I found it interesting to consider plausible objections to *Between Men*. Is it, for instance, too urban? It's a long-standing concern, to which perhaps the only fair (and ludicrous) retort is: "Are gay lives too urban?" Consider asking: "Is my life too urban?" or, "Is my life not urban enough?" and the idea deconstructs. There's a jokey reference to the worry in John Weir's narrator's flight from New York for a rural idyll. He soon realizes:

> I hate back roads and country lanes. How had I forgotten that? I hate views. I especially dislike chicken coops. Mine still smelled faintly of chickens. When I looked up from my work, through my kitchen window, I could see an open field, trees in the distance, and the sky everywhere. Not the reassuringly man-made chemical sky of lower Manhattan, but an intimidating sky so awesome and inhuman that, in order to explain it, you were forced to invent God.

In 1986, Stambolian had pointed to the confluence between the urban and gay men's growing self-awareness. He quoted Richard Sennett: "The city gives you the chance to make yourself up." It remains true for many gay men today. Still, there's nothing metropolitan in the stories by Holleran, Ethan Mordden, Tennessee Jones, and Bruce Benderson, and the city isn't integral to that many others. After all the excitement concerning the film *Brokeback Mountain*'s daring representation of desire between apparently straight men, far from the polysexual metropolis, Mordden's "The Ballad of Jimmy Pie" and Jones's

"Pennsylvania Story" in particular remind us that the film's transgressiveness originated in the E. Annie Proulx story it was based on. Moreover, fiction as good as "Pennsylvania Story" tells us much more about the threat, as well as the promise, in unreckoned longing than anything showing at the multiplex:

> Dale wanted so much to turn around, brace his hands on the coal-covered tire, feel Kenneth's hands covered with black dust and carrion wind rake down his jeans, his cheek bruised or flayed open by one of the bolts in the wheel. Instead, Kenneth pulled him forward and split his upper lip open with the force of his kiss. A moment of sacredness in a devastated place, a moment that could make you free or get you killed.

Another objection: there's a lot of youth in *Between Men*. I'm not surprised. Adolescence *is* where we situate many of our thoughts, worries, and hopes about sex, romance, and relationships. Postadolescent youth marks, moreover—and, yes, as a generalization—the period where gay men most fully realize themselves sexually ("Hello, Young Lovers" indeed). It's not exclusively true, but it *is* true—and it's as true of our heterosexual peers. Still, stories here by Benderson, Glück, Holleran, David McConnell, Mordden, Ryan, and White are as concerned with the wide range of responses to youth on the part of the—chronologically, anyhow—mature. In several cases—notably McConnell's masterly "Rivals"—part of the reader's pleasure lies in a reversal of expectations. Nobody's development could be more arrested than that of Barry and Darius's teacher, Jane. "Adulthood looks unbearably beautiful and energetic and free" to the boys, writes McConnell—but such visions of the future, we readers sense (or know), are chimerical. Alan Bennett—again speaking of his *History Boys*—"wanted to show that the boys know more than any of the teachers." McConnell's arresting miniature—as idiosyncratic as his debut, *The Firebrat* (2003)—does likewise. As in Bennett's play, McConnell's drama contains judgment everywhere, yet nowhere. It's up to the reader.

Robert Glück's narrator finds himself flattened by the circumscribed erotics demanded of his encounter with Bill, the young "Bisexual Pussy Boy": "It was just Age watching Youth, that's what it took to transform his straight ass into a sexual organ." Glück's stories and novels have long pressed the erotic into unexpected philosophical service. (Conversely, his narrator's mental processes have an orgasmic reach.) "Bisexual Pussy Boy" characteristically dares to ask: "What can be said about sex when one is old? Since each experience could be the last? It's hard not to feel sex as some mistake." Now, from youth to (non)senescence: Benderson's "Mouth of the River" offers us Delilah/Aamu, who, at 102, may be the oldest character ever to appear in gay fiction, depending upon whether you count Ronald Firbank's novel of 1919, *Valmouth,* in which most protagonists are proudly centenarian.

If *Between Men* runs the gamut of age, and traverses the United States geographically—Florida, California, the Midwest, as well as, inevitably, the urban East Coast—it also crosses national borders.

Vestal McIntyre's Rand finds his break in Montreal interrupted by Jean's insistence that American gays are, in culturally assimilating, entirely on the wrong track: "The destiny of gays is pointlessness, just as the destiny of straights is ugliness. Don't try to jump the track. It is better to be pointless and laugh." It's an arresting and cautionary moment.

Paul Russell's 1994 novel *Sea of Tranquillity* remains the only gay fiction to take readers—literally—to the moon (outside of science fiction). Still, London resident Shaun Levin's "The Big Fry-Up at the Crazy Horse Café" effortlessly spans several continents, as well as sweetly, casually, introducing his narrator's son and extended family in a manner to provoke conservatives anywhere: "Three gods it took to create our Francis. God the wanker. God the go-between. And God the girl on her back with her legs in the air." If that doesn't disturb you, try the hand job Levin's narrator gives boyfriend Mark on a flight to San Francisco. It's an original use of toast.

Levin's story closes by celebrating the "beauty of the ordinary," concentrated and perceptible when one stops moving on and on. What I most treasured was his ordering, not making-ordinary, of the mess of everyday life ("It's always messy," says friend Anne-Marie in Tel Aviv). Levin's narrator betrays his emotional investment in this ordering of the past through moments of lyrical conciseness; in a reference to "the man who broke the heart my boyfriend had to fix," or in this heart-stopping paragraph:

Jam

A moment of infidelity: Alex is a big blond giant with a thick coat of marmalade-colored fuzz on his chest.

❖ ❖ ❖

"The Big Fry-Up at the Crazy Horse Café," like nearly all the stories gathered in *Between Men,* reminds us how central women are to gay men's lives. Michael Lowenthal's "Marge"—narrated by a heterosexual, if confused, teenager—addresses his initiation into what women are, and thus what men are, too, by way of a number of freakish role models. Two are preeminent: his mother, a whore, and their transvestite neighbor, Marge, whom Lowenthal ingeniously places as beyond the "redemption" apparently offered by the growing gay rights movement:

> In some other neighborhood, or some other city, people like Marge marched and waved flags. They'd have hated him more than they hated the guys who beat him. Every time that Marge smiled at a fist, he set them back. The last thing Marge wanted was toleration.

Female—or female-identifying—characters are pivotal in most of these tales, but none more so than McConnell's "Rivals," which poses fascinating questions about what a "gay story" could be. Its erotic element is largely heterosexual, and the focus of its drama involves teacher Jane, inclusively or exclusively. It's a fascinating and original study in destabilized narration. When McConnell's narrator slyly notes that Barry's "penis was centered now," we deduce that nothing and no one else is "centered" at all. If the omnipresence of sexual desire to gay male characters in fiction has long been a cause of complaint for some readers, "Rivals" proffers a surprising antidote. It is Jane who struggles to control her longings—"sex was rare between them. Jane made sure"—whereas her chosen Lothario, Barry, not merely "could have lived with sex or without it," as the narrator understates it; he physically isn't up to it.

There are thrilling narrative moves in the stories of several of the less-known contributors to *Between Men*—Friedman, Jones, Koestenbaum, Lowenthal, McCartney, McIntyre, Ryan. The scene in "Rivals" where Jane discovers Barry's inadequacy probably trumps them all—for shock value, anyway. McConnell also inverts a staple of gay fiction and gay lives in the past, whereby romantic attachments are glossed as "friendships." Here, it is Jane who desperately and inadequately resorts to the term; Darius, by contrast (perhaps), offers Barry something more, or better.

Inversion, mockery, humor, and playfulness are hallmarks throughout *Between Men,* even if the real story remains serious. Disorientation has a key role in many stories. When Patrick Ryan's hapless Frankie Kerrigan—familiar to readers of Ryan's superb debut, *Send Me* (2006)—finds his astronautic adventure orbiting fast out of control, his sister Karen choruses: "Did this happen on planet Earth?" Alistair McCartney's "Crayons" is a ridiculous spoof detective story—or is it?—which takes us to a version of Paris during the Occupation. It refuses to adopt any conventions of fictional verisimilitude, however, and threatens to break out into your wider world, reader, as nothing more, or less, than phantasmagoria. McCartney's "Crayons" draw on himself, and then on you:

> I can't register under my own name so I register under the
> name Alistair McCartney. It's a preposterous name I know,

obviously false, but it's the first one that enters my head. The proprietor, who has a pencil mustache (Nazi), clearly despises me.

Wayne Koestenbaum's "Diary of a Quack" introduces a narrator equally in need of a reader(ship). Nothing could be more disconcerting than this opening:

My Name Is Siegfried Kracauer

Everything I do is legal. My accountability rating is high.

Anyone familiar with the crystalline beauty of Koestenbaum's novel *Moira Orfei in Aigues-Mortes* and its vertiginous narrator, Theo Mangrove, might initially feel better equipped to assess the quack/nonquack Kracauer. But our pleasure lies in being led deeper into Kracauer's absurd uncertainties, not out of them. (Aptly, one critic invoked Nabokov's *Pale Fire* in respect of Koestenbaum's novel.) Surrender your preconceptions; accept that your intuition here—as with *Moira Orfei in Aigues-Mortes*—is helpfully dry-docked.

In his introduction to *Fresh Men 2* (2005), Andrew Holleran wrote that in several of the stories featured, "being gay seems no longer to be an urgent matter; we now have the freedom to be bored." Boredom is a legitimate subject for fiction, though boring a reader remains to me taboo—and isn't what Holleran meant. Though it comes from this publishing house, I must pay tribute to the *Fresh Men* series. If, as many have noted, gay fiction is in a dire market position, then launching a volume of writings by unknowns takes special courage—or foolhardiness. I first became aware of the work of three contributors to *Between Men*—McCartney, McIntyre, and Ryan—through the two *Fresh Men* books, but great fiction has emerged from many more.

There's a lot more I could write. Nobody renders location like Benderson or Peck; nobody conveys the insiderness of our nonce gay languages better than McCourt or Mordden; nobody upsets sexual power relations as comprehensively as Glück or Killian. But it's time to trust you, reader; you *know* this. *Between Men* has been my dream job. Editing is work, but thrilling work. It's not quite like Charlie's situation in Kevin Killian's exhilarating feat of narrative control, "Greensleeves"— "'Continue!' became his favorite word, as Piers typed out story after story, like Scheherazade"—though that's undoubtedly a beguiling image. I leave you to savor what I was so lucky to be sent: eighteen outstanding pieces of fiction by the finest gay writers today. My thanks to each for their patient collaboration in the preparation of *Between Men*.

I'd like to record a few personal thanks: to those who have put me up—and put up with me—in the States; to Don Weise, a superlative editor; to Patrick Merla, a vital presence in and behind so much gay fiction; and to long-standing and long-suffering friends: Max and Mark; Marc and Richard; Billy, David, and Nigel; and especially to a great writer and outstanding friend, who read *Between Men* in manuscript and told me—as ever—everything that I actually think, Rob Beeston.

—Richard Canning, London, December 2006

Hello, Young Lovers

Andrew Holleran

There were several ways, the winter of 1981, to get from New York to the Hotel San Martin. The easiest was to take a night flight to San Juan and wait for a flight the next morning to the other, much smaller, island on which the hotel was located. People who didn't want to hang around the airport sometimes took a taxi into Old San Juan to wander around the streets looking at courtyards and churches till the sun came up. Others stayed in the airport and tried to sleep in those plastic chairs. Which one they chose often depended on their condition— since many people were sick when they left New York in January. Life in Manhattan seems to climax at New Year's in a way that leaves you run-down afterward, so that you almost always have the flu, or at least a bad cold. Coughing, sneezing, hacking, wheezing, guests would straggle up the drive to the Hotel San Martin as if they were checking into the hospital. Sometimes the only way you can ditch a cold is to just get out of town.

The Hotel San Martin was a perfect place to recuperate because there was nothing to do there—no activities, or nightlife. It was best to go with a friend who liked to read, or a couple who wanted to concentrate on each other. Dennis and Kent had been together only a few months the year I went down with them. They had met at a posh party they were both bartending. Dennis was an actor from San Francisco who had just decided to quit the theater, Kent was an Oxford graduate who'd come to New York fifteen years ago to take a year off and never left; and this was their honeymoon. In fact, I was asked along as their photographer. My assignment was very specific. "What I *don't* want," Dennis said, "is an artsy close-up of *tiles*—you know, the travel magazine thing. No shadows on the louvered doors! Nothing stark! I want a *postcard* picture, the most obvious, *clichéd* view you can find—except there has to be someone in it. Me! I want spectacular views with me and my darling in the foreground. No lizards on a balustrade, no tiles! Just the honeymoon couple with a drop-dead view! I like to see where the people are. I have never understood how a picture of a tile shows you what an island looks like. I mean, what on earth is the point of a picture of a tile when you want to see the place?"

"The point is, my darling," said Kent, "the tile is a synecdoche."

"And what is a synecdoche?"

"A synecdoche is a part that stands for the whole. The tile stands in for the entire island—it supplies a detail that lets you imagine the rest."

"But I don't want to imagine. I want to just lie in the sun. Oh, darling," said Dennis, holding his arms out. "You're not just English. You're not just Oxford. You're the Oxford English Dictionary!"

He was; or something close. Kent seemed glad, in fact, when I told him the island we were going to was an extremely quiet place: he said that was just what he wanted. He had packed a long biography of Queen Mary by James Pope-Hennessy. He liked the fact that Old San Juan was empty when we took a cab there rather around 3:00 A.M. Then, while standing outside a church, we looked up to see four men coming down the cobblestones in white pants, Hawaiian shirts, and gold jewelry, who were obviously barhopping. Dennis stared. "That's *just* what we want to avoid," Dennis said as the quartet walked toward us. The minute they left, for a bar in the Condado, we decided to hail a cab, too, and not wait till morning for the flight. Instead we took a taxi to the *publico* to Fajardo, a few hours' drive from San Juan, to get the boat.

The *publico* to Fajardo was an old Volkswagen van filled with American sailors who were all drunk, and all talking about the women they'd just had in San Juan, including the one who was still on the fingers the sailor beside Dennis held to his nose the entire journey. "Oh, darling," Dennis hissed in my ear. "I'll never have sex again." The minute we reached the island, however, the sailors disappeared in every available taxi to the American base that still occupied almost half the island in 1981, and we began to walk to the hotel in the brightening dawn. The only creatures up were the roosters: that sound that lets you know immediately you're in the Caribbean. "Is that a synecdoche?" said Dennis. "Does the rooster stand for the entire island?" "Yes, yes," said Kent happily. Even for the Caribbean, this island was particularly rural. This island's claim to fame was a movie that had been made here ten years before about a group of English schoolboys who revert to savages after they are shipwrecked. Walking to the hotel, past jacaranda trees in bloom, and horses grazing and cows with egrets on their backs, we felt ourselves reverting, in the soft tropical air, not to English bullies, but to children who just wanted to be put to bed. In our rooms at the hotel there was only one decision to make—to lie down under the ceiling fans, or on a chaise longue by the pool. But there really was no choice. Lying down under the ceiling fans was the equivalent of anesthesia—you were asleep before you knew it.

On awakening there was the most wonderful feeling at the Hotel San Martin: the certainty that you'd made the right choice—the journey had been worth it. There are certain places in life whose pleasures are so unadvertised that the mere appearance of another person like yourself creates a bond. That hotel was one. In 1981 no travel writer, with or without a photograph of tiles, or a hibiscus and a toothbrush in a glass of water, had exploited it. It had never been mentioned in the *New York Times.* It wasn't even on the list of the people who sniff out the next new thing (gay men preferred San Juan), so one was surprised, in a sense, to see anyone else at the Hotel San Martin.

Of course, there *were* Other People at the Hotel San Martin—it was a hotel—but the unspoken feeling of camaraderie at having found the place made you give them the benefit of the doubt. And that was all that was required. In fact, people there hardly spoke to one another. The atmosphere was one of trust. Guests left their doors open to get the breeze, so that, returning to your room, you would often find the very image Dennis had forbidden: a green lizard perched on a suitcase, or a frog in your shoe, or a butterfly looping across the balcony. There was no firm line of demarcation between the interior and exterior; the hotel was built around a courtyard planted with a giant ficus tree. Inside was the slightly rank odor of decaying vegetable matter, luminous shadows, echoing voices, the slap of sandals on the tiled floor, the gleam of dark wood, birdsong, and leaves: the romance of the New World. Outside, beyond the veranda that ran along the rooms, a glimpse of silver sea, tossing palms, and a woman in a blue nightgown, cutting flowers in her backyard across a dried streambed. In the rear of the hotel was a tiled terrace. Beyond it was an ancient swimming pool, its paint peeling off, and, past that, an old white horse, grazing in a field of high grass.

The horse was in not much better shape than the hotel. The swimming pool hiccuped—at least that was what the noise it emitted sounded like; unless it was the noise the diver in an iron helmet makes in an old movie where you see his breath rising to the surface in big bubbles. *Glug, glug, glug,* went the swimming pool—decomposing, like everything at the hotel. There was no concierge. No chambermaid kept your room in order. The swimming pool needed a coat of white paint. The wicker chairs on the veranda were so frayed they were coming apart. The big broad beds in the rooms you passed were made level only with magazines placed under their uneven legs. Their tangled sheets, strewn with the detritus of bathing suits, tank tops, tubes of suntan lotion, and bottles of moisturizer, spoke of one fact: this was a place people came to collapse. The retired manufacturer from Boston who had just bought the place sat at a small desk in the hallway going over accounts with a pen and pencil. No one made the beds. Even the flowers people picked—star of Venezuela, gardenia, and hibiscus— they forgot to put in water, because in the tropics, after one day, you cease to understand with the clarity one has up north why anything has to be done immediately.

Indeed, the prevailing mood at the Hotel San Martin was a vast lethargy. Few guests at the hotel exhibited the energy necessary to do much of anything. Sometimes somebody walked into town, or hired a taxi to the remote beaches one could not get to on foot. It was too much trouble to go to the best beaches on the navy base, because that required passing through a checkpoint, which required removing pieces of identification from a wallet. Most people just decomposed. Guests spoke to one another only at breakfast—and that consisted primarily of trading travel tips. Come dinnertime, they were so exhausted by the sun and sea, they sat like zombies, staring into the flames of the candles that floated in oil in seashells on each table. The terrace at that hour had an almost religious atmosphere, as if we were all waiting for a service to begin. In fact, we were starving. There was a little bar beneath the owner's desk, but nothing like a cocktail hour. Dinner was at seven—and that was that. While waiting for our food the guests watched Dulcinea flick her tail in the gloom beyond the pool. After dinner everyone went to bed, for there was nothing else to do.

The second night we did summon up the energy to take a walk after dinner to the village at the bottom of the hill, but no one was doing anything there, either. The people in the village were all in their houses watching television underneath a naked lightbulb suspended from the ceiling. The only exception was a slender young man in a phone booth at the edge of a cracked cement basketball court, talking to someone, I imagined, on the mainland, oblivious to the vast, magnificent, darkening clouds above the ocean at his back. Here we are, I thought, come all this way to see something he saw every day of his life and could not be bothered to look at. "I've never been so tired in my life," said Dennis after we fled a barking dog and went back up the hill. "Thank God there's nothing to do at night." And with that we parted in the corridor. The ceiling fans that kept mosquitoes away created a white noise so soporific their hum was the last thing you heard until the sound of a rooster the next day.

The first item of business after waking was to step onto the veranda, rub the sleep from your eyes, and stare at the hibiscus flowers beaded with drops of dew along the balustrade, and beyond them the housewife in a blue nightgown cutting flowers in her backyard, and beyond her the sea. Then one heard, with perfect clarity, the voices of the couple in the room next door. She: "You're such a *lecher!*" He: "I can't help it!" Then, like the cries of the roosters and goats, the dogs in the village below, came the familiar urgency of breath, the gasps and groans, as two larger mammals copulated before going to the beach, their only witnesses myself and the lizard perched on the balcony.

Even sex seemed incongruous on those fresh tropical mornings. Even desire required too much effort. On a short walk before breakfast the second morning there was a crew digging a ditch for a water main along the road, and as I walked past, a young man with a smooth brown chest and large green eyes stood up from his shovel and smiled at me—but there was nothing to do but murmur "*Buenos*" and keep walking. One was in love with the island. When I passed the couple from Michigan on my return, emerging from their room with rosy faces and large designer eyeglasses, on their way to toast and scrambled eggs, I felt no more envious than I did when I knocked on the door of my two friends.

"Come in!" they cried, still tangled up in sheets when I entered, their torsos covered with strips of sunlight let in by the louvered door, exactly like the photograph Dennis forbade me to take. "How long have you been up? What's happened?" said Kent in his plummy British accent. "Any scandals? Gossip? New arrivals?"

"No," I replied. "Nothing's happened—though there's a gorgeous guy digging a ditch outside the hotel—if we hurry, we'll pass him on our way to the beach."

"*That's* not what I want," he said. "I've finished my biography of Mary of Teck and I have nothing to read. I need *gossip!*"

But there was none. The guests consisted of a couple from Cincinnati who had gone to St. Bart's the previous winter; an Italian businessman looking for a lot on which to build a vacation home; a fabric designer from the West Village whose wife taught fencing to senior citizens in New Jersey; a composer from Brooklyn; and the copulating couple from Detroit. A plump, bearded man in his fifties completed the roster—a stage manager from Manhattan who spent most of the day lying by the pool on a chaise longue, wrapped in a leopard-skin-patterned cloth, coughing. That was it. A young woman named Peggy waited on tables while the owner—the shoe manufacturer who'd sold his factory to buy the hotel—sat at a table in the atrium with a morose expression doing paperwork.

The conversation at breakfast illustrated perfectly that peculiar phenomenon of travelers who talk about the places they have just been or are about to visit—everything but where they are. The woman from Brooklyn told us about a bicycle trip through Zambia she had just finished; the couple from Cincinnati talked about Barcelona; the fabric designer about Bali; the couple from Detroit Belize. This had one advantage: no intimacies were established—the common topic (travel) let everyone express himself while remaining completely unknown. This, however, was only a goad to Kent, who said, as we were leaving the hotel after breakfast, "I think we should get drunk tonight and stir things up—be rude to everyone. Let's tell Irving his hotel is a dump, let's tell Peggy the chicken Kiev tastes like lighter fluid, let's tell the couple from Michigan they woke you up with their morning screw, and let's ask the stage manager where he got that hideous caftan and the ridiculous jewelry. Let's get stinko! Let's get something started! It's all too dull!"

"Divinely dull," sighed Dennis as we headed toward a grove of sea grape trees sheltering the beach. "Divinely, deliciously, delectably dull. Just the way I wanted it!" he said, taking Kent's arm.

They were still in that stage in which the simplest act—preparing to dress for the beach in their rooms, or spreading their towels out once we got to the lagoon—was freighted with affection. Moments after running into the ocean with hands held, they were wrapped so tightly in each other's arms, their two heads looked from a distance like one coconut bobbing on the waves. After our swim, Dennis lay his head on Kent's stomach while Kent read aloud a story about Dolly Parton in the *Enquirer* and Dennis stared into space, silenced by one of those moments when at last life is perfect.

"You know," said Dennis, when Kent went back in the water, "I'm afraid my darling drinks a teensy bit too much, and I suspect his mother will never let him bring me back to the stately home—there really is one, dear, it's called Cranston Hall—but you must admit he's *aw*fully handsome. Don't you think?" He looked over at me, squinting in the sunlight: "I hope, by the way, you got a shot of us when we were coming out of the sea just now. You mustn't forget the photographs. This *is* my honeymoon, and you know how much the scrapbooks mean to me! It's all going in my scrapbooks. I want every magic moment registered! If you get my drift, *dear*."

"I do," I said. Indeed, I knew about those scrapbooks. They occupied three shelves in Dennis's apartment on Tenth Street and seemed, at times, to be his reason for living—not whatever he experienced, but the photograph of it, mounted. I couldn't decide if this was because Dennis knew more than most that life is fleeting, so he'd better record what he could, or because all that mattered to him was the visual representation of something, not the thing itself. At any rate, I was here to record his bliss in permanent chemicals, and moments later, when Kent ran out of the water and Dennis rose to greet him, I was already standing with camera in hand by the time they embraced as Dennis yelled to me, "Be sure there's no seaweed in the shot! I want *no* seaweed! And wait for the sand in the water to settle! I want it clear! Like a glass of gin!"

Click. Later that afternoon while they snored, I got up to explore a path that led through the sea grape grove to a brackish swamp in whose shallow water pink crabs scuttled to hide at my approach, a path that brought me to the edge of a coral cliff, with a view of another, blazing beach I could not reach, then back through a grove of thorn trees, where I came upon a discarded turquoise bathing suit, more erotic than any person could have been. At dusk we walked home on the path that linked three beaches, the sky above us changing color, as I allowed my friends to walk ahead, arm in arm. In the gloom horses stood watching as we passed. A man was seated on the hood of his car at the main beach, staring out to sea, as if he wanted to be somewhere else.

We were quite happy to be where we were, however; everything was perfect, so that at first it seemed of little interest that evening that there were two new guests seated at the table in the corner of the terrace. Both looked like college students. One was remarkably handsome; the other had black, curly hair, braces on his teeth, and a T-shirt that said VILLANOVA. At first they made no impression. Then Kent leaned over the little candle floating between us and said, "Well? What do you think?"

"What, dear?" said Dennis.

"Are they?" said Kent.

"Are they what?" said Dennis.

"You know, that way."

"Why, I don't know," said Dennis, as he munched on a bread stick. "It hadn't occurred to me to wonder. But I am prepared to receive vibrations." Then he fell silent while we consumed our soup, as still as a radar screen waiting for a blip to appear; Dennis was trying to receive vibrations, I realized; he prided himself on his ability to receive vibrations. "I think they're straight," he finally said. "Two friends, students, who decided to travel together."

At this point the handsome one was looking around at the other guests; the other did not look up at all.

"I remember traveling at that age with a friend," said Kent. "He was very shy. Terrified, in fact, that I might run off and leave him. It came to a head in a museum in Munich. I turned away from a painting of, what else, Saint Sebastian, and literally cut my cheek on the edge of his glasses—he had been standing an inch away from me, following me from painting to painting, like a child holding on to his mother's skirt. I told him I wasn't moving till he went off to look at paintings on his own. Travel frightens some people." He sipped his consommé and said, "That's what I think about them. One's shy, the other isn't."

"Clinging to his friend?" said Dennis.

"Exactly," said Kent.

"But this is not the sort of place college students come on vacation," said Dennis. "It's too out of the way. Maybe they are family. On the other hand, no homosexual wears braces on his teeth! Would a homosexual wear braces on his teeth?" he said to Peggy as she arrived with the paella.

"You got me," she said.

"We're wondering who the new guests are," said Dennis.

"They're from New Jersey," she said. "Will you be having wine?"

Kent said, "Yes." Dennis said, "No."

"Oh, go ahead," said the stage manager from New York, rising from his table next to ours. "Life's a banquet and most poor fools are starving to death!" For a moment we thought he was going to join us, but instead he headed for the two young men, and began to sing, in a quavering contralto, a song from *The King and I.* "Hello, young lovers, whoever you are," he sang as he walked right past them, "I hope you're faithful and true. . . ."

Dennis turned to us with his mouth agape. "That's ex*act*ly what I don't want to be like when I get old," he said.

At that moment the two newcomers rose from their table.

"Good evening," Kent said as they came near.

The handsome one stopped, while the boy with braces kept right on walking. We talked about beaches, we told him how to get to our favorite, he thanked us and said good night. The palms rustled. The pool hiccuped. The horse flicked its tail. Kent put his fork down and said: "I'm sure he's not."

"I think he's *dead* gay!" said Dennis.

"You're wrong," said Kent. "He's too relaxed!"

"Can't homosexuals be relaxed?"

"No," said Kent. "Not really. They live in a state of perpetual anxiety—for two very good reasons. One, they never know when they may be beaten up. Two, they worry that queens like us will come on to them. They live in a constant fear of predation. But the boy just now illustrated none of that. There was no fear—of punishment *or* sex. He was relaxed. A homosexual is never relaxed—because it's not easy being a ponce."

"It's *dead* easy," said Dennis.

"That may be true in your case, actually," Kent said, looking at Dennis as if regarding him from a new, anthropological light. "I think you probably are one of the few people I have ever met who really don't seem, on some level, bothered by it."

"*What's* to be bothered by?" said Dennis. "The queen got one thing right—life *is* a banquet, and most poor fools are starving to death! Those boys are deeply in love, and having the time of their young lives!"

It looked more as if they were sleeping when we came to our secret beach the next day and found that it was no longer that: the new-comers were lying on the sand near our usual spot as we emerged from the grove of sea grape trees. We stood there for a moment gazing at them. Then Dennis said: "I was wrong. They're not gay."

"And why do you say that?" said Kent.

"Because their towels aren't touching. Lovers always lay their towels down so that they're touching."

The one thing we couldn't do was ask; so instead, to advertise our presence, we ran into the ocean; and when we emerged from the water they were gone.

"You see? Not gay," said Dennis as he walked back wiping the water from his eyes. "They didn't want three old queens staring at them."

"Is that what we are to them?" said Kent.

"Yes. Age is relative, you know. It's like the beach in Mexico I went to," said Dennis, getting out the cheese and crackers, "at their age. I was still in college, traveling with friends from school. We went to this island off the coast of Yucatán, which nobody went to then— and walked miles to get to this beach the locals had told us about. Walked and walked and walked. Climbed cliffs, coral cliffs, trudged and trudged till our feet were raw, and then, when we finally got to the most beautiful beach in the world, there, at the farthest end, were these two men lying in hammocks—who looked exactly alike! The same height, same body, same tan, same hair, same bathing suits, and *reading the same book*—a life of Betty Grable! We had come all the way to this tiny island off the coast of Mexico, walked barefoot over coral to get to this legendary beach, and what did we find? Two queens from West Hollywood! I wanted to have *nothing* to do with them. Now," he said, handing us our crackers and cheese, "flash forward many years. Here *we* are on this beautiful beach. Only this time we sent *them* screaming. It's the oldest story in the book! You fly in a jet, take a boat to an island that isn't even on the map, hike for hours, finally reach the most beautiful beach in the world, and what do you find? Two decorators in white bikinis reading the life of Betty Grable."

"But why would they think *we're* queens?" I said.

"Why not?" said Dennis. "We're not wearing six scarves and a quarter pound of jewelry from Fortunoff like that number singing Rodgers and Hammerstein last night, but we are three gents of a certain age together on a beach in the tropics. Which is why I'd *love* it if you took a photo of us right now," he said, turning to me. "The light is *so* pretty, and we're not *plastered* with seaweed."

"Well," said Kent, "this island is quite big enough for all of us, wouldn't you say?"

And with that the sobering sensation of viewing ourselves through the eyes of others vanished, and we lay down and stared at the wedge of white sand between two coral cliffs whose beauty made us forget these petty, snobbish matters. An hour later the honeymooners began playing a game called Elevator, in which each one would dive down, push up off the sea bottom, and scream, as they burst up out of the water: "Lingerie!" or "Sixth floor, Menswear!" That evening we were so tired at dinner we were not even thinking about the newcomers until the handsome one said good evening as he passed our table and asked how our day had been.

"Wonderful," said Dennis. "I hope we didn't drive you off the beach."

"Oh, no," he said. "We wanted to check out some more places on the base. Really beautiful," he said, and then with a nod and a smile he went to the table in the corner, where his companion was already boring a hole into the menu.

"I have a new theory," said Kent. "The pretty one is *not* gay, but the other one, who won't even look at us, is. Why else would he avoid us so strenuously? Only people who suspect homosexuality in themselves react adversely to other homos. The genuine heterosexual is indifferent. The one with the braces, however, seems extremely uncomfortable in our presence."

"*Very* uncomfortable," said Dennis.

"Self-conscious and ill at ease," said Kent. "And depressed." After a few more minutes of soporific silence, he leaned forward and hissed: "I've got it! The boy with the braces is not only secretly gay, but in love with his friend, who isn't!"

"Could that be it?" said Dennis.

"It would explain why the boy with the braces only looks at his friend," said Kent, "and has no desire to talk to anyone else. It would explain why their towels weren't together. It would explain how unhappy the boy with the braces seems. If *I* were barely twenty-one, tall and skinny, with braces on my teeth, and in love with a friend who was everything I wasn't and wanted to be, and who could not be in love with me, because he was straight, I'd be miserable, too! In fact," he said, "I *was* all those things, minus the braces, at his age. I was so depressed I went to bed for an entire week after graduation because I and my best friend had to part. He went to Kenya to work, and I went home to my parents, where I went upstairs to my room and lay in bed for seven days, because as far as I was concerned, life had come to a complete end."

"Poor baby," said Dennis, putting his hand on his boyfriend's.

"But now look at me," said Kent as he put his hand on top of Dennis's.

"Of course," he added, "the friendly one does have a superb body."

"He has a body that would *sink ships*," said Dennis. "I'd *kill* for his stomach. And chest. And shoulders. You know, the awful thing about the gym is there is really nothing you can do for shoulders. Not really."

"The other one has a beautiful body, too," I said. "In fact, I find him really more attractive."

"That's because you like nerds," said Dennis.

I did like nerds; which meant the memory of his white, lanky body shifting on his towel in the sunlight, before they were aware of our presence, was with me now—though glance as I might across the room, he would not return the look. They sat there in silence, like a married couple who have been together such a long time they have run out of things to say, and then, just when it seemed they must look around the room to find a topic of interest, their conversation resumed—though the boy with the braces retained his melancholy mask.

"You know, if there has been any advantage to the past ten years," said Dennis, "it's been that I've learned not to pine over people who can't possibly return my interest. One simply accepts the fact and moves on. But when you're nineteen, or whatever he is, you don't know that. You can't move on. You're terrified to move on, because moving on may mean—ending up like us! That's why he refuses to look at or speak to us. He wants nothing to do with queens—all he wants in this world is his friend—which I can perfectly understand, though I'd love to walk right over there now and tell him we know what he's going through."

"That love is like a wasting wound," I said, "no tropic sun can cure."

"I think that scans," Kent said. "It does, doesn't it? That love is like a wasting wound no tropic sun can cure! We should go over right now and tell him that!"

"Well, why don't you?" said Dennis.

"Because we are all trapped in social rules, rules that maintain propriety and privacy," said Kent, as he picked up his wine. "On the other hand, I think of that lovely line of Rilke's. Rilke said the world is filled with dragons only waiting for us to kiss them to be changed into princesses."

"What a divine idea!" said Dennis, and, with this thought, they stared into one another's eyes, and then turned their gazes on the table in the corner. The couple in question chose that moment, however, to get up and leave the dining room. The outgoing one smiled at us as they passed; the boy with the braces stared down at the tiles as if being led off to jail. At that moment the stage manager in the corner put his head back and began to sing, in one of those rich, quavering voices you hear only in piano bars, "Full moooon and empty arms . . ."

"I *can't* believe it," whispered Dennis as the stage manager threw up his arms with a jangle of jewelry on his wrists.

We watched as Peggy came out with a tray of flan and delivered the cups to all the tables.

"I am thinking of another line," said Kent drunkenly, "this one from a letter by Scott Fitzgerald to his daughter. It goes: 'All life has is youth, or the love of youth in others.'"

Dennis looked up from his custard.

"Was Fitzgerald a chicken queen?" he said.

"He was a romantic!" Kent said: "The same thing, I suppose. The point is we love the mystery couple because they're young—and innocent. But the boy with braces came here to be alone with his friend—not to be leered at by us."

"Speak for yourself!" said the stage manager, who seemed to think the distance between our tables immaterial. "What you want to tell them is—there's nothing to be afraid of! I've never been happier than I am now! I'm on this beautiful island having the time of my life! And when I go back to New York I love my life there, too! You know? It's more fun, in fact, than it is at their age, in many ways, when you're worried about so many stupid things. But try telling *them* that! Try telling that to people who look at you and see only one thing—old age and death!" At this he cackled, stood up in his aquamarine caftan, spread his arms out like a great bird opening his wings, and left the dining room.

"*Awfully* chatty," said Dennis the minute he was gone. "And what he fails to realize is that I regard him the same way the mystery couple regard us!" "Three very different generations. He's singing songs to them they've never even heard. Why, I bet those boys, even if they are gay, have never even heard of Noël Coward—much less Ruth Draper."

"Ignorance is like a delicate and exotic fruit," said Kent. "Touch it and the bloom is gone."

We stared at him.

"Oscar Wilde," he said.

"I'm sure they wish the four of us weren't here," said Dennis.

"But we are, and I love to look at them!" said the stage manager, returning for his cigarettes.

"But we mustn't," said Dennis. "We must give them that courtesy."

"You can, not me," the stage manager said. "At my stage in life, there's nothing you can do *but* look." And with that he left the dining room again.

In the morning at breakfast we were careful not to stare at them, though this time they both shared in the public babble of tips on beaches, adjusting your face mask, and ferry schedules. Then they grew visibly bored as the couple from Cincinnati began talking of bicycle tours of the Auvergne and finally excused themselves, while the stage manager made ready his chaise longue for yet another day of reading beside the anti-quated pool whose bubbles rose like those from the air hose of a diver in an old adventure movie. Outside the day was dazzling—the wind tossing the palm tree tops about like shirts on a clothesline in the blazing light. Knowing he had one day left, Dennis became even more demanding about the photographs. First, he wanted pictures of them in the waves, then atop a coral cliff, then in a grove of palm trees, then close-ups beside a hibiscus and even the interior of the hibiscus itself. Then he said: "Please take a picture of that crab on my suntan lotion."

"That's the kind of shot you don't want," I said.

"I know. But I'd like the crab," said Dennis. "It's so pretty. Pretty please? After all, you are my official honeymoon photographer."

"I know," I said. "But you have more than enough shots by now. Believe me, you'll have plenty for the scrapbooks."

"Well, I hope so," said Dennis with a sigh. "I sincerely hope so. Because that may be all I have."

"What do you mean?" I said, as we watched Kent attempting the backstroke in the choppy waves.

"I mean one is simply aware that there are magic moments in life that do not last—if you get my drift."

"Like this one?" I said.

"Yes. Because—let me be frank—we both know that while I adore Kent, I don't know how much longer this marriage can last, because, like most people, he is not without his problems."

"For instance."

Dennis looked over at me.

"*A fondness for the grape*," he said.

"He's drinking?"

"Yes—which means he's got problems this girl can't do anything about—which means it's important for me to get photos while I can."

"You mean you're already planning to divorce him while you're on your honeymoon," I said.

"There's always hope!" he said. "But one does have to think ahead. That's why I want to tell the boy with braces to just get over the pretty one. Because let's face it—there's a lot more where he came from. Now, listen, dear—I will probably be asleep when the English aristocrat emerges from the water, but when he does," he said, looking over at me, "when he does, you make *sure* you get the money shot. I want him just as he comes out, *streaming* with seawater, because he's so pretty with his hair slicked down, and that glistening washboard stomach. Promise?"

"Promise," I said.

Instead I fell asleep not long after Dennis. When I awoke my friends were arguing about the couple.

"This isn't the end of the world," said Dennis. "He's going to have lots of boyfriends after this one. Lots!"

"But don't you see? None of them will mean as much," said Kent. "None of them will be what this one is—because the first time you fall in love, the world is still entire, it hasn't been split up into a thousand little truths. Your first love is your first feeling that you can unlock the door—the door of life, with all its potential for happiness, for union with another soul. It's your first ecstatic contact with the current that runs the universe!"

"So what am I?" said Dennis. "Chopped liver?"

"No, no, darling," said Kent, "you are a very fine pâté."

That evening there were several empty tables. Half the guests had gone, and the inviolate air of privacy that held sway over the diners whose faces glowed above the little shells in which the candles burned seemed slightly less inviolate. The stage manager raised his glass of wine to us; we raised ours to his. The homosexuals now outnumbered their opposites. But this hardly seemed to our advantage. In the middle of the night I woke to the sound of arguing and knocked on the door of my friends' room. Dennis stood in the doorway of the bathroom holding a towel filled with ice cubes to his head. "He hit me," he said. "He hit me!"

I looked over at his consort, who lay there with a pillow over his head discolored with vomit.

The next morning I walked them to the boat and watched it go around the headland.

The rest of my days on the island were spent in solitude; in the dining room, where I sat alone, happy to watch the other guests. Then the rest began to vanish, one by one, back to the mainland—till only four of us remained. Alone in my room I watched the woman cut flowers in her backyard: a synecdoche of domestic life. The nights continued starry, the days, even when it rained, were more beautiful afterward. The wild horses began to graze nearer the hotel. The two young men got more healthy-looking and handsome with each passing day—as if, with the departure of each guest, they could blossom a bit more, like flowers. Every day I took a road I'd not walked before and came upon another lagoon, another beach, another sea grape grove. When I returned to the hotel at dusk, however, the human wish to share these discoveries was confined to conversation with Peggy as she served me dinner: the curse of traveling alone. The two young men babbled away at their table. The stage manager read a novel by Gordon Merrick as he drank wine and smoked cigarettes, looking up every now and then to take in the youth and beauty across the room. One evening I walked back down the hill to the village. The young man ignoring the majestic sky was still in the phone booth. He was a synecdoche, too: of what I was not sure. In the morning I waited for the woman to clip gardenias, her blue nightgown blowing in the breeze. Then one day I heard the boy with the braces ask Peggy about boats back to Fajardo as she served them their toast and orange juice. When they were done eating, the outgoing one said to the stage manager, "Have a good day," as he passed his table on the way out. The stage manager turned to me and said: "Have a good day! I can get that by dialing my bank!" Then he remarked, "Lately I've begun to realize that I've seen that boy somewhere. I've seen him somewhere and I cannot remember. Isn't that maddening? I can't remember where and yet I know I've seen him before."

Five years later I found out. During that period we did not go to the island anymore; the dollar was so strong, people started going to Brazil instead. That trip involved a night flight, too. After a week in Rio de Janeiro we would return to Manhattan at dawn. The snowy streets of brownstones the taxi went down at that hour made the city look like a town in northern Germany: sober and bourgeois. The sleeping people, the cold facades, the fresh snow on the garbage cans and sidewalks, seemed to rebuke the sweaty bodies on the beach at Ipanema and in the clubs downtown. And I began to wonder why we had to go so far to find the sensual. One year I was the last person in the cab. Too awake to go home, I asked the driver to take me to a club in the West Forties where, on Sunday morning, I knew the party of the previous night would still be going. But I was wrong. Only a small crowd of people remained watching a stripper on stage. The stripper, however, looked familiar. It was the boy with the braces. Only now he was the boy with a snake wrapped around his body, undulating to the sound of Donna Summer singing "Love to Love You Baby."

It was a small club with only one exit, for performers and customers alike. I waited after closing for him to come out. He laughed when I told him about our obsession with him and his friend on the island. No one had been right, as it turned out. They had been stripping in a club in San Juan at the time—which was where the stage manager had no doubt seen him—and were taking a little vacation; and the last thing they wanted to deal with was our desire.

Greensleeves

Kevin Killian

It was Charlie's wife who introduced her husband to Piers—Moira Watson, who loved entertaining gay guys at their house in the Marina, at parties, dinners, impromptu gabfests. When pressed to account for her affinity for gay men, Moira always smiled and said, "I *am* a gay man, trapped in a woman's body." You might almost believe it, so determined was her grin. "This *is* San Francisco!" she would exclaim, a sassy gleam in her large brown eyes. Moira worked for a fledgling Web company with a large, dignified office, like a sliver of Tara, in the South Park section south of Market in San Francisco. VV5 designed advertising gimmicks for Web sites, while the money people sweated it out, hoping someone would buy some of Moira's space. Long hours, not-bad pay, lots and lots of burnout potential. And always a party to go to, many of them Moira's. Moira Watson, at thirty-five, was always at least slightly conscious that she was old—old, that is, compared to the boys and girls who flooded Media Gulch by the thousands; the children who had been born reading William Gibson novels, net surfing, and bobbing sleek heads to an unseen ribbon of world-rap cyber music; they who, therefore, had this one unimaginable advantage over her. A geometrical advantage; it was like playing Risk with an opponent who not only owns all of Asia and Europe but Mars and Venus, too. Yet many of these youngsters were lazy, hadn't Moira's drive. Their posture, she figured, was what had given them the name of "slackers." When she tried to slouch, her shoulders hurt. She didn't do badly. She tried at least to keep herself from getting into an "old attitude." Gay men gave her a kind of spark; watching them and touching them she found she could still burn down the house, without drugs. Except for her Zoloft. But everyone was on Zoloft or Prozac, almost as if it weren't a drug but another form of gravity, a law to itself from which no one would want to rebel.

Afterward, Charlie remembered the first time he saw Piers Garrison, at one of Moira's Sunday lunch parties. He'd been deputized to stand guard in the kitchen and pour margaritas. *And* keep up light chatter and pretty much play the dummy who knows nothing about computers and isn't ashamed to say so. To play Moira's husband. He would be a mirror to Moira's guests, who would receive a pleasing reflection of their own great knowledge in the silvery depths of his smiley ignorance. Naturally, since he made them feel both smart and tolerant, Moira's friends from VV5 tended to like Charlie, who worked in banking somewhere. At forty-three, he was way older than any of them, a man of medium height and build, with thinning fair hair and slate blue eyes. He was pouring a scotch and water, and Piers was looking up with eyes of dark green, through thick brown lashes, over the rim of the glass, and suddenly the idea hit Charlie—"Guy's got a crush on me." Then, before he could think a second thought, Moira slipped between them, slid one arm around each of their waists.

Piers Garrison was tall and lanky, well formed, with thick, wavy brown hair and fine-boned features. Charlie had to look up at him: his eyes were at the level of Piers's chin. Charlie could smell sexual excitation as well as most men, and he smelled it in the way Piers was staring at him, through sleepy-looking eyes, half-open mouth. His lips were red, as though he'd been drinking sangria, but his tongue was pale pink, like a doll's pillow.

Moira smiled. "You two don't know each other. Piers, this is my husband, Charlie Watson."

Charlie reached across Moira to shake Piers's hand. He could feel the warmth of his wife's fingertips fitted intimately inside the back of his waistband, between the suspenders. "I was making Piers a drink."

"Piers does computer graphics," she explained. "He's got the biggest Syquest drive you've ever seen."

Piers must have heard this joke a dozen times, but he grinned dutifully, though his green eyes remained thoughtful. Big white teeth on Piers for sure. Like Chiclets. What was a Syquest drive, anyway?

"Hey, are you pierced?" Charlie asked, with a certain thrill of daring.

"Everyone always asks him that," said Moira, with a slight frown, "because of that name. Remember, Piers, even Vanderbilt at the meeting, and Charlie, this man Vanderbilt must be seventy, and straight as an arrow. If *he* knows about piercing, then everyone does. Another example," she began happily, "of how deeply gay male culture has penetrated the straight world, right up to the boardroom."

But Piers was blushing, furiously, as if he had never, ever, been asked the question before. He shook his head no. "Family name," he mumbled. "Nice to meet you." Moira's apartment on Chestnut boasted sensational views of the Marina—and Piers retreated, with his drink, to stand beside a full-length drape and watch the sailboats darting briskly across the purple bay. The sun in his eyes produced a squint that wasn't, Charlie thought, unbecoming. When he wasn't squinting, Charlie thought critically, Piers's looks were kind of bland. It was when he was in pain that they took on the noble pallor of, say,

Peter O'Toole in *Lawrence of Arabia.* He wondered what kind of underwear Piers had on—right now. Like a flip book of paper dolls, he pictured Piers in different kinds of underwear, standing against a perfectly blank background he could cut away at will with a pair of sharp scissors. Decided he looked best in boxer shorts—white ones like his own, perhaps with tiny shamrocks dotting them to match his eyes. Whether Piers actually wore them or not was an open question.

But he wasn't pierced—*if* he were telling the truth, and Charlie prided himself on his ability to spot a liar at thirty paces.

One afternoon a few days later Charlie called his wife's office and asked the receptionist to connect him to Piers. "Remember me?"

"Yes, sir, I sure do," said Piers.

"I was thinking maybe you and I should get together."

For a few seconds Charlie could hear nothing on the other end of the line. He was about to hang up when he heard Piers's voice again. "Sir, you're right."

"What's your address?"

Piers gave it to him.

"What kind of underwear you got on, right now?"

The slight pause before Piers replied was all Charlie needed to know. It was the slight pause of the man who, though not a *habitual* liar, is anxious to cater to the erotic fantasies of another, more manly man. They made a date for that evening.

"I guess I'm at a time in my life when I need a change," Charlie confided, over a mountain of beef at the House of Prime Rib at Van Ness. Its baronial atmosphere, its smoky smells of overcooked spinach and beef and big tankers of beer, were a little out of Piers's element, which is where Charlie wanted him. Off-kilter, he thought, confusing this tired metaphor with a mental image of a kilt; a kilt drawn up over the lower parts of a naked Scots guardsman. Off-kilter. "You have family here in the city?"

"I have a brother," Piers said slowly. "He's gay, too."

"Ever have sex with him?"

Piers looked shocked, but Charlie persisted. "Why not, what's wrong with me asking you that?"

"Eddy's a whole lot younger than I am," responded Piers slowly, distracted and troubled. By this time Charlie had the tongs from the salad in Piers's lap, and was rubbing up and down his dick like a violin. "He's twenty, I'm twenty-nine."

"Well, I want to meet him," Charlie said. "Sometime." He added that Piers could be his sub if he wanted to, and Piers agreed—this radiant smile broke across his face like the sun breaking free of fog. Charlie didn't expect such instant compliance. It knocked him on his ass.

Piers lived in a cottage, set back from the street, just about in the backyard of another house, in a part of San Francisco some call "Glen Park." This is where he received Charlie, where he wrote a contract at a big mahogany desk in which he swore to serve Charlie for the rest of his life. Signed it with blood. They both did. Charlie liked to do a lot of reading, so early on he told Piers that if he ever wanted to express himself, it must be in writing. "Dear Sir, may I suck your cock?" "Please, sir, whip my white bitch ass with your thick brown money belt." Simple things. Little love notes. "I don't want to hear a word out of your mouth," Charlie said. "I get enough yakking at home."

He pointed to Piers's computer. "Type me some notes on that," he said. "Tell me about what I should do to your skinny butt." While Piers was typing, very nimbly, Charlie picked up a framed photo from Piers's mantelpiece. This was "Eddy," Piers's young brother, who was twenty and what Piers described as a "club kid." Charlie hardly knew what

27

that was, but suspected the worst. Eddy's sullen gaze and full lower lip turned Charlie on. He'd like to have half an hour making that lower lip quiver. He wondered if Eddy was a bottom, too. He looked more fleshy than Piers, whose body was rather, I don't know, aesthetic.

One evening Charlie spotted an empty crushed beer can sitting in the garbage can Piers kept chained to one side of the cottage. "You don't drink beer," Charlie said. "What the fuck is this, pal?"

"Dear Sir," Piers wrote, "the can of beer belonged to the FedEx man who asked me if he could dispose of it." Doesn't that sound like a lie? The long steady gaze he wore gravely on his beautiful face was like a dare in three dimensions. Is he taunting me? With this beer can, of all things? They watched Charlie's hand crunch the thing to a flat shiny surface. They watched the thing pierce the soft skin or web between his thumb and forefinger. They watched the two drops of blood flood to the surface, and Charlie, at least, thought he saw a vindicated sort of pleasure in Piers's steady gaze.

Charlie was the lazy kind of top who makes his slave do all the talking. Why not, it was tiring working at his office, the gym was fatiguing, Moira never stopped planning her career. "Continue!" became his favorite word, as Piers typed out story after story, like Scheherazade. Part of the fun was watching him try to entertain his master with words, since he wasn't a verbal guy to begin with, but Charlie educated him as best he could. Soon Piers was spouting off like a regular blue whale scribbling these Balzacian tales of the sex marketplace while Charlie watched TV or just relaxed. Before Charlie's arrival, Piers would ascertain what he wanted to eat or drink while visiting, and he kept his VCR supplied with a steady stream of videos, porn and others. At Piers's job he often had access to tapes of first-run movies that were still playing the expensive theaters. "I like Stallone,"

Charlie told Piers. "He's an amazing physical specimen and they say he's no dummy. So, every time Sly makes a new picture I want to see it. None of that waiting on line shit. Not for Charlie Watson." Meanwhile Piers was on the floor, writing away in the notebook of questions or typing Charlie some sentences about having to love having to be his slave. Charlie made him write so fast his sentences had no beginning or end. "I like to be fucked My ass is so tight, 'cause never have REAL sex. OK. I used some big sticks sometimes, even the U-lock of bike. Please do it. Fuck me hard. Thank you, sir!!! I'd like to do whatever you wanna me to do. Yes, sir. Thank you! I'm daddy's boy now, aren't I, Charlie? Yes, I am. Piers says, I feel proud to be your son. I belongs to CHARLIE

"Charlie: Tell me, Piers. Louder.

"Piers: CHARLIE!!! CHARLIE!!! No, you can abuse my ass anytime you want. Piers: please use my ass

"Charlie, sir, you'll just tell me drop my pants. And then spread my 2 cheeks. And Piers will do what you want with your boy I belong to you."

Charlie told him to act out his desires, whatever they were, and Piers stood on tiptoe in his own bedroom, reached for the ceiling with one hand, and with the other felt for his own cock and pulled it out to its furthest extension. A white-label dance music compilation chugged onto the stereo, some emo-boy Cleveland sobber. Charlie laughed as Piers jerked himself off, since his body was so awkward, so willing to please. He was wearing the pair of boxer shorts Charlie made him wear all the time, white with tiny green shamrocks, and his dick stuck out of it ragged, hard, and somehow still prim. His thighs were trembling under the burden of such unwavering sensuality. He concentrated on the music to take his mind off the orgasm he wanted to unleash. The unknown track that had opened the compilation had moved into the Brothers in Rhythm mix of Kylie's "Too Far." Piers acknowledged the relevance of the darkly poetic track on the moment in hand. Charlie wasn't really listening; he lay sprawled on the bed examining this picture—words suddenly made flesh.

Over Piers's mind and body Charlie had, contractually, every right but one—he had not the right to ask why Piers was doing this. Nor why Piers loved him.

One Saturday afternoon Charlie was at home flipping through *TV Guide* while Moira was on the phone in the next room, giggling. After she hung up, she said, "That was Piers. The one with the green eyes I'm sure you don't remember." Moira had convinced herself that Charlie never paid attention to any of her colleagues and pals, that to Charlie all the "gay guys" she brought home were more or less indistinguishable. And they were, to a certain extent. So why was Charlie annoyed to hear Moira laughing with Piers?

"We were talking about the magnetic door at Farjeon."

"Magnetic door?" Charlie said with a frown.

Moira blushed. Or she would have, if she hadn't told the story so often—to others. "It was at Farjeon—I'm sure I told you this story already."

"Believe me, you didn't."

"It's silly. But anyhow at Farjeon there's this antistatic room with a magnetic door, and Piers and I were there one day when this boy, this temp, this wonderful redheaded punk boy, got swept right into the door and was pinned there. As though a strong hurricane were pressing him into the door. He could barely breathe. Security had to come and turn off the EM."

"For God's sake, why?"

Evidently this was something multimedia people understood instinctively. "It was a demo magnetic door, and he—this boy—had been caught there by his piercings. I think one or two must have come out. It must have been terribly painful. I know they brought him to St. Luke's right afterward."

Charlie picked up the magazine and continued to read the story on *Star Trek,* disgruntled. "Your friends are disgusting," he said.

Finally the evening came when, as Charlie requested, Eddy, Piers's younger brother, came to pay a call. "Tell your brother who you belong to," Charlie suggested, while the three of them sat in the kitchen drinking brandy after dinner.

"I belong to Charlie," Piers said, bitterly ashamed at being so abased in front of his younger, skeptical bro. As it turned out, Eddy was intrigued at the setup. He offered to have sex with Charlie as well. "Compare how I do it with how he does it," he said witheringly. "Piers hasn't even got a dick, far as I'm concerned."

But Eddy wasn't exactly a bottom and wanted to run things his way. Charlie grunted and the two of them went upstairs to Piers's bedroom, where Charlie ordered Piers to tie himself to a chair and watch. Eddy Garrison had none of Piers's weird angularity; his body was more compact, chunkier. Eddy's hair was the color of butter, with cocoa trailed in, and his chest and butt were sculpted out of some marvelous soft marble, you wanted to eat food from them, and in due course Charlie did. Piers's eyes were the fresh color of moss, a soft bright green, filled with an open frank awareness of the world. But whereas you might have said that he was the more sensitive of the two brothers, you wanted to fuck Eddy up more.

Charlie put his hands on Eddy's shoulders and kept up the pressure, increasing it until Eddy squatted between his knees. Sulkily the boy began to suck Charlie's cock, lopped his mouth around it as though nursing. His eyes rolled, disgruntled and not amused, in their deep sockets. Charlie had to cuff him a little to get him into line. Piers looked on, expressionless, tho' Charlie did his best to include him in the conversation.

"Your brother's a good cocksucker," he said suggestively, tho' Eddy wasn't, not really.

Eddy was the younger brother Piers always felt responsible for; he always told him to take condoms with him wherever he went, tried to discourage him from hard drugs, etc. Wished he would go back to college. It embarrassed Piers to know that Eddy was abreast of his own situation, but, he thought, "I asked for it." When Charlie finally came, Piers winced as Eddy swallowed part of his semen, then dribbled the rest onto Charlie's big hairy legs.

"You two are regular sex pigs, ain't you?" Eddy guessed. "Look, guys, have fun, I'm off to a party."

After he had sashayed out there was a certain tension while Charlie questioned Piers about Eddy's sex life. He was certain—absolutely certain—that Eddy sneaked over while Piers was alone. Frantically Piers typed out, "No sir I never fucked Eddy, he's my own brother no sir I am true to you."

"Fuck you," Charlie snapped. The following week he lowered Piers onto the burner in the kitchen range as it glowed with the slightest tinge of orange. "This is for being your brother's little sex wimp," he said, as he held Piers in his arms and gently pressed his left ass cheek onto the lit burner and held it there until they could both smell the flesh burning. Charlie compared the way Piers scrambled in his arms to trying to bathe a cat. Then, a week later, he gave the same treatment to Piers's right cheek. Now Piers's ass bore two sets of spiral branding marks, brown, crackly thin flesh like pork rinds—like a strip of pork rind laid into circles on each half of his slim white butt. Piers said he didn't feel the marks, except a little in bad weather, when they creaked, but to the touch they were certainly different than the rest of that naked flesh—they were like brownish ribbon interwoven on the front of a Hallmark card, silky, as a bookbinder might underlay calfskin with Victorian ribbon. Charlie liked the look, but Eddy groaned when he saw it. "Tacky!" he hooted. "Next he'll cook you, bro." Eddy and Charlie had Piers bend over his couch so they could examine his butt. Eddy ran his beringed fingers over the punctured skin, lingered a little at the crack, giggled at Charlie. Piers started to cry, but stopped after a minute when Charlie ordered him to. As Charlie and Eddy pointed out, he was hard as a rock through the whole examination. "Almost looks like Piers has a dick," Eddy hooted.

"Charlie," said his wife, "know what's funny? Piers Garrison has been so quiet and withdrawn at the office. Almost mopey. He used to be so much fun. Do you think he's sick?" She always said "sick" when she meant AIDS. Charlie shrugged, left it at that.

"Call him," he said. "Now which one was he?"

"The real cute one with the brown hair, like Cindy Crawford with a butch haircut, but you wouldn't remember."

Charlie told Piers to place a personals ad in the paper offering to fuck strangers under his master's supervision. In this way Charlie made many new pals who would come to Glen Park to fuck Piers; all exclaimed at the perfection of this decorated ass. There were regular party nights, and Piers realized these were Charlie's way of counterpoising Moira's festive cocktail parties with some fun of his own. Late one Thursday night he stood in a corner of his house, naked but for his dirty shamrock underwear, watching some men fighting over the last pieces of Leon's Barbeque left on his kitchen table. Others were sitting watching a tape of *Friends* on TV and arguing about whether Matt LeBlanc was gay or not, while three bottles of champagne sat in the open refrigerator. Others sat at card tables spread with brown paper, drinking Diet Cokes and coffee and eating sugar doughnuts. Piers looked at them all for a minute. Then he went upstairs to his bedroom. It hurt him a little to climb. The wooden stairs creaked under his feet. The men who watched him saw the dirt on the soles of his white crew socks.

"I have a new boyfriend," Charlie said to Piers. "Young boy, studious, who I met at the Hole in the Wall. He was dancing on top of the bar in his jockey shorts."

"Maybe you'll bring him by, Charlie?"

Piers sat at Charlie's feet with a tiny knife, scraping the peels from a bushel of potatoes, one by one, in a very dim light.

"I don't know if I want you to meet him," he told Piers. "He's a very innocent boy, not a jaded roué like you. Morals infect the young. Once he rubs against you, he'll have this stain on him, gray and sour, like the inside of an old ashtray."

"Yes, you're probably right," said Piers. The peeler slipped out of his hand and clinked a mournful sound on the tile floor. "I'm clumsy today."

"Clumsy and ugly."

"I am ugly," said Piers, looking at his dusty hands, which smelled like potatoes. Later, when he had peeled enough potatoes, then fried and sautéed them, Charlie was going to make him eat them all, then hold them down.

"Know what my new boyfriend's name is? Eddy Garrison."

Piers went to the keyboard of the glowing PC. "Dear Sir," he began.

"I want those potatoes peeled," Charlie growled. "Get your hands away from that computer." And Piers complied.

Eddy liked to prance around Piers's apartment in a leather vest and pink garters decorated with roses. His bottom bare. He knew it was a pert one. It looked like someone had dashed a bowl of milk over a pair of bowling balls. "Charlie and I are going to the opera," Eddy told Piers, his eyes wide, when the two brothers were alone one evening. "Imagine, me at the opera, with all those opera queens. An opera lasts for hours and hours. And you'll be here, tucking yourself in like a good boy. Piers, I saw a mother putting her kid in a car seat, buckled him in, tucked his ears under this little wool cap, and I thought of you, bro! Don't know why . . . just did."

"I belong to him," Piers said, more or less steadily. "Don't know why, but I do."

"Know what me and Charlie call you, Piers? We call you 'E-Mail,' 'cause you have those circa brands on your ass."

"Oh, really?"

"Yeah, we laugh about it when we're out at the opera, Piers! 'Wonder how ol' E-Mail's doing tonight.' 'He's flat on his stomach for sure.'" Eddy paused, taking a drag off a big purple joint. He studied his older brother's weary silence. "You don't have to put up with this shit, bro. How much fun can it be for you, all these Hispanic dudes and old geezers traipsing up here to fuck you while some others hold you down."

"You put a washcloth in my mouth," Piers said flatly. "And it was soaked with cum."

"To shut you up, bro," said Eddy, stubbing the joint in an ashtray. "You were hollering so loud I thought the neighbors would call in the cops." He lowered himself onto the bed next to Piers and sniffed. "That

35

old pair of drawers smells, you know that? It stinks, why doesn't he let you wash it?" He took Piers's hand and placed it firmly on his own pierced cock, rubbed the limp resisting hand over his cock until it grew hard, rose from his body like a wand.

"I remember when you were little," Piers said, looking away from Eddy's erection. "Back in Austin I used to take you to Sunday school."

"Well those were the days," Eddy replied. "Now pretend I'm Charlie Watson, lick my big fat dick, bro, make it happen."

"No, thanks," said Piers, rolling away from Eddy. He remembered bringing Eddy to church, holding his hand when Eddy was eight or nine, sharing a hymnbook with him, tho' it seemed clear even then that Eddy was no reader. In those days it was easy to mistake Eddy's clear amused gaze for the insouciance of the innocent. He would give Eddy a dollar to put in the collection plate.

After he left, Piers walked to his front window, watched Eddy saunter down the steps to his bike. Eddy waved insouciantly, winked.

"Please, Charlie, just leave Eddy out of this. I don't care what you do to me, just leave him alone."

"You don't have it in your head, do you, pal? I'll do what I like with whomever I please, and to tell you the truth, that includes your brother for sure."

Piers remembered Eddy putting the crumpled dollar bill into the jingling collection plate, the pride and satisfaction on his round face. "Dear Charlie," he thought. He kept composing these long letters to Charlie, not writing them out, just writing them in his head, seeing them written out along the pale bedsheets in the moonlight. Alphabets of disjointed desire that would never see the light of day. His arms itched to type them up. But he was afraid to. "Sir, I would not complain to you for myself, but I hope that you will spare my brother some of your harder caresses, for he was reared differently than me, and he is a softer boy, his pain threshold lower than mine. If you seek to punish him, withhold your punishment from him, give it to me instead.

"Instead pamper him like a baby, because he understands no better than a baby does."

One Sunday when Charlie came to Glen Park, Piers was not present. Charlie let himself in with his own key, at the kitchen door, and padded to the refrigerator for champagne. From the CD player floated the tune of an old Elizabethan madrigal, sung by one of those countertenors Moira adored. "Greensleeves," Charlie whispered, the big bottle of Veuve Clicquot Ponsardin halfway to his lips. "Alas, my love, you do me wrong to cast me off discourteously; for I have lovèd you so long, delighting in your company." The phone rang and Charlie answered it. Moira was calling. "Eddy Garrison called me," she began. "He told me the whole sad story."

Charlie stared at the phone, then noticed the general emptiness of the cottage. The CD player stood on the mantelpiece where once Eddy's framed photo had stood. The chairs, the sofa, even the rugs were gone.

Moira continued, in a sort of drone. With part of his mind, Charlie thought, *She must be doing twice her goddamn Zoloft.* "Eddy knew just where you would be and how you'd answer the phone." Piers's big computer was gone, and his Syquest drive, his printer. The desk they once sat on—gone. All his pictures, the walls were bare. "Eddy told me how if I called, you'd pick up for sure, thinking it was some respondent to your lovely personal ad. But it's not, Charlie—not this time. In case you're curious, Eddy's taken Piers back to Texas with him."

"Who is this?" Charlie whispered hoarsely.

"Someone you've done wrong," Moira said, before slipping the phone back on the base.

In the trash bin in the kitchen he found half a dozen empty champagne bottles and the stained shamrock boxers. With a sick, shuddering sigh Charlie fell against the wall, pinching his face with his hands. The CD voice continued, mocking him, like the emperor's nightingale, exquisite, heartbreaking. "For I have lovèd you so long, delighting in your company."

Pretend I'm Here

Patrick Ryan

Clark Evans finished the talk on his NASA experience with a description of the g-forces created in a Darmotech centrifuge. He held one of his large hands open and upturned in front of him, as if displaying a crystal ball, and then moved the hand in a circle that increased in speed as he described the sensation, until Frankie, staring from the front row, felt nearly hypnotized.

The ancient librarian who was moderating the event asked if anyone had a question for their guest. Frankie, sixteen, raised his hand. There were five people in the audience, scattered over a flock of folding chairs four times that number. The librarian and Clark Evans sat on slightly nicer chairs at the front of the library's map room. She looked past Frankie and pointed a wavering finger at an old man wearing a sun visor.

"Did you find being on the moon made you want to throw up?"

"Well, as I was saying—" Evans began.

"Because Conrad or Bean—one of those guys from *Apollo 12* or *14*—said in an interview that the low gravity made him want to throw up, and I was wondering what would happen if an astronaut threw up in his suit."

"I imagine it would be quite a mess," Evans said.

"But it didn't happen to you?"

"Not to me, no. As I was saying a while back, I was lined up for three different missions, but they didn't come through. NASA politics and whatnot. But I can tell you from knowing a whole lot of guys who went up there that walking around on the moon is like nothing on this planet, that's for sure." He smiled at Frankie as he said this.

"Any other questions?" the librarian asked.

Frankie raised his hand, but the old man spoke up again:

"Are you saying there's no system in place whatsoever for when an astronaut throws up?"

"Not that I'm aware of," Evans said, and the old man, appalled, glanced at the other audience members.

The librarian cleared her throat and said in a trembling but authoritative voice, "Let's have another question."

She pointed to a woman four chairs away, who said, "God made the Earth for man to live on it, not leave it."

"How about this young man," Evans said, nodding toward Frankie. "You've got a question, don't you, bud?"

His face, Frankie thought, was a mix between Steven Carrington's and Steve Austin's. He had Han Solo's shaggy brown hair. Captain Starbuck's alluring gaze. It was a face Frankie saw every week on the back of the local TV guide in the ad Evans took out for his real estate business, which featured the slogan, "I'll circle the Earth to meet your needs!" Frankie straightened up in his chair and asked, "Can you comment on Gordon Cooper's UFO sighting and the photos he took during his Mercury orbit?"

"That's a great question," Evans said. "And, you know, I actually have an interesting story about that event . . . but it's a little long to tell right now." He turned to the librarian. "We're about out of time, aren't we?"

She confirmed this. Evans stood and dug his wallet out of his blazer, and from it he removed a small stack of business cards. He stepped forward and passed them out to each member of the audience, reminding them that he wasn't just a retired astronaut but a Realtor, and encouraging them to call if they were ever buying or selling a home in the area. There was a small clatter of applause.

Frankie was unlocking his bicycle from the rack in front of the library when he heard a voice say, "I hope you didn't think I was dodging your question, bud." He looked up and saw the astronaut standing several feet away, holding his car keys. Evans had on a pair of aviator sunglasses and he was smiling, showing white teeth.

"That's OK," Frankie said.

"I *would* like to tell you that story sometime. These public events are hell, and it's nice to run into someone who has a genuine interest in the space program."

"I'm interested in what Cooper took a picture of."

Evans held out his hand. "Clark Evans," he said.

"Frankie Kerrigan." Frankie's hand was swallowed in the grip. His skinny arm snapped like a rubber hose.

"You live on the island?"

"Yes, sir."

"Good for you. No need to *sir* me, by the way. You have any desire to be an astronaut?"

"Not for the government."

"Well, there aren't too many independent astronaut companies out there, though if there were, I'm sure they'd be better run than NASA."

"Do you think our ancestors were aliens?"

"Ha ha," Evans said. "I haven't given it much thought. How old are you, bud?"

"Sixteen. Almost seventeen."

"How about that. Well, listen, you still have the card I gave you?"

Frankie nodded and pulled it out of the back pocket of his jeans.

"That number on the front is my office," Evans said, taking the card from Frankie's hand. He turned it over and clicked a ballpoint pen and began to write. "But this is my home number. Why don't you give me a call sometime, and maybe we can get together and talk about . . . space." He handed the card back to Frankie. "Ever been inside the V.A.B.?"

"Not inside it, no."

"We could tour the facility. Would you like that?"

"Sure."

"Give me a call and we'll see what we can work out."

"Thanks, Mr. Evans."

"It's Clark," the astronaut said. He pulled his sunglasses down an inch and gazed at Frankie for a moment. Then, spinning his key ring around his index finger as if it were a six-shooter, he walked across the parking lot to a midnight blue Trans Am. He glanced back once before getting in, pulled out of the parking lot, and was gone.

Still standing next to his bike, Frankie looked down at the business card. He read the phone number and turned the card over. Beneath the name of Evans's real estate business were the words, bolded and italicized, *I'll circle the Earth to meet your needs!*

He'd begun thinking of his house as a network of pods where they all lived separately. His sister Karen's pod was off-limits and silent when she wasn't there, off-limits and noisy with heavy metal music when she was. His brother Joe's pod—formerly occupied by their older brother Matt, who'd moved away after high school—was a dark hovel Frankie rarely glimpsed; it smelled of musk and sneakers, and the only sound that ever came out of it was the faint but frequent squeaking of bedsprings. Frankie's pod (his alone now that Joe had moved across the hall) was lined entirely with tinfoil and had a cockpit at one end, fashioned out of his desk, a mounted pair of handlebars, and three dead television sets. And at the opposite end of the house was his mother's pod, where nothing ever seemed to happen but where she sometimes spent whole days off from work with the door closed.

They'd taken to foraging for their dinners, crossing paths in the kitchen like competing scavengers. Joe, his chin speckled with a fresh outcrop of zits, was leaning against the counter eating pickles from a jar when Frankie walked in. "Do we have any Wheat Thins?" Frankie asked.

"No idea."

Frankie got a soda out of the refrigerator and popped the tab. He started rummaging through the cabinets. "How are classes?"

"Awful. The worst."

"Is college hard?"

"It isn't really college. It's community college. It's more like high school, only all your friends have cleared out of town."

Frankie found a box of Wheat Thins behind the cereal and took it down from the cabinet. Before he could eat any, Karen walked in wearing her steak house uniform and grabbed the box out of his hand.

She said, "Evening, losers."

"You look like a winner in that outfit, for sure," Joe said.

"Bite it." She ate the crackers as she stared into the refrigerator.

"I met an astronaut today," Frankie told them.

"Did this happen on planet Earth?" Karen asked.

"It was at the library. He gave a talk on NASA."

"Has he been to the moon?"

"No."

"Gone up in the shuttle?"

"No. He never really got to go on a mission. NASA politics and whatnot."

"There must be something wrong with him," Karen said. "Why else would he be hanging around a library talking about stuff he never did?"

"He gave me his phone number. He's going to take me on a tour of the space center."

"Lucky you." Karen finished what was left of the crackers, took the last pickle out of Joe's hand, and ate it. Then she took the jar and drank a swallow of pickle juice.

"That's disgusting," Joe told her.

She wiped her mouth with her hand and gave him back the jar. "So when are the gay astronaut and gay you having this gay date?"

"He's not gay," Frankie said, hoping he was.

"Sounds pretty gay to me. He'll probably try to butt-fuck you in a Mercury capsule."

Joe poured the rest of the pickle juice into the sink. When he'd retreated to the back of the house and Karen had left for work, Frankie sat down on the couch and looked at Clark Evans's picture on the back of the TV guide. The picture was a head shot, no bigger than a postage stamp. Clark was delivering the same smile he had that afternoon, and his slogan was printed below his face. Frankie was staring at the picture when his mother's door opened and she stepped into the living room. Her hair was combed and she was dressed in her robe and a pair of slippers, but she looked disoriented, as if she might have been sleep-walking. "Where is everyone?" she asked.

"Karen's at work. Joe's in his pod," Frankie said.

"In his what?"

He held up the TV guide. "I met this guy today. Clark Evans. He used to be an astronaut and he wants to take me on a tour of NASA."

"Is he polite?"

"He seems to be."

She walked into the kitchen. "Well, let's hope he has common sense. And make sure they give you a hard hat if he takes you any-where where they're building something." He heard her clacking dishes around. When she reappeared, she was holding a bowl of cereal. "And don't let him speed." She carried the bowl back to her pod.

In his own pod, liquid purple from the black lights reflecting off the tinfoil, Frankie sat at his desk and extracted Clark Evans's head from the TV guide with an X-acto knife. He used his glue stick to anchor the head to a blank sheet of drawing paper, then took his time sketching a naked body beneath it: standing, arms folded, dick pointing up to the sky. *I'll circle the Earth,* he thought, rubbing himself, *to meet your needs.*

At school the following Monday, Frankie met his friend Diana in the commons during lunch. She was eating an egg salad sandwich and had a cookie and a lemonade next to her on the concrete bench. "Don't even look at me," she told him. "I'm Godzilla."

"No, you're not," Frankie said, sitting down next to her and unwrapping his own sandwich. "You look skinny."

"I'm a monster of grotesque proportions. How's life?"

"I met an astronaut this weekend at the public library."

"Only you."

"His name is Clark Evans. He gave me his phone number and wants to show me the space center."

"Haven't you seen it already? I thought your dad used to work there."

"My dad wasn't anybody important there. Clark said he wants to show me behind-the-scenes stuff. Top secret stuff. Though my sister says he's trying to get into my pants."

Diana stared down at her half-eaten sandwich as if she didn't have the energy to lift it. Then she lifted it and took a bite. "He probably is," she said. "It's probably going to turn into some steamy Mrs. Robinson affair. He's not old and gross, is he?"

"No. He's pretty gorgeous."

A boy walking past the bench stopped short and looked at Frankie. "Are you talking about me?"

"Definitely not," Diana said.

"I was talking about someone else," Frankie said.

"Faggot," the boy declared, and walked on.

Frankie turned back to Diana. "Do you really think he could be interested in me—like that?"

"Lust rules the world," she said. "It doesn't rule *my* world, but it rules everyone else's. And you're a good-looking guy, though you're kind of an oddball. You're not going to show him your bedroom, are you?"

"Why?"

"He'll feel like he's at work."

"He's not an astronaut anymore; he sells real estate."

"And he's hot?"

Frankie nodded.

Diana ate the last bite of her sandwich and let out a long sigh. "I really am going to be the last living virgin on the island."

That afternoon, at the pay phone in C-wing, he got up his nerve and dialed the number on the back of the business card.

A woman's voice answered. "Hello?"

He hung up.

A few minutes later, he dialed the business number.

"Evans Realty."

"Hi. Is this—is this Clark?"

"Speaking."

"It's Frankie. The guy you met at the library last weekend?"

"Bud! I thought maybe you'd be too shy to call. I'm glad you did."

"Me, too."

"You still interested in that tour we talked about?"

"Yeah. And I'd like to hear your story about that Gordon Cooper photo."

"Aces," Clark said, and told him to be in front of the JC Penney's at noon on Saturday.

They sailed up Courtenay Parkway in the Trans Am toward the north end of the island. The buildings thinned out and the land on either side of the road turned green and feral. Clark played the radio and told Frankie the story of how *Apollo 12* was struck by lightning—possibly twice—not long after takeoff. "The rocket generated its own electrical field on the way up. Those boys weren't even sure what had happened, at first; they just knew some of the circuitry had gone haywire. Lucky they weren't blown out of the sky."

"Which missions were you supposed to go on?"

"Well, that depends on who you believe. Supposedly, there was a rotation system in place, but it seemed like something was always mucking it up. Made me wonder if the system meant anything, since they could change it around whenever they wanted. I had a chance on Apollo 18 and again on 19, but both of those got canceled. Then I got wind of a rumor that I was lined up for 20, but *that* was canceled, too, because they needed the Saturn for Skylab. Did you know when Skylab came down, pieces of it killed three cows in Australia?"

"Why didn't they just transfer you to the Skylab team?"

"I wish I knew. Look at *those* bad boys." Clark slowed the car down and pointed out Frankie's window. Just off the side of the road, three alligators sat, half submerged in a low bank of water. "They're all over the place up here. I saw one get run over by a little sports car one day, and it just kept walking." He mashed the gas pedal. Frankie felt his back press into the bucket seat.

They passed the turnoff for the visitors' center and traveled deeper into the compound. Nothing changed about the immediate surroundings; the marshland was the same as what they'd been driving through on the last stretch of parkway. But in the distance loomed the Vehicle Assembly Building: a massive structure slotted with a pair of narrow garage doors tall enough to allow a standing Saturn rocket to exit, once it was completed. "See that American flag painted on the side?" Clark said, pointing. "You could drive a bus up one of those stripes, they're so wide."

Frankie knew this from having taken the bus tour that skirted the facility. He asked if they were going to be able to get onto the roof of the building.

"Mayhap," Clark said. "It's so tall, I was standing up there one day and looked *down* at a helicopter flying by."

Long before they reached the V.A.B., the road was blocked by a guardrail and a man sitting in a booth. Clark brought the Trans Am to a stop and rolled down his window. "How's it going, chief?" he asked the guard.

"Can I help you?"

"Is Larry around?"

"I don't know any Larry."

"Oh. Well, I'm Clark Evans. If you'd raise that bar, I'd like to show my friend here the inside of the rocket hut."

"Do you have your ID?"

"Absolutely." Clark dug his wallet out of his back pocket and displayed his driver's license.

"I meant your NASA ID."

"Oh. That's at home. In fact, it's framed and hanging in my kitchen. I used to be one of the *Apollo* boys, but I've moved on to other pastures."

"You don't work for NASA?"

"Not anymore," Clark said, lifting an index finger to clarify the distinction.

"Then I can't let you beyond this point."

"Sure you can."

"It's not going to happen," the guard said.

"Just be a nice guy and raise the rail, would you? We're not Russian spies. I told you, I'm Clark Evans."

"Sir, turn your vehicle around and head south. The Visitors' Information Center is on the right, at the overpass."

"I know that." Clark peered though the windshield at the V.A.B. "Thanks for your time," he finally said, and put the car in reverse.

"It's no big deal," Frankie told him.

"Guy's on a power trip."

"But for me it's, you know, more exciting to get to know you than to see the inside of the V.A.B."

Clark smiled at him. "Exciting, huh? You like excitement, I'll bet. Got a little bit of the wild streak in you?"

Frankie shrugged, then nodded his head yes.

"Let's get wild."

He took an abrupt right before they reached the overpass and told Frankie they were on a service road that connected to the shuttle runway. "What would be *really* wild is if we could get out on the runway and open this puppy up," he said, gunning the engine. "We'll probably just have to settle for a little look-see, though."

But before long they encountered another guard post. Clark's exchange with the guard was much the same as the one he'd just had. Again, he thanked the guard for his time. Again, he told Frankie the man was on a power trip.

He made a third attempt to get them off the beaten track by steering them onto a road clearly marked with large white signs that read "No Admittance" and "Absolutely No Vehicles beyond This Point without Advance Clearance." This time there was no guard post but a rack of metal teeth laid across the road—collapsible but presently locked in a raised position that would shred tires. Clark spotted them just in time and the Trans Am screeched to a halt.

They wound up at the visitors' center.

Frankie stood on scales that told him what his weight would be on Mars, Venus, and Saturn. He peered into a Mercury capsule (his sister's predicted setting for the butt-fuck). He wandered around the Redstones and Atlases and Titans in the Rocket Garden—all things he'd done before—while Clark trailed glumly alongside him, his eyes hidden by his sunglasses and his hands tucked into his pockets.

"It's like a literal changing of the guard," Clark said as Frankie tore open a package of astronaut ice cream. "The old boys knew me on sight. I had the run of the place."

"Want some?" Frankie asked, holding out what looked like a pink block of Styrofoam.

Clark winced and shook his head no. "Sorry we didn't get in there deep. I feel like I should make it up to you somehow."

"It's no big deal," Frankie said again.

"No, seriously. You have any interest in getting a bite to eat tomorrow night?"

Frankie felt his heart race. The artificial ice cream softened on his tongue. "Yeah."

"You could come out to the house, and we could go from there to this great restaurant I know called Pounders. It's a fun place."

"Your—your house?"

"In Cocoa. You drive, don't you?"

Frankie nodded. "I got my license this year. You know, I called your house before I called your office. A woman answered."

Clark nodded and smiled and took off his aviators. "That was Pepper."

"Who's Pepper?"

"You'll *love* Pepper. She's top of the line."

Karen's hair was caked in mayonnaise and wrapped in a cap fashioned out of cellophane and Scotch tape. She leaned sideways across the backseat of her Datsun and filled a trash bag with beer cans and Burger King wrappers and empty cigarette packs, then tied the bag shut and pushed it out into the driveway. "Can it."

Frankie carried the bag to one of the garbage cans alongside the house. When he got back to the driveway, she was sitting behind the wheel with Armor All and a roll of paper towels. "Why'd you offer to help me, anyway?" she asked.

"No reason," Frankie lied.

"Uh-huh. And where's the ass-tronaut taking you to dinner?"

"Some place called Pounders."

"Ha! I've heard about that place. Billy Myers goes there and times it so that he takes a big dump right in the middle of the meal. He really sticks it to them, that way."

Frankie didn't know what she was talking about and tried to vaporize the image from his mind. He picked up the paper towel roll from the seat and tore one off for her. She spritzed the dash. "Does Mom know about your old-man lover?"

"He's not old. He's probably around thirty-five."

"And you're sixteen."

"Almost seventeen. And he's not chasing me. If anything, I'm chasing him."

"Even sicker. Have you taken it up the butt yet? With anyone, I mean?"

"No."

"You better stick a cucumber up there or something. He's got his sights set on your Hershey Highway, mark my words, and you're going to need to be ready."

"Clark's not like that."

"If it walks like a duck and talks like a duck, it butt-fucks like a duck."

Frankie tore off another paper towel and handed it to her. "It's fun, helping you," he said.

"For you, maybe."

"Can I borrow your car?"

She sat back on the seat and glared at him. Thin rivers of mayonnaise ran down her temples. "I knew you wanted something. Do you have any idea what a hassle it is to maintain a car? I bust my ass in that restaurant five nights a week to keep this piece of junk going. I'm an adult now, you know. I've got responsibilities and a livelihood to consider."

"OK," Frankie said. "But I have to get to Clark's house in Cocoa. Can I borrow it—just this once?"

She narrowed her eyes, still glaring. "Hold out your arms." He did, and she spritzed them both, elbow to wrist, with Armor All. "No," she said, turning back to the dash.

His mother was in her pod, but the door was open, so he stuck his head in. She was on her knees in front of her closet, surrounded by shoes.

"Are you going anywhere tonight?" he asked.

She started, then returned her attention to the shoes. "I hope not."

"Can I borrow your car?"

"What for?"

"Clark's taking me to dinner, but I have to get to his house first."

"Do I know Clark?"

"You haven't met him. He's the astronaut I told you about. The one who I was with yesterday at the space center."

"It seems like you're spending an awful lot of time with this Clark. He's not a bad influence, is he?"

Frankie shook his head.

"Well." She picked up two brown shoes and studied them, discovered they didn't match, and dropped them onto the beige carpet. "Be back by eleven, and replace any gas you use."

He turned on his black lights, put Duran Duran on his record player, and rubbed himself some more over the picture he'd made with Clark's head. The paper, by now, was streaked and rippled, though he was careful to steer clear of Clark's face.

In the late afternoon he sat on the kitchen counter and called Diana.

"There's this Pepper person," he told her. "I asked about her, and Clark said she was 'top of the line.' You think it could be his daughter?"

"Did she sound like a grown-up?"

"Pretty much."

"Could be his wife."

"My sister still thinks he's trying to have sex with me. Maybe he's gay and it's some big secret."

"They might be swingers," Diana mused. "Or he might be bi. There *are* people like that, you know. Maybe I should be bi. It would double my chances, now that I think about it. Did I tell you I ate an entire package of Fig Newtons for lunch?"

"I think he at least likes me," Frankie said.

"There are even people who are into *fat* people. They only want to get naked with grotesquely fat human beings. I should find out if they have a club and join it."

"You're not fat. You just have a bad self-image."

"Well, if I *am* fat, I hate myself, and if I'm not, it means not even the people in those clubs will want me."

"I wonder what I'm going to wear," Frankie said.

He changed T-shirts three times, settling on a pink one with David Bowie on the front. Dusk was just starting in when he backed his mother's Oldsmobile out of the driveway and drove through town, over the bridge, and into Cocoa.

❖ ❖ ❖

Clark's house was on River Road, across from the island. The yard needed mowing and the paint on the shutters was flaking off, but it was a nice, two-story house with a front porch and windows that looked out over the Indian River. Frankie parked next to the Trans Am, checked his hair in the rearview mirror, then walked up the steps of the front porch and rang the bell.

The door opened a few moments later and a woman stood next to it, eyeing him. She wore jeans and a sleeveless white shirt that buttoned up the front. Her blond hair was pulled back in a ponytail. She was pretty and young looking—though not young enough to be Clark's daughter, Frankie concluded.

"You must be Frankie," she said.

He nodded.

"I'm Pepper. Come in." He stepped past her as she turned and hollered up the staircase, "Clark! Frankie's here!"

Clark's voice called from above, "Can you come up here for a second, Pep?"

"Make yourself at home," she told Frankie, then bounded up the stairs.

Frankie stood in the foyer listening to the muffled sound of their voices. Then he wandered into the living room. There was a long, lipstick-red sofa with round white pillows at either end. A black lacquered coffee table on which sat a Sears catalogue, a copy of *House and Garden,* and a glass ashtray. A treadmill in one corner. Nothing about the room indicated that an ex-astronaut lived there—until Frankie reached the bookcase. There were no books, but every shelf was crammed full of framed photos, nearly all of them pictures of Clark in his NASA days: smiling alongside a trio of crew-cutted men in the launch room; dressed in an orange jumpsuit and waving on a tarmac; sitting inside some sort of simulator and staring at a panel of gauges with a stern look of concentration on his face. In one photo, he was shaking John Glenn's hand. "For Clark," the inscription read, "—with high hopes!" and underneath it, Glenn's signature.

He moved on to the kitchen. There were beer bottles in the sink and dirty dishes stacked beside it. Evans Realty magnets on the refrigerator. Over the toaster, a large picture frame holding patches from each of the *Apollo* missions, and over the coffeemaker, Clark's framed NASA ID badge.

In the dining room, Frankie found Clark's official astronaut portrait. Standing before a wedge of moon, Clark wore a spacesuit and was looking not at the camera but slightly above and past it, his helmet under one arm, his eyes filled with glitter and promise. He looked god-like to Frankie, who suddenly realized he had a hard-on.

Adjusting himself in his jeans, he turned away from the portrait and spotted a clear glass bell jar nearly a foot high on the middle of a sideboard. Inside the jar was a pedestal, and on top of the pedestal was a jagged gray rock no bigger than a golf ball.

"Bud!"

Frankie jumped and spun around. Clark and Pepper were standing at the entrance to the dining room, smiling at him. "Hi," he said, folding his hands in front of his crotch.

"You and I are becoming a habit. And good news: Pepper approves." Pepper squeezed Clark's elbow and ruffled a hand through his hair. Clark pointed toward the bell jar. "You know what that is?"

"A rock?"

"That's a bona fide *moon* rock. Buzz Aldrin gave it to me."

Frankie turned and looked at the rock again, this time with a new sense of appreciation.

"He won't even let me touch it," Pepper said.

"I let you hold it once," Clark reminded her. "How about you, bud? Want to hold it?"

"Yeah," Frankie said. "I-I'd like to."

Clark stepped around the table and lifted the bell jar and set it aside. Then, delicately, he picked up the rock and placed it on Frankie's palm. Frankie imagined it humming against his skin, charged with some sort of space energy that would give him special powers here on Earth; though, in truth, it only felt like a rock.

He extended his hand toward Clark and said, "Thanks for letting me hold it."

"I'd say 'anytime,' but it probably won't happen again," Clark said, returning the rock to its pedestal and covering it.

"He loves that rock more than he loves me," Pepper said.

"Not true. I love *food* more than I love you." Clark brought his hands together and rubbed his palms. "Who's hungry?"

Pounders was one town over, in Rockledge. Just inside the door, a hostess stood next to a large scale with a digital readout. Her T-shirt had a cartoon pig on it, smiling, his mouth smeared with barbecue sauce. She welcomed them and invited Pepper to weigh in first. Pepper stepped onto the scale.

"One-eighteen and twenty-four ounces," the hostess said. She asked Pepper's name, then wrote it and her weight on a card with a red Sharpie.

"One-seventy-one and six ounces," she announced when Clark stood on the scale, and, "One-oh-nine on the dot," when it was Frankie's turn.

"Lighter than me." Pepper feigned jealousy.

"Nobody's hiding lead in their pockets, I hope," the hostess said.

"Not us," Clark told her. "We're tried and true."

She smiled, opened her hand to the dining room, and said, "Pig out!"

They chose a table, sat down, and ordered drinks (iced tea for Pepper and Frankie, bourbon and water for Clark), and then immediately got up again and stood in a buffet line. There was barbecue, fried chicken, fried cod, meat loaf, spaghetti, mashed potatoes, collards, green beans, rolls, and four different kinds of dessert, including an enormous pan of banana pudding that had a rubbery crust and was half gone and sliding forward like a continental shelf. "Want to compete?" Clark asked Frankie as they filled their plates.

Frankie still didn't get it. "How?"

"We weigh in again at the end of the meal. They charge by the ounce. Whoever gains the most wins."

"I don't eat much," Frankie said.

"Doesn't matter," Pepper said, reaching for the banana pudding spoon. "I'm going to win."

Clark drank four bourbons with water. Both he and Pepper went back for seconds before Frankie was halfway through his plateful of food. He'd taken too much because he'd wanted to try everything on the buffet, but he realized it didn't matter because if it didn't go into his body, it was free. "This restaurant makes the most sense of any around," Clark said, chewing. "Eating out should be like buying a shirt. You go into a store and try on a few shirts, but you only pay for the one you actually take away in a bag."

Frankie sipped from a straw sunk into an iced-tea cup so wide, he had to use two hands to lift it. He was beginning to doubt his sister's assumption that Clark was gay. As for Diana's speculation, he could only guess. Pepper smiled whenever he caught her eye. He smiled back, but felt uncomfortable. "Are you two married?" he asked.

She waved her left hand and showed Frankie her wedding band. "Seven years."

He noticed the matching band on Clark's finger. "Do you . . . have kids?"

This, for some reason, made Clark laugh, and Pepper reached over and lightly slapped his arm. "No," she said.

"Not traditionally," Clark said. He grinned and wiped his mouth with his napkin. He downed the last of his bourbon, and then pushed back from the table and lit a cigarette. "Frankie here wants to go into space, but he doesn't want to do it through NASA."

"You want to be a cosmonaut?" Pepper asked.

"No. I'd like to have my own spaceship, though." He remembered that Clark still hadn't told him his Gordon Cooper story. He asked him now if he would tell it.

"You're not going to ask me again if we descended from aliens, are you?"

"No. But I'd like to hear about the sighting."

Clark winced. "You know, not that I got to see it myself, but my theory is that being out in all that space does something to people's heads. Certain kinds of people, that is."

"What do you mean?"

"It can make them a little . . ." Clark seesawed the hand holding the cigarette, serpentining the smoke.

"But what's the story?"

"The story is, there is no story. Cooper saw ice, or something like ice, coming off the back of his ship. From what I heard, the boys in

Ground Control rolled their eyes big-time over that one. Same thing with Scott Carpenter."

"Carpenter photographed a saucer," Frankie said. "I read about it in a book, and saw the picture."

"He photographed a *tracking balloon.* He *said* it was a saucer."

"He believed it."

"Yeah, well, that's my point. Certain kinds of people . . . who get an inflated sense of their own importance . . . get blasted up there and then get a little . . . I don't know . . . light-headed. They start seeing things. It's ridiculous."

"Clark's a little bitter," Pepper said around her last spoonful of pudding.

"I'm not *bitter.* I'm realistic."

Frankie said, "I read that NASA officials told reporters not to ask questions about that stuff."

"Exactly. Because it was *embarrassing.* Glenn started it on his Mercury orbit with his report of voodoo fairy lights zipping around his head, and a bunch of those other boys jumped on the bandwagon. Most of them couldn't go up there without thinking they saw some alien . . . whatever. It's nonsense."

Frankie thought of the photograph of Clark shaking John Glenn's hand, and Glenn's inscription. Then he thought of Clark's portrait, in the spacesuit—maybe the only time he'd ever worn one.

"Jim Lovell and Buzz Aldrin?" Clark continued. "You know what they were looking at when they cried 'UFO'? Their own jettisoned *trash bags.* If that had been me, and reporters had been allowed to question me about it, I'd be ashamed to show my face. 'I saw a UFO! I saw a UFO!' Please."

"Aldrin gave you the moon rock," Frankie said.

"Yeah. Well." Clark stubbed out his cigarette in a plastic ashtray. "Even a loony can give a nice present."

They weighed themselves again before leaving (Pepper had gained the most weight, and won), and Clark paid the bill. On the drive back to Cocoa, in the backseat of the Trans Am, Frankie decided he was still attracted to Clark but no longer liked him. There was something mean about him. As for his opinions on the UFO sightings, he was just . . . wrong. In their driveway, Frankie thanked them both for dinner and said good-night, but instead of shaking the hand he held out, Clark said, "Whoa, bud, what's the hurry? Don't you want to come inside?"

"What for?"

Pepper smiled at him, but for the first time she didn't hold her gaze; she looked down at the driveway and adjusted the purse hanging from her shoulder.

Clark looked out over the river and shrugged. "Wild times. A little excitement."

Maybe Karen *was* right. Or Diana. Or both of them. Frankie looked at Clark in the moonlight. His solid shoulders. His treadmill-tended waist. The shaggy brown hair falling over his forehead.

"Come on in," Clark said, nodding toward the house.

He sat in the living room on the sofa and accepted the beer Pepper offered him. He'd never drunk alcohol before, but stepping over the threshold into the house for the second time felt like crossing a border into another country, where a whole new set of rules and customs existed. The beer tasted awful, but he drank it, while Pepper sat next to him and talked about the kindergarteners she taught and Clark drank his own beer and smoked in an armchair across from them. Clark's mood had changed. He stared at Frankie as if he might not even want him there. But when he'd taken the last swig of his beer, he nodded toward him and said, "Why don't you chug that thing and the three of us go upstairs?"

Frankie walked up the staircase between them. *Expect nothing,* he told himself, even as he became aroused. *This is a tour of the house. He's a Realtor, after all. Maybe they're selling the place.* But Pepper led them into the master bedroom, where she turned around and smiled and said to him, "If you're not comfortable with this, that's OK. You just tell us. But I thought I'd take off my clothes now."

Frankie felt Clark's hand rest on his shoulder. "Are you selling your house?"

"God, no," Clark said. "We love it here."

"Do you *mind* if I take off my clothes?" Pepper asked.

"No."

"Do you want to take off yours?" She asked it in a polite way that really did seem to leave the matter open.

"OK," Frankie said.

"How about you, Clark?"

"Why not," Clark said, releasing Frankie's shoulder. He began to unbutton his shirt.

They slowly got naked without speaking. Frankie's hard-on was sticking straight up and flat against his belly as he stood in the middle of the room, wondering what would happen next. He liked Pepper's body— but as a scientific wonder: the movement of her breasts as she bent to pull back the bedspread; the patch of hair, indented, in the absence of a dick. He looked over at Clark, who had pulled down his briefs and whose dick was half as long as the balls that sagged beneath it. Clark walked over to a leather chair in a corner of the room and sat down.

"You look nice," Pepper told Frankie. "Do you want to lie down here with me?"

"What about Clark?" Frankie asked.

"I'll be in this chair," Clark said.

Frankie started to walk toward him.

"No, no," Pepper said. "Come lie down with me."

"But—" Frankie began.

"Go on, bud," Clark said. He put his hand on his dick and started tugging.

Frankie turned and looked at Pepper. She'd climbed onto the bed and was stretched out flat on her back, with her hand extended toward him. "It's OK," she said. "This is what we do. Clark likes to watch."

"Pretend I'm not here," Clark said.

Frankie felt a little dizzy—from the beer, maybe. "I can't . . . touch you?"

"Not if I'm not here," Clark said.

"But you *are* here."

"I'm *not* here. You're doing this, just you and her, and I'm not even in the room."

"It's going to feel so horny to have you lying here with me," Pepper said.

Frankie's feet felt glued to the carpet. He glanced down and saw his hard-on begin to flag.

"Get up on that bed," Clark ordered.

After several long moments of what was starting to feel to Frankie like a standoff, Pepper pushed up onto her elbows and looked at him and asked, "What's wrong?"

"Nothing," Frankie lied.

"Do you not want to do this?"

"It's just that . . . I thought . . ."

Pepper made a little sound as the air left her lungs. "I think I get it," she said. "You don't swing but one way, do you?"

"Right," Frankie said, relieved.

"And that's not my way, is it?"

"Not really, no."

Clark peered at the two of them. "What are you two talking about?"

"He doesn't swing my way, Clark."

"Sure he does."

"I like boys," Frankie said. "Guys, I mean. Men."

"Are you kidding me?"

Pepper folded her arms over her breasts and said, "Jesus, Clark, can't you do *anything* right?"

"How was I supposed to know that?" Clark asked. His hand had stopped pulling and his fingers had opened; his dick looked like a newborn hamster sleeping on his palm.

"You're such a screwup," Pepper snapped. She got out of bed and grabbed her panties and shirt from the floor. "I don't know why I expect any different."

"It's not *my* fault if he's gay," Clark said.

Pepper pulled on her panties and sat back down on the bed, buttoning her shirt. "Sweetheart," she told Frankie, "you swing any way you want. That's just fine. I'm really sorry about the misunderstanding." She cut her eyes over to her husband again and said again, "Jesus, Clark."

"I'm supposed to be a mind reader now? If he's a closet case, that's *his* problem."

"I'm not . . . in the closet," Frankie said.

"Well, you could have told me that."

"He doesn't have to tell you," Pepper said. "You could . . . intuit. You know? You could learn for once in your life how to *gauge* people. Maybe you'd *get* somewhere." She turned to Frankie. "Get dressed, sweetheart. And please don't tell anyone about this."

"What's that supposed to mean, 'get somewhere'?" Clark asked.

"In your marriage," Pepper told him. "In your life."

"I'm somewhere," Clark protested.

"No, you're not. You're not even here, remember?" She rolled her eyes.

Clark shifted his gaze from Pepper to Frankie and just stared at him for a moment, as if trying to make sense of him. "Guess it's time for you to go, bud," he said.

"I didn't mean to—"

Clark cut him off: "No big deal."

"Well, I'm . . . I'm sorry."

"There's nothing to be sorry about," Clark all but snapped. "It's just time for you to go. The evening's over."

Frankie gathered his clothes from the floor and carried them out to the hall. He dressed there, listening as Pepper chastised Clark some more and Clark told her to shut up. She didn't, and they continued to argue as Frankie descended the stairs.

On his way out of the house, he paused in the dining room.

"There's no end to the sickness and depravity of the human spirit," Diana said upon hearing the story before lunch the following Monday, on the bench in the commons. "Maybe that's the good news."

"I guess," Frankie said.

"I wonder if people like that would go for a chubby girl like me."

"He's not nice. She is, but not him. You think he'll come after me?" He had his backpack open on the ground between his sneakers and was holding the moon rock, turning it in his hands.

Diana gazed at the rock. "Did you ever give him your phone number?"

"No."

"Does he know where you live?"

"No."

"I'll bet it's fake. Aldrin probably thought Evans was a big loser and had a laugh with his buddies, handing over a chunk of concrete. Anyway, you're a minor and they tried to have sex with you. *And* they gave you alcohol. You could go public and expose them as extreme and dangerous molesters."

"I don't feel molested."

"I know, but it means you get to keep the rock."

Frankie brought the rock up to his nose and sniffed it. It smelled like gunpowder. He held the rock an inch from his eye and peered at its knobby surface.

"He actually told you to pretend he wasn't there?"

"That's what he said. 'Pretend I'm not here.'"

"I'll probably be telling somebody that, one day."

Frankie thought about it. "I'll probably be telling them the opposite."

"Sickness," Diana said. "Depravity." She gazed out over the commons and sighed. "I'm starving. Let's eat."

A Joint and a Nice Piece of Ass

Mack Friedman

I met Jake when he was sixteen, at a volunteer recognition dinner hosted by an HIV service unit I worked for, the Central Region AIDS Project. I didn't recognize anyone. The dinners (like the organization itself) were parodies of function, marked as they were by inedible catering, incoherent speakers, and the absurd resurfacing of volunteers who hadn't done anything for the place in years. This annual commingling always made me think of parties thrown by high-ranking Nazis to honor the rank and file, but maybe I'd just talked to one too many menopausal "buddies" who loved their collies, hated their husbands, and aspired to appear philanthropic with their time. The cream of the crop hosted AIDS garden parties that made the local "Seen" column every spring. I called these well-intentioned women the Opportunistic Infections: for them, the fun didn't start until one of their buddies was losing an eye. The theme of this particular dinner was "I Volunteer Because People Are Still Dying." People were still dying? Well, glory be, and there before the grace of God were we.

My friend Natty the fund-raiser (whose days at our agency were numbered: he was sane) came up, said "Hi." We filled plastic glasses with Chardonnay and transformed cheap hors d'oeuvres into dinner. No sooner had I slipped some sweaty Swiss onto Ritz Bits than a short, pale, and winsome lad materialized by Natty's side. I'd seen this kid once at work the week before; we'd traded a quick molten stare from opposite sides of the bulletproof glass that had been installed in the receptionist's office as soon as the board realized African Americans were infected, too. I elbowed Natty and he introduced us. "Meet Jake," he told me. "Jake's been doing some volunteering for Development." I asked Jake what college he went to. He laughed nervously and said he was a high school junior. As I debated whether to ply him with wine from a cardboard box, our volunteer coordinator, Carnie, who resembled an oversize beach ball with a tassel of deep purple hair, harrumphed, and Jake and Natty ambled to the last two chairs.

Carnie wasted no time starting a call-and-response: "Why are we here?" she barked. "*Because people are still dying!*" I couldn't sit and couldn't talk and wasn't about to listen to that crap, so instead I skipped out the door into the cold rain and rode my rusty bike over God's green hills where people were still dying, home.

Ever since, my meetings with Jake have always been rendezvous; and that very word, even in this most mundane place, a steely riverfront mill town plopped down in a sooty valley, infused an exotic extract into our earliest and most banal meetings. Our next conversation occurred at the Project, in front of several witnesses. Wandering around after testing clinic rounds, I noticed Jake making sex packets (two condoms and a lubricant, stuffed into a dime bag) in the library with some girls his age. He told me of an upcoming Boston trip, and I gave him my friend Emilia's number there. Carnie waddled in and surveyed us all balefully, no doubt confused that her volunteers were actually doing something besides making a hash of confidentiality law. I asked the room if anyone would be driving to my neighborhood later, I'd popped a flat and lost my patch kit.

I waited a beat and began to leave. Jake piped up, stuttered, cracked, said he could give me a ride, and blushed blood red. I didn't even let him drop me off at home, only blocks away so he wouldn't get lost or come stalk me. The next day I was called in for a special session convened by the board of directors. They were a wizened bunch of local television person-alities and bathhouse owners who'd once spent six months coming up with a mellifluous alternative to "Center City HIV Taskforce" and had fixed on something with the acronym CRAP. "He's sixteen," noted the corporate, gray, happily married executive director. "We might have to investigate this." I told them to go ahead, 'cuz I had more important things to concentrate on. After all, people were still dying. They decided it was better not to fuck with Jake. (His dad, it turned out, was a lawyer.) That afternoon Jake sent an e-mail to my work account about his favorite bands. I can't remember what they were or how he got the address. It was the only thing he sent me that I ever lost.

Astrid had been my girlfriend and boyfriend for the last sixteen months. (She liked to strap it on—she named her strap-on Ralph—but when I suck cock I like a hole in the head.) That night I confessed: I was in love with someone else. Even though I couldn't have him it wouldn't be right to keep seeing her. She'd been idly explaining how easy it would be to pierce my scrotum when I broke the news, and she was sharp and steady about the whole thing. She talked me down, and we kept seeing each other, but it was never the same after Jake. Or only once: together in the fall at a goat farm just out of town, in a rickety old bed-and-breakfast attic reading Warhol's diaries, cedar joints squeaking, knotted boards squealing, kids bleating out on the lawn. Fucking so hard and so true . . . and I'd seen Jake clandestinely when his summer internship ended. He and I had walked around a local campus on a warm late August night and had coffee. Mostly he'd talked, about everything he liked or didn't. Yes to opera, track stars, capri pants, and his dad. No on homework, the Central Region AIDS Project, his mom. Still forming an opinion about guys, coming out, his younger brother, Judaism, and why his parents divorced. On a bridge over the hollow, I lifted my shirt to wipe my nose, and Jacob stopped chattering for an entire minute. I wondered what it would take for him to shut up for an hour, and knew someday I had to find out.

Just being in Jake's presence changed this town for me—removing the toxins, turning its rivers from sludge into silt. In the fall, when he was seventeen, he drove me back from a needle-exchange retreat. Astrid was staying the weekend, but she had gone to the lake with her best friend, a glorious sprite of a girl. I invited him in, and my kitchen seemed suddenly alien to me. Was this really my folks' old table, its porcelain so white, with edges so deep blue? Was the linoleum really this filthy? Was the cabinet really sloping off the wall? Typically I found my rented place large and drafty, but on this cool afternoon, with the light fading and the mulberries drooping against the window in the latest chill, it was confined and almost too warm. Jake held out a UCLA brochure, but turned it toward himself so that I had to stand behind him in order to read it. I wanted to reach out for comfort. Touch his shoulder. Palm his flat ass. Instead, I convinced myself I was home, here in this land of restraint.

I hated everything about these decisions. Jake wasn't saying a word. Until I was sure he'd turned eighteen, I avoided every subsequent meeting. Nothing I was doing was right. Astrid moved in on Thanksgiving and we broke up on Christmas Day. I was taking a crap. She came in to brush her teeth.

"I'm leaving you for a younger man," she grinned, twirling her labret with her tongue. "Isn't that ironic?" She pinched her nostrils and frothed through the hole in her chin.

She'd met him at the teen drug rehab center she worked for. "Do you see an ethical problem here?" I asked her, wiping gingerly; Ralph had played rough the night before, and I wasn't sure she knew.

"Fuck you," she spat into the sink. "He's sixteen. A joint and a nice piece of ass will keep him off crack any day of the week." I flushed, conceding the point, and walked into the bedroom to roll her a few. What the hell, it was for a good cause.

In the new spring, on his birthday, I wrote Jake a message. "I want what we started to happen." He wrote back asking, "What did you think the likelihood was that I would respond?" *You cocky little shit,* I felt like saying. Some things you just know all along.

After the next overdose-prevention brainstorming session we went out for an Italian ice (mango for him, lemon for me) and I led him down a hill near a subterranean park. The blackberry bushes welcomed us, thorny strangers you passed in the night on the way home from work now smiling and saying hello, come inside, pick me, take a bite.

"Where are you taking me?" he asked, vibrating slightly, then trying to sound mature and controlled.

"Into the cemetery."

I stopped my hand from reaching out to his. But when we got to a stone bench I needed to touch him. I moved to kiss him on the cheek and he turned his lips to mine. The dogs and their owners were not in this plane and they left us alone. He pleaded with me to come over again. I begged off. I wanted to savor the expectation. I wanted our plane to be delayed so I could hang around the airport and know that I was leaving, really *know* it: not yet, so soon.

He slipped a phone from his shorts and flipped it open. "Hey, Dad," he said. "Yeah. I'm coming home soon. I'm with Becky. Yeah, on her houseboat. . . . I'll be back before that. OK. Bye."

"Why did you lie to him?" I asked, and a torpid southern breeze lazed through the graves.

"My dad? I don't know. He just wanted to know I was OK. I really didn't feel like having a conversation."

We set a date for the weekend at the double iron gates.

Later, he canceled by phone—"What if I fall in love with you?" he asked, panicked, or joking.

"What if I want you to fall in love with me?"

"That's what I'm afraid of," he said. "Shit, who the hell is calling me? I'll call you back," he said, and didn't.

And that, I thought, was it: another brilliant mistake, another little death. A gaggle of boys his age started testing positive in my clinic, and I spent the fall giving them their hard-earned results and riding fast through the cemetery, trying to lift love from the dead with the wind from my spokes like the dust I raised from the paths.

There is a certain ritual to taking blood. Lift the arm. Place the latex tourniquet under the triceps, wrap it below itself in a quarter knot. Palpate the inner elbow, feeling for the antecubital vein, a small straight section of coursing plumpness. Wipe a circle on the skin with an alcohol swab, snap on gloves, wave the area dry. Screw the butterfly needle to a small plastic barrel, which has its own needle inside to puncture the rubbery red tube top. Then say something like, "You're going to feel a stick," or, "Small pinch now," or, if I really don't like the client, "Big prick here." Then a forty-five-degree angle, a quick smooth stroke, the red flush vacuuming into the tubule, and we're in. Jam the tube into the barrel's needle and listen to the miniature waterfall splashing glass walls.

You can trace this ritual to the antiquarian practice of bloodletting, venous punctures made by clerics to let sickness out of the body. The condition of my modern subjects was just as purgatorial. The invasion and blood loss was a symbol of their flaw; the blood released symbolized the expurgation of this failure; the bottling of the blood alluded to the worldly containment of such sin. Vial, vile, evil. My subjects knew I held evil in my hand.

But I did not see it as such. I saw it as water, oxygen, cells. In my vial, a substance not evil, but live.

It's OK, I would say. Talk about it. I've heard it all. I've been doing this for three years, and nothing surprises me anymore. I don't think you've done anything wrong. I will be your tester. So rest easy.

You will be, if you will, one of my testees. Something is rotten in the state of . . . well, not Denmark, exactly—everything's great in Denmark. It's a relative paradise. But here, something stinks. I'm not authorized to divulge our location. Or my name, for that matter—anonymity is a double-sided dildo. So we'll use the old standbys. You can call me Average Joe. Here in Anytown, USA, it's not too small or big, not too black or white, not too straight or gay. Just your average . . . rot.

What brings you in today? Feel free to say.

'Cuz nobody's ever fucked up here. Not in this office. Whatever people might think of you outside this office, whatever you might think of yourself in your most private moments, that doesn't transmit here. Not in my book. You never fucked up in my book.

You're just human. And you did what you did for a reason. That thing you couldn't tell your husband or wife or girlfriend or boyfriend or mom or dad or fuckbuddy or slumbergirl or hairdresser or priest or dominatrix. The shit you couldn't tell the moralists at County Health or the worrywarts on the CDC hotline, that's what you came here for.

I've heard it all, I'd say. It's OK. Nobody's ever fucked up here.

It usually worked. They usually talked. The slim young brunette, her hair a frazzled split-end mass, told me how she was raped in the car after a date. The married man cried as he recalled that day in the steam room where he sat on someone's thumb and it went inside his ass. (What fortuitous circumstance befalls those least in need!) The spinster came every two weeks for a year after she serially accepted glasses of iced tea from a man whom she suspected was HIV positive. Her situation always involved "flecks" of blood from his mouth swirling into her Mandalay. "What should I do?" she asked the last time she came. "Stop drinking iced tea," I suggested. "It's very unhealthy." The responsible bears who fucked around when their cubs were gone but came in every few months to make sure things were cool. The riot grrrls making statements: we take it up the ass, too! And the boys, always the boys, drinking and smoking and losing their teeth to crystal, wearing insouciance like cologne. "Cool, I'm not positive yet," they'd say. Or, "Oh, well, guess I should see a doctor now?" I cried for them when they left because they could not cry for themselves, and the girl who was raped returned for results and gave me a trembling, feathery hug. It felt nice then, like I mattered, but later it just made it all worse. My skull stored all the suffering of this town, and not even Astrid knew any trepanists.

"But if you want, I'll give it a go," she offered sweetly. "Just do your homework and get me the right kind of drill."

There are other ways in this modern world to approximate bloodletting. Astrid moonlighted as a piercer. She claimed to have pierced more dicks than I'd ever even seen. Piercing is a nicely impermanent way to let those evil spirits out—unless the piercer fucks you up, then it's as permanent as scar tissue. She used to be a cutter; she would slash her forearms evenly with razor blades. She told me it felt better than screaming or puking or hurting someone else. Someday we will all be as brave as Astrid. We will sizzle our shoulders with cattle branders and roll around in the dirt and bubble forth keloids. We will let pain pass through us and out the other side. We will treasure its entry and celebrate its departure. We will not bottle it so long, so evilly, inside our bodies, our capsules, our vials. And maybe we will find a new ritual for that. But for now, HIV testing, due to its lethal implications, its linkage of sex and punishment, is the best thing we've got going.

Ritual.

In the fall, Carnie was fired for stealing six hundred donated trinkets from our Toys for Dying Tots campaign. Casper, my favorite client, died shortly thereafter. He'd had HIV since he was fourteen, traced to his hustler lover who ran away to California on him. Casper's tiny tombstone read "GHOST, 1974—2000, RIP." Among the mausolea, maple leaves turned the color of Carnie's hair and bombed my face.

Once I saw Casper's most recent girlfriend, a sixteen-year-old silent albino, sitting solemnly on my bench—Jake's bench, our bench. Casper had brought her in to see me once, and she'd tested negative. I didn't think Casper could fuck by the time he'd gotten to her. He'd wasted into two dimensions, like a windowpane, and when I made him a long-simmering *pho* it went into his mouth and out his ass in two minutes flat. From then until he died, I made sure to serve him diapers with his soup. I didn't say anything to his devoted waif. She stared fixedly at the ground. I guessed she had as much right to the seat as I did; we were both doing the same thing, being here with the ghosts, trying to summon them back.

Two wayward Scots performed for me that midnight in the barren grove.

"Will there be audience participation?" they asked.

"Don't know," I replied. "Depends on the show?"

The boy getting sucked had gelled hair that stuck to my fingers, and then, his left nipple. Patriotic spotlights plastered his penis, sliding out of his boyfriend's mouth. One great view, then the squad car turned us into chipmunks. We live through somnambular law.

That night I broke down and had six whiskeys and wrote Jake a letter.

"Dreaming last night," I wrote. "You were there (what hindered truth was clothing). Where are you next summer?"

"Europe," he answered, some weeks later.

Was he accepting expatriates? He didn't respond, all through winter and spring. Then he sent me a postcard one windy day in his limbo, back here on the way from Cali to Spain.

"The cloud cover is settling. I look up and see that the blue doesn't beckon me to reach up boundlessly. There is no blue to reach for. The white pushes back, asks me to stay down here, close to the ground. To stay inside of it. Inside the thick."

I'd turned thirty and moved into an apartment much closer to the cemetery, my eye on a fresh plot for myself. *If you order early,* the commercial said, *you can save your family 50 percent!* Another pleasant June night, a year after we'd first kissed, Jake called on me again. He fairly skipped along while I gimped on a busted ankle. We circumscribed huge echoing tombs and ghostly limestone pyramids and I saw him for a short dorky overanalyzed sweet and scared Jewish kid who'd just finished his first year of college. We lay on flat headstones from 1892 and stared at the scimitar moon, Venus in its sheath. The fireflies danced around us like sentient beings from another planet, and faraway porch lights flared through the curtains of the night.

He came off in ten seconds, but it was a start. Then he said he needed to call his dad. Jake told him he was somewhere close to where we were, but not quite. Either Jake's lies were getting closer to truth or

I'd moved closer to the neighborhood he liked to lie about. In bed he quivered and stayed on after I limped off in the morning. When I got back from work, he was gone. He left me a note on the desk. It said, "Thank you for being patient with me for a few years and watching me grow up and not be as scared."

I didn't wash my sheets for a month, until my scent had replaced his completely.

I didn't know I was the scared one, now.

Two nights later, secretly, he met our friend Markos. Markos was sixteen and had been a prodigiously lyrical poet a few years before. We'd "met" in a local writers' chat room, where he'd told me he was bisexual and sent me a poem about AIDS. It's the only thing Markos ever sent me that I lost. He'd been incommunicado since his dad hired a private investigator after finding marijuana in Markos's room a year before. The family was Greek Orthodox and his parents' version of therapy was a series of consultations with the priest. Jake knew Markos through me: they both lived in half-ritzy, half-country, all-white, all-suburban Elk Abbey. I introduced them electronically soon after I first met Jake, before Markos's shit hit the fan. I'd never seen Markos in person. To me he was an amalgamation of excited electrons that made my computer screen pulse.

This time around, Jake met Markos at a public library at midnight. Jake drove them to Jake's mom's old house, empty since she'd moved to a new, smaller place. They stripped and took a shower. Then, a gap in Jake's story: use your imagination.

"If you don't hear from me for a while," said Jake's voice on my machine, "it's because while Markos and I were taking a shower at my mom's old house, his dad called my cell, whose voice mail I check ten minutes later to realize such a thing, and I am listening to this man identify the color and make of my car and the license plate (incorrectly) and he begins to threaten me before I delete the damn message and don't listen to it. I took Markos back to the high school, about a five- to eight-minute run from his house; I hope he is OK; his dad is fucking crazy. Finding my cell phone number in his son's e-mails (maybe? somehow?). That he saw my car means he saw the two of us meet up at the library for all of sixty seconds. Probably a good idea that we left rather than undressing in the woods, with Greek daddy standing there. So I'm going to flee the country. Meet me later this summer. I'll be somewhere in Holland."

Hmm, I wondered jealously, *can you really take a shower in the woods?*

Jake tried me again from the airport.

"That's messed-up about Markos," I said. *Why was everyone I knew screwing a sixteen-year-old?* "Not surprising, but still." *Was I missing something here?*

"Yeah," Jake grunted. "Fucked."

"But I think you're within the four-year gap of our consent statute." I'd read up on this quick and pro bono. "Legally, you should be OK."

"Yeah, and what the fuck." I could tell he was pissed. He didn't normally swear. "I didn't kidnap his son. He was just scared; if he were really after me he wouldn't have said that 'the police' will come to get me."

Kidnap. Something about that got me thinking. I listened to the airport page run through its cycle, *Anna Mata-Funk please meet your party at baggage carousel B, Anna Mata-Funk please meet your party . . .*

"I haven't talked with him regularly in ages," I told him. "I didn't know you still were. His family's deranged and I don't want to get in the middle. I'm already nervous about giving you his info in the first place. He's a cool kid, though."

"He is, and he's grown up since I last saw him; he was talking about symbolism and poetry and beauty in the world . . . funny guy."

"Wait." *Since you last saw him?* "His dad said the police would come for you, or Markos said that?"

"His dad's message said the police would be after me. If he really wanted to get me, and not just 'get his son back,' he would have told me that he would fucking beat me up himself." His voice was shaking but he sounded resolved. "All right, I am going to appease my dad and play pinochle with him before I have to go to the gate. I'll see you later," Jake said, and hung up.

"Good-bye," I said, "I love you," and he wasn't there, and it was probably all for the best.

There was no having with Jacob, only desire, but I guessed I wouldn't have it any other way. One August night I soared over my mercurial valley and landed in drizzly Amsterdam the next morning. I spent the day there glad for the dope. I was suddenly too anxious to see Jake. What if I *could* have him, for instance? And for how long this time, before he vanished again? I stayed at a leatherman hotel in cheap dorm digs, cruised by a naked young Frenchman in states of dreaming but no desire for anyone but Jake.

I couldn't think. I'd lost Astrid for him and needed to be right. I wanted wedding soup when he wanted a pastry. The whole thing made me nauseous. His directions were as follows.

Take the train from Centraal Station to Apeldoorn.

Catch the 110 bus to Hoenderloo.

Get off at the Apeldoornzweig stop after the first yellow bakery.

Order something. The beignets are good, light and flaky.

Take a left at the second yellow bakery.

You will be at Hoge Veluwe National Park. Keep walking.

Take a left at the first unmarked dirt road by the white house.

Walk to the end.

Find me.

22/8. Early morning I left for Hoenderloo; short trip to Apeldoorn, then long wait for bus. Walked to the farm in the downpour. Jake was bearded and drenched. Helped him haul firewood, then walked alone to the national park in the deluge, biked along heath in forest and bog and over the shifting sands, amazed by putrescent, so-bright-they-make-you-puke rough neon strokes of museum's Van Goghs and elegant skeletons of Fernand Léger's soldiers playing cards, not human troops but death masks and machines made of bone saw. J again. Smiling, wet, got stuff ready, left swampy polders for sunnier German pastures. Train ride perfect, clear, expectant, ideal. Arrived in Hannover late. Novotel. *I want what we started to happen,* Jake smirked. *You cocky little shit,* I thought, and engulfed him.

Where do you want to go? I asked before we slept.

Don't know, he murmured. *Concentration camps? Art museums? Berlin?*

23/8. Hannover, Léger, Kandinsky, Sophie Calle loves James Turrell, calm lunch and warm sun, hand in hand in hand. Train to Berlin jangled, happy, dreamy, not a minute off. A lucky room at Pension Kreuzberg: dark, Gothic, huge, pleasant, sexy, hot late-night walk along Brandenburg Gate/Reichstag/Checkpoint Charlie construction zone, history's occlusion by steel, glass, cranes, dust, spiderwebs on bicycles abandoned for months, wall remnants glued to postcards. Too late for Bergen-Belsen, no buses back from death.

24/8. Drank fucked talked loved ate walked through Viktoria Park fucked slept loved ate sunburn.

25/8. Breakfast at Obst und Omelette and Kaffee, the blond *frau* at the table across smiling for us, wistful love everywhere, angiosperms, post-fuck in the air, then Brecht's grave, Hegel's headstone, Jake's sore throat, husky philosophies, sexy, sick, sun in the meadow, blue wild-flowers after sex or sleep so hard to distinguish. Jake's pillow over his head and he finally stops speaking languages when I straddle his furry blond ass: *Shut up already shut up already shut up.* Sweetly crazy, the smell of his armpits, he wants to buy deodorant, *Shut up,* I say, *no way.*

26/8. S-Bahn fast to Wannsee beach. Deep in the FKK section the families diffuse, gay Aryans tall and fair, uncut, hairless. *You can tell we're the Jews,* Jacob cracks, but in the Wannsee Villa conference room the framed Jewish boys are the shaven ones. Jake still sick and zitty in a cemetery near Hallesches Tor kissed me beautifully with chapped lips like crepe paper, erections touch through denim, then gone, Jake gone again on the evening train to the Netherlands. Alone again so soon I find a small dorm room in a hostel, sad grateful lonely e-mail Astrid, J, say, *Love you always, and thanks.* Then smoked silly with loose nicotine, missing Jake so terribly, only absinthe helps. Wormwood, sugar cube, slotted spoon, ice water, ritual of desire and pain and forgetting. Weaving back through the streets, ask all passersby, *Do you have a Führer?* My German's not so great; all I need is a flame. Our love is a sunburn, quick and pink and taut and my nose is peeling already. The skin that touched Jake is sloughing off.

27/8. Free Internet at Hostel Transit. "I'm in the yellow bakery," Jake has written me. "It was so great to see you, if only for a bit. By the time I see you again I don't know what will have transpired. Guess that's something I keep open. But I think that I think of it as friendship right now rather than romance, if we're working with categories. We're always so far away."

28/8. On flight back I am stuck next to a lounge singer from Jersey who finally met a Dutchman she'd talked with on PalChat, some network where "you can see them and hear them." They'd had an incredible two weeks together in Arnhem, she said, during which time she'd managed to get knocked up. This explained her intermittent bouts of happy sobbing. "He says he will stop drinking so much," she blubbered, her nostalgia thick as snot. She blew her nose. "I guess I'll have to take the kids to Holland!" she wailed, exultant. "And of course, I'll need a divorce." I gave her my pretzels, it only seemed fair, she was eating for two and I wasn't at all.

Wrap the tourniquet around the biceps with one hand, bite to keep it in place. It doesn't need to be tight. The antecubital should pop up pretty well. It usually does.

Arrange two cotton filters, small and dense like birdshot pellets; one metal cooker, an empty tea light candle; one red Bic lighter, the flame. One small baggie nicked from the County Health asphalt after the needle exchange; distilled water, straight from the pharmacy; two antimicrobial wipes from the office. An eyedropper from my medicine cabinet. A diabetic syringe, blue topped, we call it a pogo stick for inventory. They won't miss this one.

Tap the baggie so half the powder falls into the cooker. Let the eyedropper pipette tap the distilled water, pinch the bulbous rubber stopper. Squirt two drops onto the spoon. Light the flame underneath. Let the mixture boil until it turns to golden mud. Water droplets race away like the impure from the pure. Draw twenty cubic centimeters, a half inch, into the pogo, through the filter. Make a fist and, with the other hand, a forty-five-degree angle. Then, a smooth straight stroke, and we're in. Watch the syringe for crimson. Let the blood's flashback be a guide. Release the tourniquet with teeth. Relax the fist.

Plunge.

The world is so far away.

Ritual.

Markos contacts me again in January.

"Don't worry, it's safe," he says. "I'm calling you from the pay phone in the library. I got your number from 411. How are you?"

"OK," I say. "Kind of sad."

"Oh, why?"

"It's about Jake. I don't know. I fell for him last summer, hard."

"Why, what did he do?"

"He's not calling me back. He's at school. He gets like that."

"It seems like he is the kind of dude that likes a quickie and then just goes," Markos tells me. Then again, I think, Markos's dad might have had something to do with those particular escapes. His parents seem to view their progeny as a sort of faulty but vaguely important appliance that keeps breaking down, like a wood-burning stove that's never used for cooking but looks great in the kitchen and can provide warmth if properly stoked. Problem is, they hired the wrong people to do the job: a priest and a PI might poke around a little, but you can't keep the home fires burning when you don't let the wood taste the air. "I really knew inside that I didn't like him because of his personality or anything," he continues. "Sure, he was nice, but my initial attraction was based on the fact that I could get a piece from him."

"I don't think he liked that thing with your pops."

"I wondered what happened to him," Markos drawls.

He quiets for a moment, long enough to hear the electric fuzz of our connection, the black crush of his thoughts. When he picks back up, he garbles, like he's chewing the inside of his cheek. "I guess he doesn't want to get in trouble."

I change the subject. "What did you get for Christmas?"

"A lump of coal. What about you?"

"A bottle of absinthe."

He is quiet again, and then hoarse: "If I tell you something, promise me you won't think differently of me?"

"Of course not," I say.

"I thought about you when I beat it the other night," he laughs, and hangs up.

Markos soon sends me a letter and a picture and a CD he burned for me. In the picture, he is grinning, a curly young Hermes standing next to a happy clown. He is wearing a birthday cone hat that reads, "17." In the letter he writes, "You better like this CD, son, because I ran six blocks in the snow to send it." The CD's first cut is "Here Comes My Man."

"You're my dream man," Markos says on my machine. "I just get high and listen to Radiohead and think about you after school. I'll buy an MG this summer and every day I'll come over and we'll smoke and walk around and you'll feel like a teenager again. Then we can go to the desert and ride horses and have campfires and sing songs and play guitar and live under the stars. And we'll have a cactus farm and grow peyote." His voice drops to a death rattle. "Listen. My dad found out about you. But it's OK because we never did anything. I'm going to write you from a safe address next time." Now a whisper: "My friend is having a party this weekend." He gives her address fast and soft. "She knows about you and she's cool. We'll hide you upstairs if we have to. I'll be so stoked if you come." The only noise from the machine is the whir of the tape wheels. Then, one last breath: "Will you be my valentine?"

The Ballad of Jimmy Pie

Ethan Mordden

If you run out of Sparktown on the north road doing 80 like Daddy and me did, hot from a scam, you get nowhere pronto, and that's where we picked up Jimmy.

I saw the kid was going to be one God's ass piece of mischief right off, and I begged Daddy to let him be. But Daddy slowed the car as we approached and looked the kid over with pleasure.

"He's a fairskin boy, Otis," Daddy told me as we braked about twenty feet past the kid. "You know your Daddy's partial."

The kid ran up and leaned against the door. He didn't give me so much as a fuckyou glance, just smiled at Daddy all slow and boylike, the kind of smile you have to practice in a mirror fore you get it right.

"How far you goin?" Daddy asked.

"Fairly." The kid pushed up his shirt to rub his stomach, give Daddy a good look. "See, I'm so young yet I don't know where I'd rightfully be headin."

"We like em young," said Daddy. "This here's my son Otis. He's twenty and big for his size."

"He's big enough, I'd say," the kid replied, finally giving me the favor of his pretty glances and such.

"We're on the move just now," said Daddy, "having lost Otis' brother Luke this morning."

The kid nodded pensively. "Cops got him?"

"Somethin like that. Whyn't you fetch your bag and Otis here'll swing into the back, won't you, Otis, and give this boy some room up front where his pale skin can take some sun."

"Aw, Daddy—"

"Scoot, now, I say."

"Thought we was goin to be just us two from now on," I said.

"Takes three for scams, you know that, Otis."

I didn't move fast enough, so Daddy's hand caught me sharp on the ear, fierce to match his eyes.

"Why you always testin me, boy?" Daddy cried, looking straight ahead. When he turned, I'd jumped over the seat into the back and the kid was makin himself to home. "Sure am obliged," he said, shakin his head to give his cute hair a show and, like, rubbin his forearms while he smiled at Daddy. Flirt! I thought. Whyn't you go down on him right here in the car?

"Throw your gear in the back with Otis there and get yourself comfortable. We're fixin to make it to Pentecost by late moon. Got a big deal waitin there." As we shipped out, Daddy added, "What do they call you, son?"

"They all agree that I'm Jimmy Pie, it seems. Cause I'm so fresh and tasty."

"Now, you hold your noise, Otis," said Daddy, eyeing me in the rearview. "Where are your manners with your new brother? Such a fairskin boy means all parties better mind their ways, or Daddy'll have to wade in with discipline and a sermonette." He got into the rearview again with "Hear me, Otis?"

I didn't say nothin back there, just locked eyes with Daddy till the kid asked, "Expectin someone? Cause I see you're lookin behind us at the road at times."

"Don't you worry, Jimmy Pie. Your Daddy's got it all figured. Take care of business in Pentecost, then who knows what we'll do?" Daddy shot a confident grin at the kid. I might as well not have been there at all with those two touching eyes and such. "Ride the skies, make our fortune. Got a thought to putting Otis into wrestling school, where they train you for tee vee. Know about it?"

"My fortune is my face," says the kid. Him feelin so dandy there, we'll just see about that. "S'what they tell me, anyway."

"Your fortune is your white, white skin," says Daddy. "Cause that is the most beautiful thing of all on a beautiful young boy. You want to get ahead in the world, you need an angle."

"I got five or six angles, I believe."

"Can't wait to know em all, Jimmy Pie," says Daddy, flooring it.

We got to Pentecost real late that night, but that's how Daddy likes it. He claims to work real good in the dark. The place was a fine ol two story job with a porch all round, hidden among many trees and bushes way the far side of town. A storybook house, you might say, right distant from fakes and jokers who snoop around and butt in at cries for help.

"Moonshine land," Daddy calls it.

We approached real quiet, and Daddy went to work on a window after checking for alarms. You have to watch the stairs for booby traps, too.

We was here before, maybe a year ago, so the guy must have taken some steps for security. Not to mention whatever else wants in on him in the neighborhood. He should of at least got a dog. But some guys don't notice anythin, so they don't learn. They're not listenin to what it is is how I see it, not ever there when it's happenin. These guys in their own world? I got not the slightest sympathy for em. Say there's a guy crossing the road with a gun in hand and a racy look in his eye at you. You don't take cover? Die fucked, asshole.

We got upstairs without a problem. He was sleeping face up, and Daddy was content to pull the covers off him real slow, so we could take him in like a stripjoint tease.

He was in real cute shape for a dealer. Most of those guys don't notice how they go around, but this one's real proud of hisself. Daddy shook his head a little, smilin in his thoughts. Jimmy just stood there.

The guy woke up when Daddy stroked his hair. He sure likes them carrottops. I don't get this color thing Daddy has, about skin and eyes and such. Seems to me a guy is pleasin to you or he isn't. It's like a scam, right? It works or it doesn't. You don't have a *luscious* scam or a *beautiful* scam or those other ways Daddy has of goin on and on about a guy's looks and his colors and his parts. It's like he's tryin to hypnotize hisself, like talkin about it will magic it up from somewhere as got no name, and then it'll be real and you'll know what to call it.

The guy's just lyin there lookin up at Daddy. He's scared, yeah, but mostly he's just waitin to see what it'll be. Daddy's like at a party, introducin us all and sayin how rough the trip was, though he doesn't mention Luke. Then he gets down to it, sayin how he'd like to dip into the guy's cashbox and if he'd just tell us the combination he won't get hurt and we'll be on our way and everyone'll be glad.

It's just talk, of course. You don't put Daddy in a room with a cute little naked carrottop all so late at night without somethin comin down. At the very least, the guy's goin to be panwhacked. Anyways, he sure isn't givin up no combination, so Daddy says, "Fetch the bag, Otis," and I get it while Daddy pulls the guy out of bed and holds him from behind, just runnin his hands over him and rubbin their cheeks together like it's Valentine's Day. You know Daddy's happy cause he's hummin as I get out the matches and the ol big ox candle of the sort Daddy likes to use at such moments and the rope and the pan, a copper number you'd cook your dinner in. The guy's doin nothin. He doesn't struggle, he doesn't go with it, and he still hasn't said a word, even when Daddy moves his cute little mop of hair around in different designs.

"He's like a model," said Jimmy, a joke on his face.

I was pulling the bed away from the wall, more into the room to give us maneuvering space. Then I set the candle up in its plate and stripped down like always. So now it's my turn to hold the guy while Daddy strips down, too. Jimmy was looking from him to me and back, but he finally smartened up and moved out of the way, settling down on a chair in the corner while Daddy gets the guy facedown on the bed, ties his wrists behind him, and turns him over.

I'm set to go, but Daddy's really into lookin at a thing when he likes it. He was hummin again and he said, "Man, oh man," all quiet and appreciative.

Finally, he does his head at me to get up there, and the guy's eyes follow me as I move to the head of the bed. Daddy pulls the guy up to place his head so lovingly between my thighs, wedged in there so he can't shout or nothin. Daddy lets out a sigh as he upends the guy's legs, which I hold by the calves. Daddy takes up the pan, hefts it a bit, then starts in quick and heavy, no warmup.

The guy's fightin it now, as they are always bound to, but somehow his struggles and the blows to his backside are merged and comin up through me like some of his soul is evaporatin. I know Daddy feels so, too, because when we switch positions his head goes up and his teeth look out of his mouth like he's comin.

When we let him go, the guy still won't give it up, though he's gasping real hard as we stand there waitin and lookin at him.

"Man, you better part with the information we require," Jimmy quietly calls out from his corner.

Well, the guy finally does talk, but it's just beggin for us to stop and such, no combination to a cashbox.

So Daddy says, "Fetch the candle, Otis," as he gets on the bed to straddle the guy and hum to him. As he bends over close, the guy flinches, but Daddy isn't going to hit him, only deepmouth him and run his hands up and down the sides of the guy.

"Dinnertime," says Jimmy.

Daddy continues to do the guy while goin into his talk thing, repeatin phrases over and over about *the worship of beauty* and *takin your love to the highest level*. Everyone's hard, Jimmy's beatin off, and Daddy suddenly takes the candle from me and gets off the guy, tellin me to hold his legs down while Daddy fires up the guy's tits and dick. Jimmy comes close to watch, but before anythin happens the guy gives up the combination and in seconds the candle's back in its plate and we're all at the little cashbox while the guy tells me, "15 . . . right to 40 . . ." and all the rest. Sometimes he loses his place because Daddy's all over him still. But we got the cash, anyway.

"We crank the guy now?" asks Jimmy.

"What for?" Daddy replies, rubbin the back of the guy's neck and smoothin his sides and ticklin his ear like briskin him up after a massage or somethin.

"He'll call the cops on us is what," Jimmy says.

"A drug dealer?" Daddy grins. "He even winks at a cop hereabouts and it's twenty years mandatory. Sides, him and us got a ongoing business process, ain't we?"

Daddy pats the guy's shoulder. "Right?" says Daddy.

The guy nods.

Daddy holds out a hand and I give him the money to count. "Otis, where are your manners with our host? Don't he need a rest after his exertions? Escort him into the other room for a little R and R."

That means tie him up in a chair so we don't have to think about him anymore tonight. Or ever.

When I come back, Daddy has Jimmy down to the skin and Daddy's at it again, talkin to me like I'm not there as he moves around Jimmy.

"Smooth all over and twice as pretty as who, that's a fairskin boy, now. The curves here. My. The little patch of hair, feel the sex crackle."

"Ooch," says Jimmy, real low.

"Or touch the Jimmy nipples . . . careful! They're pale, like all Jimmy everywhere. The Jimmy smile, so puzzling to me at times. Never know what a Jimmy boy is thinkin. Step around behind, watch. The vee shape here, so wide at the top. Whisper to Jimmy, see what he'll do."

Leanin forward, Daddy whispered so close to Jimmy's ear he was lickin it. "Can I look inside you, Jimmy Pie?"

Jimmy nodded.

"Thank you kindly. Yes. Now. Oh, my gracious Jimmy, to part the golden globes and gaze upon the eternal ring. That's rare, indeed. That's genius. That's the true Jimmy boy, so fair and kissful. Otis, fetch the tape measure."

I got it out of the bag and handed it to Daddy, who busied himself takin the sizes of Jimmy's parts, hummin and occasionally murmurin in awe at the numbers like they was holy revelation.

"Thing about a beautiful, beautiful fairskin boy," said Daddy as he dropped the tape measure on the bed, "is his secret taste, which is the sugar slick that flows out of him when he's brought to the highest power."

Getting behind Jimmy, Daddy reached around and began tummyrubbin him real slow.

"Sure would love to hear a little sigh from you, Jimmy Pie."

Jimmy obeyed.

"It's the taste of the Jimmy slick where his true self lies, for a man can get high on it. If you kiss a fairskin boy deeply enough, it livens the vein of him and stirs up the slick. Then you fuck Jimmy with a sturdy rhythm and take the slick hot and new as it flies out to you, a beseechin taste and a convertin one."

Daddy turned Jimmy to face him.

"That's the Jimmy high. Come true, now."

Daddy began, his hand heavy on the back of Jimmy's neck as he reeled him in tight for lip suction.

"You sure can smooch," said Jimmy, when he got a chance.

"Oh, the taste of fair skin," said Daddy, completely into it. "Tempt me, Satan, you win again!"

"More," said Jimmy.

"High on you."

"More, Daddy, please!"

"High on my Jimmy's slick!"

Pausing to admire Jimmy, tenderly rifflin his hair, Daddy said, "I declare I'd just about kill any fairskin boy who withheld his slick from me, or gave it away to others."

"Never," Jimmy promised.

"You can leave us now, Otis," said Daddy.

So of course it was backseat Otis from then on, just like when Luke joined us. You know, it wasn't the cops killed Luke, it was me. A scam backfired, and we were runnin, and I shouted "Go, Luke!" to pinpoint him and he took fire. Cops? It was Otis with a shotgun is all.

Anyway, I sure didn't take to the new arrangement, Daddy ravin about his Jimmy boy and Jimmy just so enjoyin that. Daddy even let Jimmy drive us from time to time. And Jimmy adored to drive, it seems. Cars were his candy.

I never got to drive. What I got was swats to the ear and Fetch it, Otis, and there was no chance to get rid of Jimmy the way I got rid of Luke.

I was so frustrated that once I threatened to beat Jimmy up if he ddn't scram.

"Daddy won't like that," was all Jimmy said, not even looking up from his X-Men comic.

"How about money, then?" I went on. "I got some."

"How much?"

"Or I could just crank you," I said, and he finally looked at me, showin that smile I surely do not admire.

"Whyn't you like me, Otis?" he asked. "I like you."

"Maybe I'd like you plenty if Daddy wasn't around."

Thinkin it over, Jimmy said, "Like how?"

"Like we could crank Daddy and ride off in a car by ourselves. I know a few scams myself by now. Or ain't we tired almighty of scammin? Soon's we pull one off we got to reckon the next one. It's endless, see, Jimmy?"

"Crank Daddy?" asked Jimmy, still grinnin. "Like if you sneak up behind while he's on me and cut his throat while he's comin?"

"Bet you'd look pretty watchin that, Jimmy Pie."

"Now you're talkin nice to me. Wondered how long it'd take. So what're you standin way over there for?"

Gettin close to him, I said, "We'll ride away."

"Where to?"

"Fame and glory."

"Yeah, like Hollywood, U.S.A.?" he said, his head turning as I moved behind him. "I always wanted to. You know guitar and singin? We'd be a brother act on MTV. Yeah, and legal for once, what a joke."

"No joke about it, Jimmy Pie," I said, smoothin him up like Daddy does. "No joke at all."

"Yeah."

"How much do you like me, Jimmy Pie?"

"That first night when we . . . oh, yeah, do that to me. That guy with the safe back in Pentecost? When we showered afterward, I was lookin at you and I . . . mmm, mighty fine like that . . . and I thought, *What a beautiful personality Otis has.*"

"I'm so flattered, Jimmy boy," I said, headin round to face him and drop to the floor inch by the inch of his skin, with some *take your time* Daddylike phrases to distract him. Didn't want him to hear the car pull up. Just don't slam the damn door, Daddy, s'all I ask.

"Oh, do more of that to me, Otis, my man," Jimmy was goin. "Yeah, crank that ol boss of ours and tool out among the people jubilatin. Find us two perfect chicks and celebrate a future. Fuck, loot, and MTV, that's how I see it. Go to town there, Otis."

"Come down, Jimmy," I said, pullin on him. "Come near for the best yet."

"Yes, Otis, I'll give it to you and you'll get high like they all. That's the real thing I was born to be."

His legs high and my hands goin up and down on his thighs, swallowin him whole till we hear Daddy hummin and I break it up real quick and worried, cryin out, "He witched me, Daddy! He made me!"

Jimmy sees how it is real fast, and he moves to Daddy in self-defense. "Said he'd crank me f'I didn't let him, Daddy!"

Daddy holds out his arms, his face blank, and Jimmy glides right in there.

"Swore to the Lord he'd strangle me," Jimmy moans.

"I see it all, my son," said Daddy, rubbin the back of Jimmy's neck. "I know how it goes with fairskin boys. The tremble. The starlike quality that redeems a sinful multitude."

"Yes, Daddy. Yes, Daddy."

Smoochin Jimmy with a heavy pull and faraway snarlin noises. Hoo, did I get thrilled! Because I knew I'd stole home. I said I knew a few scams myself, didn't I? And Daddy like to eat Jimmy up with how deep he's goin on him, that ol Jimmy Pie, who is now done with his Hollywood dreams of MTV and such.

Daddy stands back to admire Jimmy, all shiny with slick, huh, Jimmy? That one last hungry look. Daddy knew Jimmy wouldn't work right in the general run of things, cause Jimmy believes slick's to be give away without a thought, while Daddy takes his slick serious.

"Fetch the candle, Otis," Daddy tells me. "Quickly, now."

The Big Fry-Up at the Crazy Horse Café

Shaun Levin

Bacon

The butcher around the corner from my old flat in Tel Aviv sold bacon and fresh cured ham. It was one of the only places in the city where you could buy pig meat. I'd just finished college, I was twenty-four, and I was buying bacon for the first time. My friend Anne-Marie was about to become a Jew; it was part of her farewell-to-Christianity breakfast. That morning I told her I'd decided to leave Israel and move to London. Fifteen years after leaving South Africa for Tel Aviv, I was going back to live in English.

Eggs

I hate soft-boiled eggs. The yolk, the softness of it, is like eating a fetus, a chick beginning to take shape. There's too much life in a runny yolk. I like my eggs hard and rubbery. I like them chewy and bright yellow. So when I go for a late breakfast at the Crazy Horse Café on Arcola Street, I order an omelette.

"Like always?" the boss says, meaning: a bacon omelette.

I need to find welcoming arms wherever I go.

What will I tell my son when he asks how he was made? My turkey-baster boy with his father's green eyes and the blond hair of his mother. Me cycling for those five wintry months to their flat in Finsbury Park to jerk off into a yogurt pot, to have my cum slurped up into a syringe and passed on like a baton to Denise, who takes it to their bedroom to squirt into Andy. That, my son, is your creation myth. Three gods it took to create our Francis. God the wanker. God the go-between. And God the girl on her back with her legs in the air.

Beans

My boyfriend, Mark, wonders how appropriate it is for us to be saying the F-word around Frankie.

"I'm not having my son get all giggly around four-letter words," I say.

"They won't like that at school," Mark says.

"Fuck them," I say.

Mark came into the picture not long after Francis stopped wearing nappies and wasn't waking up in the middle of the night for feeding. My boyfriend is my rock and my reassurance. My son curses when he bumps his toe on the skirting board or drops his toys. Four-letter words are a way of easing the ache.

Here's one my grampa taught me: "Baked beans are good for the heart, / The more you eat the more you fart. / Fart, fart is good for the heart, / Keeps the tummy at ease, / Keeps you warm on a wintry night, / And suffocates the fleas."

Toast

Andy and I met on a residential writing retreat near Hebden Bridge. We used to go jogging together before breakfast, down to the river, over the bridge, then up the hill along the stony path to the fields with the bullocks and the farmhouse, then we'd run back down, to the edge of the town, past the school—where we stopped once to listen to the choir singing "Swing Low, Sweet Chariot"—then back through the woods, the ground soft with leaves, the air still cold and damp with dew. Back at the house, we'd shower and meet downstairs in the kitchen, where we'd make ourselves toasted wholemeal bread and eat it with peanut butter and wild blueberry jam. We often talk about that week in Yorkshire; Andy says we fell in love with each other. She says you have to sort of fall in love to do what we've done. Three weeks after we got back to London, she suggested the baby thing.

Mark and I are on an all-night flight to San Francisco—our first holiday together—on our way to spend a week in my cousin and his boyfriend's house while they're in Tokyo meeting the distributor of the handbags they make. In the morning the steward brings us French toast with tubs of "breakfast syrup," a kind of honey substitute, and Mark, because it's morning and he's just woken up, takes my hand, puts it on his hard-on, and says: "Now what?"

"Let's see," I say.

"Not here," he says.

"It's still dark," I say. "Everyone's half asleep."

And he pulls it out, his big one-eyed trouser monster, as the sun begins to rise over the California desert, and he plays with it under his tray of breakfast goodies, eyes closed, me gently pinching his nipple, until he comes in his fist.

"Milk for your tea, sir?" I say, and put a finger in his palm, spoon some out, and wipe it onto my eggy French toast.

"Ooh la la," he says. *"Le sperm perdu sur le pain perdu,"* and opens his mouth for a bite.

Shaun Levin

Black Pudding
I want to write a poem and call it: "An Ode to My Lover Eating Black Pudding."

Marmite
How wonderful to be in England among lovers of Marmite. Marmite is the taste of civilization. The civilized world is salty and smells of yeast extract. Andy says Marmite is a class thing; working-class people hate it. How disappointing for her to have a son growing up in Stoke Newington demanding Marmite sandwiches in his packed lunch.

I teach our son the comfort of Marmite and scrambled eggs on toast.

"What else could we have on toast?" I say.

"Poo," he says.

"Poo on toast?" I say, the joy of being made to laugh, the pride and relief of creating a child with a sense of humor.

"Daddy," he says, my laughter a distraction from the task at hand. "Cut my toast for me."

Tea
My boyfriend and I eat at the Kurdish restaurant on Stoke Newington Road. (Not on the nights my vegan son is with us. "Daddy," he says. "Eggs have souls, too.") The Kurdish restaurant is our treat when I've finished a story or Mark's clinched a deal (like getting a million-pound loan for some company so they can buy gas from the Kuwaitis) or neither of us wants to cook, because we've just been flying for hours from San Francisco. Adana kebab, lamb shish, hummus and salads, then small fragile glasses of tea on a saucer with two heart-shaped cubes of sugar.

During the days of my father's dying in Israel, we drank tea with mint or green tea from the box my mother kept in the cupboard beside my father's hospital bed.

I met a man once, the man who broke the heart my boyfriend had to fix, who drank only Lapsang souchong and Assam tea. For the weeks after he left—and I'd only just bought the boxes of Twinings for his breakfast—I drank Lapsang and Assam, morning, noon, and night. I was Medusa eating her children so as never to say good-bye to them.

I like my tea strong so that it looks like coffee.

"Just like my dad," Mark says.

I drink tea the way my boyfriend's father drinks it.

People say: I won't leave you for all the tea in China.

Sausages

In South Africa we called sausages *boerewors* and kebabs *sosaties*. The *bundu* was the bush and the *veld* was the open field across the road from our house on Jenvey Road, Summerstrand. Every Sunday was a *braai* day, *boerewors* and *sosaties* on the barbecue; it was the maid's day off and, as my mother would say: "There's no one to wash up after you," so we took it in turns to set the table and do the dishes. I remember my father coming in from the garden in his Speedo, the heavy Magen David pendant nestled in his chest hair, carrying a silver tray with *braai*ed meat like a Levi making sacrifices in the temple.

We were in San Francisco when Linda McCartney died. I thought: *Who's going to make sausages for my vegan son now that she's gone?*

Jam

A moment of infidelity: Alex is a big blond giant with a thick coat of marmalade-colored fuzz on his chest.

Mushrooms and Tomatoes

My father, when he was dying of cancer—although at that stage he, like us, didn't know he was dying—went on a strict diet, a regimen he thought would stop the cancer cells from devouring his body. Non-Hodgkin's lymphoma is too ugly to show its face; the killing happens beneath the skin, in the tunnels of the bone marrow. If he stopped eating spinach, he thought, all the killing would stop.

A week after he's gone, we're in the kitchen and my mother's washing three cos lettuces, drying the leaves and packing them in the crisper.

"We only need a few leaves for the salad," I say.

"It's habit," she says. "For the past year all I've been doing is washing these things for your father."

Six leaves with each meal. Fresh cabbage, too.

"Never eat your mushrooms raw," my father tells me on the phone.

I, too, believed food would save him. So my sister and I made carrot and beetroot juice, mixed in acidophilus powder, and fed it to him through the tube that hung from the hook on the wall above his bed. We'd brought him back from the hospital for what turned out to be his last three days. Three days, and then his eyes shot open at two o'clock on a Friday morning.

His spirit hovered in the house for another ten hours of grace before the men from Hevra Kaddisha came to wrap his body in a sheet, tie him to a stretcher, and take him eight floors down, stood upright in the lift like a granite Egyptian cat god.

Now, from the seeds of the tomatoes he grew in his roof garden in Israel, we grow cherry tomatoes in our back garden in London. My son calls them Grampa's Tomatoes and insists we water them whenever he's here, whether it's been raining or not. And it's been raining a lot this summer.

We go mushrooming in Roslyn Glen with Denise and Andy, and Andy's brother, John. John's girlfriend tells stories to the kids—ours and theirs—while we drink magic mushroom tea and sing nursery rhymes to a reggae beat in the drawing room of Roslyn Castle.

Bubble and Squeak

I was ten when I started shoplifting. It was summer, November in South Africa, and the week leading up to Guy Fawkes. My cousin (who now lives in San Francisco) and our friend Michael Roberts (who died of AIDS when he was twenty-three) dare me to go into Mr. Theocharus's grocery shop and steal firecrackers. So I fill the pockets of my jacket and trousers with Chinese crackers and Catherine wheels and walk out the shop. Mr. Theocharus calls me back.

"That's all I took," I say, handing over the firecrackers in my jacket pocket.

Back at Michael Roberts's house—there are always those boys who are referred to by both first and last names—Cecilia, the maid, comes upstairs shouting that Mr. Theocharus is here with the police. I throw the firecrackers out the window into the swimming pool and hide under the bed. Eventually my cousin and Michael Roberts can't keep themselves from laughing, and Cecilia comes to tickle me under the bed.

I still love the thrill of stealing things.

Spotted Dick

In the beginning my boyfriend rolls back his foreskin—a wonder in itself—and I notice little pimply things around the base of his corona.

"Is that a fungus or something," I say.

"A fungus?" he says. "They're sensory glands."

"I've never seen anything like that," I say.

"Well," he says. "Now you have."

A Serviette

"Is there anything you miss?" Anne-Marie says.

"I miss the sea," I say.

We are sitting on her balcony in Tel Aviv overlooking a paved court-yard. I'm on a rare visit here from London. I have lived away from here for seven years; the last time I returned was two years ago when my father died. Anne-Marie is still married to her computer programmer, a nice guy from Jerusalem, and is pregnant with their second child. In the courtyard, an old man is hanging up his laundry on the com-munal revolving washing line; at his feet, a plastic laundry basket overflows with faded T-shirts and underwear.

"You must miss more than that?" she says.

She's an Israeli now, and like all Israelis she wants to be reassured that their country is not a mistake; that they won't have to give it back; that history will not repeat itself.

"I miss the beach," I say. "And I miss the cottage cheese and chopped-up salad with cucumbers and tomatoes and the thick slices of *lechem chai* you get at Israeli breakfasts."

"You know," she says. "I've never *really* understood why you left."

"Isn't it obvious?" I say.

"But it wasn't just the politics," she says. "I know it was more than that."

"Everything was getting so messy," I say.

"It's always messy," she says.

"I know," I say. "But everything felt like it was getting out of hand. Remember that guy who blew himself up on the number 5 bus on Dizengoff Street, just under the bridge, and they had to pick body bits out of the trees. And then Munir telling us that he'd gone to school with the guy. That was more or less when I found out Dan was sleeping with Amir, and his betrayal felt like an act of revenge, like Dan wanted to possess something I'd had, which is basically how he put it to me."

I spent the first Gulf War in this flat, me and Anne-Marie and Munir, her Palestinian boyfriend. We'd sat on the edge of the bath in our gas masks, the room sealed with plastic sheeting and bleach-soaked towels over the plug holes, and we'd held hands while bombs fell just meters away from here. In the mornings we'd go down to the grocers on Ibn Gvirol Street for food, then stay in all day watching television and teaching each other nursery rhymes in French and English and Arabic.

"How's Frankie," she says.

"Did I tell you what he says about eggs?" I say. "And how beautifully he says 'fuck'?"

I tell my friend Anne-Marie about my five-year-old son. And while I'm telling her I realize that some of us—especially the ones who keep moving from place to place—orchestrate our lives as if they were stage plays, and that the farther we move from home, the greater our freedom to choose the characters in our little dramas. It's only when we settle down—and I think that's what's happening to me—that we stop wanting out or wanting more and our hearts can open up to the beauty of the ordinary.

Thermopylae
James McCourt

29 October, 1956
Magwyck (The Snug)

My dearest Mawrdew Czgowchwz,

In deepest gratitude for (and in consternation and chagrin at the tardy response to) yours of the 29th ultimo.

As Malevich has written, the airplane was not contrived in order to carry business letters from Berlin to Moscow (or the diplomatic pouch either from New York to Dublin) but rather in obedience to the irresistible drive of this yearning for speed to take on external form. In this line, *Fama Volat:* the Meneghini has sung. More later: it was more than just a night out.

I am off tomorrow to lonely, wintry, appropriate Manitoy to work on the outdoor-summer-night play, *The Archons.* (*Seditiosi voci* who do work of summer in winter, especially when work in question is, well, seditious, and features, as did Massine's ballet of the Seventh Symphony, the Creation of the World, the Destruction of the World, and the Descent from the Cross in between.)

"For a while," wrote Hart Crane, "I want to keep immune from beckoning and all that draws you into doorways, subways, sympathies, rapports and the City's complicated devastation." And Albertus Magnus, no less, directs "those wishing to reminisce, should withdraw from the public light into obscure privacy: in the public light the images of sensible things are scattered and their movement is confused; in obscurity however they are unified."

Added to which, Aquinas says Prudence has eight parts: *memoria, ratio, intellectus, docilitas, solertia, providentia, circumspectio,* and *cautio.* All of which (do) (does) boil down to two words: *skip town.* To work on the play. *The Archons.* That's the epic-allegory one I warned you about— the two-hour Gnostic version of the War Between the East Side and the West Side that we're thinking of staging in the park and videotaping (television in the middle '50s having become, thanks to the likes of you, something more than auditions).

You remember, it came to me that time we visited Teotihuacán with Victoria after your Mexico City Amneris and Delilah. (I can still quote the review: "*Una mujer de peso* [with flaming red hair lay extended, half disrobed, in a dark fur cloak, upon a red ottoman, bent smiling over Samson, bound by the Philistines])."

It's a little like a shorter version of the *Mahabharata* cut into Hardy's *Dynasts* with more than just a nod to Monsignor Hugh Benson's 1907 fable *Lord of the World,* a peppering of Plautus's *Asinaria* (much with restless plebs) admixed with *Coriolanus* (idea of The Voices, as in *The Cigarettes*) lines to cleave the general air with horrid speech. Boasting as it does, in addition to principals, a large cast of character men and women—Sixth Avenue will be put to work—bawds, grooms, bravos, duennas, domestics, porters, *alquazils, alcaldes,* night watchmen, municipal sanitation workers, and all the other forces of apparent good and obscure evil to be found in a great metropolis.

We in the ages living
In the buried past of the earth
Built Nineveh with our sighing
And Babel itself with our mirth.

Basically, the good archons occupy the East Side—headquarters The Sherry Netherland, and the bad the West—headquarters The Dakota, and the theater of war is The Park. Except that the bad are in secret possession of the cathedral and Fanny Spellbound. I see him sitting under a hair dryer in the shape of the papal tiara. (And ye, ye unknown latencies shall thrill to every innuendo, and after all how desperately lèse-majesté is it? Monsignor Benson has the satanic airships destroy Rome and the pope with it.) Should I give our *strategia* control in return of St. John the Divine? Do we want it? They do of course have control of The Met, Carnegie, and City Center, but The Dr. Mabuse of Thirty-ninth Street is in secret league with the enemy. The one that started out as a comic rewrite of the *Bacchae* (you remember, it was called *Revelers* until Paranoy, peering over my shoulder at the premiere of *NOIA* at the program in my lap to see written the line "Mother, *stop* it—you're tearing me to *pieces!*" groaned aloud), then veered off in the direction of the *Troades*. (You can blame your-pal-my-auntie for all this—it was she who insisted fifteen years ago I come back to New York, go to the Jesuits at Regis and learn Greek.) It's the one that now bears the epigraph from Ezekiel 9: *"Cause them that have charge over the city to draw near each other, each with his destroying weapon in his hand."*

You can see I'm hell-bent on being the next Maxwell Anderson/Christopher Fry: weighty themes/elevated expression of same—particularly the warning that New York could well disappear, exactly the way Byzantium did, and become the sore point of stories

with morals in them. (Serve everybody right, too: New Yorkers, ama-
teurs of Byzantine melodrama and *Befreiungskrieg*.) And which, due to
the success of the carnival shindig of Equinox last, and to the warm
relations obtaining between (the aforementioned) Herself The Madge
and Hizzoner, the mayor, late of Yorkville, we can get The City to let
us put it on—or photograph it, anyway, at the Bethesda Fountain.

It's the one, in which, if she takes a shine to it (or they, my archons,
the angels of the Rialto, offer her a whole lot of money, whichever
happens first in the order of consequence). Or remind her that Shaw
wrote *Major Barbara* for Eleanor Robson and she became Mrs. August
Belmost. Perhaps I'd better not, though: the Miss Robson that was got
took care of by the august August because she turned Shaw down.
Still, Bridgewood is more likely to think of capturing a Texas mil-
lionaire through her art, through spectacle (even filmed) like the one
The Redactor has made up for you in his pages, called Tulsa Buck
O'Fogatry. Not bad. I'll find out who the little bastard is if it takes
overtures to the FBI and its heinous fag director through the very
famous fag eminence I'm planning to excoriate in *The Archons*. Perhaps
Strange will help me: I know these boys, they end up telling *everything*
in confession.

La Bridgewood will be playing a cross between Mnesilochus, pro-
tagonist (in drag) of Aristophanes' *Thesmophoriazousae* (and like him/her
required to speak in hendecasyllables, but I think she does that
already), Ezekiel (aforementioned), and the Chrysler Building—all
lit *up*, the way it was to have been originally, when they molded all that
shining Krupp steel into New York's signal cathedral facade, and to
have a high priest consort called Nimrod. After all, I tell myself, and
I've told Bridgewood, Bernhardt, *La divine horizontale* in The Great War,
carried over the trenches in a litter to give performances of the last act

of *La dame aux camellias* by calcium light at night, played Strasbourg Cathedral in a pageant. "Let's make a name for ourselves"—she, La Bridgewood, will announce (in imitation of Praxagora) to the assembled throng of chic refugees speaking all the tongues of the earth, the redistribution of all wealth and influence in the metropolis, while being ferried across from The Ramble in a poop. (Anecdote: two yentas on the sidewalk at the intermission of a *Long Day's Journey into Night* matinee. One to the other: "Well, it's not really a *show*—more of a play.") I'm hoping for the reverse reaction. (And of course, lest the enterprise should be thought *allegorical,* it will be done in the up-to-the-second equivalent of New York *Togate,* and not *palliate.*)

Am hoping to feature opposite Bridgewood somebody beautiful. There are no more at home of course like your former Carnegie hall-mate. Percase whimsically did wonder were I to offer The Graybar Building to Cornell, and play John Alden Carpenter's *Skyscrapers* in the dual-piano version, might Marlon Man come back to be in it with her, as Grand Central Station, but we know, don't we, he has bid *sayonara* to the stage.

Somebody beautiful, because the part is suggested by the career of Alcibiades, of whom Aristophanes (my predecessor) wrote: *A lion should not be raised in the city, but if you decide to do so, you must cater to his ways.* (Sounds like *Bringing Up Baby,* no? Also reminds me that Marlon has already played a lion—a blond one. What we need here is somebody who looks like your current pet—he who can only act only for the camera and only under Sirk—and can act in the flesh at the level of—oh, I don't know, Tony Perkins? What *about* gorgeous Tony?) The career of Alcibiades and the melodrama of his being accused of throwing a raucous party on the eve of the disastrous Sicilian expedition that defiled the Eleusinian mysteries. The one, finally, that contains that vaudeville of elements from Greek tragedy and comedy both: Oedipus, Orestes, Elektra, Antigone; Philoctetes, Ion, Io, Hecuba; Tiresias, Pentheus, Medea, etc. Plus The Bacchae as nuns—remember I told you what I thought nuns were, and how they arose out of the cult of Isis, the Magdalen, and Maria Egiziaca. They are the Christ's bacchantes, and instead of tearing Dionysius to bits they "receive" bits of their etc. Just so you know.

You wouldn't tear a beloved to pieces of pressed white bread, would you? Anyway in the normal order of things a nun is not, despite the honorific title, a mother—pace Heloise—only I was thinking: you can always take the girl away from the nuns, but can you take the—but you took yourself away, didn't you? Anyway, Tynan, next time he comes to town nosing for a job, will be sure to say I've been influenced by Giradoux and by John Whiting. He's probably right.

Speaking of French influence, one wag said he heard it was going to be a sort of American *Soulier de Satin* spanning over a decade, and that the argument starts when Bridgewood loses one of her fuck-me pumps at El Morocco. Not bad. I'd sooner be compared aforehand to Claudel, who, even if he was a Nazi sympathizer, was also a diplomat (and used the diplomatic pouch as we do for his correspondence), than to Fry, who is really only a schoolmaster trading in on the myth that Shakespeare was one, too, which is ridiculous, because Shakespeare, the bulk of him, was the sequestered twin brother of Edward de Vere, the seventeenth Earl of Oxford, who may have run a little lyceum for young men, as in *Love's Labour's Lost.*

(And the rest of him was Mary Sidney, the Countess of Pembroke . . . but you knew that).

And then, at the opposite end of the spectrum to Claudel, some-body at the archdiocese told Kilgallen (who printed it) that what it is is a re-creation of the cast-of-four-thousand epic son et lumière enacting the downfall of capitalism in the Prater stadium in 1931.

Question: will we, come next year, be finding *The Archons* (Belvedere Lawn; two performances) anthologized in the 1956–57 Burns Mantle? Quite possibly, as he never omits a Bridgewood vehicle, some of which have actually run only one and a half performances. . . .

Meanwhile, speaking of lyceums, everywhere one goes in New York this instant October one hears talk of everything under the sun, much of it revolving around you: it is the truth. A book about you would have to include hundreds of examples—an enormous kick-line of them, as in the play *Waiting For Mawrdew Czgowchwz.*

[Further this theme: the voices of the New York night "scripting" the book of Mawrdew Czgowchwz, *The Archons,* their lives, art politics, music politics, world politics, Destiny itself in the long run. Samples overheard and copied down (everybody is taping everybody at home and between the Inquiring Photographer and roving reporters on radio and television Everyman is a player.']

If it is a defeating thing to insist on producing Art or Nothing (a new dramatic experiment, replete with *progression d'effet, charpente, facade, cadences*—and at military funerals there's always one to count the cadence—not a morality for ranted recitation), then I shall go down howling. Or perhaps, better advised, instead, and better put in the words of my favorite extinct Ulster bard, the blind Seamus MacCuarta, to the people of the Cooley peninsula, for not properly recognizing his literary worth, I shall let them be—as badgers living underground their narrow lives, gorging themselves on the sweetmeats of innutritive illusion (as in any bawdy house on any side street north of Forty-second Street between Sixth and Eight Avenues you care to name).

After the Gotham signing party for *Under Nephin* (funny the way they think they *owe* me something for cutting me out of the Sitwell picture. They cut Jimmy Merrill out, too, and I don't think either of us is going to suffer much from it: if only it *were* a sign of some transaction or other, but I can't imagine it is) I don't plan to be back in New York making the rounds rigged out in me fancy Dan until the New Year. (*"Where* does he go?" one linebacker asked another, I was told. "Oh, you know my dear, that island, somewhere off Massachusetts." "Hm. He ought to be going to one off New Hampshire, called *Smuttynose*.") Except of course to check one or more further Meneghini apparitions—the Tosca, the Lucia—and perhaps to spend an afternoon with her and Leo Lerman. (She's not much for the *passagiata*: the publicity has been wormy—the *Time* cover, Dolores, the coy attentions commencing to be paid, we are told in appalled whispers, by "The Old Oaken Bucket in the Well of Loneliness"—and really, what a vicious parody of the divine Marie Dressler that one's turned into: Cole Porter is a disillusioned cookie to think her fun; Johnny Donovan, drunk at Madame Spivvy's, doing imitations of the Hy Gardner interview—like that.)

There was a gag going around that the ghost of Toscanini had appeared to the Meneghini the night before the opening, wailing, "The music is too great—it is beyond human powers. Cancel!" In any event, it was not a great official triumph, but details anon. One interesting theory had it that it is the only role she will not have a great success in at the Metropolitan, because the gods (which is to say the Elohim, dear, and not merely the Family Circle) will not have it. They will have it that Rosa's triumph in her greatest role will here and only here go uncontested—her statue up on the Miller Shoe Building and all. I'm reminded of what you said of MMC, quoting Chorley wasn't it, on Malibran, that nature had given her a rebel to subdue and not a vessel to command. I'm going to the second one, of course—we all are. Shame about her and New York—even about her and the Met. After having been treated as an anagram of Scala itself, and breezing of an aftermath into Biffi to be met as if she were *Iside-stessa* by those gaggles of gorgeous and ecstatic *melochecche*—well, schlepping it with Tony Arturi and Frances Moore from the Old Brewery across to the Burger Ranch, or down to Macy's could hardly have been her idea of fan romance, and the Gotham City High Life, though it may attract her attention, can never do for her what the Milanese have done, for she lacks your (and Milanov's) flair for the Ringling Brothers aspect of *thuh opra,* and for corralling private citizens in significant numbers (and Leo could make her welcome *anywhere* that mattered in New York, save Nuncle's elevator at the Chelsea).

As a matter of fact, at Herbert Weinstock's party for her last week (fully of those people from the kick-line, momentarily diverted from talking about you to talking about her) she was terribly quiet and shy—and when I mentioned you (I had to: she wasn't wearing glasses and didn't know who I was, not that it's in her interest to recall me, especially from three years ago in Mexico City) she gave that odd look composed of complicity and awe: the awe I saw on her face on stage when in the boudoir scene you down-winded her with that open chest *"figlia di Faraoni!"* Open chest, incidentally, is something she should give up using: she is of breath too short for the gesture. So there.

Meanwhile, the father pulled us into the kitchen and announced summarily, "In my daughter's breast there beats the spirit of Thermopylae!" (Not to be confused with the Spirit of Marathon—q.v. *Under Nephin*—who was in fact The Pythia herself—of Delphi—who raised a fog that confused the invader under Brennus—by the way not a *Boi*—most likely an Illyrian *Keltoi*—so that they fell about, and taking one another for the enemy, slew their own in overwhelming numbers.) "*I* don't know if *he* knows what he means, dear," I heard Leo L. whisper to Robert Giroux, but I hope to God nobody tries to convince Maria to sing *Xerxes!*" I thought to myself, self-immolation at the hot gates of hell?

Absit omen. Sounds to me like her fantasy runs to mass suicide after her final performance—and to think that this underground epic accuses *you* of *Stuvwxyzchina*—with notes left all over town, reading *Go, stranger-to-this-mystery, and tell the* Times, *the* Tribune, *the* Journal-American, *the* World Telegram and Sun, *the* News, *the* Mirror, *the* Post, and *the* Brooklyn Eagle, *that here, obeying her behests, we fell* (or were burnt to crisps. Really, she should leave Marfa's scene to you, even if you have poached on her Violetta). Whereas you're content with bringing them screaming to their feet, she must have them paroxysmal, fetal, trussed in straitjackets, begging for surcease of sorrow and for merciful death—and you never know: if the kick-line runs out of steam, if you stay away more than a single season, if you retire to have children, she could prevail—which, after all, might be, well, as the Princeton boys are said to say, *only fair*—because as for life as you—and I, sometimes, construe it, she is, I'm afraid, maladapted.

Which leaves her high and dry on Art's cushioned pinnacle. I prefer your approach; I do. But I have an idea she'll never be happy here, never can be; it's my belief that something very Greek happened to her with daddy, and that all this with the mother is, truly, the cover story.

The *Time* cover story was vile, and obviously threw her. (She is *a very nervous woman, pace,* spirit of Thermopylae, and it ought to be remembered that the *size* of New York, compared to that of Milan, or Chicago even, is enough to throw anybody, not to mention somebody it's already thrown out, so to speak.) Neither is she terribly well educated—but you knew that. She is witty—or caustic—but for instance, she missed the point entirely when, in some banter at Herbert W.'s about the fee controversy, it was mentioned that Tucker was reportedly outraged and might not do the *Tosca* because she was getting secret outside help, as it were, Leo Lerman snapped, "Doesn't he realize Maria wishes to emulate the virtuous woman of the Bible whose price is above Ruby's?" One thinks of what you yourself might have said of the Meneghini (in relation to the Frankly Dowdy Diva from above the *Gelateria* in Parma) countering the charge that the fondness for luxury and couture seemed to sit ill on a supposedly dedicated artist. "Sure, where's the harm at all—and a bit of class."

And, after all, although it's a shameful truth, *Time* is a great part of New York: a vile part, but a significant one. I must tell you, it did occur to me that, feeling the way you've felt all these years about her, we might have mobilized something preemptive—but who knew that Luce would do what he did, in the holy name of motherhood? (And he likely entertains some confused notions about her premature antifascist activities during the war.) He would have done the same thing to you, you realize, when you landed here—unable as he was to disentangle the skein of your story, buying the story that you had been singing in Omsk, in Minsk (as opposed to Minsky's, in Jersey City; it is known you went there with Auntie, Consuelo Gilligan, and Grainne de Paor, but whether or not you gave them a song is not recorded), in Vitebsk (and probably convinced in his own alleged mind that you pushed Masaryk out the window like some Bohunk Tosca), had you not *known what you know*: had you not given that private warble over in Jersey, and enjoyed that fortuitous deep-dish tea with Lucy Moses and Lila Tyng, who'd so adored you that winter in Paris as Amneris, as to the true authorship—and the exact remuneration involved in the transaction—of *The Women*. (I remember how you said, "But there is a copy of the script in the Library of Congress with her handwritten corrections, and Paranoy's pointing out how easy it was to sit at rehearsals and transcribe the action of director and rethinking and cast rethinking and rewriting to keep the audience from leaving the theater. And you said it seemed so much her story and how hard it was to imagine a man writing it. Well, perhaps now, in the light of what's been coming to light you wonder what *your* story is, in relation to the said text—and so perhaps does Neri [see below].)

Pity all the same we couldn't have foreseen the attack this fall on your friend—or the remake of *The Women* as *The Opposite Sex* (and the *Variety* headline Ralph made up trumpeting the hoax: "Luce Lip-Sync Gyps"). She might well have paid a courtesy call on the American ambassadress in Rome, sipped a companionable Campari or two, and spoken a few straight words—delivered a few home truths (as Dawn Powell says), something like, "Listen, bitch, we *know* who wrote it, and for how much." Especially since the noise about Trovaso Corradi being interested, because of Visconti's admiration of the Cukor pic in Mrs. Luce's (of, for forty thousand bucks George S. Kaufman's) American comic masterpiece. (Rather diverting it would have been, too, than the Barber-Menotti opus for Jurinac—and you know the full *T* on that, don't you? They showed it to your friend, hoping to make it her Metropolitan debut, and she said: "Rewrite it so that Erika is the heroine, and I'll think about it." As the watchword hereabouts nowadays goes—taken direct from your devoted bodhisattva, Panama Hattie-Three-Sheets, or M. Chowderhead Bahadur Baksheesh: *Tee-hee-hee-hee-hee-hee-hee.*)

Notes from the Hotel Chelsea: Uncle Virgil, Lone Defender of the Mitigated (aka the Countess Razamowsky) wasn't there—or claims not. (Paranoy said, "No, he wasn't there; Nuncle prefers—*trahit sua nunque voluptas*—to fall asleep nine stories up at home on Twenty-third

Street these days rather than in public parterres on Thirty-ninth and Fifty-seventh streets—where love no longer beckons. Not to mention the fact that some people are beginning to say *Who?* and even to confuse him with the *other* T, the one with the *P* up in Cambridge who writes those chorales and sanguine, gusty symphonies that flirt with dissonance but are not besmirched." He, Nunc, has however *heard she's a hoax* and has apparently written to—get *this*—Mary Garden [they being *'on s'en passerait'*]. Yes, dear old Mary, that pillar of strength, sanity, and perspicacity, known to the world, as was Jenny Lind, for piety, modesty, charitable good works, intrinsic worth of heart and delicacy of mind, and a spotless private life—aka to her intimates "Little Egypt" and "Isadora"—she learned dancin' in a hurry, and 'fore the days of Arthur Murray.) Written to say so (she is a hoax) in so many words: apparently he is in his own mind the *Flugelmann* of that small band of vocal connoisseurs convinced that the rising tide of superstition and Kabbalism is too damaging to society to be ignored. This gives him a *cause* to which he can append his energies, lest he subside altogether, like any number of old bags around town, into beadwork pillows, sailor's valentines, gin, and jigsaw puzzles.

(Not to mention the fact that he would much rather dish with Mary over some really *significant* and *timeless* issue involving for instance her art versus that of Povla Frisch or the realization at long last of her ambition to sing Kundry—which he could easily arrange with a single phone call to Josephine La Puma and what better venue after all for *Parsifal* than the Palm Gardens [Madame Middleton would surely graciously demur] than deal with these upstart blow-ins—except to point out of course the fact that Sabatini, after all, did create frissons in her, Mary's, honor at the Ambassador, whereas what has been created for this Callas at the Ritz, only some new kind of greasy doughnut.)

Remember, Nunc was all set to denounce *you,* in *Aida* (probably for waking him up so rudely in the boudoir scene, with *"figlia di Faraoni!"* For that and the unfortunate contretemps with the Neri transformation). "Nothing, I fear," he was heard to whisper to Olin Downes in the can after the Triumphal Scene, "but a rather more hysterical Herta Glaz, costumed in an overexuberant and yet, for a royal personage surely underclad manner, fielding a performing style and a blazing *pyrean* headdress together suggestive less of Miss Gladys Swarthout than of, say, Miss Margie Hart—and reminiscent of that of the gigantic red-haired harlot impersonated by Bert Savoy." (*Did* they run that back to you, at the interval to send you into V-8 overdrive in the Judgment Scene, reducing the presbyter to a mass of quivering mandarin jelly? He later denied saying it at all—claimed he was maliciously misquoted by a rival; that what he'd actually said was "an uncanny portrait of a mysterious heart: she is a fiery Amneris who calls to mind no earlier exponent of the role, but rather the greatest of all Aidas, Theresa Stolz, the toast of the House of Savoy.")

("A likely story," Paranoy was heard to comment; "the raddled old iniquity *was* probably *at* La Stolz's debut in that role, at Scala, on his Italian journeys. It's certain he was, with Walt Whitman, an Alboni fanatic—went to *both* of *her* Normas!")

Nunc is of course most famous—apart from giving Lou Harrison a nervous breakdown—for his pronouncement on another of your favorite pieces of Americana, recently reimmortalized by your favorite new American soprano. "A libretto," he said of *Porgy and Bess,* "that should never have been accepted, on a subject that should never have been treated, by a composer who should never have attempted it." (Clearly, he was aching for two more *nevers* to make up a resounding Lear-like crescendo, but Rhetoric, the tease, failed him.) Paranoy says

Nunc has become like an old Roman *principessa* (perhaps he's been influenced by the creation of the mythical "Principessa Oriana Incantevole, deaf since the bombing of Rome, in *MNOPQR STUVWXYZ*), living on the *piano nobile* of her mind's crumbling palazzo, amidst the fantastic wreckage left behind in the wake of bands of marauding visitors (which gave me the shivers, for I've always liked the Chelsea).

This you will like. I heard one old dear say to another on the way out, "It's true, life is like that. She makes you see it." And Frances Moore said something I might have said as well of you, had I thought to. "When Maria sings, the painted scene clouds *move* across the painted moon!"

Many things said to have happened never did. This, for example, so eerily reminiscent of exaggerations published in the aforementioned text relating to yourself and companions as to invite.

"The whole theater was an insane asylum—fists waving, pummeling, hoarse guttural exclamations and anguished cries filling the auditorium. Strangers fell sobbing into one another's arms; delirious women clinging to one another staggered toward the exit doors. There was an undeniable sense of a universal chaos out of which some entirely new era was being created."

Paranoy said, "Sounds like Marcia Davenport losing her broadcast mind at Gina Cigna's debut" (which of course really *did happen,* on WOR).

Somebody said Marcia Davenport *was* there, telling everybody who would listen that this woman was a flash in the pan and that the real news was Jolanda Meneguzer. Paranoy said, "That wasn't Marcia Davenport; that was Rodney Bergamot's new drag." But we know for a fact it was the only child of Alma Gluck, not merely from the way she sat out the intermissions in the stark attitude Dostoyevsky (who really should be raised to render the scene) made the derisive mouth of

Nastasya Filipnova decry, to wit: "If I sit in a box in the French theater like the incarnation of some inapproachable dress-circle virtue . . . etc." Not only, but also because she dropped her program on the steps leading down from Sherry's on the way out during the final curtain uproar and some deft queen retrieving it for her and spying script, *pulled a quick switch* then disappeared up the secret Thirty-ninth Street side stairway to the Family Circle. (It all came out the next day on the Line, along with the following.

"Marcia Davenport? She claims to have once been a member of the highest councils of state."

"Surely more a membrane than a member, no?")

What was written in the white space in the Steinway ad opposite the billing page went something like this:

"Bellini.

"Suddenly, Vincenzo began to sob. He doubled over and buried his head of golden curls in the bent crook of his arm. All of Paris was humming out the window. *'Qu'as-tu, cheri?'* the Countess whispered, putting down her needlepoint and turning to him in alarm. 'What is it? *Que (Qui?) fait-tu mal?* What has disturbed you so?' *'Niente . . . niente,'* he muttered (for though joy is a convulsion, grief is indeed a habit, and emotions had long since become his events) his wet face gleaming with tears in the *demi*-lune. *'Sono trieste—e straniero!'"*

And yes, your pet lunatic standee (or is that *slandee?*) was there for the seasonal opening: the one we call Bartleby; the one you and the countess maintain lives in a broom closet at Patelson's and forges antique baroque scores. Dressed in the usual semiclerical black, with the worn collar reversed. Listened, as always, to everything from the Fortieth Street lobby, sitting under the bust of Caruso, clutching *Fear and Trembling & A Sickness Unto Death,* reading from them at intermission, acknowledging (in the piercing and haughty luster of that gaze enjoining any notion of fraternity) *nessuno.*

Then a snatch of dialogue: "The *theater?* Please, my dear; the lights go down, the curtain goes up; people are *talking.* Boring."

When Dolores and Gloria Gotham walked down separate aisles and greeted one another, one wag remarked, "The meeting of Erys and Enyo." (In the Irish these ones—Strife and Battle Axe—are called Nemain and Babh. They, with the Morrigan, constitute the Major Triad in Big Earth Trouble. O. W. will expatiate for you.)

Whereupon I myself saw, wreathed in blue cigarette smoke, either Dalí or the false Dalí (the latter, I'm inclined to think, as there was no version, true or false, either of Gala at his side, only a gaggle of the living foredoomed). Whoever he was he was heard to proclaim, much to the consternation of the score desk gnomes, "The music is *irrelevant* with Callas—she is *elsewhere* from the first measure. I have in my life in the theater come upon only two incarnations of the tragic muse, this woman, Duse and Margarita Xirgu." "*Who?*" one score desk gnome wailed.

(I might have told him, but Lorca's ghost came floating at just that moment out of the men's room, flashed his eyes, put a finger to his lips, and yet I heard him say, "You know how I have suffered in this city, I cannot bear to be here, I don't know why, but do not allow this terrible man to profane by speaking it the divine name of Margarita Xirgu!" I promised him I would prevent all further discourse of the only woman he could ever love, and then I felt his chill ameliorate and indeed his dark and diminutive ectoplasmic form dissolve in the light of Sherry's chandelier.)

Ralph nearly slugged some old transparency on Saturday who stood there cackling, "Darling, when Bellini said, 'Bring death by means of song,' do you suppose he meant *this?*"

All right, I can't not talk about it all night. She may have three voices, all of them archetypes capable of defining for a generation the music she sings, but for me—to keep the triad argument going—she is everything in *two* of the three great essential manifestations of the Triple Goddess as envisioned by Mozart in the letter to his father wondering if he could snag Da Ponte after Salieri was through with him. That is to say the *seria* and the *mezzo carattere.* I don't see that she can ever be the *buffa,* which you can and have been. I'm sorry, but there it is.

The immediate problem, according to one seer, is: she is at the Met up against the psychic remnant of the greatest Norma of the early century, and cannot, for all her genius, best it. (She's even known to have given on the subject of the sometime vaudevillian who once gave voice lessons and sang a piece of the Verdi Requiem with Joan Crawford, "with her voice you can't compare us—it's *not fair."* Fair? Sounds like the canard about Princeton boys and a certain specified reciprocal erotic configuration.) Whatever the reason, this Norma, unless it undergoes a metamorphosis (or unless she starts some class of blazing affair in Gotham) is not going to be the one. Anyway, according to everybody that's already happened, yes? In London—twice: and that's the second part of the argument, that having done *that,* she simply will not be given what she was given there: so that the two great Normas of the century as it turns out will have been Ponselle here and her there. You know how people go on. (It's true, life is like that.)

Fortuna favet fortibus. (Aloha.)

"This is not a job for a music critic," one vilificator avowed, "this is a job for a *plumber!* When she did *Butterfly in* Chicago, I said I'd rather be listening to Ganna Walska. Tonight I'd rather be listening to Ina Souez singing with Spike Jones! I am inclined after hearing this performance to believe the rumor that it was this voice—this woman—who gave

Anita Cerquetti a nervous breakdown! I mean *really*. What has issued from those distended jaws is a voice such as it would be madness to attempt describing. There are indeed two or three epithets which might be applicable to it in parts. One might say, for instance, that the sound was harsh and broken and hollow, but the hideous whole is indescribable, for the simple reason that no similar sound can ever have scorched the ears of humanity. There are two particulars, nevertheless, which might fairly be stated as characteristic of the intonation. In the first place the voice seemed to reach one's ears from a vast distance—as from some deep cavern under Broadway. In the second place, it impresses itself upon the sense of hearing as gelatinous or glutinous matters impress themselves upon the sense of touch."

An even more coquettish exchange took place outside Sherry's between gentlemen (unlikely ever to marry). "Well, obviously a reputation as full of hot air as the Hindenburg, and likely to meet a similar end." Pause. "Oh, I don't know, darling, not unless she gets *really* desperate and tries dropping anchor in Jersey."

And then a knowing—maddeningly knowing—apprisal. "Shot to shit in seven years; terrifying!"

For my part, I'll tell you that I have *never—not even from you,* not even from Lady Day (who is the only one finally to compare either of you with) heard emotional deprivation voiced with more molten anguish, whether in one voice worried into three folds, as you insist, or from the three voices the Italians demark, whichever. At white heat, which *I* felt she reached nearly as often here as at Covent Garden, she is the end of the known histrionic world. The mint of the musical genius—the way, like you, she does her count from within, and is so always and never marking; the way her preemptive attack and swell to full volume in next to no time allows for split-second, almost improvisatory variation

125

from phrase to phrase within the context of the line . . . all that exquisite finesse that gives bel canto the stamp of a particular performer in a particular strait. She is with you and Victoria one of the trinity of exponents of that *ars subtilior* in which the giddy pleasure of rhythmic invention explodes. Such amazing, hard-won control veils only somewhat her dangerous and forbidding affect: a raging, and not so musical torrent (hence the "argument" in performance between her art and her ballistics) in contrast to your dark still well that could make me lose my mind, were it not lost.

(In fact there is some confusion of effect between you. One knows that *fiatto* is as distinct as a fingerprint, but were not the grain of your instruments so nearly opposite: were not her voice so molten and yours so *radioactive,* one might be forgiven for arraigning you in the court prosecuting her for mass audience illusion-homicide, and vice versa.) If I found any fault at all, it was in the occasional end phrase: she tends nowadays to run out of steam (the operative word, I'm afraid, among the naysayers was *scrannel*) certainly in relation to London, in '52, and the consequence seems to be that she dwells a fraction of a second too long on certain final notes, until the fevered brain refires. That and (I know we don't talk about wobble, but) the wobble you can at times now indeed play jump rope with, and the undeniable fact that she sometimes sounds absolutely like a *coyote.* (Somebody cackled, apropos the much-mooted Dallas engagements, "They are gonna *love* her out there—she *yodels!*") Like a coyote or like an egregious example of the notorious *bad fifth* (of which I know something myself, coming from a family of *poitin* distillers) in Henri Arnaut's fifteenth-century treatise on the Pythagorean tuning—and that is frightening. (And reminds me, though I never thought I would be reminded, of Mark Twain's description of that animal as "a living, breathing allegory of want.")

During the first intermission a combustible discussion of the sort much valued nowadays in existentialist New York got going at the bar in Sherry's—not over anything so insignificant and *contingent as* La Divina's wobble: rather over the question of Norma and motherhood. One or two loons posited that you had to have been a mother, and three or four more took the opposite view—the Golgotha Church organist (redolent of vetiver and inhaling Benedictine like Vicks) going even so far as to insist you shouldn't even have *had* one. Team A cited Ponselle and the big Z as non-moms, and Neri and thee as moms (both with lost children). I thought Ralph would choke to death on rage and spit. I found it riveting: in my experience it was the first time in the history of categories that you and the Old Foghorn have ever been put in the same file, except as *women* or as members of the cast of *Aida*.

I of course could only think of the truth of the matter, of that boy in Jerusalem, who has certainly passed the age of the bar mitzvah. Will he remember you? Does he realize who you are? You never said you were his mother, only the neighbor, fair enough, but he must remember his years with you, your tutoring him in the Torah like a Deborah in the wilds of Ruthenia. Deborah is "swarm of bees." "Busy little bees full of stings, making honey." You could never have stung the boy, only fed him on honey. I wonder do I sound jealous when I speak of this great work of yours. No, I don't think so, only mindful that I myself was in another context a boy fed on honey. Incidentally, apropos lineups, I thought you'd want to know where they put her in the rogues' gallery in the lobby. Right next to *you,* flush left of the north, or Fortieth Street box office window. It took me a while to remember whom they had moved: Mary C-V, who's now batting her eyes between Milanov and Blanche Thebom. So there.

Electing to abjure the felicities of the recessional (the gangways were, as Ralph declared, "*imbedded* crowded"), I cut out through the pass door to the executive offices (my prerogative now that I am an employee of the place—if that's what the translator of *Salomé* is entitled to call himself [and what else can I call myself, "Bosey"? Or put another way—the way of wit: "I never call myself, dear; I'm always in; too bad. I'd like to be able to give myself a piece of my mind once in a while, but my answering service is down on strong language"]). Whereupon, the big Z, with that ample vestal Maisie Halloran in tow, loomed up in the prospect (evidently having just left the Del Monaco dressing room, where God knows what . . .) very like the Queen Mary emerging from a North River morning fog into her waterfront berth. "*Zo, vot* are you *doink, smilink* like it *vuz* your *vedding?* I am goink to cabel Mawrdew Czgowchwz on you!" "Madame, don't bother, I'm confessing. How could I live with myself and keep such a passion secret?" She looked balefully from Maisie to me. "You Irish could do anything." Poor Maisie looked *pilloried* (after decades of selfless toil organizing socials, and especially after the latest salvo against Z by the Callas lobby in *English Opera,* calling Mama's Aida in particular ridiculous, and excoriating the Slavic pitch. Mary was heard *screaming* only last weekend, "She's the *only* Aida in *history* who sounds *Ethiopian! She researched* that pitch—it's the way they *sounded!*").

Ralph said later, "I love her like a two-reel silent, but has anybody heard any Haile Selassie records lately?"

(Of course the uproar when Madame Milanov walked down the aisle must have unnerved the debutante: you could've heard it at Carnegie—where of course the young Miss Price, Madame's obvious successor in Nilotic melodrama has sung Cleopatra.)

However, concerning the woman, she is a primitive woman, for all that she is a musical genius and for all that she has fallen in love with the Audrey Hepburn look and means to achieve it. A poorly educated, self-doubting (and therefore in respect of the genius perhaps all the more touching), primitive woman who has been terribly punished, whose overriding idea of punishing retribution makes her finally less compelling than a woman like you (well, there are no other women like you, so you) who having gone through hell is able to find a kind of restoration through kindness.

I could say more—all the nasty speculation about the weight loss from devotees of warblers at least four axe handles across the pistol pockets. Let suffice that everything you've held about the Meneghini all these years is still true, and the only thing to be done about it (at least until the Pope opens The Letter from Fatima in 1960) is to put the two of you back together and charge a hundred dollars a ticket to raise cash to elect the first American president who likes to go to *thuh opra.* *Herodiade* alternating the mother and the daughter? Or are you currently so steeped in mother/daughter cross-referential melodrama that all you yearn to do is—but you declined *Dialogues,* didn't you? (It's going to be a *succès fou,* but I never did see you in it.)

Aftermaths and post-mortems: this morning, on the line (reported on the telephone by Ralph and Alice):

"Did you love it, dear, love it *live?*"

"I loved it."

"Were you *moved?*"

"I wuz, deah . . . so moved they had to move me back."

And so *skip town—but first,* the last First Friday of 1956. They'll just have to do without their December: those who have not already made nine in a row must begin again. I do hate leaving town, just in case Winchell does decide to blow his brains out on television: it would give me as much joy to behold as did the public humiliation and death of the senator from Wisconsin. I know, hatred is a wound, and I pray to have it lifted . . . one day. In the meantime I am so delighted with the sponsors of his vile show for canceling him that I may take up smoking Old Gold *and* give myself a Toni ("which twin?"). Also, I'd love to crash the parties the debutante has lined up: the noise is she's going in Harry Winston's rented rocks like a showgirl. Glad I was at Herbert W's: she came looking like Audrey Hepburn in *Funny Face.*

I could go on in this vein, but I'd best abrupt myself if I'm to regroup my forces for the day and face life (I wonder will it ever get to the stage again when I sit down and look at that thing the way we did last winter?). Best of luck with *Pilgrim Soul* and the ways of *Eire-wohn mo bhron.* Remember that Maev means intoxication. And don't worry about playing your own mother; Gloria de Haven did it with no after effect (that one can detect).

Do write c/o General Delivery, Newport, or telephone the general store. (Massachusetts is a far cry from New York, but not so far as that from Dublin.) After last summer, they'd send out Indian runners in the winter storm to fetch the eremite off his lonely hill, down from his own Tor Ballyhoo where on the widow's walk in the howling nor'easter Calliope is right at home amid the travails and flails of any number of wailing Whaling widows, see above.

Si da mi stesso diviso
e fatto singular di l'altra gente to talk to you.

Your ever-loving pal,

S. D. J. (The O'Maurigan)

His Seal

Bisexual Pussy Boy
Robert Glück

My middle years were going by so fast—I seemed to be swept into a Max Sennett frenzy of manic gesture and locomotion toward the cliff and over. I was fifty-four years old: how durable the urges to fuck and to write about it. I responded to an ad on Craig's List during one of the periods that Rich left me, October 2001. "We have problems," I thought, as though to confirm our success as a couple. Rich was just a floral motif. Something pretty to give away. He turned away. The replication of that moment—a civilization founded on a gesture.

I longed for the days of general condition, average situation, but the complex was also compelling, to be impossibly sundered, hands thrown wide apart, the gesture of grievance and loss. I'd stood at the sink, saying, *Oh no I won't!*—but what did that mean? *Get away! That's what you think!* Now, where is this?

I had not been attracted to the photo on Craig's List: his smock is gathered at the chest like a housedress; he wears round glasses and his limp, sexless hair is tightly gathered, but he stands next to an energetic painting—a huge grasshopper—and after a few e-mail exchanges he wrote, "My experiences with men so far have been pretty anonymous but very thrilling, and it seems like the next step is to find someone who I can trust who is educated, interesting and experienced enough to boss me around and make me a masterful cocksucker. Can you do that? I've read a little about you online and it seems pretty clear that you possess a sophisticated creativity and gratitude for your life which is unusual. This makes me optimistic."

His response made *me* optimistic. I felt honored to be initiating Bill into the homo mysteries, although setting out on the drive to Oakland was making me even angrier at Rich. For some reason, it took me decades to learn that nothing is better than sex with someone you love. I learned that with Rich. As for Rich, anyone would probably have been a better mate, any guy walking on the sidewalk of the degraded street that leads me to the freeway. I thought I would be with Rich forever, so now forever seems to be in the past. All my future was chased away by the monster arbitrary. I hate the psychic drudgery of crossing the bridge and I resented the waste of time promiscuity takes.

I brought some champagne. I learned that from Kathy. Late one night, she asked me to stop at a corner store. She emerged with a bottle of Veuve Clicquot. Her boyfriend was coming over later, she explained. Thrillingly late. I'd felt so strong a pang of love for Kathy and her ways that it knocked the wind out of me. I was happy for her night of romance, relief from romantic desolation, and I looked forward to her report the next day. I needed to take care of someone, and here was a national treasure for me to nurture. We took baths together. She talked about her breasts, that they hung so thoroughly she called them worms, that they were murderers, that they would kill her. We were both confident in our nakedness, our sexual organs, little Napoleons. My own worm floating wanly. The jumble of limbs. But I was driving across the bridge in the middle of a random afternoon on the way to some stranger's body. I envied those writers for whom meaning is evident. At that moment, they were putting the finishing touches on poems and novels with favorite pens and drinking cappuccinos in favorite cafés or they were symbiotic with their laptops at home, basking in the bright screen of their own mentation. They were gripping the world with ideas and power. Blasts of wind buffeted the car. Now Kathy was on my mind, and her mountains of pills. Twenty years earlier, I started crying in Safeway. I could not go on, and sat down on the floor next to the chips and bottled bean dip. I felt intense relief when I learned it was a disease and not a breakdown. I retreated to blankets and sheets, pajamas and soup. Kathy needed a place to stay for November and December till she left the city, so we had the absurd idea that she would take care of me. Kathy needed to be taken care of, always, but that did not amount to a debt in her mind, any more than it would to a child. I felt a pervasive nausea, partly because I undoubtedly got the disease from rimming some guy—my favorite activity in those days. What was I living on?—how did I run my classes?

The flat oily odor of Kathy's vitamins and obscure supplements filled the house as I drifted for weeks in a nausea that sharpened my senses. My disease did not interest her. I could not convince her that I was really sick. She came home from the party at eleven o'clock instead of nine with a paper plate of leftover Thanksgiving dinner, just scraps that she seemed to want herself. I felt like a pig trying to get them down quickly. "I have friends who *died* of hepatitis," she said. Liver disease reduces testosterone, and I floated through the year with no desire at all, prepubescent. A roaring, clanging noise had been silenced. No more wheel of fire. Instead of killing me, hepatitis saved my life, since HIV was spreading through the bathhouses at that time. As Kathy was leaving—for London?—she thrust a cheap gray windup rabbit in my hands and turned away without a word, a gesture I could not interpret. She had a menagerie of stuffed animals, so perhaps she wanted to comfort me? I found the rabbit in a closet five or six years later and realized at once that she was letting me know that I was acting like a baby. Like someone who needed to be taken care of.

Best girlfriend.

Bill and I sat on a broken-down mohair sofa next to a space heater in his chilly studio in the industrial section of Oakland. He was trembling and it was an honor to take his fear and excitement into my arms. He was the perfect WASP. No more smock, good-bye pony tail. I exalted as though with the first swing my pick had struck a fantastic vein. I felt the skin of his back under his shirt; his skin was luxury. The parts of a mobile started turning on their own inside my chest. I had been invited as a teacher, the limit of my role and function. That made sense of the disparities. Bill was twenty-eight; he had a preppy face, bred for centuries to retreat from the arousal it generated. His variation on that theme: he was comfortable alone, he desired to be alone. He took off for weeks in his four-wheeler, camping in the desert, feeling connected to the earth. Also, he swam in the bay. Was this like an adolescent taking too many hot showers to cleanse his raddled spirit?

Bill explained that he had a girlfriend who encouraged our meeting. "Without her this would have been impossible, because I need a certain balance." His emotional life belonged to her. He wanted to forestall emotion in me so urgently that it amounted to an emotional request. Despite his appreciation, he did not want me. That is, he wanted my age, my attention, and a hard fuck. It was intolerable that I should feel anything beyond excitement. It was a mistake to build on my hope that we might speak the same language. He wanted me to shut up. It was a mistake to think that I could protect him and guide him. He wanted me to fuck him carelessly. I told him what would make me feel good, but my words carried no force and we both knew they were beside the point.

Bill led me to a mat in the middle of the dark space, protesting a little because I dragged the space heater with me. He did not want to give our sex an association—not with the sofa, not with the tidy bed against the far wall, which I looked at with longing. He did not even care if I got undressed—it was just Age watching Youth, that's what it took to transform his straight ass into a sexual organ.

I thought this was something to tell Ed about, but he had been dead for x years. This was something to tell Kathy about, though she had been dead for x years, and estranged from me for years before that. She would call the operator to break into my conversations if she wanted to talk to me. That was later—in 1987, say. I was running the Poetry Center then. Her food was utterly erratic, now she was eating only potatoes.

Two figures—Ed and Kathy—they are complete in themselves and have no relation to each other—just to their own narrative and inner drama, like Bellini saints. I gave my life away freely to Ed, Kathy, and Reese, then I suppose I needed some payment. Loneliness creates an excess of self. I could not give any more life away without getting some back. A group of her friends went looking on Twenty-fourth Street for a container for her ashes. I thought the floral Mexican box from the craft store would do, but the others fell in love with a nineteenth-century bronze dripping with flowers and cherubs. Kathy's ashes would inhabit the urn for what—only four or five weeks?—before we scattered them at the beach. This was a sin against thrift. Reasoning with the others in the overpriced antique store, contorting inside, I realized two things in the same moment: the urn was exactly the sort of excess Kathy loved, and *I* will end up in the stupid Mexican box. The pure jealousy I felt for Kathy's urn reconnected me to her more than anything had since her death. Like any extreme emotion it replaced what was in front of me. I had the sensation of falling. I inhabited a resentment that had always been too expensive, slightly out of reach.

I was supposed to be writing about Ed, but Kathy intruded, the real unfinished business at that point, if that's what you call a ghost.

Bill had a beautiful stomach, taut and small. He liked to show it off, this prize, this flesh. His pubic tuft, a bit of loose fur. His penis was a detail, even to him. I use the word *penis* because it was so cold in his studio. I put the hard curlicue in my mouth but that did not seem to give him pleasure. The studio had been some vast industrial warehouse. He blew me, lightly keening. That turned the day upside down. The footlights dimmed, and a silver shaft fell on us through a crack in heaven's floor. Bill's face was held up to it by the activity of our two bodies finding their way together, slow and deliberate. That is, Bill defied the future, then put his trust in it. In that blow job, his reality was realized. His faith scared me because I feared the depth of his loneliness and my own, in this barn, in the heaven of his flesh. Its strict beauty was like a happy sermon, like the peaceable kingdom. How extremely strange to find heaven and hell so mixed up. There on the wall gloated the devil with washboard abs and a forked flame for a prick. And there was the giant grasshopper—God had stretched out his hand.

After the blow job, my cock was returned to me. I poked it, the skin slick and cold, like fell on a lamb. Bill showed me his asshole and what he liked to do with it, and why not? He achieved what few can claim outside porn fantasy, the complete transformation of an asshole into a sexual organ. It didn't really have a name any longer. Pussy. It was bubble gum pink, clean as a whistle, and without the suggestion of scent, as though it existed in the imagination or as a photo. His rickety daddy long legs cantilevered outward at odd angles so his weightless torso seemed to bounce on them.

I am telling this to Ed and Kathy. Long ago at the baths I saw an old man gazing slack jawed into the vortex of a churning butt of a man who was fucking a man beneath him. The old man's head was tipped at an odd angle, as though a strong wind blew out of the butt, and now I understood that he was using the bottom correction of his bifocals to keep the ass in focus. My head was tipped back as well in order to read the fine print on Bill's little butt. His fingers were inside it, displaying it, running rings around it. He said, "It's repulsive, right?—what we do."

"Sure," I said. I felt shocked, but I hate to disagree. Bill probably needed our sex to be repulsive, and repulsive sex was not automatically undesirable. My first thought was that my age disgusted him. "Can I have some water?" I asked. And, "How about some music?" But Bill didn't want to be sidetracked, or to ruin some favorite CD by associating it with our sex. I didn't think our sex was disgusting—his desire not to communicate was frustrating, but not disgusting. It produced a question. Why do young men want old men if not to learn from them, since experience is what we have to offer? Possible answer: young men want power over old men. Communication upsets that dynamic and every dynamic of power. I was that much more an old fool, he was that much more a young slut. Anyway, I began to feel pleasure, and pleasure made our sex normal. Does arousal make things strange for some people? It is my native home.

At some point, when Bill realizes that his inner life is so disjunct, won't that equal terror? It seemed very 2002, the sense of bodies coming apart, sexuality parsed out, yet intensely lived. States of being can't be averaged out—is living in a disjunct condition a kind of heroism? The front of my body whirled, feeling a greed satisfied, I had forgotten it existed—waking from the sleep of marriage. He pulled his asshole open an inch with his forefingers for my eyes. It was time to come, but every few minutes I was distracted by this strange vaudeville show, the finger drawing the membrane outward as if throwing a tiny pot.

Then I fucked him as carelessly as he wanted me to do. I entered him from behind, my strokes were so hard I was spanking him with my thighs. His intricate lower back and the jiggling flesh of his ass made me feel surges of tender lust. Inside he was hot, I was in a well-heated room at last. Bill had only enough flesh to jiggle a little. I felt the complexity of generating excitement in a body that interests me, an alphabet of sites. I plunged and probed like a prospector losing his cool, made frantic by the growing richness of his vein of gold. Then I fell into—what?—a spatial fallacy, looking at our aroused bodies where there was so much interaction, if only along a few inches of skin. But from the point of view of the vast empty space, our little bodies expressed a contradictory stillness or timelessness, our two fragments, our two little hard-ons like levers that start the toy engine's senseless rotation: the organic reality of our bodies did not survive the cold darkness. I felt the grief of separation, as though time islands were drifting apart, me with a foot on each. And weirdly I also felt merry, like Slippage the Clown. Nature made a mistake. Nature *speculated* when it gave every one of us a temporary meeting place of bone and muscle. Why shouldn't life be as forever as a Martian landscape? Why should the inorganic remain and the living change and perish? That is, emptiness saw *through* my senses. A new model: desire, the creator of ghosts. His barn of a studio, his huge works, his space heater. I had the thought that one day Bill would understand his disjunction as grief and kill himself—say, vanish in the desert. Until then he would never make a unit, never come to rest—

I told him to touch his toes and to stand on his toes so his muscles were taut and he relinquished his balance to me. I bent him in half and really gave it to him, bringing forward another measure of time, sort of fast-forward. My goodwill counted for nothing. He felt compromised and humiliated, his ass taking the place of his head. Half of our bodies sizzled in the space heater, half froze like planets without atmosphere. The flesh on his body was intelligent and knew what it was doing, except for the mounds of his ass, which were ignorant and required tenderness and direction. Stupid in the sense of giving blind access and needing to be organized by a penis. That is the penis speaking, but what did it do but disorganize? I wanted to keep him from coming till he was desperate. I grabbed his tiny waist, pulling him up, he wouldn't, I pulled harder, and then his huffing noises told me he was coming. "Why didn't you say so?" He stood. Bill said that was the first time he was penetrated by a cock, and I was surprised. I would not have been so rough, but he was glad. To return to my shame—orgasm.

When I looked in the mirror in his bathroom, I didn't see the conflict inside me that seeks resolution inside some man's rump—the strange continual urge that suffers so much from its simplicity. Instead, I saw my father, who'd died two years before. Would I be writing more if I had less sex? It's an idea from the fifties. I shove gratification down, and up pops a force that pushes civilization forward. I suppose sublimation was the last gasp of empire and the Freudian version of republican restraint. Certainly, peering at Bill's butt hole from a distance of two or three inches, I felt unbelievably lucky, though at the same time I wondered what I was doing to myself, and where my body came into it, as though mixing some grief into my excitement made the excitement honest, as though this sex were duplicating something that made me teary. I had not allowed myself to put my mouth on his asshole because that was not safe sex, but I wondered if I was harming myself in some other way. Early sexual experiences torque one's sexuality because they are the expression of all sexual need. What can be said about sex when one is old? Since each experience could be the last? It's hard not to feel sex as some mistake. Some extra fear has gathered around the sexual urge. Testosterone drips from a leaky faucet that someone forgot to turn off. It's rotting the foundation of the structure. Will I want sex when I can no longer move or speak? Would I be spending my old age trying to remember some boy's butt hole seen first through my bifocals? A vague tear burning miles deep inside the empty sky of my chest, world too large, a pang of emptiness, delicate terror.

Bill wore an alarmed expression when I kissed him good-bye. I had forgotten that he saved all kisses for his girlfriend. When I told Denny about this part, he said, "God, I hate when they do that."

The Piers

Dale Peck

The past makes for a bad traveling companion. It can't be led but drags
you back with every step, distracting you, slowing you down,
throwing you off course. What I mean is, I'd needed to change at
Ninety-sixth Street for the local and I almost slept through the stop. I
opened my eyes just as the bell signaled the doors' closing, and I threw
myself out of the car and ran straight into the hot sucker punch of the
station. For a moment all I could do was waver on the platform like a
blade of grass. The heat seemed to have left me paralyzed, and only
instinct kept me upright. The first part that came back was my hand.
My wrist really: it was a quarter after eleven; and then I checked the
security of the key around my neck. The sun dripped through the sidewalk gratings, painting shadows that mockingly resembled the bars of
a cage. Voices fluttered down as well, the shed feathers of conversations floating somewhere above me, and as I followed the words down
I caught sight of a fat black woman whose breasts were underlined by
twinned crescents of sweat. She was eyeing a thin shirtless Puerto
Rican man a few feet away from me, something that looked like jealousy filling her eyes. When the Puerto Rican man caught the black
woman looking at him, she turned belligerent.

"Whyn't you put your shirt back on?"

The man shifted position with exaggerated nonchalance, scratched his balls. "Whyn't you mind your own business?"

"You think that turns me on?"

"I'd like to turn you off," the man said. "At least turn you 'round."

A few people standing nearby chuckled. Headlines fanned faces, eyes darted back and forth; the woman had at least a hundred pounds on the man and she moved in a little closer.

"You think I like seeing your skinny-ass chest and itty-bitty stick arms? You know what you should do? You should take a bath more often. I can smell you from here. And whyn't you pop those zits stead-a leaving them whiteheads all over your chin? You got herpes, boy?"

The man looked angry but distinctly intimidated. "Lady, I'm-a pop something besides a few zits."

"Yeah, I'd like to see that, you skinny runt." She stepped closer to him, and I heard the schmear of sweaty feet sliding in sandals. "C'mon, twiggy, let's—"

The downtown local roared into the opposite platform then, and, overpowered by its noise, the woman seemed to lose interest. She wandered away from the man with her hands on her hips, shaking her head, and as she walked away I remembered the confrontation between the cabbie and the men in the van the night before, and it occurred to me that *here* was New York. New York was always interrupting itself. New York was an accident waiting to happen. Even now, the woman was listing toward two boys who were throwing a baseball back and forth. She was talking to her shoes, the boys were oblivious to anything but their game, the *pop!* of the baseball against their palms measured out the moments to the impending disaster like a leaky faucet and it seemed to me if the ball did strike her then the ensuing bloodshed would be on a par with "Carnage on the GWB." But how did one yell "Look out!" in New York City?

I looked at the woman's back. I wondered if Trucker looked like that, from the back, standing: thick and shapeless as a stick of unpulled taffy. I wondered if Trucker had walked into his own baseball as blindly as this woman, and I looked behind me then, saw that the downtown train was still in the station, and quickly, before the baseball struck the woman and she exploded in a shower of blood—before I could stop myself, and before anyone could stop me—I jumped onto the tracks, one palm pressed to my chest to keep the key my mother had left for me from bouncing around. I hopped over the third rail, pulled myself up into the joint between two cars even as the brakes belched a jet of hot air and the train lurched toward Eighty-sixth Street. I thought I heard someone yell behind me but I didn't turn to see if it was the woman being struck by the baseball or someone exclaiming at my recklessness. I just opened the door, sat down in the first empty seat; I refused to look at my fellow passengers, keeping my eyes down until I was convinced we were safely in the tunnel. No newspaper would report this story, I told myself: as far as I was concerned, the fat woman, the thin man, the two boys and their baseball, and Trucker were now and forever safe. I only had to worry about myself.

At no point during my flight had I actually thought I was skipping out on my appointment at the clinic. It had simply slipped my mind. As soon as I remembered, I told myself I'd get off at the next stop and catch the uptown line. But the next stop came and it was Eighty-sixth Street and I didn't get off because I wasn't sure if there was a free transfer to the uptown train until Seventy-second. And, too, I'd broken out in a sweat, and the air-conditioning just felt too good to give up. New York, I was learning, was much easier to deal with when it was just a headline and three or four smeared graphs.

So the next stop was Seventy-ninth, the next Seventy-second. As the train was pulling out of Seventy-second I was still telling myself it was OK—it was early, I told myself; I'd have a bite to eat and then head back uptown, the testing center was open till four, maybe only three, but according to Trucker's watch it wasn't even noon and I had plenty of time, I told myself, plenty of time. When the conductor announced Christopher Street, I got off the train with the feeling I could eat a little something, do a little window-shopping, and still make it back uptown with time to spare. What I was thinking was that I was a gay man new to New York City and I still hadn't seen Christopher Street or the West Side piers, and so I walked down one to get to the other. Along the way I acquired a juice, something beet purple but tasting more of ginger and carrots, some candles, and the phone number of a middle-aged man who'd chatted me up at the juice bar (he was wearing his own jump-suit, yellow rather than orange, and he used the coincidence as his pickup line). The morning's drama was gone and in its absence a weightless calm had taken me over. I stuffed the phone number in my wallet, dropped my half-full cup of juice in a trash can, and then, my feet bouncing in *those shoes* as if I walked on balloons, I crossed the West Side Highway and saw the Hudson River for the first time.

I'd read about the old piers, seen pictures even, or one picture. It must have been taken from a boat far out in the river, and it showed a swaybacked ramshackle structure that looked like a section of an old-fashioned white-beamed roller coaster, but a roller coaster built for giants. On its maze of warped scaffolding had sat or leaned a half-dozen shirtless men whose baskets and brush mustaches were visible across a hundred yards of water. My fathers, I said to myself, my gay dads, for they'd had as large (or as little) a role in my upbringing as my real father. But the pier was long gone, in its place was an asphalt strip that stretched from Chelsea all the way down to Battery Park City, a tar ribbon as flat, black, and ugly as any Plains highway. It was the province of joggers, skaters, bicyclists, dog-walkers, hand-holders even, of all persuasions; but where the men who once came for an anonymous fuck now went I didn't know. Maybe they were all dead. Maybe, for the same reason, their descendants now preferred to score in juice bars or gyms or online, but as I made my own slow way down that ugly promenade—it was the very antithesis of the Yellow Brick Road—what I found myself wanting was a quickie, something to stop the normal flow of time and erect a little wall between the morning's misadventure and what still lay in store for me uptown.

What I got was a splash.

In the movies there are shouts when this sort of thing happens, but in the real New York, I was discovering, no one shouted when you expected them to. They ran, they gawked, they even pointed out the scene to anyone who did or didn't care to look, but they discussed the situation in a seen-it-all-before tone of voice, and as I hurried toward the confluence of bodies and bicycles at the river's edge, I, too, felt strangely unexcited; curious, but not aroused. Snippets of voices came to me.

"Did he fa—"

"I think he ju—"

"Where di—"

"Over the—"

And then I saw him. He floated face up, not more than ten feet out, his arms wafting on either side of his body, his legs pale shadows beneath the surface of the water. Save for the current's rollicking southward drift and the membranous movement of his white shirt and pants, he was still, and for a moment I felt it as well as saw it, the tranquility of floating. His eyes were open and he stared straight up. I could see the sky as well, its cloudless expanse reflected in the smooth water around his face, but it was the man's face that held me, his blank eyes, his hair like seaweed darkly haloing his head, his lips puffing out like rising dough with his refusal to answer the shouts from people on shore.

"Are you OK?"

"You need a hand?"

"Can you make it over here?"

"Man, what the *fuck* you doing?"

Then someone mentioned the police, someone else mentioned the fire department. A skinny man in running shorts ran off to find a pay phone even as a half-dozen other spectators pulled cell phones from purses and pockets and belt-slung holsters, but that was all the help anyone seemed willing to give. With a weak gesture, the man in the water used a fingertip to pull a splayed lock of hair off his face, and all the while the current carried him steadily south—toward, I saw then, a dark tangled mass of pilings, the jagged base of some long-gone pier, perhaps even the one I'd seen photographed. For a moment its ghostly specter hovered above the river, the ghost of a ghost, and by the time the apparition had dissolved I found myself on the chain-link fence separating the walkway from the river, my feet, freed of *those shoes* for the first time in nearly a year, pinched in the tight little diamonds, my fingers curled like grappling hooks and pulling me up with a grace and strength and speed I didn't know I possessed. *This can't be happening,* I was thinking, but that thought was erased by pain, belied by it, as the jagged top of the fence pierced the fabric of Trucker's ridiculous jumpsuit and seamed my leg like a plow opening up the soil. For a moment I saw the river below me, as black and impenetrable as a chalkboard, and then I saw my reflection, the boy I'd seen two weeks ago in the barber's mirror, the fleshless struts of his bones outlined inside the jumpsuit like the crossbars of a kite, his hairless skull as unadorned as a death mask. I wanted to say something to that mask, but before my brain or my tongue could find the words, my real mouth bestowed a rushed kiss on its reflection, and then I was in the river.

I was underwater.

There was a moment then, I don't know what to call it. I don't know what you'd call such a state. An ending, or just a transition? A suspension? Maybe "lapse" comes closest. For a moment time stopped, and for that moment I was at peace. I didn't feel it, didn't hold it anyway, I couldn't actually call it my own, but I still felt it around me, as palpable as the river's water. It was like the moment I crested the Rockies and let gravity roll me down to the plains. This much I can tell you: the closest this world comes to perfection isn't some kind of willed, built-up thing. It's emptiness. It's absence. I heard my heart beat while I was down there. It was the only thing I could hear, the only thing I could sense in that dark plunge, my heart's outward press and the water's inward push. For the first time since I'd arrived in New York I had a clear sense of where I ended and the world began. I thought of The Well then. I thought all the water that had never come out of its dust-clogged spigot was right here: I was suspended in it. I floated in the water that wasn't sex. And then I gave in, for the final time, to Trucker. On our last day together I'd done what I always did. I slipped my shorts off without taking off *those shoes,* and then I scooted across the seat and straddled him. It was easier if I faced the steering wheel, but that day I knew I needed to look at him. My ankles rode on his thighs and my knees flanked his hips. "Hey," Trucker said as I undid his belt. "What are you doing?" I didn't answer, just took what I knew would be there, curled my spine, bent my head so far to one side that my ear was practically touching my shoulder. Friction and the roof of Trucker's car filled my hair with static electricity, filled my ears with its crackle. On more than one occasion in the past Trucker had burst out laughing at my hair standing on end—Albert Einstein he called me, Don King—but that day all he said was, "Come on, now, don't be crazy." But I ignored him, just rocked up and down as I always did. "James," Trucker said, "don't you realize things have changed?" And, when I still ignored him: "James? Why are you doing this?" It never took Trucker very long and it didn't take him long that day, and it was only after he'd finished that I said, "Because it was there for me. Because you had it to give to me. Because nothing's changed," I said, "and I never could refuse a gift."

It was the flavor that brought me back. The oily stuff filling my mouth tasted like . . . like what? Like a slightly caramelized petroleum-based soft drink: repulsive, yet also sweet and compelling. It tasted like semen, and I almost swallowed a mouthful of it. But I spit it out as soon as my head cleared the surface. I'm not sure how I cleared the surface. Maybe it was just the air in my otherwise empty stomach ballooning my body upward. Swimming seemed to have started automatically, a sort of messy breaststroke, and it was only when I looked in front of me that I remembered the man.

He was a half-submerged beacon, his white clothes glowing under the river's surface, and as I swam toward him I felt the salty water stinging the wound on my leg and it was the only thing real to me, that little pain, but even it had the soft focus of a fever dream, as my mind filled with an image of blood inking the water each time my legs frog-kicked me forward. I performed as if following a script. I swam to the man, and as I got close he turned his face toward mine. "Please," he said. "Just keep away." But I ignored his words. I pulled up to him, ducked under the water, and with seal-like agility flipped myself over and came up beneath him so his shoulders rested on my chest. I looped an arm around him. "Please," he said, struggling feebly, "please just let me go." His words were in my ear along with the sound of the river, and I could feel his heart beating against my forearm. "Let me *go*." I turned to him then. Saw up close whiskers and wrinkles, the softening profile of a man slipping into middle age. I kissed him then, on his cold cheek. I pressed my lips against his skin and just held them there until the man said, "Oh." And then again: "Oh." He stopped struggling then, and with my free arm I paddled us to the shore, and there waiting for us was a slimy but still solid length of rope or root just sticking out of the earth as if it were the anchor of the city itself. I grabbed on to it, and then we waited for what would happen next.

What happened next was that a couple of men scaled the fence and reached their arms down to us. The hero act is catching: there was lots of *We got ya*'s and *Here comes the cavalry*'s on the part of the men, lots of *Look out*'s and *Careful*'s on the part of the watchers, but even with all the acting it was only a moment before they'd clasped the man's limp hands and pulled him off me. He had begun to cry, a mewl of shame and chagrin, and the sound only reinforced the idea that I'd made a mistake, that I hadn't saved this man but condemned him to a fate worse than drowning. The man's crying became a wail as the men on the shore slung him over the fence's barbed top like a sack of animal feed; his sobs were all I could hear as they reached to help me. I tried to avoid his eyes, but they were all I could see. He was hung over the fence like something already dead, but still his head lifted up and he fixed me with a sad stare and he said, "You shouldn't have, you shouldn't have, you shouldn't have."

For the first time I looked at him. His hair was dark and he was about forty and although he could have been my father I knew he wasn't and would never be. As I backed away from him I felt hands on my back and shrugged them off more successfully than the man who wasn't my father had shrugged off mine. When I'd backed all the way through the crowd and felt the space empty out behind me I turned and, shoeless and sodden, ran for home.

By the time I made it back to Dutch Street I was nearly delirious. My bare feet were blistered and bloody, the cut on my thigh had opened up again, and closed, and a long thick brown streak showed where the hairs on my left leg were stuck to the fabric of the jumpsuit. What was worse was that it was dark, and it had still been morning when I'd jumped in the river. Where had the time gone? Where had *I* gone? My keys were missing from my pocket, also my wallet. I entered the building through the shop and screamed Nellydean's name until she materialized from one of her secret dens. In response to my demands for another key she walked to the box of ostrich eggs I'd found on the long-ago day I'd gone looking for a touch-tone phone, and when she cracked the egg open a key as rusty as its predecessor fell into her palm. I snatched it from her, stumbled upstairs, and the first thing I saw was that Trucker's computer had finally found its way to me, sprung up on the vast surface of my mother's desk like a pox that had been incubating for weeks. My impulse was to throw the boxes out the window. "Fuck you, Trucker!" I screamed into the empty room. "How could you do this to me?" But what had he done? What was his fault and what was mine, what had *I* done and what had simply happened? *What* had happened? It was all confusing, and it was all I could do to lift the computer boxes to the floor, all I wanted to do was sleep, to slip if I could into the lush psychedelic comfort of a fever dream. I climbed onto my mother's desk and closed my eyes; the stone was hard but the coolness was like a pillow cushioning my hot body. Like the last, this chapter ends with a disembodied voice delivering a cryptic message. But this time, at least, I knew it came from a dream. It was just a gurgling at first—or was it crackling? Was it a fire, or was it the river, or was it the voice of the headless statue in the garden? I strained to make it out. I opened my ears as if they were my heart itself, and the words fell into my soul like medicine from a dropper:

You're safe here.

Neorealism at the Infiniplex
John Weir

My friend Dave died of AIDS in the fall of 1994. I had planned to be sad about it, but it turned out I was relieved. I'm not proud of this. In my fantasy, he would have died in my arms and the screen would have faded to black, like in a movie. It was an Italian neorealist ending, a grim death but a noble one, suffered in a time of war, or shortly after war. What happened instead was that he was so mean for the last three months of his life that I stopped liking him. Not just at the time, but for all time, both in the season of his death and retroactively, forever. His dying wasted our five years of friendship, and I lost him in retrospect. I don't remember what I ever liked about him. People say they can't believe their beloved husband, mother, son is gone, but I had another feeling. I couldn't convince myself that I had ever known and loved someone named David. That was the worst thing that happened.

No, the worst thing was that he left me some money that took a long time to clear. In 1997, three years after he died, I got about three thousand dollars, and I decided to rent a place in upstate New York. Because I teach school, I have my summers free, and so I sublet my East Village apartment, bought a used car at a police auction in Jamaica, Queens, and signed a three-month lease on a converted chicken coop. It lay on the grounds of an old Dutch farm, and it was vast and cheap, with a high ceiling and a sleeping loft. There was no furniture, so I bought a futon and a table. I put the table in the kitchen in front of a window with a view of the mountains. On the tabletop, I set a borrowed laptop computer and a stack of books I had never finished reading: *Paradise Lost,* Proust, *The Naked and the Dead.* I was going to read the classics, write things, eat right, go running every afternoon on the back roads and country lanes, and finally lose the weight I had gained while Dave was dying.

Of course, I hate back roads and country lanes. How had I forgotten that? I hate views. I especially dislike chicken coops. Mine still smelled faintly of chickens. When I looked up from my work, through my kitchen window, I could see an open field, trees in the distance, and the sky everywhere. Not the reassuringly man-made chemical sky of lower Manhattan, but an intimidating sky so awesome and inhuman that, in order to explain it, you were forced to invent God.

When I fell asleep over *Paradise Lost,* sitting outside in an Adirondack chair that had bark clinging to its arms and legs, I woke scraped and sunburned and covered with bug bites. A mile down the road at the food co-op, the cashier was so vegetarian she wore rope-soled shoes, and she would not sell me bug spray. Within days, I was aching for anything lethal or synthetic. I was nostalgic for pizza and car exhaust and Avenue A. Of course, there were people living in my apartment—German students on summer holiday—and I couldn't go home. Twice, I drove down to the city and paid eighty dollars to sleep in the Jungle Room at the Kew Motor Inn. Obviously, I couldn't spend the summer traveling back and forth every day between a New Paltz chicken coop and a by-the-hour motel off Grand Central Parkway in Queens.

So I loaded Proust and Milton and Norman Mailer into the trunk of my car, and I went to the movies.

I moved to the multiplex. To many different multiplexes, which are so abundant in the wilderness that I began to think of all upstate New York as a vast infiniplex. From late June to early September, I went to every several-screen movie theater from Kingston to Yonkers, listening to Billy Joel songs on the car radio and crying because I was old enough to remember liking them without irony. When I was not in my car, I was seated front row center with a bucket of popcorn and a Coke watching Bruce Willis in *Armageddon.* You see how entertainment was not the point.

If I kept going back to *Armageddon,* I thought, it would eventually turn out to have a plot. I saw it six times, and it never did. Of course, I was grateful. It was a relief to be spared the pain of cause-effect. Thank God for a plotless world. Watching the scene where Bruce Willis, draped in an American flag, waves good-bye to the world from the floor of a crater in a huge piece of orbiting igneous rock was the most satisfying emotional experience I have ever had. I'm through with stuff that really happens, like, people die and you don't. Or, they die and you don't feel bad in the way that you want.

Which is how I got in trouble with *Saving Private Ryan,* Steven Spielberg's D-day massacre movie. I saw it twice a week for two months, like short-term therapy or a lover who beats you every time you go back, despite your insane faith that one of these days it will end differently. *Saving Private Ryan* is more believable than *Armageddon,* though this, for me, was not the point. I didn't care about World War II. Isn't it a film about a bunch of gay guys who take a summer house in Fire Island in 1983?

Look at the evidence: it opens with a few hundred handsome young men in expensive outerwear squeezed into a boat approaching the shore of a famous beach, where people casually speak French and stern

Nordics are lurking in the dunes with their hands on their weapons. We meet eight guys, just enough for a half share in the Pines. Most of them are midwestern. Once ashore, they go from house to house in uniforms, carrying accessories, singing Duke Ellington songs—"In my solitude, you haunt me"—and listening to Edith Piaf, all the while searching for just one cute boy. And every few days, one of them dies.

It's the same plot as *Longtime Companion,* one of the first films about AIDS. A bunch of men with no special talent or need for intimacy or closeness have to deal with the fact that everyone they know is dying all around them all the time. Sometimes they abandon their dead. Sometimes they mourn them. They do what they can given their uneasy sense that the next person dead could be you. Later, the dead men are buried far from their hometowns, out of sight of their folks, gone in a way their parents can't, or won't, understand.

When Dave died, his mom and dad came up from Florida in a rental car. He died on Wednesday and was buried on Friday. They left their house Thursday morning and drove, they said, straight through. Nonetheless, they were two hours late for the funeral service at Riverside Memorial Chapel on the Upper West Side of Manhattan. The service had to be finished by sundown, because he was Jewish, it was Friday afternoon, and the parents had insisted long-distance—even though David hated God or even the mention of God—that there be religious last rites.

So we waited in the chapel. It was the fifth time I had been there for a dead friend. And we went through two rabbis. Each of them stayed an hour and then had to leave. The place was rented, it was full. David was naked in a pine box loaded with ice to keep the body from stinking. The coffin was sweating as the ice slowly dissolved. We had a bucket under the corner to catch the drips. I thought of Dave floating inside this cocktail like a lemon wedge. All the mourners, David's friends and co-workers and cute guys from the Chelsea gym, were sitting quietly in the pews listening to the drip, drop, drip into the bucket.

The stage was set, in other words, and the effects were starting to melt, and we had no parents, and now suddenly no rabbi.

Try finding a rabbi free on Friday afternoon on the Upper West Side of Manhattan. I made an announcement in the chapel, really a plea. "Does anybody know——?" How would I ask it? I felt in need of Mel Brooks. He would have struck the right tone. But it turned out that somebody had a cousin who knew somebody, who knew . . . And I made the calls. "You don't know me, but I need a rabbi."

It took ten calls. The sun was setting. Thank God some Jews are not observant; people were answering their phones. Finally, we got a rabbi. I never said "AIDS." I didn't know what to say about AIDS. I wasn't sure he'd do it. I said nothing. I said, "Dead guy on ice," which sounds like a hard-core band. And he understood, he came to the chapel. Why wasn't he busy on a Friday night? I didn't want to know. Cut-rate rabbi. Though in fact he cost just as much as the others. We paid for three, we used one. Not the star, but the road-company replacement. We started with Nathan Lane, ended up with Steve Guttenberg, it's better than nothing. He's available.

He showed up five minutes ahead of Dave's parents. Their rental car had broken down in Philadelphia. Never mind that the quickest route is not through Philadelphia. That's why God gave us the New Jersey Turnpike, it's a straight shot from Jacksonville to Bayonne on I-95. Why tour Philadelphia? Whatever. I had avoidances of my own. Just before the parents appeared, the rabbi took me into a small room and said, "Quick, tell me about your friend. Say what he was like. Say three things. I don't need more than three. Add some color, make it personal, and make it fast."

And all I could think of was, "Well, he spent a lot of time at the gym." It was an awful thing to say, that he was a gym-going muscle queen, a gay cliché. Though it was true, he went to the gym the way Baptists go down to the river. Still, there were plenty of other things to say about him, and why was this my first thought? He was a writer, he had published several books, what prevented me from listing these accomplishments? Grief is sneaky, not sobering, it refuses to suppress your worst impulse.

Then the parents appear.

So there is the sudden attention to the parents. Who presumably have precedence. Though they had not visited David even once, had not in fact seen him in more than a year, hadn't called except when the rates were low on Sundays, and had sent, as a token of their concern, only a package of home-baked chocolate chip cookies. For a guy who could not digest so much as a piece of dry toast without soiling his shorts. David made me eat the cookies in his hospital room while he swore at his nurses. Then he swore at me. Then he died, and we had a ten-minute funeral service where the parents got front-row seats.

The rabbi ripped cloth from their garb in honor of some tradition that did not include my dead friend, who had wanted to have his wrist tattooed at the last minute so he couldn't be buried in a Jewish cemetery. Kaddish was said, and the rabbi made some remarks. He said, "David was a man who loved sports, especially at the gym." And a roomful of people, not his parents, burst out laughing, because he was famous, at the gym, for cornering cute boys in the steam room and asking them to lunch.

The Kaddish was endless. I don't know when I've hated God so much. I had tracked down the last photograph of David taken before he went into the hospital, and we got it blown up, and it was standing on an easel next to the rabbi. An awful picture. Dave looked shrunken and rabbity and pale. He had shaved off his '70s-era Christopher Street gay clone mustache, and though I always hated that mustache, he was unrecognizable without it. He lost almost half his body weight in the two months before he died, dropping from 150 pounds to a little less than 90, and this photograph was how I would always remember him, now: barbered and desiccated, a huddle of bones under sacked skin, which happened to be my dying, now dead, friend.

His body had nothing to do with him. His funeral service had nothing to do with anyone who cared for him. It was an appalling farce. I had to be polite to his parents, who, if they loved him at all, nonetheless could not manage to visit their dying son. They knew he was dying. If he were my son, I would have moved into his hospital room. I would have postponed my life to be with him, which is basically what I did. And they were his parents, they sent cookies, I despised them, I wished they had died instead, I hope they die soon, lost and alone and uncared for by their own flesh and blood.

Afterward we talked like I thought they were human. They barely registered my humanity or my closeness to Dave. They had me down as "good friend," official funeral parlor role. I was not family. It was their loss, not mine, and I had exactly a minute to cry. It happened in a closet. No kidding. I was not going to cry in front of someone's suddenly visible parents. I found a coat closet, oddly empty for November. I thought, *Well, as well here as anywhere else.* I thought, *This is where it turns out I was always going to have my private sorrowing moment.* I don't believe in God, but I do believe in the fated emptiness of coat closets and private moments of sequestered grief. I leaned in a corner, folding myself into the crease of a papered wall as if the angle of the building could hold me.

In a minute, I was going to have to walk out into the reception room and answer questions, give directions, to the cemetery in Queens, to the ice-skating rink at Rockefeller Center. That's what the parents wanted to know. They had driven all the way from Florida and they were not leaving without seeing the sights, buying souvenirs, "MY SON DIED OF AIDS AND ALL I GOT WAS THIS LOUSY T-SHIRT." But for now, avoiding them, crouched under coat hooks, I cried, it was almost the only time I cried about AIDS. Half the people I knew when I was twenty-five years old are dead, and I cried while Dave's parents waited, and I cried at sixteen different showings of the last scene of *Saving Private Ryan*.

The scene that Amy Taubin of the *Village Voice* called "creepy."

I thought that was the whole point.

Actually, the popcorn was the point. It was my steady diet. Every movie theater in upstate New York sells a version of the Supercombo Special—a huge bag of popcorn and a giant soda—always served by an underpaid teenager who stares at a point slightly to the left of your head and slowly asks, "Do you want the special it's only fifty cents more than the medium size the soda comes with free refills—"

And I say, "Yes. Now. Immediately. Please. I want, I want, I want," I say, interrupting them, slapping money on the counter, exact change. God forbid I should have to wait for them to make change. Give me a giant-size popcorn, I say, soak it in butter to ruin my heart and salt for my tears, so I can taste it on my face hours later when Steven Spielberg makes me watch an old guy walk through acres of white crosses—a military graveyard in France—and drop to his knees in front of the headstone of a friend who died in battle instead of him.

It's the end of *Saving Private Ryan*. World War II's over, we won. Spielberg has returned us to the framing device, a scene taking place more than fifty years after the war, in the present moment, a summer day in 1997. Private Ryan, who was saved by his buddies, is now an old man, no longer played by Matt Damon. He is white haired, slow moving, unglamorous. Since the beginning of the film, and presumably all through the two-hour-long flashback to World War II, he has been walking with his family—his wife and son and his son's wife and his grandchildren—up and down the rows of headstones in the military graveyard.

Suddenly, he stops in front of one of the bone white crosses. The John Williams music swells loud and an American flag whips overhead—though we're in France. Whatever. You're right, Amy Taubin, it's schmaltz. Obviously, I've got bad taste, I'm moved by schlock. In front of the headstone, the old guy seems to be tossed to his knees by an electrical shock. He is on the ground before the grave, weeping, not dead. He turns to his wife.

"Tell me I'm a good man," he asks her.

His family stands behind him, kind of appalled. They've got no idea what he means. Clearly, he has never mentioned the war, or how he was spared, or why his friends died.

His family doesn't have a clue what he's talking about, but I do. He wants them to know what it's like to have the worst thing happen, to lose everything and never discuss it, so that you lose it twice, both in the moment, when it actually goes, and afterward, in the official record of its going. So two things are gone, Dave is gone and you're gone. And maybe you get a moment to cry for what, now, you will never be able to tell: that all the people you loved for a season had died, and that you, for years and years after, quite simply, had not.

Rivals

David McConnell

Darius was neat and prompt. He arrived early in homeroom and sat quietly while the other boys played chess or flicked triangular paper "footballs" across their desks. Sometimes he made a flowery gesture to himself before recomposing his hands on the glazed plywood.

In his teacher Jane's opinion he had an average mind, but every so often he spoke at length in class. On these occasions he was riveting and made no sense at all. He'd twitch. He'd flinch at the loud ticking of the clock as the words poured out. He'd only go still when his eyes rolled up at a patch of the acoustic-tile ceiling and he looked ready to faint. "Sharks are animals! Sharks are animals! You look at them and they have these major senses we don't have. And they're animals, so . . . Also, the fishermen don't know about the cancer cure thing!"

Waving for his attention, his teacher put in, "Are you saying they'd be more careful not to overfish sharks? Our speaker made the point that even though sharks are dangerous, they may benefit us." Jane Brzostovsky knew the sense she tried to make for Darius wouldn't calm him.

The student who'd just given his "homeroom speech" on sharks and who was still jumpy and flushed in patches squealed, "Yeah, because of what *I* just said—the cartilage!"

"No, no," Darius groaned. "Because sharks are animals!" His gaze made an appealing but haughty sweep of his audience before drifting to the ceiling again like oracular smoke. He made a passionate gesture with one arm in a way that caused giggles. He seemed not to hear them. "This, *this* is not what they see!"

Jane began to wonder, as always, whether he were making sense too sophisticated for his age. Then she heard, "They're as scared of *us* as we are of them!" An age-appropriate banality.

And then, again Darius: "I have a tooth from an extinct shark two thousand feet long." Snorts of disbelief and *No way*'s went unnoticed. "I threw it in our pool. I won't say why." Was it a contentless compulsion to perform? Pure, childish rhetoric, in other words? "I know he loved his tooth." Much laughter. And Darius laughed, too, as if for a moment allowing this was all a joke. The moment passed. "But he's an animal—was. So you guys might be useful for cancer. You could be! *This!*" Thrillingly he seized the homeroom speaker's hand and tried to hold it up. But the boy shook his arm free with a stormy look and blocked-sinus wheezing. Darius talked on. What could one say?

When the boy finally wound down and the bell rang, Jane reminded him to stay after class to discuss his own speech, next on the schedule. Darius sat, crossed his legs tightly, and put a jaunty hand on his hip. He looked exhilarated, proud, which somehow annoyed Jane. The truth was, she disliked him. Jane disapproved of irony, the vice of the age. And unseriousness bubbled up from Darius—like that moment of laughter today—even when passion had seized him. Most ironical and maddening of all, he adored her. She was his favorite teacher. He took her winces, her reserve, her dutiful encouragement as some kind of hilarious flirtation. She sighed, "Maybe you should think about doing a follow-up, more on sharks, since you feel so strongly . . ."

"I'm doing it on the Borgia family," he said, raising an eyebrow. He'd moved to the desk closest to hers. "They've probably never heard of them." He chucked his head at the empty room.

"Darius, don't be so arrogant. You come off looking foolish. I'd wager some of them have heard of the Borgias."

He smiled at her, an oddly prying expression, and repeated, "'Foolish'?"

"I only mean it takes a lot of hard work to do well and . . . to explain your thoughts clearly. I do get a sense that you have something to say sometimes. But let's get on with it. What about the Borgias?"

"Well, the Pope had a homosexual incest relationship with his nephew, who was really his son."

"I think there was a lot of nasty gossip about the Borgias. I mean . . . a very evil family."

"And the son was in love with his sister."

"I don't think you need to be . . . sensationalistic in your speech."

Again he raised an eyebrow at her.

"Darius, do you know what all that's about?"

"Of course."

"What?"

"Sex. The Borgias, you mean?"

"I don't know if that would be such an appropriate thing to dwell on. Maybe if you talked about the dark side of the Renaissance."

"You want me to hide the truth?" he asked in the most insinuating tone.

Jane made a face at the window. Outside, healthy-minded boys were playing flag football, plastic streamers, red and blue, dancing from their narrow hips.

"Don't look out the window on me," Darius said, outrageously, baselessly intimate.

"Darius!" Jane snapped. "A little respect!"

His face went slack. She closed and rolled her eyes briefly, causing herself an invigorating pain. The boy's global ignorance didn't make him endearing. He had no clue about her feelings. Or his own.

The bowdlerized Borgia talk didn't go over well, but Darius seemed to get the taste of stardom anyway. He talked in almost every class in the days following. When he was on the brink of one of his talking ecstasies near the end of homeroom, Jane Brzostovsky called on others and tried to overlook his waving arm, double-jointed with yearning. At intervals a grainy, silvery thunder of cheering came through the open windows from the middle school playing field. "I know everybody wants to get out, so I'll try to wrap up," Jane said.

"I have something to *say*," Darius couldn't contain himself.

"Not sure we have time, Darius." Jane tried to sound offhand. She snuck a glance. Sure enough, Darius looked betrayed, his brow pinched.

In a snide tone of voice he addressed the class, "She just doesn't want you to hear the true thing that will go against her small-minded—"

"Hey! Watch it! I don't like the sound—"

"Of course, she doesn't. She's—"

Jane grabbed his upper arm and flung open the classroom door. She dragged Darius into the hall. The other students, vocalizing like monkeys, peered after them.

The door had revolved on its hinges and struck the outer wall. The pewter glare from a glass pane shuddered on the tile floor, and an aqueous clangor re-echoed up and down the hall. Jane's muscles felt like frothed milk, her eyes actually hurt in their sockets—she was so enraged. Darius's head rolled with flowerlike indifference. "You've been wanting to touch me for a long time, haven't you, babe?" he said.

She struck him with the flat of her hand. His expression wrinkled up. "And all of you, shut up," Jane snapped at the murmuring class.

The slap was a serious matter. Jane dutifully reported it to the head of school. Together they settled on a risky course of inaction: not even a phone call to the parents, the exceedingly rich Van Nests. The calculation paid off. Darius never told anyone what had happened. Pleased with their discretion, the head of school bunched his lower lip whenever he saw Jane over the next few days. It looked like he meant, "I do feel for you—these kids sometimes. . . ." Other parents who might have heard about the slap would assume a disciplinary word had been spoken. And that was that.

Jane felt an irritable sort of remorse. Maybe she wouldn't have been so hard on him, maybe he could have aroused her compassion—by all accounts his parents were horrendous—if only he hadn't been so close to Barry Paul. Barry was Jane's favorite student by far. She often laughed to herself about her more or less full-blown crush on him. Or "crush"—when it came to Barry her stream of consciousness bubbled with giddy scare quotes and, she had to admit, sputtered with irony. Seeing the two boys together drove her crazy. Annoyed her, she told herself, on Barry's behalf, because even he might be affected by exposure to such a "twisted" companion.

The two boys were always together. Inseparable from the first day of class at Lawrence Academy. Jane had no clue how their friendship suddenly sprang into existence. It was one of those kid things. It had to be very pure, very beautiful, and very mysterious. At least on Barry's side.

Next to Barry, who was husky, Darius looked svelte and crafty. He effaced himself. Chin scratching his clavicle with feline strokes, he'd eye his friend. If he needed attention, there weren't any outsize ecstasies. A rapid whisper passed his lips. Then, as soon as Barry turned, frank and grinning and, for some reason, amazed at what he'd heard, Darius's fingers squirmed. They formed a white-knuckled spider on the white denim stretched tightly across his thigh. He smiled at the floor. Jane didn't care for the too-tight pants or the flowered shirts the boy, or his mother, went in for.

Since Jane's thoughts about Barry were over the top as well as energetically secret, her love was also funny. To her anyway. The scare quotes tickled. Self-deprecating amusement creamed inside her, becoming more abundant affection for the loved one, then diffuse happiness, then a barely visible smile.

Barry had a special quality, didn't he? Who knew what it was? Jane tried pinning it down. Too simplistic to say he lacked irony. The universal mistake people made—this was Jane talking to herself, for she really believed Barry's appeal was widespread and that was no joke—the universal mistake people made was thinking that the quality didn't belong to him. They thought *they* were content, *they* were having a good day, *they* were interesting, *their* personality was bearable, even admirable, whenever they had some little dealing with Barry. Since he wasn't memorably beautiful and never said anything a suburban New Jersey boy wouldn't say, he was able to go about his business in the healthful anonymity that suited him. His star power—that's what Jane called it—was slow-acting, subterranean. A tribute to her, in a way, that she'd picked up on the—uh, "star power," no? She tried laughing but failed. In subtle stages, she'd given up the notion that sometimes *she* was content or interesting or to be admired or that she could ever become that way through an effort of her own. It was objective, this quality Barry had. Like those naïve maps that placed the Garden of Eden exactly here, so many miles northwest of Ur, fulfillment seemed to be local, tangible, the fragrance of sour candy on this one boy's breath. She was like any of us when we're starstruck. We squirrel away tiny facts about our idols, whether to take them down a peg or draw them closer is unclear. But sometimes all the detail in the world is insufficient. They have one more thing. An invisible thing. And we swear it's real.

Barry's eyes were set wide. He squeezed the right one closed when he didn't understand something—often enough. In repose his mouth looked straight, grim, and countrified, but it was always moving. He was an avid, poor skateboarder. He sometimes tied a spare wheel truck to the flap of his backpack, a sort of tradesman's token. He had no particular passion for any of his classes, though he liked the biology unit of science best.

Even at eleven, a year older than most of the boys in his class, he seemed lumbering. He wasn't above trouble. Somehow, bigger in body, the trouble seemed a bigger deal than it was, too. He was caught shoplifting *Rock Climber Magazine* from a 7-Eleven. There were plenty of successful thefts, as well.

No matter how amiable, he liked popping out a cruel remark from time to time and thought them pretty funny. Jane and Darius were both—independently—shocked. Like the time he mimicked his grandmother's Alzheimer's a week before she died. He wasn't not good-hearted, just not mincingly good—a distinction neither Darius nor Jane happened to be strong on. Plus, the down at his ankles and another patch of down that often showed over his huge red-eyed death's-head belt buckle were going coarse prematurely, a little too sexy for a kid. When you glimpsed it, you imagined he was secretly manly, despite the beardless baby face.

He had one quirk. He claimed to be a communist. He insisted on it. Though he knew a few Maoist aphorisms and pretended to celebrate

May Day, his communism wasn't a thought-through political position. Sometimes the most normal boys in the world develop a healthy consternation about being *so* normal. With a simplicity that's really anything but eccentric, they seize on a single eccentricity and make a hobby of it. Being a communist, especially at the time, 1989, made Barry feel more like a particular person. And of course, it suited Jane, a brazen leftist till reality dumped her in the hallowed halls of Lawrence, perfectly.

All the humor—the irony, ironically—mostly shielded Jane's "crush," her love, from her own eyes. But Jane wasn't stupid. She knew there was something out of hand about so unwieldy an emotion for a student. She once tried to finesse it. Too smart for her own good. As all the world knows, secrets want to come out.

There happened to be a scandal that got a lot of play in the *Star-Ledger* around this time. Thuggish football team. Slip of a boy raped with an Eskimo soapstone carving of a seal. *Then,* comfort in an assistant coach's arms! A two-year chronicle of forty-eight "incidents" between man and boy. Jane wasn't the only one to follow this story. But she stayed up late one night typing a memo to fellow faculty members. "Thoughts before We Formulate a Policy on Inappropriate Behavior" was the long title, and "Glasnost! Openness!" was the short first paragraph.

The memo went on about a friend of Jane's, a first-time mother who discovered that her nurturing feelings toward her *infant* actually had an erotic component. "Perhaps new parents often give up having sex for a time, because they're experiencing a perfectly normal displacement of erotic feeling onto their children. Nor should any of us feel alarm if we acknowledge that this might be part of our 'job description' as teachers. Not that anybody's talking about reviving the Greek example! Ha ha!"

Jane got through six revisions and had made thirty copies of her memo without ever realizing that to stuff the thing into the banks of cubbyholes in the teacher's lounge would be insane.

A prudent sixth sense took control of her body, and she handed the sheet to elderly Emmett Drinkwater (New Jersey history, lacrosse). "You have a minute, Emmett, to take a look at this for me?" Why was she clearing her throat so much?

After skimming it, then reading it through again while he tickled a wrinkled earlobe, Drinkwater hemmed, "I'm not so sure, Ms. Brzostovsky." He grimaced as if a strong wind were coming from the memo. "Do we want to get into this? Seems a bit of a personal statement."

"Personal?" Jane said, with a note of miffed laughter.

"I'm just not sure it's something you ought to embark on. Though you . . . you make some points."

Two months later felt like a thousand years when she found the thirty pages at home, read the first couple of sentences, and started hyperventilating. She threw the sheets away as if they were thirty pieces of silver. What on earth could she have been thinking? The alarm passed eventually, but to this day it could come over her like malarial fever.

There was another time that her crush struck her as not such an amusing thing. Maybe this was when love began to elbow "crush" out of the way. Jane was renting a small house in a so-so section of Monmouth County. Her neighbors were all old, mostly working-class retirees who reminded her of her parents. So it seemed a dream when she was sipping coffee at her kitchen window one Saturday morning and saw Barry Paul, wearing only white jockey shorts, mowing the lawn of the backyard next door. She felt a flood of . . . loving concern. He could easily be injured. His big feet were bare and he was handling the flimsy mower carelessly, snapping the orange cord over the grass like a bullwhip. She watched him until concern for his toes spiraled off like steam and her coffee got cold. She moved from window to window watching him. A secret seventh sense had taken control of her body as she studied him, a little thick and well made for so young a boy. She eventually woke from that dream. Even though it wasn't a dream.

It turned out Barry was a friend of Hi and Betty Malcolm, the elderly couple who lived in the house next door. He'd gone with them that morning to inspect some dreary square footage their son-in-law had rented for a card shop. Because Barry wore dress clothes to meet the son-in-law (and his mother always made a stink about taking care of dress clothes), he sloughed them later to do a chore for the infirm couple. Hi had a sore arm, Betty an enlarged heart. Thus yard work in underpants.

Jane didn't make herself known that day. But Barry visited the Malcolms from time to time, and months later Jane flagged him down, "Look who's here!" He gave her his squinty, one-eyed look. She put her hands on her hips and heard a flutter in her long sigh. They were both clothed. They were bemused seeing one another in the civilian world. Barry seemed to find it funny. Not Jane. She was horribly depressed all that afternoon.

What was that very pure and very mysterious connection kids can form? That just uncurls like a leaf? Jane felt, frankly, excluded, and it almost made her angry—anger she turned on Darius, no matter how unfair. She just didn't like him. It happens.

The two boys didn't even notice they were particularly friends, until Jane smirked one time, "You're as thick as thieves." Several other adults dropped similar aren't-you-cute comments. Which made friendship feel disgusting, but the boys had to admit, now that they thought about it, they were always together. Other kids were matter-of-fact. If they wanted to know what Darius thought about something, they asked Barry. And vice versa. They addressed the two, even when one of them wasn't around, as "you guys." Poetry was written about them: "Very hilarious / Are Barry and Darius."

The boys even traveled together. When she heard about their trip, Jane got perfectly jealous. The emotion shocked her. It was torture how each boy came to her to report happily about spring break. And even worse torture hearing herself needle them about it over several days like some—well, some Claggart. Needle them and also probe for more and more detail. She wanted to know everything.

Barry was unusual in getting along with people of all ages. Not just the elderly Malcolms. Another pal was a cousin, a freshman at Rutgers, who invited Barry to tag along on spring break that year. The cousin rented a clapboard house in Belmar with ten schoolmates. Because parts of explanations were omitted and because the Jersey shore was so close and because "cousin" sounded all right, Darius was allowed to go. Then Barry, who hadn't been given permission himself, was allowed to go, because his mother savored the fancy Van Nest family connection. The boys handled the circular permissions nicely. As for the cousin, he had two contradictory reasons for wanting them along. Partly he meant to use the boys the way a lady-killer uses a puppy. Partly it was a sincere and sentimental pantomime of fatherhood.

Like most New Jersey shore towns, Belmar is built along a narrow beach in strips, boardwalk, traffic-congested street, jostling bars and shops facing the Atlantic, then a quieter swath of modest summer houses. The town is overrun with black teenagers during Greek Week, white during spring break.

Neither boy had the words to get the idea across to Jane, but the world is marvelous when a bunch of doting teenagers are the grown-ups. Adulthood looks unbearably beautiful and energetic and free. Belmar wasn't anything like the madhouse locals grumbled about. Barry and Darius were so happy they panted when they talked. The first day they spoke as loudly as possible.

"SHAKE IT, DARE!"

"I AM, BARE." Darius turned to a voluptuous girl in a green bikini and purple kimono. She was the only one who was up at that hour. She'd fixed cereal for them and was now fumbling with a cigarette. "Should I help clean up?" Darius asked her.

"Uh, no," she answered, unsure about letting them run off to the beach on their own. But Barry was so determined.

"I GOT YOUR TOWEL, DARE!"

"COMING! WEAPONS?"

"GOT 'EM."

The girl made an expression like, "Yikes!" She blushed when she noticed Darius staring at a couple of black curls peeking from the bikini-strangled apex of her thighs. Tugging at her kimono, she turned abruptly and blew an uninhaled mouthful of smoke through the screen door. From the humid dimness of the house a mucous-y, male voice said, not unkindly, "Get out or shut the fuck up."

On the beach Barry shouted, "SEE THAT OUT THERE?"

"NO. WHERE? WHAT?"

"THE BOAT UNDER THE BANNER-TOWER. HURRY! UNDER THE TAIL OF THE BANNER—'QRL EASY-*PISSING* MUSIC' I THOUGHT IT SAID!"

Darius laughed, gripped his belly. His too-large mirrored sunglasses, already askew, slipped off when he bent forward. "OK, YEAH. I SEE IT. SO?"

"ILLEGAL DUMPING. THAT'S WHAT HE'S DOING." Barry shrugged and pretended to inject his forearm with a hypodermic. Darius squinted at the horizon. He couldn't see that the ship was dumping anything, illegal or not. "CAPITALIST *SCUM!*" Barry screamed.

"Hey!" a stranger in headphones barked. "Pipe down, f'Chris'! S'with you, you two?"

Barry and Darius gave one another a long look. Barry arched his back, thrummed his belly like a duffer but deftly lifted his towel to his hand with a foot. "THINK WE CAN PIPE DOWN, DARE?"

"DON'T THINK SO. THIS IS JUST THE WAY WE TALK."

"WE JUST TALK THIS WAY?"

"YU-U-U-U-UP!" Darius screamed.

The stranger pulled off his earphones and feinted getting up. The boys ran down the beach. Half an hour later they were still escaping him in fantasy. Darius pretended the reverse of the "Belmar Daily" beach tag safety-pinned to the hip of his Speedos was a video screen. He sat on the gritty boardwalk and pulled his towel over his head. One of the stranger's earphones was a camera (planted earlier), and Darius could observe the man's thoughts on the screen. "SHIT! HE'S COMING!" He scrambled to his feet and shoved Barry in the small of his back. The boards made cooing thuds as they trotted off toward the bridge that led to Avon-by-the-Sea and Bradley Beach.

Fantasy was heady stuff for Barry. He enjoyed Darius's knack for it like he enjoyed watching movies. Left to his own devices, he was curious about everything that wasn't fantastic. He almost preferred talking with the teenagers. When they'd exchange looks and teasingly make as if there was really too much he didn't understand yet, he took it good-naturedly.

He was fascinated by work. He pestered a pizza boy with questions about hours and wages. The pizza boy was standoffish at first, but he let himself be drawn out, scratching flour from the messy scar of, perhaps, a patched harelip. He said he'd gotten his GED. This job was a stopgap, of course. He was vague about his recent discharge from the navy. Somehow Barry had really started him thinking about his life. Barry wore an expression so adult that his smoothie's straw in the corner of his mouth looked like a gangster's cigarette. The pizza boy noticed the brown gaze sizing him up and was suddenly self-conscious.

Like an uncle slightly out of true, he asked, "So what do you kids think you want to do, be, whatever?"

Barry and Darius answered at the same time. Darius said, "Actor, I guess." Barry's response was a question: "You ever, like, put stuff on the pizza if the guy that ordered it's a real jerk?"

Darius had an inkling that his friend was a few steps ahead of him. He wasn't too young to pooh-pooh Barry as boringly normal (privately and only if he got in a funk), but the being normal was, in fact, what he most loved. It exerted a powerful fascination. Barry—maybe all normal boys—seemed hurtling and unprotected in a way that caused Darius a kind of . . . loving concern. This tenderness was almost painful. It could make him cross with Barry. Or it could make him neurasthenic. As if Barry and he and the teenagers and a kid he'd known who'd drowned in a golf course water trap years earlier—as if they were all on a spree, splashing and ducking in the ocean, and Darius suddenly needed everything to stop. He needed to be up on the beach away from it all. Because death was going to get one of them, no matter what.

He couldn't explain this part to Jane and didn't even try. He started feeling homesick, and by the fifth day the anxiety was pretty strong.

The two boys and six half-naked teenagers piled into a car and sped off, jamming the clutch and bucking, speeding, swerving—Darius had no idea where they were going. Everybody talked at once. Darius was queasy.

Toward the Atlantic the lights of freighters and Jupiter pricked the lavender evening. The car was full of scent. The crammed bodies touched with secret alertness. Cowardly, exhilarated, saliva pouring down the back corners of his mouth, Darius sat dumb among these extraordinary strangers. Even laughing Barry was a stranger. Where were they going? Anything might happen. A crash.

They pulled up alongside the big park in Spring Lake, safe and sound. A band was playing under a panoply of Irish flags. An upstanding crowd of picnickers was scattered across the lawn. Pulling on T-shirts, the teenagers formed a sheepish group and pointed at the clarinetist, their friend.

Barry and Darius ambled down to the pond. Their approach seemed to bump two swans onto the black water. The boys sat brushing the last feather-shaped patches of sand from their skin. Barry made Darius hold his hand an inch from the skin of his thigh, not touching it. "My soul," he explained. "It got so hot today it's leaving my body. Feel it? Let's . . . yup. You're losing yours, too."

"Bullshit . . . Shit, I am!" He tried to sound amused, play along. But the rich boy who could take Borgia evil in stride was upset by Barry's teasing hint of irreligion. This evening he was. Barry's fantasies weren't like his own. "What'll we do without a soul?" His tone wasn't so broad.

Barry smiled. "I guess we'll go to hell." He threw a dried pea of excrement at the swans. A gluttonous carp made rings in the water, slow and slowing.

"But you have to have a soul to go to hell," Darius said. He was recalling a childish nightmare about *nothingness*. "I just remembered something . . ." he trailed off.

"Oh, right. Well, I guess, maybe, we'll be like wandering souls. And our bodies'll be like zombies. Maybe like that."

"Whoa, Bare! Your foot!" Darius pointed.

Barry examined a black crust between his toes and along the edge of his scuffed left foot—dried blood. The sole was wet with it. He recalled wincing on a broken cockleshell at some point that afternoon. Strangely, he'd felt no pain whatsoever. Then or now. A moment ago he'd thought vaguely he was stepping in mud. But he said, "Oh, yeah." As if he hadn't deigned to mention his suffering. The wound was too horrible and painful looking to waste. "No big deal." He shrugged in contentment.

"You want to wash it?"

"Not in there! I just threw a swan turd in there."

"These things?" Darius stirred the pellets with a stick. "These aren't from swans, they're from fish."

"What? The fish come onto the shore to take a crap? Bull."

"No, they just come in this far." He splashed the shallows with his stick. "I had a bunch of them in my fish tank at home. But they all died. But this special kind of fish, it sticks its tail out of the water and farts, and that kind of shoots the turd on shore. 'Cause they don't want to swim around in their own . . . obviously."

Barry grinned appreciatively.

"Seriously, Bare, you have to tell me for real. Do you think your soul is leaving you?"

"Wait a second! You had these fish in your tank? In your bedroom? With all that shit flying out of there?"

"Yeah, it was gross. Tamala cleaned it up, though."

"Oh, right. The ruling class. With a housekeeper! I forgot for a second you were the enemy of the people."

That evening Barry made a big deal about his injured foot. He was mewled over by four teenage girls. They bandaged the wound, and the elaborate bandage caused him such pride that he started limping and kept it up till he went to bed. Darius had gone to bed a little before. Darius—no one knew this—cried to himself. For two seconds he cried. He was imagining that no one knew him or knew where he was, and that if he died during the night, the teenagers would just say, "Who is this kid? Or *was?*" and roll him aside with their bare feet.

At Lawrence Academy one or two teachers may have wondered. Especially after Barry and Darius came back from spring break and seemed closer than ever. Innocents are never as innocent as we think, or are they? Jane was irritable if anyone turned to her for the lowdown on the two boys—home situation, sports, homework load. Why did people think she knew specially?

Even if they wondered, the teachers virtuously insisted you could never predict how a kid would turn out. So they said. In their bones most of them felt adulthood was going to be an isometric mapping of the shoulder-high personalities of middle school, or all but. With fair confidence they picked out the lawyers and the screwups.

Sexuality was a more interesting guessing game; no longer too charged even to think about. But bets were taken only in short-odds cases like Tom Gelertner. No one wanted to consult openly the handful of teachers everyone knew had an eye for these things. After all, who's asking? Ostentatious shrugs stood for tolerance. They may have wondered about Barry and Darius, but the obviousness of their crush made it seem less diagnostic. Tom Gelertner tossed his head in tragic isolation. Barry and Darius got only friendly, pro forma attacks as "You two faggots."

Sometimes the obvious thing is true. Or maybe half true. Barry and Darius got into an argument about chicken skin. Whose scrotum looked more like supermarket chicken skin? It had to be settled. In a couple of dreamlike steps their pants came off, and they kneaded their balls, pulling the skin over their knuckles like saran wrap. Barry's scrotum was bumpier, more chickenlike, they decided, holding them side by side to compare. The stiff penises got in the way, dumb-seeming as puppies on Christmas morning. Wryly, Barry strangled his with one hand and knocked Darius's in a meditative rhythm, gradually losing his smile and just watching.

At least that was a step in the right direction. Usually Barry found Darius's bashfulness aggravating. It was the only thing Barry got angry about that whole vacation at the shore. Salty and dusty and scraped after a long day at the Belmar beach, they were about to wash up. Barry sat on the toilet examining his foot. He tugged the shredded, filthy plastic bandage away. He picked curiously at the ring-straked gauze, red, brown, and yellow. "Hey!" he said crossly, spotting his friend. Darius had turned shyly to the corner to peel off his Speedos. "Don't do that," Barry said. He really seemed angry. "We should just strip down and jump in the shower. I think that's more normal, if you're buddies." For some reason Barry was put out by Darius's shyness. Maybe it made them seem less close. Or he was concerned for his friend. Maybe he hated seeing Darius give in to unhealthy habits of mind.

Knowing whose scrotum was more like chicken skin was a step in the right direction for Darius, too. After that issue had been decided, they spent a long afternoon together, getting well bored halfway through a game of Stratego. They were sitting on Darius's bed. Barry was losing through sheer indifference. Darius tried to keep interest alive by talking. A loud, old window fan filled the bedroom with noise. Somewhere in the complex sound the thing made was a regular heartbeat. The doomlike rhythm distracted Darius. The strands of a bamboo curtain he'd hung in his doorway swayed and pecked their own time.

Seeing it through Barry's eyes, Darius was aware of something dreary, even prisonlike about his bedroom. Listening to the ticking bamboo and the beating fan, he stopped talking, just like that, in the middle of a sentence. He realized that, try as he might, none of his relationships was quite real. That old "love" he'd felt for Jane Brzostovsky wasn't real, was it? He was experiencing one of those unnameable key changes of consciousness, which children may be more subject to than we are. He went from nothing to grief to near dizziness in an instant. He heard himself asking, "Do you ever like getting stuff stuck up your butt? 'Cause I actually do sometimes." It felt odd to be sitting there after saying this. He listened to the fan and gently pressed the fanged token "General" against his knee.

Barry seemed to stop what he was doing, though he'd been perfectly still. His stopped expression, a smile, looked a little like pleasure, a little like mockery withheld. He shrugged finally, and started moving his bendable mouth. "Hadn't really thought about it," he said, clearly thinking now.

"Oh," Darius jerked his shoulders, which made his loose-jointed old spool bed creak for a long time, and the creaking was an additional marking of time—like the fan's heartbeat and the ticking of the bamboo strands. "It's weird, I guess."

A weekend morning a little after this the two boys had been on the phone for what felt like hours. It got to the point where they were just breathing to each other and going about their business. Barry was particularly bored again, which made him cranky, so in a speculative, nasty tone of voice he threw out, "You know, I think Ms. B. is losing her mind."

"Yeah?" Darius had taken the phone into an attic room to rummage through a broken Empire sideboard. The sideboard was full of old silver, tarnished black and blue, and bundles of ancient family letters containing creepy, beribboned curls of hair.

"Yeah, she asked me if I ever woke up sticky."

"What? Sticky?"

"Right, and then she laughs like an insane person."

"What does that mean?"

"You know. And she said not to worry about it 'cause it was like protein or something and if I didn't want to get in trouble with my mom, I should wash my underwear in cold water 'cause if my mom washed it in hot it would, like, cook the protein and turn it brown."

"What the fuck? I don't know what you're talking about."

"*She* was talking about it. Not only that, she's . . . I don't know. I think she's turning into a bitch."

"Barry! Shh!" Darius sounded wounded. He still felt loyal, even if love was dead. "Don't say that." He opened a manila envelope full of old travel guides and spilled them onto his lap. Dresden decked out with swastikas! "Oh man! Oh man! You won't believe what I just found. I've got all this Hitler stuff here."

At the end of the year Barry got in some trouble—drugs—a little bit blown out of proportion because of his size and the way he acted. With dour super-seriousness a juvenile referee ordered him to call her *ma'am* and to write a personal statement for a court psychologist. "What's to keep me from just writing whatever to make you happy?" Barry asked.

"'Whatever, *ma'am*,' and you're in no position to be snippy."

Barry frowned, insulted. He got Jane to help him write the statement, and thinking of the snippy judge, he told her, "You should put down something like—maybe—being a kid doesn't jibe with me."

Jane swallowed. With healing insistence, as if the remark made her worry for him, though, curiously, she liked it, Jane said, "Oh, Barry, you don't think that's true, do you?"

"Sure," he smiled. "The only outstanding thing about being a kid so far is being friends with Darius. That's awesome. Maybe we should write about him some."

Strangely, Jane's heart froze. "I don't think . . . well, maybe." Her hands had stopped on the word processor keyboard. She looked down.

They were in a small ground floor office in the "new"—1967—wing of the Lawrence middle school building. Several teachers shared the room, using it to scribble class plans, grade homework, or meet with students, though the space was cozy for two. The glazed brick and blond woodwork, the turquoise-painted door, and the crank windows (oxidized shut) made modernity feel painfully outdated. Barry had twisted in his seat and rested his elbows on the desk. He wore a monster truck T-shirt and khaki pants. When Jane looked down, just as compassion for her hooligan was welling up in her, she glimpsed—it was almost unmistakable—a khaki tumescence lounging along the crease of one of the boy's thighs.

She turned away, of course. She tried to look like she was hunting for a word. Unfortunately, being shared space, the room had almost nothing in the way of decoration to occupy her eyes. She felt an ardent . . . embarrassment for Barry.

When she opened her eyes, he was looking at her candidly. "We don't have to write about him, if you don't think it's—you know—appropriate."

Jane looked out the window. "No. No, it's—whatever . . . what about him?" she said randomly.

He shifted wonderingly in his seat as he answered, "He's a great guy. Sometimes I feel bad about that whole Richie Rich thing he's got going on there. Not that I usually get worked up about the oppressor. You just got to string them up at some point, even if they never *meant* to do anything."

"Are you—starting to be enemies, then, or . . .?"

"Nothing like that. Come on! No, I'm just messing around. I'm getting bored with this thing." He reached out and gave the paper in the word processor a fillip. He arched his back. His hands made fists and reached for the ceiling. He closed his eyes and inhaled.

Jane got a good view. The bowed thing shifted unmistakably. He even scratched at it with an ultraquick peck of a forefinger. Jane looked out the window and answered him a little sharply, "Barry, look, this is important. Please, take this seriously. Because if you don't, I have an awful feeling . . . with the way this year went—with this, that, and the other thing . . . Well, your mother's a bit fed up. I offered to tutor you next year. If she—if she thought it might help."

Barry looked at her quizzically a long moment. "My grades are really bad, huh?"

"No, it's just . . ."

"Yeah, yeah, yeah. So should we say Darius is, like, a good example? Like, I want to be a good kid like him?"

"Barry. You are a good kid!"

"I mean more like smart. You just said I need to get tutored."

"Barry, wake up! You've got *so* much more going for you than . . . Darius Van Whoever-he-thinks-he-is." She dared to lay her fingers encouragingly on his knee, though she didn't look at him when she did and lifted them at once. She brought her hands together in bony prayer and kicked her wheeled chair as far from Barry as she could get. Not more than a foot. The back of the chair butted the aluminum windowsill.

The boy appeared to notice something odd and looked at her. Really looked at her. Even before he spoke, she snorted self-consciously. He said, "You don't look like you used to."

"Same me," she said in quiet hysteria. "Let's get back to it."

"I think you dress different. Like, this whole year you dress different than you did at first."

"'Differently,' but I'm not sure what you're talking about." She did know. Coral nails. How had that started? She was all but certain Barry couldn't figure it out. He was a kid, for God's sake.

"Well, like those," he said uncannily. He meant her black stockings.

"This is just a French style. Tights."

"And that stuff," he said unerringly.

She wiggled her fingertips. She softly clapped several times. "OK, OK, OK, Barry. Let's get back to it, please." She looked at her watch for effect. But she had the fluttery idea that he didn't care in the least about his tumescence. That he knew she'd seen and didn't care about that, either. Or he did, just not in an embarrassed way.

Apart from glimpses and waves when Barry visited the Malcolms, Jane and he saw each other only once over the summer. Barry had been thrown out or ran out of his house after calling his mother "Marie Antoinette" one time too many. Although he'd never had bratty, childish thoughts of running away from home, now that it had happened, he liked it. Solely out of pity for his parents, he decided, he wouldn't stay out the whole night.

At a strip mall Barry let himself be picked up by a police cruiser—two mustachioed, friendly cops. Reluctant to go back home so soon, 9:00 P.M., he gave them Hi Malcolm's address. He made up a story, not too elaborate, about Mother leaving him at a store—she'd had to rush home, sort of an emergency. For some reason he faked a limp. The cops, as is their way, appeared to believe nothing. Turning onto Meadowlark Lane, their eyebrows rose. They saw an ambulance flinging its drunken, unfestive lights across the somnolent housefronts. So the kid hadn't been lying.

"Shit oh shit oh shit. See!" Barry couldn't resist acting a little, even now. But he was also trembling with nerves. He was more or less certain Betty's enlarged heart had burst (as it almost had). When the cruiser pulled up he saw Hi Malcolm, fluttery as a snared heron. Barry didn't run over and shout "Dad!" or anything grotesque. He hung back with the officers. A very bewildered Hi climbed into the ambulance without ever seeing him. "Barry! Oh, Barry . . . isn't it . . . scary!" came a familiar alto from the tree lawn. Seeing a responsible-looking woman, short hair and a terry robe, the two officers melted away with mumbled condolences. And Barry was left in mother Jane Brzostovsky's hands, still faking the limp. In fact, the story became much more elaborate. He'd spotted some kids trying to break into a Sam Goody's through a mall loading bay. He'd been chased. He'd taken a spill down a ravine. To Jane, his clothes did look, at least, messy.

This is how it happened. Eat? No? Bed? Her rapid-fire ideas caused her to jerk. It was a little disturbing. She put him to bed. She washed his clothes. She sat in the kitchen in wordless argument with the telephone, looking at it reproachfully, as if it were at fault for not being used. Her heart was pounding. She had a glass or two of Chardonnay. Silent as a mouse she crept upstairs. She fore-fingered ajar the door to the darkened bedroom. She sidled in and stood there a long time.

"I'm not asleep, you know. It's really kinda early." Confusion about Jane's twitchiness and worry about Betty and Hi had made Barry tractable about going to bed so early. Though how this had gone from striking out on his own to a weird sleepover escaped him. "What are you doing? You get my mom?" he asked.

Jane sighed a tragic, an operatic sigh. She posed a hip on the bed, then tipped over softly onto the pillow. Her trembling made the whole bed shudder. She lay facing him, parallel, a foot and a couple decades between them. Her hunched shoulders were in awful pain, but the trembling got worse if she tried releasing them. Her eyes adjusted to the dimness. She saw that he couldn't bring himself to look at her. His dark eyes hovered at her throat. He frowned slightly. He was bashful beyond belief. More bashful than Darius, even he realized it.

In the slowest of slow motion Jane plucked a corner of the duvet at Barry's shoulder. Just as slowly, she folded it off him and tipped it to the floor. "I don't know," he mumbled. His tone, meant to sound like humorous skepticism, sounded oddly like a whimper.

He was holding his body awkwardly, rigid. Any more tense and he'd start trembling like her. But the luster of his skin, flawless as a new baseball, seemed to illuminate the room. It was shining, however dusky. The angelic freshness of his scent was like nothing Jane had ever smelled. He lay so the front of his Jockey shorts was partially hidden, shyly turning his buttocks to the ceiling. The white cloth twisted and rode up between his legs. Still, what he was hiding wasn't so hidden. In the confusion of gray tones, Jane could see an untimely swelling stretch at the cotton fabric, causing the elastic to yawn in a shadowy gap at his hip. His wisecracking whisper came again, "I don't know." His mouth worked. He shut his eyes, crumpled them tightly in the way of children. Jane slipped her hand between the mattress and his unbreathing chest. The nipples seemed as hard as jujubes, the skin as soft as—ha ha!—kid. She pried. He seemed unable to move himself. As her hand went lower, his hip obediently rose until he was facing her. Her trembling hand rode over the swollen cotton, and, though he didn't recoil this time, he started trembling, too. Which made them both laugh a little. Barry's eyes were still tightly closed.

A moment later—or so it seemed—Jane was downstairs, arms folded, staring at the duvet she'd left trailing on the carpeted steps. Her shoulders were killing her, and there was something familiar about the hunched way she held them. Wildly, for some reason, she analyzed this. She stood in front of the window, in front of a desk, now over the stove in the kitchen, now bending slightly into the open refrigerator. All the time she was holding her shoulders more and more tightly. Then she pretended to remember what had caused her shoulders to hurt like this before. (She believed, hysterically, this was a real memory.) She dropped her shoulders and laughed in horror. She'd only hunched her shoulders exactly this way when she used to play with the miniature people in her dollhouse as a little girl!

Back upstairs, the duvet wrapped around her like a wedding gown, she found Barry sitting cross-legged on the stripped bed. He stared at her with his cheery, know-nothing, raised eyebrows. This expression kept morphing, like a candle flickering, into a stagey version of his old cockiness. He shrugged a few times. His penis was centered now, sticking straight up past the waistband as if he'd arranged it there with simple-minded artistry, as he had. Jane let her eyes fall closed tragically. She let the duvet fall. She fell to the bed, curled on her side, abased her head at the boy's crossed ankles. She was crying.

"I'm sorry about two seconds ago," he said. "Really, I'm sorry." She turned her head to look up at him. Her eyes were streaming. He crossed his pale arms and shrugged, making the mattress bounce. "I wish you didn't feel bad. I hate that. I'm really, really sorry."

"I love the way your ankles smell, Barry. I love you," she whispered.

After this Jane would have been wise to cancel. It almost came as a surprise to her when tutoring began on schedule at the start of the school year. Barry and Jane met at her house.

Three times a week for weeks and weeks, everything passed with Jekyll-like civility. Jane's schedule was light, so she was able to drive back from Lawrence to meet with Barry in the afternoons. Barry was dropped off after school by his mother or biked over himself. On warm September days Jane and Barry went out in the backyard and were full of innocent waves for Hi Malcolm staking his delphiniums in hopes of a second bloom. When they met indoors, Jane was inhumanly patient with Barry's flirting: his obstreperous and/or continuous erection, the tickling of his sneaker toe under the table, sudden bouts of exhaustion when his head and arms fell to the kitchen table and his overgrown child's fingers accidentally brushed her shoulder or trapped her hand. He was pushy, except when Jane occasionally fell into a sort of trance and they got to real sex. Then he was immobile, awed by her.

He tolerated the suspense. Maybe the game of being held off wasn't that different from what it always feels like to be a child, and Barry assumed this affair was the natural sequel to childhood. Besides, what he was after, or what he played at being after, though he was getting a taste for it, was still a bit much for him. Jane realized this early on. The odious mother stopped in for chats at first when picking up her son and once let slip, "He didn't want to do it! As usual he fought me and fought me. I told him, 'Barry, don't be an idiot like you always are. This is your favorite teacher! Or was. And she's nicely offered. . . .'" Barry shrugged hugely and gave Jane, who blushed with shame, a raffish smile. "Furthermore," Jeanette waved an envelope in Barry's face. All demure sweetness, she turned to give it to Jane, "I'm more than aware fifty an hour is about as low as any sliding scale can slide. We're enormously grateful. Even this idiot."

Jane later whispered to Barry, "If you don't want to come . . .?" He was able to convince her he did. Still, coming was a problem—his coming but not coming, that is. Jane became scientifically obsessed, though quite emotional, about this hydrologic detail. (Moralists make the best sinners. So twisted!)

The first time they had sex, Jane had no greater inspiration—no thoughts in her head at all—than to mannequin Barry into missionary position with her hands. Her hands were busier and more aware than she was. Propped on his arms for a lazy push-up, he did it, swaybacked, arrhythmic, eyes closed. After a short while he stopped. He rolled off her. With a pleased grin, he wiped his brow and lithely sat cross-legged. He flipped at the fat penis rising past his ankles, stiff as ever, gleaming and insistent, and made an uncertain stab at humor, "Boing, boing." He seemed to feel the same friendly companionship for it as he did for Jane. He lowered his voice, quoting some movie, "That was . . . amazing." Though she had no idea why he'd stopped, Jane didn't dare suggest they go on. The boy didn't seem to realize there could be any going on. Was he too embarrassed to leave a puddle on her or in the bed? Over the months, the next three times they had sex ended just as inconclusively, with the same childish and abrupt change of subject. Since he never made the first move (beyond general and constant flirtiness), Jane was confused by the decided way he kept breaking it off.

Then Jane grasped something awful. She'd been premature a year or so ago with her zany, nerve-wracked question about nocturnal emissions. However knowingly he'd pretended to answer at the time. He was—the problem was moral, not hydrologic, after all, and Jane almost fainted—too young for the sap to be flowing yet! Or else he was so painfully innocent that he knew of no connection between blurting at midnight in his own bed and what it was he and Jane had started to do in hers. He knew nothing!

Barry could have lived with sex or without it. But now that it was happening to him and Jane was making him happy on the whole and he was getting all the adoring attention he could want, he tried to reconceive this as something he'd decided on. He tried on outsize words like, "my love affair." Though he didn't have much gift for fantasy, he came up with an enjoyable way to imagine the relationship. He adopted a cool, James Bond-like persona. In bed he made odd facial expressions, cold seeming or supercilious, which mystified Jane but were supposed to "drive her wild." When given an opening, he stroked Jane's chin with avuncular tolerance. He either didn't guess or ignored her power.

When he started opening his eyes, there was too much for him to admire. The breasts with their forbidden, V-shaped pallor lurched in drunken, separable ways. Their sponginess needed so much restraint that it worked on his nerves. Even the slightest touch sometimes made her cringe. And the miraculous tubular muscle her hand led him to (because he didn't have the confidence to look and wasn't even sure how the link was supposed to be made)—when he knelt over her and did look at it for the first time, leaf upon leaf upon leaf parting, until she had him just graze the jack-in-the-pulpit with his ink-stained finger, he wore no expression at all, his heart in his throat. The thing was like some minute dungeon-master secreted behind pink curtains that were half animal, half fluid like honey. He tried raising his chin to give her a taste of Bond-like arrogance, but he couldn't stop staring. He was under her power. After pulling his hand back, he reached out again, measured her, or concealed her, with his palm. For a moment he seemed to rest his eyes, really rest them, on a blue haunted house rubber-stamped on the back of his hand. His mind couldn't take so much detail all at once. Or he was so young he didn't know the words for the details he did see, which may be the same thing.

But sex was rare between them. Jane made sure. To a surprising degree she was still his teacher. Except in the darkest recesses of her heart—where who knew what wounded and virginal drama was playing out?—Jane refused to "play" at anything for Barry. He got no Miss Moneypenny, at least none he ever observed. She calmly stared at him across the kitchen table's piles of dog-eared worksheets until she was sure he really didn't know whether a comma was needed before a prepositional phrase. "It's not. Generally the fewer commas the better," she smiled. With an identical expression and calm, she'd pull away his inky finger, "Don't be a brute with a girl's clit, Barry." The uniform matter-of-factness went over well with her student and lover.

This sort of thing has to blow up, doesn't it? As long as it was tutoring, as long as they only met in the parallel world of her house, Jane could go on. Not that the situation didn't take a toll. She had the occasional panic attack. She had a trailing and ominous bout of hilarity when she and Barry once conferred with the mother about progress and the truth seemed *right there* on the surface, obvious to anybody. Apparently it wasn't. But when she and Barry relaxed, left the house, close calls became closer. A Schwarzenegger movie at the mall after wrestling with the Pythagorean theorem: "Mr. Drinkwater! Hello!"

At Lawrence Academy, Jane was in a constant agony of indigestion, waspishness, and gloom. She'd arranged to have no classes with Barry and never drove him to their sessions after school. Still she mistrusted herself. She assumed she was trying to get caught. Other teachers commiserated that she was obviously having a tough year.

Barry was insufferable. She walked past him in the hall. "Yo, B, you bringin' that Coke for me?" His insolent wink caused some surprise, only kids, thank heaven. The Coke can made a metal *ribbet* as Jane swept past. Her sandwich had deep finger marks when unwrapped. She told herself Barry was stupid. Not even attractive compared to the obvious standouts, who left her cold.

Then again, she and Barry might cross paths, and it would be just them. Alone together in the hall after school let out, reduced to black flickers in the consuming glare from the overwaxed floor, like shadowy wisps of soot rising in a candle flame. Jane reminded him severely, "Barry, I have *total* confidence in you." The way he nodded looked so manly. His smile, just too faint to be cruel, struck her as an impossible combination of love and wisdom. Washed out in the glare, his blue T-shirt, collar deformed and blond hair and his glinting brown eyes—he looked more apparition than real, and it was easy for Jane to think her way into her dreamworld. "I don't know if you feel like biking over later, we could watch something on TV." Appalled, rapturous, she assumed he could see her heart kettle-drumming through her blouse, and she didn't care.

That spring Jane took a cruise of the Chilean fjords by herself. Lifevested, she was shuttled by Zodiac to a briny crag colonized by seals. She ignored the Iowa retirees in the boat with her, even the handsome guide. She ignored them and studied the seals. What *animals* animals were! This wasn't a virtuous nature show. The seals stank. They bleated. They farted. They fought. They bled. Long yellow "fingernails" twisted over their flippers. But all around, the crushing sublimity of the fjord remained somehow unaffected by their uncleanness and their crimes against each other. Since this lonely trip was mostly a trip away from Barry, Jane couldn't help holding up her own crime in comparison. Strange to say, seeing how it, too, had no impact at all on the sublime inattention of nature and time made her crime seem *less* pardonable to her than ever before.

When she got back, Jane moved a pot of basil to the left side of her front door. That was her and Barry's signal. Jane never had to phone the Paul home, leaving pesky records. A day later she heard Barry rustling in the lilacs outside. Hiding his bike from the Malcolms. She sat him down, and his knees fell apart in the cocky way he had. Though he could tell it wasn't going to be that kind of a visit. And if it had been, oddly, a breath of shyness would have come over him.

Jane brought up something they'd never mentioned before. "Our . . . friendship, Barry. You know, people don't think it's OK. They really don't."

He asked how dumb did she think he was. Of *course* he knew that.

"No, Barry, just let me . . . if this happened in . . . I don't know—in China—and someone found out . . . they might . . . whatever they do—execute us, cut off our heads. I don't mean to be terrifying, but . . . On the other hand, of course, if we were in a different time and place, like Rome, maybe it wouldn't be a big deal at all. But we are where we are, right?"

He gave her a shrug. He looked off. She had a horrible reminiscence of justifying an F to some kid.

"We know we have to stop. Absolutely stop. Don't we?" Jane collapsed in a chair with a sigh of regret and unpleasant clarity. Barry crossed the room. She sat up. He stood over her, chin bunched up. For a second she thought he was going to hit her. Then she smiled at such a ridiculous fear. She'd relaxed completely and expected a caress when his arm floated toward her slowly, involuntarily almost. He pinched her biceps. His nails felt like needle-nose pliers. She shrank into the cushion, so shocked she couldn't not laugh and frown. She rubbed the sore spot. She looked at him, "Barry! What's gotten into you?"

"Oh." He gave her a twitchy version of Bond's raised chin. His eyes—Jane stared with incomprehension—had watered up. "You're done with your toys, so you just throw 'em away."

Jane couldn't speak. The idea that he had feelings, strong feelings, anyway, had never occurred to her. He was a kid. A pang of guilt made her heartbeat stumble and start kettle-drumming painfully. Would he tell? But this grief of his was sure to blow off in an afternoon. He was a kid. Besides, he was the one who cheerfully teased *her,* got under *her* skin, in the Lawrence halls. She was the one with a full set of adult emotions.

His eyes narrowed. Tears bulged like glass matchsticks. He was a child. Wildly, Jane imagined him laughing in a week. She even felt an iota of anger about it. She was so confused she could barely read his expression or hear what he was saying. What was he saying? "—but him at least—and I know you think he's a spoiled brat and a faggot— him at least I could take seriously something he said. If he said—you know . . ." The tears flickered to his cheeks. "With him, it was never like you and me being 'friends,'" he spat the word out bitterly. Jane almost didn't grasp that when he shook his fists in the air, he was also trying to make meaty, violent quotation marks with his fingers. So she'd know he thought that word was a complete joke, not a funny one. The gesture wasn't like him at all.

Crayons
Alistair McCartney

In the detective story, a park-keeper has discovered a corpse in the Bois de Boulogne. The good-natured park-keeper was off to collaborate with the Nazis when he heard little hissing noises. Following the strange sound, he happened to stumble upon the corpse. The park-keeper was so stunned that he dropped the gifts he was carrying: a link of sausages and a brightly colored toy boat.

The corpse belongs (or no longer belongs, having been confiscated by death) to a well-known Viennese doctor. The Viennese people were known for their charm and their ability to hate Jews. Most of the doctor's patients were nervous boys. When people asked the doctor what he did, he said, *I work with nerves.*

Bees are gently buzzing around the doctor's corpse. Pieces of a broken hive lie nearby. His corpse (or *the corpse*) is covered in bright red crayon dust; the crayon dust is so bright the policemen must place their polka-dot handkerchiefs over their red mouths.

This job is especially hard on the younger ones. One of them has been stung in his lips, which were already full.

Even the more experienced ones, who thought they had seen everything, are horrified by the sheer violence of so much red crayon.

This will surely be a job for the Inspector, who specializes in crayon forensics.

The bees get red on their wings. The policemen do not have wings (they only have shoulder blades, which are like the sawn-off stubs of wings) but they are also coated in red crayon. When the policemen go home they immediately jump in the shower to wash the red and waxy muck off. But as they lie in bed they are unable to sleep. They are haunted by the image of red crayons.

Because I am nervous, and was sent to the doctor to be cured of my nervousness, and due to the fact that I am a mediocre artist who works primarily in red crayon, it is natural that I am a prime suspect.

The Inspector is in hot pursuit of me. This displeases Madame Inspector, who is wearing a black crepe dress and folds of pink flesh. Five strings of fake pearls. She has taken a lot of trouble over dinner. She has spent the afternoon polishing her husband's magnifying glasses and cleaning his fingerprinting kits. She is sick of her husband shadowing young men and taking their pictures for purely official (sexual) purposes with his miniature camera. She is sick of him taking boys' fingerprints.

She remembers when he used to take her fingerprints. The thought of him taking someone else's fingerprints drives her insane with jealousy.

Every night the Inspector comes home stinking of crayons.

Madame is very angry. As she leans against the mantelpiece. To get back at her husband she is going to collaborate (make love) with the Nazis.

Let them shave my head so the world can see my skull, she thinks.

I am wearing a gray felt overcoat and a gray hat. It is a ready-made coat. There is a big yellow star on the left pocket. The star has been sewn from felt. As I try to figure out what to do next, I suck on the soft tips of the star.

My hat is also made from felt. Felt is my preferred fabric. I find it to be very flattering. I think if the ugliest boy in the world wears a garment sewn from felt, he may not become the most beautiful boy in the world, but he will surely rise a few places on the scale of ugliness.

Felt is derived from the fur of rabbits and muskrats. I would like to think that their souls continue to reside in my felt coat, my felt hat, even my felt star. I would like to think that their soft little souls are intensified during the lengthy felt-making process, particularly during the extended period of time the fur must spend in the slowly revolving cone of the forming machine.

Yet somehow my felt star is causing me to like felt a little less; I am beginning to think I need to find another fabric.

On my coat and my hat and my star, red crayon stains here and there. These implicate me, like saliva, like the fingerprints on my fingers, like my footsteps in new snow. I go to a movie theater with worn red velvet curtains. The theater has a buttery stink to it. I'm unsure if this is the odor of popcorn or boys. Perhaps it is a delicate combination of both.

I watch a newsreel of Hitler invading Vienna. All the Viennese (who are known for their charm) are crying and laughing so hard that their noses are running. None of them seem to have discovered handkerchiefs. It's difficult to tell if they are happy or sad about this new arrival to their city. But the voice-over says: *The good people of Vienna are extremely happy. They are so happy they will never know sadness again.*

In one scene, a fat little boy offers Hitler strudel. Hitler bends down and takes a bite, getting flecks of pastry caught in his mustache. The little boy licks the crumbs from Hitler's mustache. The other people in the movie theater all go *Ooh, how adorable.* But I can't help thinking that the fat little boy really shouldn't be eating strudel, not even the crumbs of strudel.

In another scene, standing very close to Hitler (so close they are almost touching, but not quite) is a man who looks exactly like the Viennese doctor. He is sobbing. His tears are falling on the sleeve of Hitler's coat. Again a voice-over says: *The good people of Vienna are extremely happy.*

Yet somehow I sense that the tears of this man (who must surely be the doctor) originate in a sadness so huge he will never know happiness again.

Up on the screen Hitler moves a little to the left, probably because he is sick of being wept upon.

The doctor continues to weep. To weep and to shake. As I watch the doctor weeping, I begin to question whether this man is really the doctor. Perhaps he simply appears to be the doctor, just as a crayon that is shaped like a pencil may from a distance appear to be a pencil, but is not a pencil, just as the so-called French chalk used by tailors to measure the inner legs of boys bears no relation whatsoever to actual chalk, with its tiny seashells, but is a form of talc, just as the substance popularly known as chalk, those crayons children use to solve (or to not solve) mathematical formulas on blackboards, has nothing to do with the limestone scraped and gathered from the bottom of ancient seas, but is (like this man's tears) of an entirely different nature.

And I begin to wonder, which is saltier: tears of grief or tears of joy? Is there an instrument that can compare the level of salt?

The man in the newsreel who simply appears to be the doctor is now talking to a boy who is wearing what appear to be brand-new lederhosen. The lederhosen are green, with a border of appliquéd apples. A price tag dangles from one of the straps.

The boy seems very nervous. He keeps fiddling with his yellow star. He must be one of the doctor's patients. The boy starts to fiddle with the doctor's star, but the doctor slaps his hand away. The boy's lederhosen are tight around the thighs.

Perhaps the boy is nervous because he believes the lederhosen don't suit him. Perhaps the boy has not yet cut off the price tag (with a pair of big scissors) because, despite the many sincere compliments he has already received, and in spite of all the wolf whistles from the anti-Semitic construction workers, the boy is still not convinced that the lederhosen are flattering.

That is, maybe the boy is still uncertain in regard to the absolute nature of the lederhosen.

The boy is handing the man who merely appears to be the doctor a pink cardboard box. Surely it is not appropriate for a doctor to accept gifts from his patients. The man opens the box. His mouth pops open like a trapdoor. Inside the box, at least fifty red crayons rest on white tissue paper. The crayons are obviously expensive. I would kill to own those crayons. The man is gasping with pleasure—understandable, considering the quality of the crayons.

As I watch the newsreel, a mysterious boy sits down in the seat next to me. He offers me some popcorn. I politely decline his offer. We begin to kiss. His lips are full and cold. They make me think of rivers frozen over and animal traps set in the snow, waiting patiently for animals.

The boy is wearing a blue fox fur coat. As my hand gropes beneath his coat, I wonder if the fur was produced as a result of selective breeding. I almost ask the boy if he knows, but my shyness gets the better of me. I can sense already that the fur is not wearing very well, but I do not have the heart to tell this to the boy. Besides, if I point this out, he may recoil from my advances. So instead, I whisper in the boy's ear: *This fur is wearing very well.*

I realize (or my hands realize) that beneath his coat, the boy is wearing skin-tight lederhosen. In the dark of the movie theater, my boy looks very much like the boy in the newsreel. The boy sitting beside me is similarly nervous, which of course arouses me even further. I carefully unbutton the straps on his lederhosen. Big buttons. My fingers trace over what is without a doubt a border of appliquéd apples. My hands caress the boy's hips, which bring back fond memories of riding on the handlebars of a bicycle. The boy's skin is covered in scratches and little jewel-like scabs.

Finally, at midnight, I decide to go to a hotel. I want to take the mysterious boy with me, to draw a nude portrait of him in red crayon on a sheet of butcher's paper. But the mysterious boy has dissolved, leaving nothing but a sweet little feeling.

As I walk the streets in search of a suitable hotel, I find myself wishing the boy was walking beside me. I would have liked to spend more time with the boy. Actually, I would have liked to spend my life with him. But then again, he wasn't really my type. Generally I am not attracted to boys who wear lederhosen.

I go alone to a dirty hotel. It is a second- or even third-class hotel. There is only one bellboy; his uniform is frayed at the edges. I can't register under my own name so I register under the name Alistair McCartney. It's a preposterous name I know, obviously false, but it's the first one that enters my head. The proprietor, who has a pencil mustache (Nazi), clearly despises me.

I go to my room, number 7. I pass by boys of the night and banisters.

The boys of the night are dressed in pale yellow cross-fox coats. Although the hotel is bleak, it makes me happy to think that today, because of modern methods of collecting animal pelts, almost everyone can afford fur coats.

I try to flush my crayons down the toilet, to get rid of evidence I suppose, but the toilet is broken.

The red crayons float in the bowl menacingly.

I fall asleep and dream that the Inspector is looking at me through a huge magnifying glass. Watching everything I do. Then I dream of a room in which there is nothing but a huge heap of red crayons, going up to the ceiling.

The next morning I wake up full of hope, and with a positive attitude, until I notice that the bedsheets are covered in red crayon stains. The maids (boys in frilly caps and aprons) will be annoyed. The thought of this makes me anxious, because I am profoundly attracted to all maids.

I get out of bed and go over to the chair where my felt coat is. I put on my coat and begin to suck on the points of my felt star.

The last thing in the world I would want to do is displease a maid. But then I remind myself that such an establishment as this probably doesn't have a maid, and if it does, it would most likely have one exceedingly unattractive maid, a maid so plain even I could not desire him.

I go to the bathroom to splash some water on my face. That will be refreshing. The mysterious boy I made love to in the movie theater is lying in the bathtub, dead. He is naked. His skin is waxy. His body is plump and more shapeless than I remember; last night he gave me the impression that he was quite athletic.

Though of course nothing is shapeless: everything has a shape. This does not, however, automatically place the boy within the category of shape*ly*.

The boy's lederhosen hang on the shower railing. They are soaking wet. I stop for a moment and listen to the dripping. While I am listening, I tell myself that now there is no possibility of spending the rest of my life with the boy, watching him grow old in his lederhosen.

It's then I notice the boy has a big red bruise, in the shape of an apple, on the inside of his left thigh. I have never liked apples, but suddenly I feel as if I could grow to like them.

Red crayon lines have been drawn neatly on each of the boy's wrists. The water in the bathtub is red from the violence of so much crushed red crayon. The boy appears to be comfortable.

I leave the hotel in a hurry and go to a library. I grab the first book from the shelf; it is a book by someone called Sappho. I seat myself at a reading desk and switch on the little lamp. It makes a pleasing click.

For a second I remember the clasp on my mother's penny purse, the way it would click when I opened her purse to steal money, to buy crayons.

I open the book to page eleven:

My heart broken[

[ ]

Bright crayons[

Leave even brighter[

[ ]

Stains
In the snow

By now it is evening, and the library must close—the librarians must reorganize the Dewey decimal system. According to the head librarian, this is an overwhelming task—one they have been putting off for ages—but they can put it off no longer.

The head librarian is a young man but happens to be suffering from premature balding. I begin to suggest to him that he purchase a nice felt hat just like mine, but think better of it.

I have never found young men with premature balding attractive. On the contrary, I have always found it disconcerting to be in the presence of such unfortunate young men. The way their hairlines recede reminds me far too much of the sly manner in which life recedes.

Yet somehow I am deeply attracted to the head librarian. It must be the look of sadness on his face, which is all creased like crepe paper. He also has very nice hands, probably from handling all those books.

I despise work of all kinds, but I ask the head librarian if I can be of any assistance. He says no, reorganizing the Dewey decimal system is a treacherous and sensitive business, one that requires years of training. But as he says this, he throws me a look, pale and sharp as a paper plane. In my heart I know that the head librarian would have liked very much if I could have worked by his side, throughout the night.

Outside, snow is fluttering down in the street. There is snow on my coat collar. How aggravating! It might stain the felt! I go to brush the snow off my collar before it melts.

As my fingers make contact with the snow I discover (or my fingers discover) that the snow is not real snow, but little pieces of white felt that have been carefully cut out and sewn into the shape of snowflakes. I take a closer look at the little impostors. There are three of them. Just like real snowflakes, none of these artificial snowflakes seem to be alike.

As I finger the so-called snowflakes, I think about how strange life is. There was a time when I lived for felt. Now I feel almost indifferent to it. I suppose the allure of felt lay in its relation to all fabrics that were not felt. But what with them manufacturing everything in felt these days—stars, snowflakes—felt was rapidly beginning to lose all its appeal. Or perhaps my love of felt was just a passing childhood fancy, and this disinterest a sign of maturity.

I cup my hands and check to see if all the snowflakes have been sewn from felt, but the rest of it appears to be real.

Trying to figure out where to go next, and if indeed there is any-where else to go, I walk over to a lamppost and lean against it. Snow continues to drift down. I find myself wishing my mother were around. Not that she would be able to help me. She was never very good with advice. But just the fact of her being here would make me feel a little better.

If she were here with me now, she would brush the snow from my coat collar.

Once again, I wonder where they took her. I had gone out to buy some red crayons. When I returned, the door to our apartment was open and my mother was gone. She had left a note on the table saying:

Keep mastering the art of crayons! I love you. There is toffee cooling on the stove.

Feeling tired, I close my eyes. I open them to find the Inspector standing a few feet away, peering at me through a huge magnifying glass. In his trench coat he cuts an impressive figure; I can see why boys find him so irresistible.

The game is up my friend, he says, licking his lips. Some of his spittle lands on my cheek. The Inspector pulls out some big shiny handcuffs from a leather bag and places them on my wrists. Then he takes my fingerprints.

While he stoops over to look for his miniature camera, a handful of red crayons falls out of his pockets, onto the snow.

He finds the camera and proceeds to take my picture for official purposes. The tiny flashes hurt my eyes.

There is only one thing to do! Surely it will be better to join the ranks of the doctor and the boy than to fall into the hands of the Inspector.

As the Inspector places a fresh roll of film in his miniature camera, I run over to the bridge.

For a moment I hesitate.

Not because I desperately yearn to keep on living. I had always found living to be an unpleasant experience, simultaneously mysterious and monotonous, an experience made bearable only by the constant use of red crayons. Perhaps I would have felt differently if I had done something meaningful with my life—a miniature pony that acts as guide to the blind must feel quite attached to living—but I had never been interested in making myself useful.

Gazing down into the river, I realize that if I take my own life, I will never get to visit the great chalk deposits of western Kansas that I have always dreamed of visiting. I will never get to see the extinct (yet wonderfully preserved) skeletons of sea serpents and flying reptiles trapped in the deposits' soft chalky walls.

Nor will I get to see my mother again.

Yet somehow I have the feeling that the chalk deposits will not live up to my expectations. And that I will not get to see my mother again, whether I am alive or dead.

I throw myself off the bridge and into the river. As I fly through the air I remember that as a child I used to call suicide "silver side."

When I hit the cold water, I make a modest splash. I don't sink immediately. I float a bit.

The snow has stopped falling. On the bridge above I can see the generous silhouette of the Inspector. I look past him, up at the stars.

Unlike my star, which is dull and flat, those stars are twinkling. But of course they are not really twinkling. They only seem to be. In actual fact, they are caving in. And what appears to be twinkling is nothing but the motion of air, scattering the light.

Mouth of the River

Bruce Benderson

I turned up one of those steep inclines toward Stapler's ramshackle Victorian mansion in Astoria, Oregon, suddenly feeling quite happy to be in the oldest U.S. settlement in the entire West. The house, once gracious and stately, was in dire need of repair; it had become a dowdy old spinster, full of cobwebs and busted-spring furniture. Although it was unlocked, as if expecting visitors, it wasn't particularly welcoming with its thermostat set to 62. The first thing I did was twirl the dial up to 76. I could hear the old furnace groan as if in astonished protest, then burst into rumbling flames. Stapler had said he had no intention of coming out until the following weekend and had crisply requested I be sparing with the heat. But no one would know until the bill came. By then I'd be back in New York, I figured; let them take it out of my salary.

The next thing I headed for was the liquor cabinet. It was quite well stocked, to my delight. I poured myself a scotch and took a sip to swallow a morphine tablet, then headed for the sinking porch, which creaked under my feet. Since the house hadn't warmed up yet, I'd be no less comfortable in the damp and drizzle. It was noon, and the view in the encroaching fog revealed only the sharp edges of roofs, between which one could catch glimpses of the leaden water of the mouth of the river. However, in some areas of the sky, the droplet-saturated air caught the rays of a struggling sun and diffused them into a lustrous wash. This was reflected in the wet black asphalt to create a disorienting, mirrorlike sensation, similar to the one achieved by staring directly into silver. Dimensions and directions get lost in the watery glare, and you plunge blinded into its metallic dispersal. With the help of the scotch and the morphine, I floated into this melancholy evanescence until a female voice startled me out of the watery feeling.

Claiming to have been sent by Stapler as a sort of local guide was an ancient, shriveled woman with elfin eyes and crudely cropped hair, who introduced herself as Delilah. Was I ready for a trip into the heart of Astoria? she wanted to know. But first, she said, eyeing the scotch, would I be willing to supply a little "fuel"? I felt surprisingly profligate with the borrowed bottle, and I led the old witch inside to pour her a stiff one. As we entered, her wrinkled face burst into an expression of astonishment. Was I planning on opening a sauna? For her, the place was stifling! I compromised by turning the thermostat down to 69, and we settled into one of the broken-down couches in the high-ceilinged Victorian parlor. She clutched the glass of scotch with knobby, arthritic hands and toasted me with the Finnish expression "*Kippis!*" Then she bottomed up faster than I could raise my glass to my lips.

A half hour later, we were in Delilah's strangely well-preserved Studebaker. I could hear her gasp and wheeze as she struggled with the clutch, but each time I looked at her with concern, she shook the glance off with hostility. Then the sun suddenly broke through the clouds, revealing one of the oldest faces I'd ever seen. Above a mass of deep wrinkles were two cataract-clouded blue eyes, and from them glimmered a silvery light, producing the same effect as the silver-tinged sky of Astoria I'd noticed earlier. Perhaps I imagined that the eyes seemed to be sizing me up, and her mouth, which was little more than a thin, rigid line, seemed to curl at the corners with a hint of perverse amusement.

"How . . . old are you, Delilah?" I heard myself blurting indecorously.

"A hundred and two," she barked. "Now put that behind your ears and cogitate on it!"

Delilah was part of the large community of people of Finnish extraction who still lived in Astoria, Oregon, many of whom had ancestors who'd been squashed by the government and the industrialists during the climax of the labor movement. She was, in fact, no real Delilah, but a Finnish immigrant, appropriately named Aamu, who'd come to work in a salmon cannery at the age of thirteen and had moonlighted more than eighty years ago in the offices of the Finnish communist newspaper *Toveritar*,[1] a publication with strong connections to the Wobblies as well as to other labor organizations and the Communist Party.

We were heading in Aamu's pickup for the docks because, as she explained, she had a very special surprise in store for me. Her great-grandson, Jukka, whom most people called Johnny, had just received his certificate as a bar pilot and would be guiding his first Japanese container ship under the Astoria Bridge. It was a lucrative, but potentially very dangerous, job. Hidden under the swirling waters of the river's enormous mouth were treacherous bars, which could act like sucking mouths that created huge, voracious swells. A good number of even experienced sailors had met their deaths there, riding one moment on the flat surface of the sea, which seemed as stable as a floor, and then suddenly swooning downward, with enormous walls of liquid rising up menacingly on either side. That's why a supply of highly

1. Finnish for "Woman Comrade." It was the sister newspaper of *Toveri*, or *Comrade*.

trained local captains was needed in Astoria, to get the ships safely past the river mouth and take them upstream.

The thought of our upcoming adventure sent a thrill coursing down my spine, and I wondered, perhaps wildly, how such an experience could have been prepared for me. Was not the river, with its predictable downstream course, lined on either side by the punctilious settlements of commerce, the perfect objective correlative of the predictable, bland cultural tyranny I so deplored? And wasn't it just and natural that when it met the swirling id of the sea, a violent and ungovernable reaction should occur? But how, in a million years, could all of those who seemed to be shaping my trip out here realize that this represented the distillation of my imaginings, that I myself had been slipping downstream on a dull, predictable path of aging, only to find myself suddenly facing an inexplicable unmooring, dark, full of exciting, perhaps treacherous currents?

Aamu had parked the car a few blocks from the pilots' pier, to give me a better feeling of downtown, I assumed; and as we walked past the Maritime Museum on a neighboring wharf, I saw that the adjoining harbor, which was full of sailboats and recreational cruisers, had been invaded by a colony of enormous sea walruses. They were sprawled on the docks as if drugged, some belly up, morosely staring at the heavens. At the sound of our walking by, several of these tubby mammoths flipped to a standing position with surprising speed and charged along the dock toward us with raucous, rageful honks. Inebriated as we were, both Aamu and I broke into startled laughter, and together, our noise and the animals' seemed to shatter the moist air like glass.

With this feeling of libido and spontaneity rippling through me, I followed Aamu onto the small pilot boat, which immediately took off from the dock and headed toward the bridge. Three men were with us, the driver of the pilot boat, his assistant, and the river pilot. According to the usual procedure, Aamu's great-grandson Johnny, the bar pilot, had been driven out earlier beyond the bars to meet a container ship coming from Japan. He would navigate the freighter past the bars and under the bridge, whereupon we would meet him at the ship with the river pilot. It was the river pilot's job to relieve Johnny and then guide the ship a hundred miles along the river to Portland. Both bar pilot and river pilot had months of rigorous training under their belts. Only they, and not, for example, the Japanese captain of the freighter, knew every current, inlet, and shallow of the Columbia and its mouth, a necessity for getting it safely from the ocean to Portland.

The light, euphoric feeling of release still dominated my body as we skipped across the waves toward a speck in the distance. Droplets of rain made glimmering, blurred patterns against the windshield of the boat; its pilot was in a merry mood, as well, spouting river tales of past gales and sailor bloopers, flirting with Aamu, whom he'd known since he was a child, as if she were an attractive young filly, by peppering her with harmless, macho banter. Each time he turned to gaze out the water-spattered windshield, Aamu would make comic gestures of contempt in his direction, then swiftly slip a flask that she'd filled with Stapler's scotch from her purse, take a quick swig, and rapidly pass it to me.

Slowly, the ship we were heading for came into view, enlarging almost imperceptibly, until it finally revealed its full nine-hundred-foot length, the size of three city blocks. It was a faceless, windowless gray hulk, rising several stories above the level of the sea—like a monstrous steel anvil that had the miraculous ability to float on the surface of the water. The closer we came, the more its menace increased, dwarfing our small pilot's craft to the proportions of a fly, making it clear that if just the wrong swell of water were to thrust us against it, it would shatter us like a sledgehammer could crystal. There it stood, almost motionless, as if glued to the ocean, a fragile rope ladder hanging from its wall of a side like a few strands of a spiderweb.

"They must be carrying, say, about four thousand Toyotas," said the driver of our boat with a slightly ironic gloat. "Looks pretty stable now, but when they get out to sea, they're so top-heavy that they really roll."

The gray, floating mammoth sent a shiver of awe through me, not so much from the imminent danger of getting close to such massive bulk, but from the realization that every feature, aside from its utilitarian function, was designed to repulse. Faceless and sealed to the environment, its only purpose was to protect and transfer six thousand tons of steel, plastic, and rubber; and inside this windowless prison, which moved at only twenty-two miles per hour at top speed, was a crew of about twelve or fifteen, who spent several probably dismal months at sea. It was commerce at its ugliest and most oppressive; but this didn't mean that it, as well, couldn't be deceived and destroyed by the vortex at which nature met civilization. The thought of this afforded me a perverse pleasure.

Slowly, our small craft inched toward the hulk, more and more slowly until we were side by side, almost touching. Then the river pilot bid us a cheery good-bye and hopped onto our deck. Seizing the rope ladder hanging from the container ship, he climbed up the side of the boat with the agility of a monkey. According to the driver of our boat, we now had to wait several minutes during which the bar pilot, finished with his task, presented the river pilot to the Japanese captain and turned over direction of the freighter up the Columbia River to him. Then the bar pilot, who was Delilah's great-grandson Johnny, would come back down the ladder and we'd transport him back to shore.

Just as predicted, a body appeared at the top of the container ship's rope ladder. It moved even faster than the one that had gone up, because it was younger and slimmer. As it stepped from the bottom of the ladder onto our deck I caught a glimpse of the oval face beneath the black wool cap. It was beaming with excitement, probably from the fact of having accomplished its first journey past the bars by itself. It was a stirringly handsome face, strong and sculpted, with just a touch of Billy Budd vulnerability; or at least that's how I saw it in the trembling excitement of the moment. Then the shadow of a darker thrill passed through me as I studied the large, blue, tempestuous eyes, which seemed to hold that same wild energy I'd seen earlier on this trip and been so startled and confused by; my entire soul fell into those eyes, and my whole journey compressed in my mind into one wordless, insane realization that I cannot describe.

There was, however, another surprise in store for me. Instead of pulling away, our boat hovered, still unmoving, inches away from the container ship.

"Aren't we going now?" I ventured.

The question was met with a tense silence.

By now Johnny, the bar pilot, had entered the boat. Was I imagining that he kept staring at me with a playful, teasing smile? Aamu spit out some cursory introductions, after which silence reigned again, while our boat stayed inexplicably in place and Johnny kept staring at me, almost challengingly, I thought. To avoid his glance, I studied his large, dry, but somehow sensitive-looking hands, letting my eye trail from them up his arms to the curves of his muscular shoulders. Then my gaze slid downward along his broad, flat chest, pausing irresistibly at his crotch to discover that the material of his pants was raised like a tent, signifying an erection.

Just a few moments later, another figure appeared at the top of the rope ladder and scrambled down to our deck even faster than Johnny had. He was dressed like the two pilots, in down jacket and work boots, but he had tied a black bandanna around his chin, which had been pulled up to the level of the top of his nose. As he hopped onto our deck, a second, almost identically dressed figure appeared at the top of the rope ladder, and it, too, scrambled down to our boat. Both of them were much smaller than Johnny, wiry and crouched, as if ready to leap up and bolt at any moment.

Immediately Aamu extracted her flask, and both strangers in bandannas took a gulp from it. Tension was so thick you could cut it with a knife as we headed back to Astoria. No one had introduced me to the two extra passengers. The waves had risen, and we leaped swiftly over them, like a weighted cork; but while the other passengers and I were tossed upward a bit each time we hit a wave, the two strangers remained in place, their knees spread, their feet planted firmly on the floor. They still had not removed their bandannas, and everyone in the boat seemed to avoid their and my glance, except for Aamu and her great-grandson, who seemed to be gazing at me with a gloating, almost jubilant expectation.

As soon as we got back to shore, the two extra passengers scrambled to the deck and hopped onto the dock, sprinting toward the street until they disappeared. It was as if they hadn't existed; the thickness of tension suddenly broke, and the driver of our boat resumed his corny, homey banter. Aamu began chattering in her croaky voice about celebrating her great-grandson's first successful run by taking him back to the Labor Temple and Café for a few more drinks. She commanded me to meet them there in an hour. "You just got to," she bid me severely.

"Delilah," I managed to croak out, "who were those other two men?"

She let out a raucous peal of laughter, as if my question were absurd, and Johnny turned away to gaze at the street. "You know," she said offhandedly, avoiding my eyes, "sailors used to have a ball when they finally got to port. It made up for all those dreary days at sea. Nowadays, with the terrorist threat and all, most of 'em are confined to the ship."

"But who were they?"

A note of exasperation crept into her voice. "Silly man from another land, there's still a lot of solidarity among people of the sea." And with that, she waved good-bye, but not until her great-grandson, to my astonishment, had given me a playful slap on the ass.

It was growing dark as I trudged back up the hill to Stapler's house. Now the setting sun had become powerful enough to inject strong shafts of rose through the watery sky, which seemed to writhe with the pleasure of it. Then the play of light deepened into a lid that weighed heavily on the city, congealing into a black viscosity that made it hard to see my feet below me. The house, which I'd left set at 72 degrees, was toasty, as I liked it; and as was my wont when I was indoors, I kicked off my shoes and stripped down to my underwear. My memory of what had just happened seemed to crawl over me like an insect, or was it like the feeling of colliding with a spiderweb in the dark: invisible sticky strands that are impossible to remove and cling in places that are difficult to pinpoint? For the first time, a terrible sense of confinement began to close in, the feeling of becoming a pawn in someone else's diabolic game; and the fact that I seemed to be the last to know suddenly filled me with an impotent rage. But I certainly didn't plan to show up at the Labor Temple and Café; they could find another East Coast imbecile to use as their patsy.

I stalked back and forth in my underwear in the dark house,

windmilling my arms at invisible fears, then hurried to my luggage to extract another tablet of morphine and threw open the door of the walnut cabinet of the bar, which struck the wall, chipping the plaster. Grabbing what was left of the scotch, I swilled it down, then doubled over coughing, letting the bottle crash to the floor.

It was in this tortured position that I noticed the seashell on the floor below the couch, and something metallic gleaming from it. The shell held a large key, the classic type that had been used over eighty years ago. That's when I realized I hadn't yet bothered to examine the house.

Muttering and with head bowed, I walked up the stairs in the dark until my forehead collided painfully against a door. At first the key didn't seem to fit, but after jiggling the handle and key at the same time, I felt the door give and pushed it open. Behind it was a narrow, very steep flight of more stairs, almost vertical, of a type I'd seen only in the cramped houses lining the canals of Amsterdam, leading to the attic. In my inebriated state of bewilderment and rage, it was all I could do to pull myself up them, sputtering for breath. At the top, I fumbled for a light switch and flipped it on, which illuminated only half of the immense space. Beneath the sloping walls of the attic was a single gigantic room, which looked almost like an army barracks, mostly because of the rows of about thirty cots that filled the center. The walls were lined with books, and stooping under the sloping sides of the roof to examine them, I began scanning the titles. Everything was impeccably arranged, in alphabetical order: from Bakunin, Bey, and Goldman to Debord and Zerzan; but pop marginals were there, as well, such as McVeigh and Manson. Stacks of clippings recounting attacks and arrests that went all the way back to the Symbionese Liberation Movement and the Panthers had been carefully paper-clipped together in folders.

At the far end of the room, which was still plunged into gloom, was a large, white board on a wooden stand, blocking the triangular window, the kind of board used in kindergartens on which you could write with a felt-tip pen and then erase by wiping off. On it, in the semidarkness, was a childishly drawn multicolored drawing. I stumbled toward the light switch on the opposite wall and flipped it on. A brass Revere chandelier, hanging precariously from the ceiling and outfitted with flame-shaped bulbs, illuminated the room with a wan glow. On the whiteboard was a felt-tip map of the Oregon coast; it was obvious that it had been painstakingly but rather inaccurately copied and enlarged from a smaller map in a book in an artless attempt to reproduce the many inlets and tiny peninsulas that jutted from the shore. Red dots had been used to indicate the cities, and blue lines depicted the highways connecting them.

It took me a moment to realize that the green line running north/south was a visual rendering of my itinerary. There it was, beginning at a little asterisk next to the city of Seattle, advancing down along the Washington and Oregon coasts to Portland, then dropping further down to Eugene and back up to Portland, zigzagging west to Astoria and then across the bridge to Washington State on toward Canada.

Through the numbness of alcohol and morphine, I stared dazedly at it, mouthing the strange words in brackets next to each stop on the itinerary:

1) Pre-Assignment: New York—Background Investigation
2) Seattle: Brush Contact with Target—Cold Approach
3) Portland: Maintain Cover—Plant Drugs If Necessary
4) Eugene: First Contact, with Cell—Begin Biographic Leverage

5) Portland: Honey Trap (Use Raven for Co-option)

6) Astoria: Employ Usual Stringer; Contact Is to Maintain Deep Cover; Some Disinformation Could Prove Helpful; Raven May Use Pressure

7) Aberdeen: Continue Attempt at Reeducation

8) Vancouver: Target Should Be Ready for Enlistment (Employ Multiple Ravens Again, If Necessary); If Recruitment Negative, Burn[2]

But why should anyone believe me? Why should I believe myself when I know my blood was saturated with more alcohol and morphine than even I was used to imbibing, when I found myself lying in my underwear among shards of glass from the broken scotch bottle in the middle of the downstairs living room floor the next morning, without any memory of getting back down there, if I had, indeed, ever gone up?

Moments later, as I was loading the rest of Stapler's liquor supply into my duffle bag, I felt a large, rough hand with a strangely sensitive touch gently caressing the back of my neck with its big knuckles. Then the hand grasped my neck and turned me around, after which I saw enormous, wild blue eyes staring into mine. They were, I decided, the eyes of Delilah/Aamu's great-grandson, Jukka, if you'll allow me to use his Finnish name, and they pulled me toward him with a strange magnetism, until my lips were crushed against his, tasting the flavor of the licorice *snus* he kept in his mouth between cheek and gums, then opening to the plunge of his tongue.

After we pulled away, the look on his face was in no way in accordance with the amorous gesture he'd just completed. His features

---

2. Slang term for deliberate sacrificing of an intelligence agent, usually a newbie.

were hardened into a blank, militaristic impassivity, and the blue eyes had dulled into the impenetrable color of tin. "I've received instructions," he said. "I don't believe his car can make it all the way to Vancouver, so you'll be leaving it here and riding with me in my Jeep for the rest of the itinerary."

Without answering, I took a step to the side so that I was in line with the open door behind him, through which the first truly sunny day of my visit glared; but he rapidly shifted his position, forming a barrier between me and that portal of freedom.

"Get your bag," he required in a flat, staccato voice that bordered on the sullen, then folded his arms over a puffy chest and stood blocking the door with legs astride. I'll never forget the image of his backlit, unmoving, booted body, in its khaki green clothing, transformed into a two-dimensional dark silhouette by the constriction of my pupils to the harsh light outside the door. It changed everything around it into a fable, within which he became the central golem.

"You should have showed up at the Labor Temple and Café last night," was all he said. "We were expecting you." The severity of his tone was enough to make me follow wordlessly with my bag to the Jeep.

The Jeep rattled down the steep incline toward the water and then swerved left toward the bridge. Jukka had lapsed into a stony silence, which complemented my emerging sense of being held prisoner. He answered my few questions in monosyllables or short sentences, almost the way a superior briefs a petty officer. In such a situation, others might have been fixated on the possibilities for escaping, or at least be trying to unravel the web of manipulation that had put them in this perplexing position. But amazingly, my entire mind was occupied by the notions with which I'd arrived in this region and how artlessly "off" every impression that I'd had was.

This was all I thought about as we drove over the Astoria Bridge toward Washington State, not so very far above the steel-gray, thrashing waves of the mouth of the Columbia River below. It was a thrilling experience, almost like driving across the surface of the water itself, because of the relative thinness and astonishing length of this truss bridge. We were headed, Jukka informed me, for the eastern end of Grays Harbor, on the banks of the Chehalis and Wishkah rivers, to pick up a "shipment" (human, I suspected) before continuing on to Vancouver; and as the spray stung my face through the open windows of the Jeep, as well as after, I had the impression that I was finally understanding this region for the very first time. It was neither an Edenic natural paradise nor a smug, opportunist hub of commerce; but actually an accidental, brilliantly grotesque collision between the two. Again and again in the fine mist of sea and rain, huge stretches of forest and water would hypnotize me into a state of awed surrender, whether I saw the gloom-ridden, totalitarian majesty of a stand of old Douglas firs or waves slashing a desolate, pebbly shore; and then all this would be interrupted suddenly by the baldness of a clear-cut hill or the sinister smoke-spewing stacks and tangled juggernaut of a power plant. Unlike the East, where, in many places, such sights had long ago tamed and supplanted nature, here the struggle aggressively raged in all its blatant and elemental vulgarity. Everything seemed accidental and random, and at moments I chastised myself for my naïveté in thinking that I'd been assigned to an insipid territory that was energetically working in an orderly manner to spread the com-modified North American dream. No, by some accident I'd fallen upon another form of chaos—I, the critic who had always lauded the chaotic adventure of the Eastern urban scene. This was a place—I finally had to admit—of violence and struggle, a thrillingly ugly battle between the land and humans that produced a rich, stupefying sensory experience. Here there would never be a chance for genuine order; only the snarl of nature echoed by the discontent of the human condition—and all of it hiding under a featureless mask of progressivism because the people here were well aware that their struggle could never be completely expressed in words.

Having read a fair amount of literature about the next stop on my itinerary, I knew what to expect of Aberdeen, the small city at the eastern end of Grays Harbor: a drab southern Washington mill town not many miles from the other side of the Astoria Bridge, population approximately seventeen thousand, a good amount of whom, after losing their jobs in the declining lumber industry, must have declined into alcoholism, which the surprising number of taverns and bars in the nearly deserted downtown area clearly confirmed.

Jukka parked the Jeep on the main street, informing me that we were about to "make our choices from the shipment." He led me into the only establishment in downtown Aberdeen that seemed to have any activity: a pool-hall-cum-newsstand in which a collection of savage male adolescents, fated for dereliction and homelessness, loitered, playing pool, bumming cigarettes, and breaking into occasional scuffles until the proprietor, a pallid, middle-aged blond woman with ringed eyes, bellowed at them over the sound of The Doors' "People Are Strange."

Never before, even in the ghettos of the East, had I seen such ebullient desperation. Scraggly haired and scrawny, jittery with rageful anxiety, the shoulders of their shirts and their cigarettes drenched by the rain outside, they marched up and down the length of the pool table, often hitting the ball with such force that it went flying off to strike a wall, an event that produced catcalls of perverse jubilation.

Others stared glumly with slackened mouths at the "game" in process, calling out acidic insults every time someone missed a shot. The majority had the habit of rubbing their crotches during an idle moment, not in any gesture of sexuality but in the bored spirit of passing time evoked by a cat licking its fur. They were speed freaks, I assumed; but they were also casualties of a failing economy, more than likely to have been abused at home by working-class parents who were victims of the new service economy, wore sweatshirts calling for the frying of the spotted owl, and spent the endless rainy season unemployed paging through copies of *Soldier of Fortune* magazine, which one of the youths sat perusing at that very moment.

Jukka picked several of them, drew them into a corner of the pool hall, and whispered an inaudible proposition into their ears. I sat across the room studying them, interrupted regularly by one or another bumming a cigarette, until my pack was depleted, while I continued my meditation on my journey in a new, demoralized way. Once again, I was seized by the impulse to escape the subversive activities of this outfit, which now seemed to have become increasingly apparent at each stage in the journey. Yes, I was through with my "research." There had to be a moment when Jukka would forget his vigilance.

Jukka's new recruits, he informed me, would meet us the following morning at the garish motel he'd chosen for us, with neon signs promising pleasures that ranged from waterbeds and mini-gyms to cable TV. It was less than a block from the local casino, and Jukka specified that it be booked in my name, traveling as he undoubtedly was under cover.

It was very early evening when we checked in, even too soon for dinner. Despite the orangey light of the bedside lamp, Jukka's perky features—which included a small, regular nose, dimpled chin, blue, enormously lidded eyes, and pink, sinuous lips—suddenly took on an exhausted pallor. Then a strange gleam of compassion crept into his formerly opaque irises, and he gently motioned me to him on the bed. Quite rapidly, his entire face was contaminated by this new delicate emotion; he took my head in both enormous callused hands and stared into my face with a disturbing frankness. The words that followed astounded me, because despite their liberal use of euphemisms, they contained an uncanny awareness of my own mental processes. I seemed to be, he said, about to fail at the accomplishment of the project for which I'd been drafted. This, he had to admit, was causing him an uncustomary feeling of consternation; it was not often the case that he developed a sense of protectiveness about his "targets." It was in fact downright unprofessional of him; nevertheless, the task he'd have to perform if I did not swiftly progress in my "reeducation" was one that he now dreaded.

Taking a different tack, he made some references to the prejudices with which I had arrived but said he wanted to make it clear that he was, in fact, quite impressed by my intelligence. However, I seemed to have a tendency for a certain kind of emotionality that the "drafters" hadn't considered. I wouldn't call the tone that followed "pleading," but the tiny tremor in his voice rather closely resembled it. All I had to do, he explained, was open myself to the struggle of the people of this region. Then his voice darkened, returning to its robotic frigidity, as he added, with a strange casualness, "Otherwise you're finished."

I suppose that the gesture that came next was an attempt to color what he'd said as convincing, and I will not describe it in detail because none of this really has much relevance to my story. I won't dwell on every feature of his deliriously silken, wiry body, nor the two hard melons of his buttocks, which tightened into steel with each thrust into me as we lay together on the still-made bed, because I doubt anyone would believe me, and because my state of confusion at the time would not make me a very reliable narrator. I will admit, however, that despite the swooning surrender necessary to accommodate such maneuvers, I did not lapse completely into the manipulated subject that was the intended goal because, shortly after he fell asleep, I crept to retrieve his olive khakis on the floor and gently extracted the key to the Jeep. Then, with no idea of where it would take me, I sped up East Market Street and northwest on East Second, where I found myself in a lower-class residential neighborhood and a frustrating cul-de-sac.

I threw the Jeep into park and sat anxiously staring through the dirty windshield at the eternal drizzle, wondering about the easiest way to find egress. Those thoughts were quickly interrupted by the sight in my rearview mirror of an approaching taxi, quite far off, but driving much too fast for the transportation of a normal client. Fearing that it was indeed Jukka in the backseat of the cab, in search of me, I leaped out of the Jeep and looked around wildly. For lack of a better idea, I crept under the small overpass bridge at the end of the street, happy that the drizzle had turned into an angry torrent and might keep anyone from spying me.

It was a low-slung bridge, and I had to stoop to keep from hitting my head as I scaled the small incline of bare dirt beneath it. Dizziness caused by the excesses of the night before, as well as a sudden rush of fear, suddenly overcame me. The rain was coming down in sheets, and I doubted I could make it back to the Jeep and attempt a belated getaway without falling in my suddenly enervated state.

Halfway up the bare-dirt incline under the bridge, there was a depression in the earth. It was almost the exact shape and size of a mummy's coffin, with what could have been the outline of a human head at the top and a swelling in the curve halfway down to accommodate the arms. Just like a preserved, bandaged corpse, I lay down inside it; its curves fit almost perfectly around my prone body; and it was deep enough to shield me to some degree from the spray-laden wind, which came in gusts through the open spaces on either side and concealed me as well, I hoped, from any prying eyes.

From my position, I couldn't make out the person who jumped from the back of the cab through the sheets of rain, so I stayed pressed into the earth. But I supposed there was as good a chance as any that it could be Jukka.

Then I don't know what happened. The rain suddenly began to come down with such ferocity that all images and sounds beyond the underside of the bridge were cut off by it. With each gust of wind, sheets of it were flung at me under the bridge, and my body was bathed in its iciness. But for the first time, I blessed the rain, because I knew it was my only chance of remaining concealed. There even seemed to be something ritualistic about it, a strange, violent baptism toward which other experiences in this region had been leading.

As those in a panicked state of suspension are wont to do, I let my eyes move around in an attempt to distract myself from the eternity of those moments. If I thought about it, it really wasn't very different from the inside of a mummy's tomb. There were calligraphic scrawls on the walls that from that distance could have been thought of as cuneiform, and around the rear side, where the incline at its steepest met the bottom of the bridge, which I could see by straining my head backward with all my might, someone had left a trail of artificial flowers and leaves. One of the inscriptions was large enough to make out from my position. It said, "Thank you, Curt. All I knew I learned from you."

Who was "Curt"? And why did this place, punctuated by the continual hammering of rain and the hysterical gurgle of the river, with a view of broken pilings like stalactites in the water beyond, feel so sepulchral? I wrestled with the thought only for a few moments, before passing into unconsciousness.

Pennsylvania Story

Tennessee Jones

There is a town in central Pennsylvania that has been on fire for twenty years. A vein of coal ignited underground that no one could put out. The town is an almost unnoticeable spot on a gray asphalt highway, yellow lines faded away to nothing. Most of the houses are gone, and the ones that are left have been taken over by a strangely symmetrical overgrowth, kudzu obscuring what was once front-yard trees, chimneys, and crumbling storage sheds. Some days the smoke from beneath the ground is visible, other days it is not.

Kenneth and Dale searched for that smoke during a weeklong camping trip. They drove a pickup Kenneth had bought and fixed up with beet harvest money. Kenneth knew about the fire in the way he always seemed to know about things, as if he had simply been born with the knowledge of them. They found the town easily, saw a red fire hydrant growing from a squall of grass, a desolate bus stop bench, but could not find the fire. They talked to an old lady who still lived there, but she claimed she didn't know how to look for the fire. *Talk to my son,* she said. Her voice was like bits of freshly dug potato hung on the tines of a fork, bleeding clear juice and covered with mud. She said they were two of twenty people who had decided to stay.

After talking to the woman, they drove over miles and miles of two-lane blacktop to find beer in the middle of the country on a Sunday afternoon. They came upon a mining town called Shamokin, two-story houses stacked up on each other, squeezed between the road and the mountains. They looked like they would fall over, pushed forward by the shadows of the mountains in their backyards.

Just before a little bridge leading out of town, they saw a slag hill with a mining road winding up it. Dale realized many of the big hills they passed were giant heaps of slag coal with trees and bushes taking root in it. The mountains growing themselves up again. He had expressed surprise, but Kenneth had only nodded and told him a little about coal-mining history. The town of Shamokin seemed half made up of those displaced hills.

Kenneth parked the truck by the side of the road and they walked up the mining road. It was creased with big tire ruts, bits of dried red clay crumbling into the crow's-wing black of the coal. The mining equipment at the top looked like it hadn't been used in a long time. The debris of teenagers was scattered across the hilltop: fire pits, grayed-out beer cans, turned-out, blackened condoms.

They separated wordlessly to explore. Dale was overwhelmed by the feeling they shouldn't be there, and it made everything that much more precious. That was one of the things he loved about traveling, how being in a place you would never expect to be in collapsed time, made the past and future converge on the now. Even the ruined mountaintop, invaded and destroyed, became sacred again. He touched the machinery, marveled at it. They had taken many trips together over the years, and the silence of discovery was one of the things they loved sharing with each other.

Landscape tugged at memory in ways that were unexpected. A mountaintop a heartbreak, the desert a forgotten memory, a reservoir the anatomy of someone you've always longed to be. Each place was distinct, but sometimes conversation and landscape ran together, so that a certain idea was always bound up in a certain place.

Dale climbed into the sooty cab of a Caterpillar bulldozer. He watched Kenneth poke around in the trash around a ruined building with tin walls, a crooked roof. From that altitude, he could see the matchsticks of trees that had been felled by forest fire on a nearby mountain. And farther away, the horizon defined not by city lights, but by shades of green and purple that would disappear with the setting sun.

Dale heard Kenneth scream and saw vultures, greasy and half-dead looking, boil up into the air above his head. The air touching his spine shimmered and turned cold, the same way it did whenever he saw a big black snake crawling through grass. Kenneth ran back toward Dale, sliding all over the loose slag.

"Fuckin' vultures flew right in my face," Kenneth said. "I smelled 'em. Felt 'em." He reached up for Dale's hand.

Dale slid down off the bulldozer, trying to cover his smile. He curled his hand into Kenneth's, pulled him so that their chests almost touched, grinned against his ear.

Kenneth looked back over his shoulder, breath heavy. "Man, that scared the shit out of me." His heavy knuckles pressed against Dale's smaller ones. Dale's body shook and he could not stop himself. He laughed until tears brightened the coal dust on his face.

Kenneth pushed him against the giant tire and put his forearm against Dale's throat. "You gonna stop laughin'?" he asked.

Dale smiled. "Uh-huh."

Kenneth smiled back at him and pressed him back against the giant tire, knocked Dale's feet further apart with the sweep of his boot. He twisted the hand he held behind his back and stepped in so their foreheads touched. Dale sank into the shadow of the wheel well, relished the heavy smell of grease coming from the machine's guts. From the road, they would look like two men in a fight.

Kenneth dropped Dale's arm and put both hands around his throat, body pressed tight against him. He felt the shadow of Dale's erection, was careful not to rub against it too hard. Kenneth's smile sharpened, his eyes narrowed. Dale's eyelids fluttered and he looked toward the sky, his head resting inside the wheel. The sky blue, the vultures gone. His fingertips began to tingle, and he sensed the onslaught of what he had experienced with Kenneth in so many different places, the sensation not of leaving his body or consciousness, but of truly finding them, gone almost as soon as it happened.

Dale wanted so much to turn around, brace his hands on the coal-covered tire, feel Kenneth's hands covered with black dust and carrion wind rake down his jeans, his cheek bruised or flayed open by one of the bolts in the wheel. Instead, Kenneth pulled him forward and split his upper lip open with the force of his kiss. A moment of sacredness in a devastated place, a moment that could make you free or get you killed.

The summer after Shamokin, Kenneth invited his dad to visit him at a summer cabin Dale borrowed from an old girlfriend's grandfather. The cabin was about fifty miles from his dad's house in Portland, Maine. They hadn't seen each other in five years, despite Kenneth's travels. *There's some things I need to talk to you about,* Kenneth had said and his father had agreed to come, no questions asked. Kenneth wanted Dale to be there when his father came, but he would be introduced only as a traveling partner.

The plain walls of the cabin stank of the spice of the old man who owned it. Thin, early sunshine filtered through the trees and dappled the floorboards of the porch with light and shadow. On the lake side of the house, the parted curtain allowed a long bar of light the color of warm butter to melt on the kitchen wall. Dale stood with his feet apart, holding a cup of hot water with whiskey and lemon in it. He stared out the open door at Kenneth's wide back, covered by a hooded sweatshirt too heavy for the season.

Kenneth heard Dale's heavy boots come toward him over the kitchen linoleum before he swung the wooden screen door wide.

"Want some whiskey?" Dale asked.

"Too early for that." Kenneth turned around. "Gimme a hour or two."

Dale grinned. "Be time then to fry up the fish you caught yesterday." He saw them, split and silver, sizzling in a cast-iron skillet. "Wonder if they'll taste as good as the ones we had that time in New Mexico."

"Doubt it. You remember those guys on Birmingham Road, the ones whose house burnt down? They caught it somewhere above the goddamn tree line. No pollution." Kenneth stopped talking, and his jaw settled into a hard line.

"You know what time your dad is coming here?" Dale asked.

The jaw muscles flickered. "Later on tomorrow, I figure. Probably 'round dark."

Dale turned to go back into the house. Kenneth picked caked mud from his shoes and was bombarded by smells and sounds that threatened to close up time, to turn the present back onto his childhood, even though the area around him had nothing to do with it. It was a more intense version of the presence he usually found when he traveled, and the timelessness he experienced was the thing that made travel so ultimately appealing to him. It was where real life happened, instead of the other way around. He turned a beer tab in his fingers and wondered how the hell to tell his dad what he thought he knew.

Dale sipped whiskey in the mottled bright kitchen. He poured two dollops of oil into a black iron pan and turned on the flame. His morning drink had turned lukewarm. The cabin was filled with different bits of debris: a rusted hoe with a handle gone so gray it was the color of barn dust that hasn't seen rain or light for decades; a heavy, opaque whiskey crock; a collection of cloudy glass bottles. There were also what must have been the artifacts of the grandfather's dead wife: a red-handled potato masher, chipped teacups too damaged for household use, a paring knife with blade worn utterly concave, the handle dark as the shell of a black walnut. It was this last thing he stared at as he cracked two eggs into the heated oil.

Kenneth, less than ten feet away, seemed halfway across the lake, even though Dale smelled the thin smoke of his cigarette when he lit up.

"Got eggs in here," he yelled. "How many you want. How you want 'em?"

"Gimme two. Fry 'em hard. Brown on the edges if you can get 'em to do that." He spoke from the doorway, outside the screen door. The way the light fell made him half a silhouette. "'Bout time for some of that whiskey, too, but I can do that."

Kenneth opened the door and the cigarette smell came with him. Dale loved the smell even though he hated to smoke.

Dale stuck a couple pieces of cornbread and butter into the oven to warm, and cracked two more eggs. Grease spit everywhere.

Kenneth poured two big splashes of whiskey over ice in one of the little ruined teacups. "Cup's probably fifty years old, wouldn't you say?"

"I was thinking about that. Maybe. Ellen's grandma was way up in her seventies when she died." Dale watched the stove doggedly. "They had this place before anybody else ever thought about coming around. They used to stay here for the entire summer sometimes."

"Yeah, we had summer people in Kentucky, too. Only they moved in and stayed the whole year. Then after a little while they started making fun of the people who only stayed for a month or two. Nobody thinks of themself as summer people."

Dale grimaced, slid two brown-laced eggs onto a plate. A piece the size and shape of a thumbnail was missing from the edge. "But everybody is, at one point or the other. Everybody wants a piece of something they ain't got a right to every now and again."

Kenneth took his plate and laughed. "Don't I fucking know it," he said.

Dale smiled and followed him out the door. "Don't you wanna take off that sweatshirt?"

"I'm fine." Kenneth shook his head and turned to the plate resting on his knees. Silence fell between them. Dale watched the sun twinkling on the lake and was irritated by the sharp, flickering light. Kenneth emanated the same distance as before, and Dale realized that was the true source of his irritation. Kenneth's way of dealing with reality—a kind of flatness that took everything as it came—had a tendency to pervade everything, to make the people around him question their own relationship to the world. The way he read a book or rolled a cigarette was dogged and deliberate, and seemed infused by an understanding of reality both difficult and satisfying. It was as if he had no natural filters to protect him from the onslaught of information he experienced every day. He was doomed to notice everything, and his reactions were slow and distant because of it. Sometimes he seemed to get beyond this when they fucked, in a certain way Kenneth might touch him, as if he was trying to get to a place where being deliberate would no longer exist. In that formless place deliberateness, along with all other things, would be obliterated.

Kenneth finished eating and lit a cigarette, his eyes fixed on a far point on the lake ahead.

Dale cleared his throat. "You wanna talk to me about your dad before he gets here?"

"I decided this after Shamokin. Somethin' about those vultures got to me. Kept dreaming about them. You know me and my dad ain't been on the best of terms for a long time. This is a story I ain't told you, 'cause it was one I just started to remember, the day after we was up on all that mining shit. It's still hard for me to talk about, but it's what I got to talk to my dad about.

"I got this picture in my head of being in Texas with my family when I was little. Brown sand, a hotel room right on the beach, big pool right below our window. Me and my mom's friend's kid got a room to ourselves. He was about a year older than me. The way I remember him now wouldn't a been the way I thought of him as a kid. He was tan and real muscley for a kid that age. It made me jealous.

"That kid got ahold on me on our second day there, middle of the afternoon, and pulled my swimsuit to my knees. He grabbed my dick and started working it. I didn't know what to do, so I let him. He got me on my knees and told me to suck his dick, and then he turned me around and fucked me up the ass. The thing I remember most about that is stuffing my bloody underwear behind the stove so no one would know what happened. I felt guilty. I hadn't really thought about this in so long, but I can see and smell everything, even the fucking towels they had there.

"That kid fucked me over and over the entire week. He pretended like it was a game, and I'm not entirely sure I didn't like it. My mom was pissed at me when we got back home because all my underwear was gone. I put it everywhere except for the trash, because I figured that would be too obvious."

"Nobody ever found out?"

"That's just the thing, man. I'm pretty sure my dad saw it happen, at least once. Unless I was dreaming it. There was this big window, and that kid would draw the curtains on it so no one could see in. But I think I remember my dad standing in the hallway while that kid was going at me, his reflection on the glass in the lamplight, watching us and jerking off."

"Holy shit."

"Yeah. So I think he let it happen. And I think he must have let it happen other times, too. I just don't understand why.

"After the thing with that one kid, it was like everybody could tell. It's almost like if it happens once and some part of you secretly likes it, the rest of the world can tell. And then they come to you, they find you whether you want them to or not." Kenneth finished his drink. "So that's what I got to talk to my dad about."

Dale touched Kenneth's knee. Silence fell between them again and Dale stood up. "Let me go in and get you another drink," he said.

Dale broke ice out of the metal ice tray and dropped it into their cups. He opened the screen door with his shoulder and handed a drink to Kenneth. Dale sat down beside him, not too close, just so the fabric of their jeans touched. That bare separation seemed to almost hum, and Dale thought, as the smoke from Kenneth's cigarette swirled around them, that sometimes it isn't getting exactly what you want, it's just being able to want with the force of the world.

Later that night, after Kenneth poured water over the fire they'd built at the edge of the woods, they fucked like they were camping high in the desert, red sandstone grit blowing into their eyes and hair. Kenneth grabbed up Dale, punched him in the mouth, and brought his lips to knock against the bloody teeth. Big knuckles squeezed tight on Dale's throat, until his fingertips and eyelids fluttered and one of them shot across the other's stomach, and then the throat was released, those same knuckles smearing blood across Dale's cheek. They fell asleep on the weathered mattress in its wrought-iron frame, each dreaming memory. Every movement had already been made; they were just waiting to rediscover it.

Kenneth fell asleep with the smell of a million grasshoppers in the desert in his nose. A few years before they had driven through Utah, and on their way to see the only undammed river in the West, they had come across a migration of grasshoppers. They were huge, black, covering the asphalt completely. They made a sickening popping sound under the tires, and the smell was so pungent they had to turn the car around. He had felt their bodies were right between his teeth, the dark alien blood in his mouth. The thin vein of fluid between his brain and skull turned arid as the shelled wings on their backs.

Where they had turned the car led them to something unexpected: a crater in the earth from some ancient meteorite, two blackbirds over the abyss who had abandoned their wings. They clutched each other talon to talon and let themselves drop, uncoupling and flying at the last possible moment, again and again. The two of them had stood side by side, watching, for as long as it lasted.

The next day Kenneth watched the one-lane road for the approach of his father's truck. Jake had told him what to look for: an old green F-150. When he finally saw it a couple hours after lunch, he stubbed out his cigarette and immediately lit another one. He wished for an endless row of drinks. "My fucking dad is here," he said, just loud enough for Dale to hear.

Dale came out onto the porch and watched Jake's slow approach up the road. The sound of his truck door slamming reminded him of every family dinner he'd ever been to: that little bit of dread at the arrival of each new person. He wore jeans and work boots. His hair was silver, still cut the way he might have worn it as a teenager in the fifties.

Jake must have been a young man when Kenneth was born, Dale thought. He walked up on the porch with the wide gait Dale had copied from other men his entire life, similar to the cocky and defensive walk of his own father. If that way of walking were a story, it would be about escaping from the police, but having to crawl through a quarter mile of shit to do it.

Kenneth met his stride, hating the way he walked differently because his father was there. His steps were just a little too wide, his shoulders squared off too much. His hand clapped loudly on his father's back. The sound was like a flock of birds lifting off at the same time.

Dale half expected something sinister to snake out of Jake's rough palm when he shook it, but his smile was genuine enough, the lines around it and his eyes not so much crinkled as greased, and his grip was warm and easy. Dale was immediately aware of how little Jake knew about his son's sexuality.

"Nice to meet you, Jake," he said. "I've heard a lot about you." Dale didn't quite smile at him, but held his rough hand a little too long.

"You, too," Jake answered. "I mean, nice to meet you. Today's the first I ever heard anything about you."

"You want a beer, Dad?"

"Yeah. Bring us a few out here. It's hot as hell."

Jake sat in one of the two old iron chairs on the porch. Someone had painted it many times years before, and the thick layers of paint were visible where it had peeled. He crossed his arms behind his head, and Dale noticed the dark patches of sweat in his pits.

Kenneth opened the screen door and gave them their beers, dripping from the five-gallon bucket of ice in the kitchen. He loved ice, made special trips to the store just to get it. He leaned against the porch railing, too uneasy to sit down. Dale sighed and took the iron chair beside Kenneth's father.

"So how long you boys been on the road?" Jake asked.

"We ain't really on the road," Dale said. "Just borrowing this place for a little while. It's in one a my ex-girlfriends' family. We've been on lots of other trips though. Out West and through the south. I'm not much of a hiker, but I like to camp."

"Oh, uh-huh. I used to have a big army tent, weighed thirty or forty pounds, I used to take Kenneth and his mom out in. 'Member that?"

Kenneth nodded and drank from his beer. He watched how his father's big hands moved, and looked down at his own.

Dale, terrified of what might rise from silence, kept talking. "Me and Kenneth spent a lot of time out in the desert, too. Two months one time, camping out every night and driving all day. There's a helluva lot of country to see out West." Kenneth glared at him from his perch on the porch railing. Dale felt like a child again around Kenneth's father: the peculiar pull that had plagued him as a child—to both be someone like Jake and to touch someone like him—confounded him in a way he hadn't felt in years.

Kenneth opened his mouth to speak and closed it again. The afternoon sun leaned onto the porch. The shadows were the fat, edgeless shadows of summer.

"I was thinking we oughta go fishing," he finally said.

"Sounds all right to me," Jake said. "As long as there's more a that beer to take with us."

"Yeah, plenty a that. Dale, you wanna come?"

He looked at Kenneth's face, but it told him nothing. It was the same blank look he wore when he was reading to kill time and thought no one was looking at him. "Yeah. I'll come," he said.

They pulled an aluminum boat out of the shed and dragged it down through the grass in the yard. The sun did its melted-butter trick, and the summer people filled the air with the smell of their barbecues, the noise of their radios turned to the classic rock or new country stations, the trill and bark of their voices, the roar of motorcycles and Jet Skis. They paddled to a quieter place on the lake, a recess of cool and shadow out of sight of the summer cabins. In not too long, that part of the shoreline would probably be developed, too.

Kenneth sat in the middle slat of the boat, with his back to Jake. Dale faced both of them, and he tried not to look into their too-similar faces. He slit his finger baiting a hook with a fat, sluggish grub. Its split body poured sap onto his bleeding finger. Kenneth watched him with trapped eyes. The water close to the shore was colored with the reflections of trees.

Jake chose a long pink night crawler to bait his hook. Dale watched him past Kenneth's shoulder. The worm sent out little ripples in the water. Kenneth impaled a grub straight through its entire body and cast his line. They shifted uncomfortably, trying to find a way they wouldn't get their lines tangled. The silence lasted for a long time before Jake spoke.

"This a nice place your old girlfriend's got, just for the summer. What'd her family do to get the money?"

"Grandpa had a big paper mill. He sold office supplies."

"How the hell about that! Knocked down half the state and got a freaking summer cabin for it." He turned up the long neck of his beer. "Glad you all get to enjoy this, at least."

It was after dark by the time they pulled the boat up the dew-damp yard. It didn't matter they had come back empty-handed. They'd all had too much to drink to care about eating.

They sat on the porch for a while, drinking and smoking, before they went back inside. Most of the lights around the lake were out before Kenneth flipped on the kitchen light. They settled into the living room, and Kenneth and Dale both watched Jake, careful to keep their eyes hidden by the bills of their caps.

Jake made the cabin seem more like home to Kenneth, the home he missed and knew he could never quite go back to again. Jake emitted the spice he and Dale were still growing into. It was a smell Kenneth remembered from childhood. It made Dale think of his grandfather at the end of a day in the field, new sweat layered on old dried sweat. The smell was enough to knock you down some days.

The light in the living room was dim. Yellow enough to hurt all their eyes. Dale turned up his beer, cold from the freezer, and looked down his nose at Jake's sledgehammer fists. He had to close his eyes, and took another long swallow of beer, cold enough to stab his forehead with an ice pick. Memory flooded in, and he immediately thought of how he might tell it to Kenneth; it was too big to keep inside of himself.

There had been a day in the fall when he was a kid that he'd lain on a sledgehammer for hours. He'd been curious about the strings of drying chili peppers strung up on his grandpa's carport, so he slid one off the string and split it open. Knowing somehow the meat would be hot, he had put the little white seeds into his mouth instead. They lit into his cheeks like embers popping off a campfire. He ran around the house, grass cooler under his bare feet, turned the spigot like it was salvation itself, so hard his white hand would hurt the next day, and found no relief in the pouring springwater. He ran up the cold concrete steps, mouth burning, and in desperation laid his cheeks, first one then the other, on the cold reddish brown sledgehammer that belonged to his grandfather.

He had told the story occasionally for a laugh, but hadn't remembered what had come after it until seeing Jake's hands hanging between his knees. He remembered something that had been forever bound up in the heat of where the pepper seeds had touched the insides of his cheeks and burned well into the orange and purple dusk. His cousin, Morgan, the one whom he'd visited a few times after he'd finally packed up and hitchhiked out of the mountains, came upon him and asked him what the hell he was doing. Dale, his cheeks painful, had only sobbed. He had held out the crushed pepper pod, still in his hand, and Morgan had laughed at him. The concrete was too cold on his bare knees, but he couldn't take his face off the sledge. It smelled like icicles just starting to melt. It might have tasted like chilly sunshine if his tongue hadn't been on fire.

His cousin had taunted him while he lay there, in too much pain and half panic to move. Then he grew quiet, and the air became heavy and silent the way it might before an especially bad summer thunderstorm, the colors of dusk brought on early, the silence of midnight in late afternoon. They had sat on the lichen-splashed concrete steps a hundred times before, hid in the giant boxwood their grandpa had planted in the backyard when he was just a boy, cracked beechnuts that fell there in late summer. As if it was just as familiar, Morgan lay down on top of him, stuck his warm and acid fingers into Dale's burning mouth. Dale had felt shock but no real surprise, and the day, warm, but with the hint of coming cool and promise of crisp leaves, had simply become nothing at all. Dale was not there, or here, or anyplace, and the awful burning in his mouth momentarily ceased, even as the air between them mirrored two warring fronts, one hot, the other cold. The feel of Morgan's hard dick hot against his back and the cool of the concrete as his shirt rucked up over his belly was not something he'd thought about for a long time before seeing Jake and his ham hands. That storm feeling was similar to the heaviness he and Kenneth had experienced in many different landscapes, when it was uncertain whether they would clash together. It was the gravy-thick feeling just before teeth hit skin and blood was shed.

Kenneth watched Dale from his seat beside the little woodstove in the common room of the cabin. The tin flue had been welded clumsily around a hole in the wall. It made him feel a certain affection for the old man with the dead wife who had built the house. They were among the artifacts of their lives; he couldn't take a step without feeling like he was rattling bones.

He looked at his father's face and saw they were similar. He was beyond finding something to say to fill up the silence in the room. He looked at Dale, his beer empty, staring at different points of the room. Kenneth saw how he looked at his father, and realized Dale was angling for him. Maybe it had been there since the moment he'd arrived or maybe it was just the booze. He could feel it in the air like poison oak on a vine rubbing against his cheek. Dale, wanting to touch the man who may or may not have been responsible for the way reality would forever be like a freight train he could never quite get on board of—Dale, wanting surely to touch the valleys between the relief maps of his knuckles, wanting to know the shape and line of his pulse. Those were the kinds of things Dale would think about before sucking a man's cock.

His own hand, wrapped around his almost empty glass, felt tight enough to shatter it. But it wasn't anger so much as the familiar feeling of reality folding in on itself. Time, forcing itself back up through the rings of trees, announcing, *Everything is always here.*

When Dale looked up, Jake's almost-gray DA made him feel peculiarly exposed. There was his older cousin, still hanging over him, a lit bottle rocket dangling from his teeth, daring him to come forward. The smell of beer was suddenly new, the same as when he'd first smelled it, like ocean foam when Morgan had poured it against the resin-veined trunk of a pine tree after he'd taken his first drink.

The silence in the room gathered weight. Dale sucked the bitterness from his brown bottle of beer, but the taste could not hold back the murky undertow of memory. Kenneth sat in a far corner of the room, his beer warm as bathwater.

"Anybody else need a drink?" Jake asked. "Never mind, I'll git you all a drink. Always need another one." He stumbled off to the bathroom.

He lumbered out of the room, but his presence invaded every part of the house. They heard his long stream in the toilet, the way he moved heavily in the kitchen. Kenneth expected to hear one of the old woman's teacups break.

Dale wanted Kenneth's father to be gone, and for him to fill up the room at the same time. Something about him reminded him of his cousin, and something of himself. Something he'd always wanted to be, tried to be, was wrapped up in the way he moved, smiled, talked, the easy way he drank a beer. It was the edge of masculinity that shapes itself as archetype, the line of a jaw so perfect it becomes more than just flesh and bone, and is strong enough to reroute desire itself.

Dale imagined himself bending over his lover's father's knees, unbuttoning his old jeans, slowly taking out his cock and easing it between his lips. One heavy hand clasping a bottle of beer, toes of his boots pointed toward the far wall.

Kenneth and Dale looked at each other across the room.

Because Kenneth had thought of the desert the night before when he had punched Dale in the mouth, and did not know what else to say, he asked, "Them birds we saw in the desert, you remember them?"

Sounds came from the kitchen; Dale saw the old woman moving within it. He saw her young, saw her in a flash being worn away like the blade of her paring knife. The smell of apple dumplings filled his nose.

"I remember them."

And he did. Two blackbirds, in the sky over the desert in Utah. They had picked their way over rocks to sit on the edge of where a meteorite had crashed into the earth and made a deep, colorful gouge. So deep it made Dale want to throw up, sitting with his legs dangling over the edge of it, but they'd had to get as close to it as they could. Those birds had come up flying out of nowhere over the chasm. They locked blue talons together and folded up their wings. Then they plummeted downward, toward the center of the stardust crater. They dropped like stones; they dropped like they wanted to die, until they let go of each other and opened up their wings to catch an updraft. They came sailing back up and did it again, over and over. Kenneth said those birds were laughing, making fun of them. Dale had reached out, like he thought he could touch them, and inched closer toward the edge. Kenneth grabbed him roughly, said, "No, don't do that," but they'd both been near hysterical, laughing like they could make death a funny thing, the cavern below them the color of sunset. Kenneth let his fingernails bite into Dale's sweaty forearm, so there were still half-moons in his flesh the next day.

Dale wanted to talk about those crows, but his tongue felt too thick. He wanted to say, *That's exactly what it feels like sometimes when we fuck,* but the words hung in his mouth.

Instead he asked, "How're you holdin' up?"

"I'm all right," he said. "Better than I have been for a long time, if you can believe that. Just seeing him again is helping me figure things out."

Jake walked back into the room with their drinks then. Instead of sitting, he staggered to the other side of the stove, put his hand on the sheet metal flue. His gesture made Kenneth feel protective of it. Jake turned up his beer and swallowed, one hand in the pocket of his jeans. Kenneth remembered some of the stories his father had told him when he was a kid: running through the woods and coming out on a cliff, not being able to stop himself before he went over the edge, saying prayers and then not knowing what had hit him when he landed in cold, black water that carried him until he could pull himself to the shore. Hiding between the mattress and box springs when the cops came looking for him, a couple years before Kenneth was born, the time he'd watched someone in his company go crazy and shoot someone in an alley in Vietnam. The time he'd almost killed a man in their hometown for looking at him the wrong way, touching the snap buttons of his shirt with fingers still grimed with grease, offering to buy him a beer. The way he imagined his father's knuckles had felt across that man's face had crept in to the way he hit Dale sometimes, into the way he himself wanted to be hit, to see the clear water of the last undammed river in the West.

"Be out a booze soon," Jake said, and slumped down into a ruined chair. Kenneth's hands tightened around his beer again, and he drank it deep.

Dale was bound up in disgust, felt his head begin to swim. He rose from his seat on the old man's couch. The empty space of it had been bothering him the entire night. The dim light of the small room, the punctuated screams of summer people in the night, radios playing across the lake. Everything. It was late enough for the cool of night to have burned off the heat of the day.

"Kenneth, will you go get me a drink of whiskey to go with this?"

Kenneth looked at him and nodded. He got up and left the room, knowing he could wait as long as he wanted to before coming back. In the kitchen, he closed and opened the refrigerator without taking anything out. He didn't bother making the drink. The light was too dim and hurt his eyes. He pulled open the dark wooden drawer of silverware and took the butcher knife, long and old and oil dark, and held it in his hand. He waited, his other hand grazing the bucket of mostly melted ice.

Kenneth heard Dale's boot heels clump against the wooden floor in the next room. He imagined him walking straight up to his father, crowding him, pulling the beer from his hands, setting it onto the floor. Dale would come on to him just the way he would to any man in a bar, direct but gentle, the kind of way that if he wasn't into it Dale could just back away and turn it around on the other guy if he needed to. Kenneth didn't feel anger, but a kind of wonder and befuddlement that had been with him for most of his life. It was an interest, a curiosity, to know what would happen next. If Dale did fuck his father, would Kenneth get something back he'd been owed for a long time?

Kenneth stepped quietly across the faded linoleum floor and looked into the living room. The doorway was made with wood that had obviously been cut by hand. It might have come from the woods in the backyard. The wood was the color of the shadows lamplight throws in summer dusk.

His beer sweated cold in one hand, and he squeezed the dark-handled knife with the other. Dale was on his knees in front of his father and Jake leaned forward in his chair, like he was waiting for Dale to tell him something. Dale brought forward the bottles, grazed Jake's cheeks and lips with the round mouths of them. The sound in the house was the change of the seasons.

Jake jerked back his bottle of beer and swallowed long. Dale, distant enough to just be about to tell him something a drunken man would say, was also close enough to kiss him. Kenneth's heart jumped. His memories folded over.

Jake's hand dropped, twining tendons, the marks of years of hard work, and he leaned farther back in his chair. Dale said something to him Kenneth could not hear. Dale took Jake's beer and set it onto the wooden floor, the only sound in the house. Kenneth watched him lay his hands on his father's brown leather belt. He wondered if it was the one he'd unloosed in the reflection of the mirror in Texas, the same one he'd used to beat him. Jake leaned his head back in the chair; Kenneth couldn't tell if he'd passed out or not. Kenneth raised his hand to his cheek, almost expecting to find blood.

Kenneth remembered all his summer evenings, suddenly pressed together, the way night had stretched out long and black and made him so lonely, the way he had felt when the boy in Galveston had turned him over. He saw how all the things he'd wanted had not been obliterated but changed, by only a few afternoons.

Kenneth could see his father's boot heels, worn on the outside, pointing toward him. He thought of the light of storms coming in not over the mountains, but over the ocean. That was why he'd been able to see him, he realized, not because the curtain had been drawn, but because it was dark enough outside to cause his reflection to appear in the lamplight on the glass. That storm had rolled in over the beach in Texas. He'd never seen anything so gray or angry. Nothing with so much hard beauty and potential to kill.

Kenneth stepped backward into the kitchen. He put the knife back on the counter, listened hard for what was happening in the next room. He felt revulsion so deep it turned within him, took him to the place he was always trying to go, that place beyond. He leaned against the counter and unbuckled his belt. He imagined everything happening in the next room by the sounds he could not hear. Kenneth took his cock in hand, and became both wretched and free.

Dale, in the warm lamplight of the living room, existed in the pit where Kenneth had seen the vultures emerge, the shadows of the slag, the fire smoldering beneath a town burning for twenty years. There is a place where damnation ceases to be damned, and he had always searched it out—and occasionally found it—with Kenneth. He glowed the color of a dying star. Nothing had ever come up between his ribs the way touching that man's belt had. At the same time, he wanted to take it back, to take everything back. That split second before he hit the ground was perhaps more than he could stand.

Marge

Michael Lowenthal

Marge had long blond ringlets and eyes like poached eggs. He only ever wanted to be a housewife: the slippers, the curlers in his hair. Plus I think he maybe craved an accent. He talked like he was trying to keep from downing a bite of mush.

His mother had won the lottery years back and bought a building with ten rental units Marge could manage. Pronto he hired a crew, turned the ten into twenty-five—so measly, folks said, that if you sneezed in one apartment, everyone God-blessed you in the next.

Marge rented to pimps and prostitutes. The first of the month he slippered through the halls: "Pay-up time," would come his porridge voice. The pimps rarely paid. They beat him up. He loved it.

He left his door open so the guys who loathed his type could stomp in and fuck with all his stuff: light his stove, melt his plastic plates. Next day, he'd chip the melted plastic from the stove and bustle right down to the five-and-dime, where he'd buy a new set of pink plates. Ah, he'd say, the landlady's life!

He also adored the young boys. Eleven, twelve, thirteen. (Marge himself was always not quite turning thirty.) The whores and I would sit downstairs and watch the kids go in, then watch them come out twenty minutes later. If a boy left with a chocolate kiss in addition to

251

his cash, it meant that he was very, very good. A tangerine or a gumball, only so-so.

"I want to die smiling," Marge said. "Boys make me happy."

Sometimes a boy gave me his tangerine as he left. Maybe he knew he'd been a disappointment. He would ask if that dude's name was really Marge. Someone would say sure, of course it is. It might not have been the name that Marge got from his mother. How much of the truth do our mothers ever give?

Mom and I lived in the building next door. Mostly I stayed home alone. Who cared? Mom worked for one of the guys who clobbered Marge on rent days. My father was dead, or might have been.

One day I was cutting school, ants were in my pants. Hotter than it should have been for June. Crank a hydrant, maybe? Suck some ice? I went down to the street in my boxers, nothing else. Sunlight sharp and dogged as an itch. There was Marge, lounging on his stoop, next to ours: flimsy housedress, hair pulled back and tied. It made his face look bigger, flexed like muscle.

Out from Marge's robe came a leg as long as lightning. Now I saw the bowl, the shaving cream. He used a Lady Schick, just like Mom's. Stroke, stroke—one leg, then the next—stroke, like harvesting a crop. His skin got pearly, catching all the light. I peered into the rinse bowl: bits of hair sprinkled, all those zillion tiny twists of fate. It felt like the legs he stroked were mine.

"I'd shave you, too," he said. His voice made me sizzle. "But your thing's more a *toe* than a leg, ain't it?"

He pointed down. It poked clear through my fly.

I ran inside, locked the door, and panted prayers to God. I begged him not to let me be like Marge.

The old neighborhood, two decades on, is getting chic. Bargain hunters troll the streets with ponytailed Realtors who talk about *upswing, vested interest.* Switchblading open their silvery cell phones, they call their mortgage brokers and say "Buy." Way back then, we could have used those cells. One day Ma Bell came and yanked the public phones—stripped for coins too often to be worth it. Mom couldn't afford a private number. How was she supposed to call for help?

We were natives waiting for our continent to be found. Street signs said NO STANDING, so we sat. Best seats in the house for Marge's show. *At last, would Marge discover true love?*

Merge was what I dubbed him in my mind: part one thing, part another, all mixed up. But the pimps always called him Marge of Dimes, grand marshal of the freak parade.

He joked about the colors of his bruises, naming them with catalogue-type terms. Strife, he called a certain purple shade just shy of black. Yellow tinged with blue: Mottled Remorse. Beneath the flippancy, was that his mood?

Looking back, I think of him as Marginalia. His commentating made life almost graspable. "Prodigious!" he might say of a scorching August noon. "Hot as the hole of an overtime ho!" He evangelized his own low-down church. "Jesus and the holy-rolling three-way," he once barked at a b-boy who wouldn't mind his paws. "I'll whup your ass to dingleberry jam!"

Most everything reminded Marge of food. The moles on a preteen Puerto Rican kid's cheek were currants in a bowl of oatmeal. A *chulo*'s backside was his hot cross bun. (Best to lick it, Marge assured us during Lent.) Once, fifteen yards before I turned onto our block, I heard him call someone's face *tragically shapeless.* "God must've forgot," he said, "to preheat his griddle before he poured in *that* bit of batter." From the way that he cackled when I cornered into view, I figured he was talking about me.

I was already too old for his taste, maybe. My upper lip was fuzzed with hair like lint. I was a tall drink of juice, he told me once. In two years, I grew thirteen luckless inches.

I was a good enough cheater to just get by. I studied boys: how they strutted, pop-'n-locked; the way they picked their hair but not too much. I cribbed moves and epithets, snuck peeks.

The juice was in my privates. Did Marge know?

I learned people like all sorts of things. There was the bald guy who forked over two crisp Franklins weekly for Mom to twiddle her thumbs up in his ass. Another man—she called him Reagan, rich and overtanned— wanted lead fishing weights hung from his nipples. All manner of noises came from next door. People craved. People paid. There was no shame.

Except for me. My itch for Marge? I couldn't.

Where did he find the guys who would? The Y, maybe. The chop shop by the river. I envied their brassy finder's-keeper's view of pleasure, their bootleg happiness.

In some other neighborhood, or some other city, people like Marge marched and waved flags. They'd have hated him more than they hated the guys who beat him. Every time that Marge smiled at a fist, he set them back. The last thing Marge wanted was toleration.

The plate-melters asked me along once. Damon, whose crackerjack moonwalk I'd tried to copy. Pedro, whose track pants always bulged. It was Halloween. The air reeked of dried-up country stuff. The smell of plastic jack-o'-lanterns melting.

Shaving cream was part of the night's plan, and rotten eggs. A can of Crisco, too—who knew why? This would be my chance, I thought, to look at Marge's life. My chance to prove what I didn't want.

I'd been in his building a bunch of times before, but now it felt a shade of unfamiliar. The light was like a stain on normal light. Behind a hollow door, someone's hand slapped someone's something. I heard: *Feels good.* And: *No the fuck you don't.*

SWAT-style, we slithered up the stairs, down the hall, rotten-egg grenades set for launching. As per legend, Marge had surely left the door unlocked, but Damon karate-kicked it anyway. In we blitzed, screaming skinned alive.

And when we slowed enough to see past our own bluster, there was Marge, in his bathtub, knitting. His creation, pink and cabled, looked to be a baby blanket. He might have had a niece we didn't know.

The room was all lace and fake flowers. Flesh-colored candles like dildoes on every shelf. Foil-wrapped kisses in a pink plastic bowl. You know how, when you're sick, puking actually feels better? I wanted to spit up my whole self.

"Trick or treat," Damon said, with goblin eyes.

"Nah," corrected Pedro. "Dickless freak!" He hawked hard, spat into the bath.

Marge just kept on knitting. He locked his jaw.

"Faggot," Damon said. "You a man, or what the fuck? Stand the fuck up, show us what you got."

"Yeah," I said, wanting the guys to know that I was with them. Plus because I hoped to catch a glimpse.

Damon cocked his fist. "Hear me? Up!"

Marge grimaced. Knit one, purl two.

The bath soap smelled like killing us with kindness.

"Let's fuckin' stomp him," Pedro said.

Damon's arm stayed cocked but didn't move. Above his elbow's hinge, a tiny pulse showed. It fluttered. He wasn't yet fifteen.

"Fuck 'im," he said. "Her. Whatever the fuck: it. I hate the way it won't quit lookin' at me."

"We're just giving it its jollies," added Pedro.

They scrammed, spurting foam across the walls and on the bed. Damon hurled the Crisco at a lightbulb-bordered mirror. Two bulbs popped like back talk: *yap yap.*

"Ready, aim," yelled Pedro.

On "fire" they launched their eggs. I chucked mine, too, a wicked sidearm fling.

The way you see a lightning bolt before you hear the crack, at first I watched the yolk ooze down in streaks. All three scored: the jaw, above each eye. Pretty in a certain way, like drippy abstract art. Then boom! came the thunder of the smell. A death stink. Abortions, gangrene.

"Get the fuck," yelled Marge, then caught himself.

Egg yellow clashed on the pink of baby blanket. Red, then: blood above his brow. I guess his skin wasn't all that thick.

The other guys hoofed it out to the hall, and I followed. But when I hit the threshold I stopped short. My brain was a coal that Marge was fanning.

I turned back and found one of Marge's bath towels, as soft as my grandmother's cheek. (Bull! I never met my grandmothers.) I stepped up and handed it to him.

Closer, inside the smell, it wasn't quite so bad. Nasty still, but flowery, too, perfumed. Marge had his left eye half closed like a wink, which made him seem forgiving, even charmed. Slimy white stuff dripped along his cheek.

"Much obliged," he said in a dinner-party voice, and dabbed the towel elegantly on his brow. Then the bubbles parted and he rose. He stood facing me. His skin shone.

For the first time I understood that shameless isn't bad, but maybe an ideal, an aspiration. Marge was so much taller than I'd thought. His hair down there was reddish—the parts he hadn't shaved. His thing curved like a smirk. It looked like mine.

I'd never run so fast in all my life. I caught up with the other guys and said the freak had grabbed me. "He's stronger than he looks," I said. "I swear."

I kept waiting for Marge to say something. One day. Another. A week. I was mortified and hopeful and confused. What I wanted was to never see his fuckhead face again. What I wanted was reassurance, an invitation.

The boys came and went (Marge joked: came, came, and went). I searched their faces. Triumph? Resignation? They had a talent or a recklessness I lacked.

The country reelected an old actor. I didn't know a single soul who voted. Plus there was a referendum on a new subway line, an extension into our neighborhood. The verdict? It wouldn't kill us to keep walking.

Clementine season came: for a month that's what the so-so boys left with. One kid, with freckles and a harelip, gave me his. "Sick," I said, and threw it at his ass. He dodged into traffic. The fruit missed.

Marge couldn't find enough boys who were willing. He had to make do with real men. Their moods were unstable, their knuckles harder. New shades of bruise were soon coined. Misdemeanor (grayish). Loss of Face.

For Christmas, Mom surprised me with a leather basketball, too nice to dribble on blacktop. I kept it in its swanky box, unopened, like a wish that still has not come true. Mom split for a week with José, the guy who kept her. Reno, she said. So they could tie the knot. (What she tied, I'd find out, was her tubes.) All week, I ate SpaghettiOs and whacked off.

My body was like a TV that someone was channel surfing, sweat and hair and hormones, click click click. Everything was changing, up for grabs.

Pedro and Damon formed a gang. *Which side are you on* was now the deal. With heated pins and ballpoint ink they tattooed their right forearms: a time bomb with a clock face that read SOON.

Marge proclaimed that tattoos were for fools. Mutilations must be mutable, he said, and momentary, flaunting his own latest laceration. (Flaunting and flinching sometimes look the same.)

I took Marge's advice. I resisted. For two weeks, I kept my sleeves rolled up as living proof that my loyalties lay more with him than with Damon.

If Marge noticed, he didn't give a damn. I'd stood in his room, face-to-face, seen his all. I'd almost apologized. I'd almost begged. But that moment, so monumental to me, for him was nothing. Battered and bare was Marge's every night.

"Chickenshit," Damon said one day, grabbing my inkless arm. He twisted an Indian burn. Thrilling pain.

"Do it," I said.

"Now," I said.

I'm in.

That spring, I tailed one of the chocolate-kiss boys. I'd seen him around school but didn't know him. He was a mutt, skin the rust brown of the grates that barred our windows, but whetstone gray eyes: they sharpened you.

He was probably sixteen. Me, too, almost.

Leaving Marge's, he walked with an extra fuck in his stride, tossing his silver kiss like a coin. He had braces that yanked sunlight, beamed come-on when he grinned. With each step, he kicked his own future.

I followed him down Washington, then behind the Laundromat into an alley that was Bomb Squad turf. The week before, Pedro and I had bopped a kid back there, a smart-mouth who called us "fucking cretins." All we shook loose was a pack of Camel Lights, but the heat of his cheek on my fist was worth it. Recently, we'd also lifted pints from Sully's Liquor. We practiced pickpocketing each other. Damon talked big about going back to Marge's and nailing him this time, no retreat. My tattoo was the color of a vein.

In the alley, a rat nosed a Zero Bar wrapper. A broken mirror cut the sky to bits. The kid—I couldn't think of his name, but he looked like a Leon—bent and fished fivers from his sock. Counting, maybe. Maybe glorifying.

His money wasn't what I was after. But how do you ask for what you really want? I gunned my hand and jabbed him. "Fork it over!"

Leon didn't flinch. Didn't budge. A headband kept his curls out of his eyes.

"Now!" I said. "Give it up. Cocksucker."

When Leon stuffed the cash back into his sock and stood up, I felt like someone'd swiped my cheat sheet. I was tall, but he was taller. Awfully thick.

I hadn't really thought it through this far. Follow him, and watch, and then what?

"I know where you've been," I sort of croaked.

He snorted and said, "You don't know shit." Half of his mouth smiled, and the other half stayed mean. His braces looked made of razor wire.

Laundry steam hovered like something consequential. I thought about bolting, but I couldn't. "How does it feel?" I might have asked.

He grabbed my arm, his thumb on the double O of SOON, and pressed like he was digging clear to China—to the opposite of wherever he lived now. I remembered that his father coached the basketball team at school, and his name wasn't Leon, it was Darrell. Darrell was the youngest but the best varsity player. A power forward. All-city. Eyed by scouts.

"I want," he said—then paused long enough for me to wonder— "to hear it come out of your mouth."

"What?"

"That you don't know shit."

"You're right," I said. "I don't. Let me go."

He tippy-toed nearer, his mouth up in my face. I saw a smear of Hershey's on his teeth. His breath was like the Y locker room at closing time: bleach trying to hide a human stink. I made a guess about what he had swallowed.

"Say what?" made a breeze that kissed my chin.

"I don't. Don't know anything. C'mon."

The rage in his eyes was so fierce I almost heard it, the *shick shick* of steel being edged.

"I'm not," he said, still pressing, even stronger than before, "what you think I am, or what you maybe are. I'm gonna be huge. I'm gettin' outta here. Is anyone gonna try and mess with that?"

I could feel my flesh giving under the pressure of his thumb. What would I name the bruise's hue?

"No one," I said.

He knocked me to the ground.

Friday: a few of us loafing on the stoop, tiddlywinking beer-bottle caps. Mom was there, bra cups stuffed with cash, painted smile. Alley drafts tickling our ears.

"Thank God for the weekend," said José. He cracked his knuckles.

"Thank God there *ain't* no God," said Mom. "Otherwise I'd meet you shits in hell!"

Laughter all around. High-five smacks.

Damon and Pedro had some Bomb Squad mischief planned: a rooftop, a case of beer, some girls. I wanted time to shower, clean my teeth.

Just when I stood up, I saw him leaving: flash of silver fang, scissor stride. Darrell, headband skewed, making tracks from Marge's building. Darrell, both hands empty at his sides.

"That one of Marge's boys?" asked Mom.

"Dud, I guess," José said. "Where's his chocolate?"

Mom said how you never knew, it might be in his pocket. Boys hide lots of treasures in their pants.

They chuckled, but I couldn't. Already I was scrambling—into Marge's building, up the stairs. The door was open. Fruity smells leaked out.

I stepped inside. I blinked hard. Then I looked.

It's been twenty years, but I still see it. I see that scene more clearly than my high school graduation, the first diploma in my family. More clearly than the day I finished Rutgers. It's sharper than my wedding, six years later, to Samantha, whose hair, when it's damp, curls like Marge's. Sometimes when we're making love, I twist some on my finger, and Sam has no idea what I'm thinking. It's clearer to me than this now, today.

Shards of pink plastic bowl were scattered on the floor, half a dozen chocolates smeared around. Centered in the midst of it lay Marge: long blond ringlets free like sunlight in fast water, cotton robe bunched around his hips.

His mouth, stretched past normal, was crammed with chocolate kisses. Two dozen? Three? Maybe more. Most still in their foil, some smushed out.

I checked for breath and pulse. Nothing doing. Already his skin was going gray. Then I saw the thumbprints on his neck.

On cop shows, they're always saying not to move the body. Don't touch a thing. Call 911.

It's not as if cops would have rushed for Marge.

I straightened out the robe so his legs were mostly covered. I spread his ringlets nice around his face. Then, with my finger, I dug into his mouth to clear away the mushy, melting chocolate. At first it felt nasty—scooping giblets from a chicken—but then it felt OK, then almost good.

When all of the kisses I could reach were emptied out, I saw his mouth had fallen to a smile. I tried to smile at him, but couldn't. I faced a long lifetime of restraint. Backing away, stumbling, I sucked my messy finger. It's still the sweetest thing I've ever tasted.

A Good Squeeze

Vestal McIntyre

I lay on the floor of my apartment rolled in a Persian rug. With every inhalation, I smelled my own hot exhalation mixed with the woody smell of rug fibers and a hint of feet—that very human stink of dirty socks. (I asked my few visitors to leave their shoes at the door and I myself was usually barefoot.) But to inhale that recent exhalation, that wet, oxygen-poor air, seemed to be the goal now.

I waited quietly.

It was comforting, this pressure from all sides—a firm embrace but without the complications of human emotion and response to emotion, that ping-pong game that set my jaw to clenching. Only the crown of my head and the tips of my toes were free. Which school of belief said spiritual energy flowed into one's body through the top of one's head? And which old mystic was it who said she could see the angels treading air in the space above her followers' heads? And how many of our holy figures besides the obvious and her son, did not descend into the earth, but took the A train to Sugar Hill way up in heaven? Thin air above and below me, but the air that I kept resharing with myself was thick with wetness it picked up somewhere in climbing my respiratory tree. Comforting. And sometimes a little comfort was as much as one could ask of life. But other times one could ask a little more.

The embrace weakened. The pressure lifted and I felt both relieved and disappointed. Belinda had stood up.

Now I was rolled over, whump, and over, whump, and again, whump, and I could breathe freely and light struck my closed eyelids and illuminated those bubbling lava-lamp paisleys.

"Rand, are you OK?"

"Yes."

"I was getting worried. It had been a long time."

I sat up and held my knees and was dizzied by a head rush. More paisleys. "There was no reason to be worried," I said and opened my eyes. "None. It was really lovely. Thank you." I put my fist before my mouth and coughed.

"You enjoyed it?"

"Yes. And now we know that I can go longer next time."

"Right," said Belinda. "Time's almost up."

"Oh, really." I looked at the clock in the kitchen. "I was in there longer than I thought."

"Almost forty minutes," she said.

"My. Well, yes, the time's almost up. I think we're done anyway." I stood and made a motion of dusting myself off, although there was no dust on me, since my apartment was kept very clean.

I went through the pockets of the jacket that hung by the door and found my wallet. Belinda nodded and accepted the folded bills without counting them. When I went to open the door, she stopped me.

"Rand," she said, "I've been meaning to ask you something. Are you still practicing alone?"

"Yes," I said.

"You shouldn't, you know."

I nodded. Her concern amused me and tapped the enormous, unspoken affection I felt for her, and I couldn't repress a smile.

"But I've been thinking, if you must, you should at least have someone check up on you. There are cases where people have been trapped, alone, for days. You could die, Rand. It's not funny."

"I know," I said. "That's not what I'm smiling about. Go on."

"Give a friend keys to your apartment. Tell the person to come check on you if he or she goes for a day or two without hearing from you. I insist, Rand. This stuff has its risks."

"I'll do it."

"You won't."

"I will, I promise. Thank you, Belinda, I know you're right."

She smiled. "See you Tuesday?" she said.

"Tuesday."

I didn't mind obeying Belinda. The problem was, though, whom to ask. I had very few friends. Connie was the first who came to mind. She was orderly, responsible, aware of my practices, and nonjudgmental about them. She knew that I had hand restraints attached to either side of my bed, and that I had trouble sleeping without my hands safely enclosed in them. She knew sometimes I needed to gag myself or be gagged to feel at peace. I was sure she would be willing to be my "check-up person." However, I usually only spoke to her once a week—a phone call on Sunday—and saw her about once a month. To make her my "check-up person" would have forced me into closer contact with her and, as much as I liked her, this was not my intent.

As I went down my mental list of friends, again and again this was the case—it would have forced me to call them more than was my habit. All except Frank.

At first, the thought of entrusting Frank with my well-being made me laugh. But then again, why not? He lived out in Queens, but found an excuse to come into Manhattan nearly every day. He had nothing better to do with his time, I supposed, than come over and make sure I wasn't dead. He was irresponsible, but in this he might be trustworthy.

In many ways I considered Frank a special case. He drunkenly stumbled through life from boyfriend to boyfriend, still depending on the youthful charm and good looks that the alcohol was slowly ruining. He had been in a minor car accident some years earlier and had swindled his way into living on disability ever since. He was obviously well, but he kept up the act, even with friends like me, occasionally remembering to wince and put his hand to his lower back when he rose from a chair. But he had a good heart, and that is what bought my patience and made him a special case.

So I invited Frank over for takeout and a chat. When he arrived at my door, the rose in his cheek and the blur in his eye told me that he had already had a drink or two. "Happy May Day!" Frank said, holding out a neon blue bunch of Gerber daisies, the variety available at the corner deli.

"Is it May Day?" I said. "I didn't realize. Come in."

Frank would be embarrassing if he was capable of feeling embarrassment himself. If he ever apologized for showing up to my house drunk at five in the afternoon with a three-dollar bouquet, I wouldn't be able to forgive him. But he would never apologize.

I put the flowers in a vase, where the dye immediately began to seep down the stalk into the water. "Lovely," I said, which wasn't completely tongue in cheek, as the swirls of blue in the water were as beautiful as the flowers were ugly. "Before we order food, there's a favor I want to ask."

"Anything," said Frank, plopping onto the couch.

"Belinda says I need a *check-up person*." As I began to explain, Frank laughed as if I were making a joke, although he knows I don't make that kind of joke. Then, like a child that slowly realizes the gravity of the subject, he reassigned the expression of his mouth into a determined frown and his eyes into a concerned squint. "I'm certain you'll never have to use these, but all the same . . ." I placed the two linked key rings into his cupped palm, and he took them, fingering the keys—again, as a child would. "This set is for the door here, I've marked them with a red marker, and this set is for downstairs. I rarely do these things down there, but you never know." (Years ago, I had bought the floor beneath mine, telling my parents it was an investment and that the rent I could charge a tenant would cover the mortgage, all the while knowing I would leave it empty, as a barrier. Now I stored a few pieces of furniture down there, nothing else.)

Frank knit his eyebrows and nodded, then he rose and placed the keys carefully into the pocket of his backpack, which was hanging by the door.

"You'll never have to use them, Frank. It's just a precaution. Now then, what to order for lunch?"

"Oh," said Frank, "I'll have to owe you one. I'm kind of short on cash at the moment."

The lunches that Frank owes me at this point must number in the thousands.

Sometimes I wonder if I would be attracted to men if I hadn't attended boarding school. I'll call it Tenderwood Boys' Academy. Despite girlfriends at home, real or invented, everyone there was gay.

The first hint of this penetrated my terrified thirteen-year-old brain during the tour, when the admissions officer nonchalantly pushed a bathroom door, letting it swing wide as we passed by, ". . . there are two bathrooms on every hall . . ." and, there being no barrier (why, in the boys' bathroom in a boys' dormitory in a boys' school, would there be?), I saw an alleyway lined on either side with stalls that led to a shower room glowing with golden tiles and seven? eight? showerheads pointing impudently toward a central drain hole.

Gang showers! I silently gasped.

And gang showers they were.

How many svelte young asses endured the sting of a towel-whip here? How many shy boys turned toward the corner to hide a boner, and how many brazen faces turned proudly toward the central drain hole to expose one? How many times did a boy glance at the source of echoing laughter to find that one thread of the hot stream was not water, but the yellow arc of his neighbor's piss? In short, how many adult fantasies, nightmares, obsessions, and neuroses were born in this shower room?

The door swung closed on gently sighing hydraulics and the admissions officer continued: "The boys live two to a room, and often find their roommate to become their first and best friend."

Indeed.

I loved Michael Prescott, my first roommate freshman year, who would creep from his corner to mine where we would cuddle and rub under the down comforter my mother had bought me after being shocked during that same tour by the solemnity of the folded and tucked woolen blankets.

Hunched and acne faced, Michael was almost as tall as I and a much better student. We traveled in different packs, and didn't talk much even when we were back in our warm den, each wearing his earphones and studying under the lamp that lit his own opposite corner. But often, after the lights went out at ten, sometimes even hours later, after I had fallen asleep, Michael would make that dark journey, and I would never turn him away. Sometimes he would even fall asleep with me in my narrow bed. We would arrange ourselves in the bed to make the most efficient use of space—his feet by my head, my feet by his—while still enjoying each other's warmth. He never complained about the very restless sleep that had plagued me since early child- hood. (It wasn't uncommon for me to find, upon waking, knotted sheets I had cast on the floor, or scratch marks on my face.) If I tossed and turned too much, he would simply wake me, I would calm myself, and we would both return to sleep.

Then, only a quarter into the school year, tragedy struck. Michael's father, age fifty-one, dropped dead from a massive heart attack at his desk in a Manhattan law firm. Michael went home for two weeks, and when he returned he had changed. Now he wanted to sleep in my bed with me every night. Sex took secondary importance to sobbing qui- etly while I held him. Again, I never turned him away, but quietly asked the administration to assign me a new roommate at semester.

Later, I loved Chris Medici, the slender, girlish asthmatic whom, in leaving my bed to take a piss, I discovered taking a midnight shower. As I washed my hands and lingered in front of the mirror, his shower sput- tered and ceased, and he began shyly toweling off in the shower room.

"What's with the late-night shower, Medici?" I asked in a perfectly offhanded, abusive tone. (I assumed that it had to do with his being too shy to jack off within earshot of his roommate.)

"They let me," he said. "It helps my wheezing." As proof, he emitted a high-pitched, gravelly cough.

The next night I stayed awake, then, just before midnight, put on my bathrobe, grabbed my towel, and headed to the bathroom, reasoning that if I was caught in this minor infraction I would claim asthma. I had a feeling Chris Medici would know to meet me.

I was minutes into a nice hot shower when, sure enough, here came Chris. He hung his towel on a hook, then his bathrobe and, avoiding my gaze, charged up a showerhead on the opposite wall. Keeping his back turned, he touched the stream, adjusted, touched, then stepped under. I ended my pantomime of scrubbing and stood gazing at Chris as he heaved deep breaths of steam, his narrow back swelling, his tucked-under buttocks tucking further under. He glanced over his shoulder and, seeing me, blushed and went immediately back to his breathing. Then he dared to look back, dared to look down, dared to turn toward me. I walked across the room, shared his shower, and touched him.

We turned off our showers and ran, naked, into one of the stalls where, for the first time, I saw up close how some scrotums, when shivering wet and shrunken, are not pink like my own, but a lovely shade of brown.

To this day I have a habit I picked up in grammar school when a volunteer instructor came to my class every Wednesday for two months to teach us some basic sign language. Lesson one: the alphabet. Our little voices sang and our right hands raised in a strangely shifting pledge: fist to fan to cup to point, *OK,* pinkie, two, *L,* fist, fist . . . Now my hands, which were already delinquents scrambling for something to do, could spell. *F-U-C-K Y-O-U* they giggled to my practice partner when the volunteer looked away, *G-O T-O S-L-E-E-P* they told me from under the covers, *I H-A-T-E Y-O-U* they repeated under the dinner table, and, as I walked alone on the beach that summer in Newport, repeating in unison just for the comforting fists the word made deep in my jacket pockets, *S-T-E-A-M, S-T-E-A-M.*

Now, walking through Washington Square Park, past the dry fountain that served as an amphitheater for the overeager sunbathers (early May, sixty-five degrees and cloudy), my hands did a simple *A-Q-A-Q* in my pockets and my mind said, *knit, knit, knit,* then, *purl, purl, purl:* I was practicing on the way to my first knitting class.

I had been teaching myself from a book I had found at the library, and had done well producing two large scarves. It was a perfect occupation for my hands while I listened to music, and it being May, I thought, I could have an entire collection of sweaters by next winter, if I could learn ribbing, buttonholes, and more complex stitches. For these complicated operations the book proved useless.

When I emerged from the park onto Eighth Street, I heard someone call my name. It was Frank.

"What are you doing out?" he asked, as if I were a naughty puppy.

"Oh, nothing. I'm in a bit of a rush, though."

"Rand, this is Nori," Frank said, indicating his companion, whom I had not noticed. I looked at this tall Asian man and for the first time in ages was immediately dumbfounded by attraction. I reached for his hand. I might have said hello. His face was solemn and gorgeous—narrow jaw, protruding bottom lip, serene gaze. He bowed slightly as we shook hands—that wonderful Japanese style of greeting, a subtle, respectful bow which I vastly prefer over the messy strength-play of handshaking.

"Well, we won't keep you," Frank said, and they were gone.

In class I tried to pay attention as the instructor demonstrated the slipped-rib stitch and the seed stitch for the entire class by holding her hands high and exaggeratedly digging the needles and tossing the yarn while her long white braid wagged in reply, but my mind kept returning to Nori. Was he Frank's new boyfriend?

At home, I forgot what I learned, returned to my simple knit-one-purl-one scarf and continued to wonder.

Then, one night in mid-May, I descended into the corridors beneath the porn theater on Third Avenue where I went during my rare moments of boredom and desperation for physical contact. Cruising for sex is one of the most awkward occupations imaginable, and one that ensures failure to those whose appearance betrays this awkwardness. So I found myself moving through the smelly, uncomfortable maze trying to convey the ease of an evening constitutional until the awkwardness won out and I lodged myself in a corner. As usual, I was not bombarded by solicitous leers, but the few glances cast my way carried a hint of worship. Square jawed and shaved bald, I have the type of features that many consider unattractive, even sinister, and some consider strikingly handsome, with no one falling in between. I considered this a luxury.

Five more minutes, I said to myself finally, shifting from foot to foot, then *I'm going home.*

Then, at the far end of a corridor, Nori appeared. He meandered slowly up the hall in my direction and almost ran into a column. Maybe his eyes hadn't yet adjusted to the dark. In any case, there was no discernible attempt in his tall, somewhat bent form to mask the awkwardness.

He chose a spot against the wall perhaps ten feet from me and surveyed the hallway. He wore a smile of playful, perhaps drunken, embarrassment. With that smile he transcended all awkwardness and coolness and emerged simply beautiful. Everyone saw it; the men slowed as they passed.

Here was what I came for. I decided I must approach him or leave. I launched myself from the wall, thinking I would leave, and instead walked over to stand beside him. When our eyes met and he recognized me, I greeted him. He nodded. "Do you remember me?" I asked.

"You are Frank's friend," he said.

"Yes, Rand." I didn't reach for his hand, but gave a slight bow.

"Nori," he said and returned my bow.

"Yes, I remember," I said. Then I stood waiting for something to say.

"You want to go in?" he asked, indicating a doorway.

"Yes!" I said, perhaps too eagerly. I was shocked; nothing in his demeanor had betrayed an attraction.

I followed him in and we made fumbling attempts at sex that resulted in ejaculations but not much pleasure. Small dark closets can be entertaining for one person, I believe, but two's a crowd. Nori was someone special; I wanted to hear his hesitant voice and feel his eyes on me as I undressed him.

I asked for his number, he told it to me, and I immediately committed it to memory.

In the cab home, I again wondered about the extent of Frank's involvement with Nori. I had brought up the subject casually during a phone call the day after I ran into them on the street. Frank had said they weren't dating, but offered no further information. I didn't know if they had been or would be, or if there was any other reason I should consider Nori off-limits. If there was, I wouldn't phone Nori. I would bury my attraction and quietly mourn. But if there wasn't—and I tipped the cabbie extra in this hope—I would pursue. I hadn't pursued anyone for a very long time.

At Tenderwood Academy I loved Tony Cole, the soccer star a year my senior who I always assumed was too handsome and athletic to have eyes for a goon like me. But then one hot afternoon near the end of my sophomore year, he found me away from a group of swimmers (swimming legally, in bathing suits, under the sun) in a bushy nook of the pond. I had been emptying my lungs to sink and sit lotus-style in the mud. He invited me to race him out to the island and, aware that I'd lose, hiding my eagerness to do so, I accepted the challenge.

Halfway there, it was obvious I'd never catch up. The race must have lost its thrill for Tony because he turned and swam back to me.

"You win, Tony."

"You lose, Rand," he said, not with pride or malice but with bone-dry boredom.

Then, for some reason, he shook his wet head, rose in the water, exposing his shoulders and those hairs that fanned out from the center of his chest, held his breath, and plunged down. He swam beneath me, thrust his head between my legs, and clutched the meat of my thighs. Confused and delighted, I rose as he rose and was sent into a sideways dive that painfully clapped my body against the surface of the water. I resurfaced and we treaded water together, laughed and panted and waited for what would come next.

Then some boys called Tony's name and we swam reluctantly toward them.

For the rest of that warm month, I wished again and again that he would come recklessly groping toward me (how little I shunned physical contact back then!), maybe on one of those nights of illegal swimming, naked, under the moon. He never did.

The next year I loved my roommate, Richard Victor, who, as heir to a Pennsylvania smelting dynasty, might have been the richest boy of all.

Nearly all the Tenderwood boys were rich. Some made embarrassing attempts at acting like real teenagers, others showed their shame: they wore Birkenstocks and Greenpeace T-shirts, although their fathers were executives at Exxon. Still others were aware and haughty. Richard was one of these. He would walk into a classroom like a house cat, never rushed even when he was five minutes late. Then, in his wonderfully deep, faggy voice he would make purposely obscure comments and leave it to the teacher to justify them to the text because—Richard's arched brows seemed to suggest—he (Richard) was paying him (teacher) to do so.

One evening in October Richard pulled his trunk out from under his bed, dug under his winter sweaters, and pulled out a small collection of gay porno magazines—gifts, he explained, from his uncle in San Francisco. Although this was in, what . . . 1987? these men were from the seventies—hairy chested, thick mustached, their big, lolling cocks basted with baby oil. *San Franciscans,* I remember thinking. Ten o'clock came, lights out, but we pulled out our flashlights and continued flipping the pages frantically until it was too much for us and our trembling hands abandoned scenes of firemen fucking and red-assed leathermen receiving spankings to find each other.

That year we became something like boyfriends. But, more than Richard, more than anyone else at Tenderwood Academy, I loved Mr. Drake.

Mr. Drake. That name conveys the longing, the schoolboy crush that colored one little corner of our relationship (but I loved that corner as I did every part of what we had) more than the name I called him in private—Will. Mr. Drake was an artist in residence at Tenderwood, a painter. Mr. Drake's residency began after winter recess my junior year and ended in November of my senior year.

"He looks like a young Montgomery Clift!" I said to Richard Victor after the assembly when Mr. Drake was introduced.

"Montgomery Clift *after* the accident, more like," answered the jealous Richard.

Part of Mr. Drake's residency requirement was that he hold informal hourlong painting lessons in the late afternoons while most boys were playing sports. I swallowed my pride, put aside my fear, and started attending every lesson he taught.

I was not then, never had been before, and never will be an artist. Although I love art, music, poetry, etc., I haven't the slightest interest in producing the stuff. The paintings I made were ugly. I would hide them, sneak them back to my room, look at them one more time just to feel the disgust, then destroy them. You can imagine the humiliation of standing at an easel during an outdoor class with the man for whom I felt an all-consuming passion looking over my shoulder, giving me suggestions on how to capture landscape in watercolor. I would pretend to take the suggestions, pretend to care about the hateful thing, just in the hope that he might, in his instruction, lay his warm hand on my shoulder.

It became too painful to attend the lessons. I abruptly quit, and two days later slid a note under the door of Mr. Drake's apartment. "Mr. Drake," I told him, "I am completely blissfully painfully in love with you. I cannot bear to take your lessons anymore. I must know if you love me, too. Late tonight, I'm going to come here and tap on your door three times. I can't tell you what time it will be, as that depends on when I can sneak out of my dormitory. If you love me, open the door." (I think I was reading Jane Austen at the time.)

So late that night, I snuck across the wet lawn and up the darkened back stairwell to stand trembling before his door. I gave three light, measured taps, and almost immediately he pulled me in.

"Did anyone see you?" he whispered hoarsely.

"No."

"Are you sure?" He thrust his head out the door to check the hall, then closed and locked it.

Although I was trembling, I was conscious of exuding a confidence, the confidence that comes with true love, and this began to infect Mr. Drake's troubled expression. We both broke into a laughter of disbelief and joy. Then he kissed me and held me tight and we laughed again. Then he made love to me in an intense, beseeching way that I had never experienced. We were silent, both out of necessity and in order to witness more clearly the dramatic arc of the act. Then we lay naked together and Mr. Drake told me to return to my dormitory, which I did, happier than I'd ever been before or have been since.

I was soon in the middle of an affair with the resident artist. We actually spent relatively few nights together, he was so afraid we'd be caught. But those blissful nights, the recollection of whose every detail stole the sleep from subsequent nights, became my one and only objective. My studies, which were never a priority, were jettisoned completely in favor of imagining our next night together, and all those nights to come when we would be free from Tenderwood.

Needless to say, I never went to his lessons again. It was imperative that we seem completely unaware of each other. I watched him teaching from the woods, though, just as I watched him eating in the mess hall at the long table with the other instructors, whose drabness so contrasted with his brilliance it was hard to imagine them the same species, much less the same occupation. He shouldn't eat with them! was my angry and somewhat deranged conclusion. He should eat only with me, out of doors, on hillsides. But, of course, that was impossible. I felt that conflicted pride—he was beautiful, he was mine, but no one knew it.

No one except Richard, and this terrified Mr. Drake. But how could I keep him from knowing? He was my roommate! I continued to screw Richard, just to keep him from getting too jealous and snitching.

Mr. Drake asked me if I thought the other instructors suspected anything. I told him I didn't, and to further ease his mind I related rumors and truths of other faculty-student contact I had heard over the years. These stories, like every other word we had spoken since our last art lesson, were whispered. Nothing calmed his fears, though, and he broke it off. I cried, left him crazy letters, tossed in my sleep. His mood darkened and he left his post a month early.

Was it during this period of longing, hopelessly, for Mr. Drake that my sleep became so torturous and I flailed my arms so violently that I finally devised my first system of self-restraint? I took a towel, tied the ends, and laid it across my bed. Then I lay down on it and put my hands through the loops created on either side, and felt somehow comforted. Was that the first time? That would make sense. And I try to make sense.

Unlike most people, I turned from a child into a man in a matter of weeks. I graduated and, four days later, turned eighteen and received my first check from my trust fund. I defied my parents' command to go to Dartmouth, where I had been accepted (it seemed too much another Tenderwood), and moved to New York City. On my one-month anniversary of living there, I decided it was time. After three brief conversations with other William Drakes in Manhattan, his unmistakable voice answered. To this day, I still remember the phone number.

"Hello?"

"Will? It's Rand. I'm here in New York."

"Rand? *Where* are you?"

"I'm here. I live here now."

There was a long pause, then three sentences: "I can't talk. I'm not alone. Don't call here." I stood frozen, unable to put down the phone. Nine words in three sentences, the last I would ever hear him speak: statement, statement, command; whispered, of course.

I wandered New York for some time chilled to the bone, then slowly embarked on the series of disappointments adults call "dating." Where were all the men I had assumed would be waiting in every café and gay bar? (I was never denied entrance to any bar, gay or otherwise, having always seemed older than my years.) I started to discover that in this city that seemed to be so crowded, one still had to go out in search of people. And in this adult market the currency was no longer just kisses and body fluids; safety, diversion, status, the future—things such as these were on the block, and every transaction left me feeling either guiltily indebted or, more often, robbed.

The next time I saw Frank, I told him. "Remember that guy Nori you introduced me to?" I said. "I met him again."

"Yeah? Where?" he said.

"At that porn theater on Third Avenue."

"I didn't know you went to porn theaters." Again, the naughty-puppy treatment.

"Well," I continued, "we fooled around there at the theater, and he gave me his number. I want to call him, but I thought I should ask you first. Do you mind? You said you weren't seeing him, right?"

For a moment it was as if Frank had turned to stone. His face drained of color and I could see the gin blossoms at the tip of his nose. Then he shook it off.

"Um, sure, Rand. Do whatever you want."

"You seem unsure," I said.

"No, it's fine. Do what you want."

It was clear to me that something very sad had passed between Frank and Nori, and it was only my own selfish desire that kept me from investigating it further. I asked no more questions, and called Nori. We had a short, friendly conversation. It seemed he was busy working on a project (he was in civil engineering at NYU) but would complete it and present it the following Thursday, which happened to be the eve of a three-day weekend. He suggested we get together then, and I was flattered that he postponed our meeting until a time of leisure.

Then it very impetuously and prematurely occurred to me to invite Nori on a weekend road trip to Montreal.

I had had a lovely time there with Connie a year and a half before. We had spent the days together exploring the city, then after dinner our paths would part—Connie's to theaters and lesbian bars, mine to gay bars, jazz clubs, and saunas. The city was chilly and magical, populated with beautiful, scrawny, dark-eyed, French-speaking men. Ever since, I had thought that if I ever found a worthwhile boyfriend, I would take him there.

Not that I presumed to consider Nori even a proto-boyfriend, but he was certainly worthwhile, and at this moment in life when I had decided that a companion would not distract me from my search, that was enough.

I arranged to meet him for breakfast Friday morning, explaining that I was going to leave town. I reserved a car and hotel rooms with king-size beds, making sure everything could be canceled with minimal penalties.

Over breakfast, Nori proved to be as bright and charming as I had sensed, and at a perfect moment near the end he asked, "You are leaving town? Where are you going?"

"Well," I said, "I'm going to Montreal, just for a relaxing weekend. Have you ever been there?"

"No, but people say it is nice."

"Yes, it's very nice. I like it very much. Would you like to come with me?" I was sure the answer would be no, in which case I would politely finish breakfast, then flee, never to call him again.

"Um," said Nori, cocking his head and looking down at the corner of his place mat, which his fingers were repeatedly dog-earing and smoothing, "this is so nice. But I do not have lots of money, so I cannot."

"Oh—well, everything's paid for already—the hotels and things," I said. "I mean, I'm going with or without company. So it wouldn't take any money really, I mean. Things are cheap there."

"You don't mind?" he said tentatively.

"Oh, no, in fact I'd really love the company." *S-A-Y Y-E-S*, said my hand under the table.

"All right," Nori said, and he laughed.

He told me it would take just an hour for him to pack. I gave him my address and told him to meet me as soon as he was ready.

Again, I was surprised at his willingness, and wondered if I should consider it a warning sign. But, I said to myself, a sign warning what?

When Nori arrived at my door, the look on his face told me he was reconsidering. He came in and set down his backpack. I hugged him tentatively and kissed him on the mouth but, still, he frowned. "What is it?" I asked. "Is everything all right?"

"Do you have downstairs neighbors?" he asked.

"Um, yes. Why, did someone stop you in the hall?"

"No."

"Is everything OK? Do you still want to go?"

"Oh, yes. I still want to go to Montreal," he said.

And we left.

After leaving Tenderwood Academy, I kept in touch with only one friend—my jealous junior-year roommate and boyfriend, Richard Victor. He had gone to college in England, where he found a handsome Irishman to love, and for a while after graduating they lived in a stone house in the Irish countryside, which is where I visited them.

"This place is very rustic," Richard had warned me before I went, but I assured him that simple, rustic beauty was what I craved.

The house, the rolling hills, the silence were all beautiful. I visited at the end of the summer and, though everything was still green and misty, there was a chill in the night air. Only the john was too rustic for my taste—an outhouse at a short distance behind the house.

I usually flush several times during a bowel movement, whispering an apology to the water gods. I consider the ability to immediately whisk away our shit the greatest wonder of the modern domestic world. How could I endure shitting into a cesspool?

The first time, I nearly panicked. But I calmed myself, held my breath, and did it. After a few days it was almost bearable.

Richard and his boyfriend were very much in love. They had vigorous sex almost nightly, and through a gap in the rafters, I could hear every thud of flesh against flesh, every sharp inhalation. Usually, I would put on headphones and patiently listen to music until they were done, at which point I would fall into fitful, unrestrained sleep. One night, though, near the end of my visit, the sounds aroused me sexually.

I began to guess at the exact position Richard and his boyfriend were in; from my experiences junior year I knew Richard could be quite innovative. I wanted to masturbate. Doing it there, while listening, felt too shamefully lonely and prurient, but where could I go?

I went to the outhouse. I sat over the cesspool and jacked off. It was a windy night and, just as I came, some of autumn's first-fallen leaves were blown under the door. In the moment of orgasm, in that ecstatic rush of whatever it is in our brains that makes us feel joyful, everything was unspeakably beautiful—those leaves, the outhouse, even the smell.

I returned to bed shaken and stayed awake for hours thinking about my experience. I wondered, are we fooled by our orgasms into loving whatever is before us at the moment? Or is the orgasm a doorway to a transcendent state where we see the true essential beauty of things? Where shit smells delicious?

Somehow I was reminded of my childhood. I had never thought much of it, but when I was very young, there were moments when I was so wracked by the beauty of the moon, so overwhelmed with love for the family dog, so enraptured by the taste of cherry cordials that tears would fall from my eyes. How had I come so far from that joy?

When I got home from Ireland I did some experiments. I would choose an everyday object, say, a spoon, and I would place it before me as I jacked off. I would force myself to concentrate on the spoon at the moment of orgasm.

O the beauty of the silver! The functionality! The subtle bend of the neck just before the dipper! The awesomely distorted reflections!

Later, I opened the *Times* to a photo of some particularly repellent figure in city government. I jacked off and focused on his face at the moment of orgasm. His offenses against the people of New York fell from his back like a heavy load. He was human, forgiven, and beautiful.

As I cleaned up, I glanced at his face again in folding the paper, and felt my old detestation.

The thing that kept me from shooing away these thoughts as the handiwork of serotonin was the similarity they bore to the simple love for things and people I remember from my early youth. I began the arduous process of collecting memories, trying to decipher the process that led to my mind and body's insulation. How, for example, at Tenderwood Academy, was I able to live closely with so many boys, and love many, like more, and tolerate the rest? I didn't remember hating one boy among those hundreds. And now I had to create imaginary doubles for my friends—assemblages of their best qualities that kept my ambivalence from slipping into distaste. At the occasional dinner party to which I dragged myself, I had to turn away from the other guests when they spoke while chewing. As my other senses had been numbed, my sense of smell had become strangely acute, to the point of sometimes triggering a gag response when presented with other people's odors.

Still, it would be a mistake to imply that I wanted to return to some previous mental state, as I was generally happy with my worldview; I wouldn't reverse my insulation any more than I would actually forgive that city official his offenses. What I wanted was solely interior— to distill from the world, for my own enjoyment, the beauty that I cautiously hoped to be its true essence.

On the way up to Montreal, Nori and I stopped for a picnic at what was advertised on a roadside as a "Historical Shaker Village." The visitors' center was closed, though, and only two of the buildings appeared to have been restored. They were locked. We walked past them, through the tall grass buzzing with insects, to the largest building, or shell of a building really, as it had experienced a fire that had left it roofless and without upper floors. Stone walls thirty feet tall surrounded an interior of lawns and thickets at different elevations, separated by the rubble of walls. We climbed down into an inner room, sunken five feet into the ground. The afternoon sun blazed down. Nori lay back on the grass, and I set down our lunch and reclined beside him.

"Do you miss Japan?" I asked after a minute.

"Sometimes," he said. Then he wriggled and took from the billfold in his back pocket a tiny photo. "I miss Hitoshi." Nori handed me a picture of a very handsome silver-haired man.

"Hitoshi?" I asked.

"He is my lover, um, my husband."

I looked more closely. There was deep tenderness in the smile Hitoshi gave the photographer, marred slightly by a cringe at the lens. He wore a black suit, and his hair was oiled back from a narrow forehead, a pointed, intelligent face. He must have been several years older than Nori.

"You took the picture," I said.

"Yes."

"He loves you."

"Yes. He has my heart, you know? I am with him in Japan. I miss him. But I have other boyfriends, so I don't get too sad. He wants that. He knows it is good for me to have other boyfriends, because he cannot be here." Nori's English was that of someone who had studied it for years before speaking it—near-perfect grammar, but a Japanese rhythm forcing sounds together in odd combinations.

"Why doesn't he come to America?" I asked.

"Maybe someday, if I am rich, he will come to America. Now it is very hard because he does not have lots of money."

"He can come and get a job, it's not so difficult, is it?"

"It is very difficult. Hitoshi has HIV. He gets help in Japan with medicine that he cannot get here. When I am an engineer and I make lots of money, then he will come."

I looked back down at Nori's handsome husband, whose tenderness embarrassed me. This was a picture meant only for the photographer, to whom I returned it.

"Does he have other boyfriends, too?"

"Well, I tell him to. That it is good. He tried, but it makes him very sad because it makes him miss me more. So he does not have other boyfriends. He waits for me."

Nori rolled onto his elbow and looked at me. I moved my head under his so it would shield me from the sun. He kissed me. "It is all right that I have a Hitoshi?"

"Of course," I said.

"I thought it is good to tell you, so you should know."

"Yes, of course."

That night, I made love to Nori in a hotel room overlooking Lake Champlain. I touched the length of his lovely, smooth body. The ridges of the hips that, on skinny boys, create graceful lines that frame the flat abdomen then curve toward the cock, are actually the edges of the upper pelvis. They have the beautiful name they deserve: the crests of ilium. I lay my face against Nori's left crest of ilium and kissed his belly. There was only a wisp of hair under his navel; otherwise his belly was bare and flat. A small patch of scrubby pubic hair, then a thin penis, simple and precious.

Sex was more somber than I had imagined before Hitoshi entered the picture. Less flights of fancy, less reckless exploration. Now that Nori loved and was loved monumentally, I felt my meaning had changed, swaying toward serious pleasure in the shadow.

I took Nori's penis into my mouth, put my hands to his sides, thumbs resting along his beautiful crests of ilium. I knew their name from an artists' anatomy book that Mr. Drake had had on his shelf. The models were red-faced athletes of the twenties with strings around their waists and single, fake fig leaves hanging over their genitals. Lines led from their bodies to wonderful words: *sternum, abdomen, internal oblique, crest of ilium.* Somehow these stern-faced men were infinitely more exciting than the nude and lusty seventies sailors of Richard Victor's porno. Maybe it was just that they were citizens of the land of Will Drake, who was sleeping quietly a few feet away, and who, even in sleeping—or, especially in sleeping—radiated beauty.

Nori lay behind me and I let him penetrate me slowly. Breathing hard, I stopped him once to let me catch up, then let him go all the way in, until his body came flush with mine, his chin on my shoulder and his breath in my ear.

What did I want from him? It hadn't occurred to me to wonder this until now, making love to him. The third party, I supposed, must always have an agenda. Only two can blindly explore. Maybe it was better this way. The sex, with its frankness and intensity, was almost certainly better. Maybe I would be able to enjoy Nori more in every sense now that I needn't concern myself with his heart.

Afterward, Nori fell asleep against my shoulder and, unable to sleep while touching another, I gently eased his head onto a pillow and moved away. I realized I had no idea what I wanted from him or from any man. I had no blueprint. I wondered, had I never known a real adult relationship?

I tucked my hands under my legs. If I hadn't been exhausted from travel and sex, this would have been difficult, but now the illogic of sleep started to weave itself easily into my thoughts. Not knowing what I wanted, I allowed myself to be Nori, longing so desperately for his steady and melancholy Hitoshi. Then I allowed myself to be a child again and longed for Mr. Drake.

But, I decided after my many jack-off experiments, the orgasm is so short-lived! If I was to go anywhere with this I had to extend the period of ecstasy.

I took Ecstasy, but even as I explored the wonderland of my apartment feeling surge after surge of goodness, I was aware of an artificial tang to the flavor of the experience, a bitterness that lingers on the tongue after one takes a pill. And the aftermath, two full days of sorrow spent in bed and in movie theaters, as I was too sad to read, was more than I could bear.

I read books on transcendental meditation, and even went to a class at the Open Center, but found the effort to divorce the mind from the body contrary to my goals.

Then I wondered, what if the answer was, again, encoded somewhere in my past?

There was a certain type of activity that I had always been drawn to. I remember being five or six and taking all the clothing off the hangers until there was a massive pile on the closet floor, then crawling under the pile and feeling a perfect stillness and satisfaction in the thick, warm dark. Whenever I went swimming, I never played with the other children, but made my own game of swimming to the deepest point, emptying my lungs and sitting on the ground for as long as I could. (This usually brought the bitter reproach of whatever nanny or lifeguard was present.) I have countless memories of being alone and impulsively wrapping a blanket around my head; or lying on the floor and thrusting my feet deep between box spring and mattress; or coiling whatever rope, towel, or bathrobe belt that came into my grasp around and around my wrists until they were drawn together in a happy bond. And at different points since puberty I had asked lovers to place their hands over my face during sex, or fill my gaping mouth with their fingers, or smother me, gently, with a pillow.

But these were examples of indulging a taste I otherwise tried to ignore. Only with my sleeping arrangements, out of necessity, did I allow myself to create an elaborate system of restraint. Had I stifled the very impulses that would lead me to that state of transcendence?

I decided to completely indulge myself in whatever self-restraining activity I could successfully and safely accomplish alone.

Also, I cautiously answered a few personal ads, inviting gay sadists to come bind me, gag me, etc., but each experience left me feeling unfulfilled and a little sore. Then, in a different section of the personals, I found Belinda:

Strong intelligent mature redhead. Available only for advanced role play and bondage. Experienced. Will work with clients to develop unconventional methods of satisfaction. Serious calls only.

How difficult it is to reconstruct a broken frame of mind, no matter how recently it was broken!

What would I have done with Nori in Montreal if there were no such man as Hitoshi? Holed us up in the inn and held him until it felt like he was mine? Spent money on him? Been bored by him? Climbed Mont-Royal to survey the city and the gray Saint Lawrence beyond and convinced him to hide here with me until his friends stopped calling and NYU forgot his name, then return to live quietly in my loft?

It's impossible to imagine how he would have responded to a radical proposal. As it was, he was uniformly, cheerfully willing. We visited the cathedral where English-speaking Canadian tourists took flash pictures next to NO FLASH PHOTOGRAPHY edicts in French while mournful singing echoed from a hidden side chapel and a grandmother wept, prayed, rocked in her pew. We ate delicious Vietnamese food for lunch, then bad French food for dinner, and Nori insisted he liked it all. I couldn't imagine the hard, resolved side of him that perhaps only Hitoshi saw—that chose to leave Japan; that chose to take on lovers.

Would I have taken him to the sauna? Who knows? But I did.

That night as we walked the halls, our bare feet making kissing noises against the tiles, I imagined how we looked together. To these diminutive Montrealers, we were tall as lampposts. In the mist we could have appeared as different versions of the same stooped, hollow-chested but handsome man, one the color of tea with milk, the other the color of, well, milk. Or as one man followed by his ghost into the swirling mist of the steam room. The man sits and adjusts his towel as his ghost does the same, then the illusion is broken as the man leans in to share some quiet English words with his ghost, who is really his pale friend. Then they both respond to other men's greetings in French. Were they Torontonians? No, Americans more likely.

Nori and I had discovered earlier in the day that our French was about equal, and although this was a few degrees worse than Nori's English, we *merci*'ed our way through the day, enjoying the equal footing, bypassing the momentary resentment, the speed bump a Montreal waitress goes over before she lists the specials in English. And now we talked with the three other residents of the steam room in our halting French about New York and about Montreal.

"Gay men in Montreal," said Nori, "seem to be friendlier than gay men in New York."

"You're not speaking of us specifically, are you?" said the hairy-chested man with stubby, nervous fingers. "We're friendly because we're hitting on you."

We all introduced ourselves. These three were friends—two accountants who were talking up Nori while the third, a musician named Jean, had taken a shine to me.

"Montrealers and French Canadians in general," Jean said, taking up the subject from his friend, "are friendly out of pure tackiness. New Yorkers can afford to be unfriendly."

"That's silly," I said.

"The beauty of New York and New Yorkers is an unfriendly beauty," Jean said with wavering authority, causing me to consider that patently non-American trait—the willingness to try out theories in casual conversation. To most Americans it seems intellectual, pretentious, un-Christian; I loved it. "The beauty is in the street noise and in the way buildings lean against each other. But," he said, taking on a dramatic sadness, "there is also a problem with the New York gays, and American gays in general . . . they're becoming straight. It's like a science fiction movie, really."

"Oh, hush, Jean," said one of Nori's accountants. "Always talking." The man turned to Nori and me. "We just came here to relax before a party. Would you like to come? It is our friend's party. There will be lots of boys."

Nori and I looked to each other. "Well . . ." I said hesitantly.

Jean suddenly broke into English: "You were hoping for some action here?"

I nodded.

"It's too early. Midnight on Saturday? Everyone's still at the bars. It'll be hours before this place gets going. Come to the party with us."

It was a couple of hours and several drinks later, as Jean and I stood in a dim corner of a crowded living room, that I was able to return to the subject he had raised in the sauna. "Jean, you said that gay men in the U.S. are becoming straight. What did you mean?"

Now he spoke in English. "Gay men in the U.S.," he said, "they talk out of two sides of their heads. They say, 'You straight people must respect us—we want rights—we want to live by our own rules,' then they say, 'May we please live by your rules? May we please get married and have children and live in Ohio? May we join the army? We don't want to be outlaws anymore. We want to be just like you. We want to have a day at Disney World.' And in this I mean Torontonians, too, because they want to be Americans. Long before Quebec secedes from Canada, Toronto will secede and join the U.S.

"Are you like this, Rand? Do you want to marry some man and have little gay babies?"

"No, definitely not," I said. "The impossibility of procreation has always been one of my favorite aspects of gay sex."

"Yes," said Jean, and raised his wavering glass in salute. "And do you talk out of both sides of your head? Or do you talk out of your ass, as you should? As I do?"

We were both drunk—I for the first time in years. Usually I am satisfied by a little cognac or some scotch, but tonight I had drunk untold amounts of god-knows-what, as the host merrily wandered his party with pitcher after pitcher of fruity concoctions.

Jean continued. "Maybe we Quebecois are old-fashioned, but you see we still have our gay village where we laugh at everything. It's always been the same neighborhood; the straights are not interested in coming here. It's not like New York where the straights chase the gays from this to that part of town until they all give up and, what is the word . . . integrate?"

"Hm," I said, "there goes Nori." A man had led him by the hand into a side room.

"How old do you think I am, Rand? Guess."

"Thirty-five."

"Thank you, angel. Forty-eight. Surprised? Yes, I'm very well-preserved. You are, maybe, twenty-nine?"

He had guessed it exactly.

"When I was your age, my lover and I, with six of our friends, had a bridge club. We met the first and third Wednesday of every month. There were penalties for missing a game, penalties for conversation at the table, big penalties for cheating, although that was very rare. With the fines we would buy sherry and cheese for the next game. No gambling, of course. We were like little old ladies. Naturally, it was funny, but when we were on the phone planning the event, then together playing the game, we were very serious about it. It was like we were practicing. But, for what? Were we paying tribute to the little old ladies or making war on them? All those men but one—Andy, he is here, maybe you met him?—all those men but me and Andy are dead now. My lover, too, in 1990. It is sad, but it happens. Little old ladies die. But I tell you this, my friends did not die for the right to go to Disney World. They didn't die for anything. Their deaths were completely, utterly pointless. That's the only way to be at peace with it. Accept it as complete pointlessness. That's what I'm saying about the Americans—they're trying to change their destiny, to have a point. The destiny of gays is pointlessness, just as the destiny of straights is ugliness. Don't try to jump the track. It is better to be pointless and laugh. That is our job, I think. Like they say in blues songs, laughing just to keep from crying."

During this Jean had wandered, but now he seemed to remember to whom he was speaking. "So you will promise me, handsome Rand, that you and Nori will not go to Provincetown and get married."

"Out of the question," I said. "Besides, I think Nori is already married. He has a lover in Japan he called his husband."

"Ah, so you are the other woman, so to speak." Jean ran his fingers along the underside of mine, lifting them, and sang the Nina Simone song: "'The other woman finds time to manicure her nails. / The other woman is perfect where her rival fails . . .' Do you like the party?"

I put my hands to his hips, then slid them under his shirt and up his back to feel the ribs under his shoulder blades. "Yes, it's quite a party." I looked over his shoulder and past the trees. Men in twos and threes were kissing, fondling, shedding clothing.

"Where is Nori?" asked Jean.

"He was lured into a bedroom earlier," I said.

"That's a pity. I'm sure he's nothing but a pile of bones now. We're a bunch of cannibals, you know."

"And old ladies," I added.

"Yes, old lady cannibals." He kissed me, then pulled back and, in a wicked-witch voice, said, "Delicious."

I woke up sore and naked, having cast off the blankets in the night. I went to the bathroom and vomited sour fruit juice, alcohol, acid—last night's party gone rancid. I wiped the lip of the toilet bowl with a starchy hotel towel and washed my face. When I returned to the bedroom I saw that Nori was sleeping on the floor. Sometime during the night he had made a bed by folding the extra comforter into a pallet under the window, and now he lay stiffly on his back, wrapped in a sheet, with lines of trouble in his brow. Or was he squinting to keep out the sun? I stepped over him and closed the curtains, then knelt down.

"Nori, why are you sleeping on the floor?" I whispered.

He frowned and turned away from me.

"Come back to bed." I put my hand to his shoulder, but he jerked away. I was startled. "Nori, what is it? Why are you down here?"

He leveled an angry, bloodshot gaze at me. "You don't remember?"

My thoughts struggled through the mire of the previous night. Had we had sex? I barely remembered returning to the hotel room. We had had sex in separate groups at the party. Was that what upset him? No, now I remembered holding each other, chuckling conspiratorially in the elevator, and then we had collapsed onto the bed . . . right?

"No," I said. "I don't remember. What happened?"

"You hit me in the night."

"What?"

"We went to sleep and then I woke up. You were hitting me."

"Oh, God," I said, squeezing my eyes shut. "Nori, I apologize."

"I didn't understand. I thought you were dreaming so I said your name to wake you up. But you kept hitting. You were awake. You were angry."

"No, Nori. I . . . it has nothing to do with you. I have trouble sleeping. Or . . . trouble while I'm asleep. It's kind of like sleepwalking."

He looked at me with fear and disbelief.

"Nori, please forgive me. I would never hurt you intentionally. I think you're fantastic. It's just me. I've always been like this."

I put my hand on his shoulder and he softened, just slightly.

"I thought maybe you were asleep," he conceded. "I thought you were mad that I had sex at the party, or you were jealous about Hitoshi, and maybe since you were asleep it . . . came out. I was scared."

"But I wasn't angry! It would have happened whether or not you were here. You see, I'm used to sleeping restrained. It's very complicated."

He didn't understand. "How do you know you weren't angry if you can't remember?"

For a moment I was speechless. "Because I'm not angry now. I have no reason to be angry with you, Nori, I like you very much."

"Maybe you are not angry when you are awake," he replied, sitting up, "because you don't have a reason. But when you are dreaming, things happen without reason. When you're dreaming, you're angry."

"Nori, I'm so sorry." I put my arms around him and drew him up to stand. Then the room rocked and he supported me. We were both naked, and there was something vaguely delightful about the sickness and his body next to mine. "If it's true and I'm angry in my sleep," I said, "it's not at you. I promise. It started years and years ago."

His gaze shifted and he turned to sit on the corner of the bed. He probably thought I was insane, and in that, he was certainly not the first.

I stretched out onto the bed, my mind limping to catch up to where my body had taken me: How were we so intimate here? How had I come to beg and how had he become so stony?

There was nothing more to say. I thumbed the flesh of his buttock with my big toe. He lay down, but with his head at the opposite end of the bed from mine. I propped my head against his ankle to gaze up the foreshortened and shifting landscape of his body until it rolled, dizzyingly, away, and he said, "It's late. We've got to drive."

And so, with my heart broken, just a little, I drove. We got into the city late, and I woke Nori to direct me to his building.

"Did you have a good time?" I asked dejectedly when we arrived.

"Yes, I did," he said. His brightness had returned. "Thank you."

"Again, I'm really sorry. . . ."

"Please, it's OK. Don't worry. I had a good time."

"Well, I hope I can see you again. Maybe . . . we could get together with Frank sometime. The three of us."

The silence that followed allowed me to consider what this offer, which had spontaneously leaped from my mouth, meant. The best hope for Nori and me now was to relate on that level—friends.

"Frank is your good friend?" asked Nori.

"Yes. We're very close," I responded.

I wondered if he was about to tell me about their relationship. If so, I would stop him. At this point, it was so unnecessary. But he started in a different vein: "Rand, the apartment under yours—no one lives there."

"Right."

"But it is yours."

"Yes, why do you ask?"

"Maybe I shouldn't say so, but Frank is not a very good friend to you."

"What do you mean?"

"Do you let Frank use that apartment?"

"No," I said. With a wave of sickness, I realized what Nori was telling me.

"But Frank has a key," he said.

"Yes."

"The night we met, he took me there. We had sex there. I'm sorry. He didn't tell me it was your place. He pretended it was his. He said we had to be very quiet, not to wake up the neighbors. But it was *you* he didn't want to wake up." He fiddled nervously with his keys, which he had already taken out. "Maybe I shouldn't have said. But, you know, maybe I should."

"I've dealt with Frank's problems before," I said. "It's good you told me."

Nori reached for his backpack in the backseat and set it in his lap.

"Thank you, Rand. I had fun in Montreal."

"And maybe," I said, "we should just leave it at that?"

"Maybe." He leaned over, kissed me, and left.

Shaking my head, I pulled back into traffic. Something made me laugh. As I wondered what it was, I remembered Jean's theory about gay men, that it is our job to laugh.

Exhausted from the trip, I went home and got in bed, but then lay awake for hours. I imagined going downstairs and finding that Frank had moved in—that I opened the door and it was his apartment in Queens, only now it was here. I finally fell asleep as the sun was rising and slept late into the morning. On the way out to return the rental car I peeked into the apartment and, of course, everything was as I had left it.

Later, while unpacking my bag, I noticed on the answering machine's blinking display that I had eleven messages. I didn't even know that it could hold that many! I pressed play, and what unrolled was as comical as it was grotesque:

Hey Rand, it's Frank. Haven't talked to you for a couple days. Doing the old check-up. Give me a ring.

Rand, it's Frank, give me a call.

Frank again. Call me.

Look, Rand, give me a call. Is everything all right? Don't make me come over there. Bye.

On and on it went, like a bad radio play. The pitch of his voice increased with tension, like a violin string whose key is being turned and turned.

Rand, it's Frank. Did you go out of town? Call me.

I had forgotten to tell Frank that I was leaving town. Had he come to check on me and found the apartment empty? Wouldn't he have left a note?

Then it struck me: he knew I was going to call Nori, and that Nori might end up here, and that Nori might tell me. The cowardly whine of Frank's voice, which was still being played by the machine, nauseated me. Years ago I had removed the possibility of a friend betraying me. I never asked anything of anyone. How had this happened? I felt sick and profoundly unsafe.

I would have all the locks changed. I would do it today. But first, I had to calm myself.

I went to my closet and found the racquetball on the top shelf. In the kitchen I wrapped the ball with cellophane and pushed it into place in my mouth. A length of cellophane around the back of my head secured the ball in place. Then I went back to the closet and pushed the clothing to either side, creating a snug space for myself. I stepped in and bound my ankles and knees with old shirts. I drew the doors carefully closed, put my hands above the rod, and coiled a light cotton shirt around my wrists, then attempted to tie it. It was clumsy, but it would do. Slowly, I relaxed the muscles of my legs until I was hanging by my wrists, my body supported on either side by soft cushions of clothing. After a few moments I was sure that the knot at my wrists would not give. A warm pain began to spread from my armpits down my back, and I found a little stillness.

To put it simply, I sought simplicity, which is to say, a complete form of complexity, unified and elusive. I had realized years earlier that the layout of my apartment was the layout of my mind, and that it was cluttered. I had gotten rid of everything I didn't need—which was most of what I had owned—by giving it away or putting it downstairs. I felt calmed. There was room for sunlight to flood in.

I didn't waste words or time. I ordered in, and I usually ate alone. All of this aided in my search for something that I couldn't name, something inside me. I believed I'd recognize it when I found it.

I think this search began with something I misheard my father say over the phone, many years before. Late in the series of arguments we had had over my refusal to go to Dartmouth, my father decided to make it personal. He accused me of sending my mother into a nervous breakdown with my decision.

"Rand," he said, "how can you be so coal-hearted?"

I had been cleaning my fingernails as I argued, but now I put down the nail file. I was struck by that image: instead of a shiny, red heart pumping away in my chest, I had a dull lump of black coal, like one a bad child got in his Christmas stocking. For the first and only time, my father gave me pause.

Of course it was a mistake. My father had used the hackneyed description "cold-hearted," and I came up with a boring defense he would understand: it was my life, my decision, my money, etc.

After the call I toyed with the idea, imagining myself a bad boy's Christmas stocking. Who, then, if not my parents, those very accusers, dropped into my empty body that lump of coal that would be my heart (denying, as we must, the existence of Santa)? And if I had a coal heart, how much pressure exerted equally from all sides would it take to squeeze it into a diamond, the world's hardest and most beautiful rock?

Now, years later, I wondered something similar: if I gathered all the evidence of life's beauty (which, I'd found, I could only begin to do if I am surrounded by emptiness), and gave it a good squeeze, embossing my heart with all those memories and sensations, was there a moment (or eternity) of transcendence, when I touched the beautiful truth of life? When I was comforted? When I held up to my face and was illuminated by that tiny jewel, the hope of whose existence compelled us—all of us—*not* to hang ourselves with extension cords from light fixtures?

A crack, light, the knot at my wrists gave, and I was out onto the floor.

"Oh my God!" screamed Frank. He knelt over me and cradled my head. "Rand," he wailed, "are you OK? How long have you been in there? I'm so sorry!"

I blinked my eyes, trying to focus. Then I saw Frank's frantic expression and laughter began to bubble up from my chest, but my mouth was still gagged so it must have sounded like I was suffocating.

"Shit! Fuck!" muttered Frank, as he tore at the cellophane, scratching my cheek. He plucked out the racquetball, sending saliva flying, and I burst into a deep, cleansing laughter.

"Are you OK? How long have you been in there?"

"As long as I can remember," I howled as I pushed him away and rose to my feet. I laughed and laughed at the fear on his face. Finally I settled down and told him I had only been in there an hour. He was quiet and bewildered, and I almost pitied him. "Let's get takeout," I said.

After Frank left I called the locksmith.

The more salt one adds to water, the greater a submerged body's buoyancy in that water. And the greater pressure experienced by a body forcibly submerged.

Facedown, I wore an oxygen mask attached to a pliable plastic hose, which was taped loosely to the tiled wall. This was an apparatus of my own invention created from supplies found on Canal Street, and based on the design of a snorkel.

The water was tepid, and I could taste the saltiness. Belinda flattened black industrial-strength garbage bags against my back and the backs of my legs. She gently lowered bubble-wrapped twenty-five-pound weights between my shoulder blades, into the dip of my lower back, onto the backs of my thighs, into the cradle of my loosely bound ankles. She placed a Ziploc bag of ball bearings onto the back of my neck.

She was done, and I was quiet.

It was somewhat bothersome that my hands were unrestrained. Belinda had insisted that I keep the index finger and thumb of both hands pressed together in OK signs. If the hands relaxed and the fingers parted, she'd assume I'd lost consciousness and immediately end the experiment. I had assured her I'd be fine, but she had insisted, and, of course, I appreciated her concern.

It usually started when I ceased to think of what I saw as darkness but, rather, a shade of neutrality.

I felt a wonderful displacement: which way was I facing? In which direction was my head pointing? The mental map of my surroundings became a maze; I lost the layout of my apartment. Which way was which? I let it go.

The bubbling lava-lamp paisleys came and I lost myself in them for a while, then they divided and revealed a great open expanse. I entered it and, softly, so as not to break the stillness, said, "Yes?"

Diary of a Quack

Wayne Koestenbaum

My Name Is Siegfried Kracauer

Everything I do is legal. My accountability rating is high.

I see patients for a form of "talk therapy" that includes touching. Licensed, I charge $80 an hour. Rents are cheap in Variety Springs.

I had a brief acting career—commercials, soaps, summer stock. I lack a middle initial. I'm five foot five. That's small, for a masseur. It's difficult for me to get leverage.

Current favorites: Aeneas, Killer 69. Patients, protégés, friends.

My mother used to say, "You have no sense of humor!"

What stern, authoritarian handwriting I have! Like a religious studies scholar. Which religion?

I'm a Marxist, Sexually Speaking

I'm single. Sexually, I discombobulate inherited structures.

I'll undergo this self-analysis for five months.

Momentarily my suicidal tendencies and my hypomania have abated.

Don't Jab My Balls with Your Umbrella

My treatment room: purple velvet tacked to its walls. A small electric waterfall, always in motion: white noise machine. Massage table. Two Eames chairs.

My curly red hair: attractive feature. Not dyed. I don't look like a freak. My patients trust me.

Just now I pressed my ear to the floor to hear the shouting and smacking (spanking sessions) in my downstairs neighbor's apartment: Benjamin Levi, sadist.

Once, he told me, "Don't jab my balls with your umbrella."

I wasn't holding an umbrella.

Smack Smack

During sessions, I must sometimes assume a mime's silence, to allow the patient's verbiage to fill the room.

Smack, smack, again resounds: Benjamin Levi's hand on some navvy's buttocks.

Here's My All-Purpose Eulogy

Max, drug dealer in the house next door, was found dead—OD—in his kitchen. Body left there to rot for a half week before discovery. Light-skinned black guy, messianic gaze, nimble on his dirty-sandaled feet: I never forget a dead man, even if we weren't close. Minor acquaintances who die—their disappearances prove most wounding. Where's the pockmarked woman with Carmen Miranda flip-flops— the one I'd see daily, holding her ratty pooch, in the park? Cancer? Dementia?

For Dinner: Chicken Legs

Variety Springs, New York: small town with a big-city density. High percentage of gays. Loose morals. History of countenanced prostitution.

Absence of police action. High percentage of Jews. One orthodox shul. Not my scene. Many of my patients are Jews: fine with me.

Aeneas owns a used-CD and -record shop, Miracle Music.

Or chicken thighs?

Future Topics

my psychiatric training (keep it sketchy)

sadness of being an only child

my libertarian philosophy

my illustrious namesake, Siegfried Kracauer

I Jumble Chakras

I stepped into Miracle Music, empty of customers. Aeneas did my astrological chart. My "Sun Q" is in Sagittarius, "by ecliptic," Aeneas says, which explains my cheerfulness. My S is "in Scorpio H," which means, says Aeneas, that I am secretive, reclusive, and easily hurt by imagined or actual rebuffs.

Aeneas is thirty years old, 163 pounds, from Lisbon. Some days his voice usurps mine.

"Have you visited Karl Marx's birthplace in Trier, the oldest town in Germany?" Aeneas asked me, after doing my chart.

Massaging his feet in our last session, I noticed incipient hammertoe, right foot.

His brother has cerebral palsy. Aeneas feels guilty for pursuing an independent existence in Variety Springs, thousands of miles from Baton Rouge, where his brother and their widowed mother live together. After Aeneas's father died, the family, seeking opportunity and amnesia, emigrated from Lisbon to Louisiana. Aeneas's mother loves a tornado sidetracked and dissipated before it can lay waste to the city, as the inept Cassandras of the weather channel had foretold.

O Aeneas, your *horror vacui* is only exceeded by my own.

Hair patch above Aeneas's butt: sweat marks the spot.

Aeneas told me that his father's spirit, postmortem, overtook the son's body and ruled it for weeks. A turquoise glow outlined the boy's torso. Eventually the aura faded and the family left Lisbon.

My lot: *unlikeability.* Quoth Benjamin Levi, downstairs. (Why trust a sadist? Because he has freckled shoulders: visible in tank tops.)

Aeneas's penis: not overlarge. Often erect. My bush is red; his, black.

I Am Pink

Death of Jed, owner of Tunnel Traffic Books, in Variety Springs. I never deeply cared for him, though he could forecast my reading tastes. Jed vanishes: in response, go to the pharmacy for a refill. Adelle, druggist, who looks like Sylvia Miles in *Midnight Cowboy,* says, "Siegfried, take these pills with food." She forgives in me the retrograde dreamer who chooses what Soviets call "inner exile" over the pioneer rigors of nation-building.

I am communist at heart. I am stilted in verbal expression, nasally clogged. I am a peony somewhere between white and red.

Two o'clock appointment with Stavros. A newish patient. Aeneas's longtime lover, friend from childhood. So far it's been mostly talk. Today we might proceed to lightweight erotic healing. His nonverbal connection skills (eye contact) are excellent, but his speech is disorganized and he shows avolitional tendencies—unwillingness to open the treatment-room door by himself, unwillingness to call the dentist to make an appointment to clean his decaying teeth. I will tell Stavros, when the session begins, as I tell each of my clients, "Be aware of what you want from me, and why you want it, and from whom in the past you have wanted the same."

A Characteristic of Stavros's Speech Is Over-elaborateness

In today's session, Stavros said, "My childhood friend's father, Mr. Petrucci, drove ninety miles an hour on the highway through Baton Rouge, Interstate 10. His speed—and his hairy forearms, oyster blue shirt rolled above the elbows—didn't bless me, but ushered me into unpleasant vertigo. I was frightened by Mr. Petrucci's speed and hirsuteness, where Interstate 10 fails to mollify Interstate 12, or fails to conquer it absolutely, like Catherine the Great. I prayed that he would take the Prairieville exit, but he kept speeding on Interstate 10, and my vertigo took the alarming, exciting form of a wish to relieve myself. He eventually arrived in Gross Tete, where, at a taverna, while Mr. Petrucci and his son Lonny ate gyros, I found my first glory hole."

A Heavy Concentration of Healers

Variety Springs is stained (but not fatally) by former industry; is capable of utopia; is one hour from the Atlantic; is a pocket of economic idealism in a nation headed toward ruin. Here, home attendants make as much money as lawyers. Not a litigious community. Zen centers, Korean restaurants, Kosher butcher, leftist newspaper, a tradition of grassroots philanthropy and low-level activism. History of accidental electrocutions (live wires). Variety Springs, where amorality reigns. Our mayor sticks up for transgendered rights.

My income comes from private practice and guest gigs at healing institutes. I do not seek a permanent appointment at Variety Springs Community College. Nor has their search committee approached me.

Wayne Koestenbaum

Family History
Father: Jacob Kracauer, psychoanalyst. Mother: Bettina Kracauer, psychoanalyst. Sliding scales. I was born in 1964. Only child. Mother had a hysterectomy an unspecified time after my birth. Mother's maiden name: Gold. The one independent gesture I ever made was to leave the Upper West Side, fortress of Kracauer and Gold, and emigrate to Variety Springs.

To discuss: why Tom Cruise's penis has come up in several of my patients' sessions this week.

At Least I'm Not a Victim (Today) of Hypomanic Flight of Ideas
Last year Benjamin Levi's lover slashed his wrists in the shower and died. Benjamin's freckled shoulders, light (clipped) hair on upper arms and chest, preference for tank tops, long penis (I've seen it at Baby Snooks Baths).

I need nonstop touch. My father, Jacob Kracauer, hates to be touched. When we hug, he raises one of his shoulders, like a raptor in flight. I inherited none of Bettina Kracauer (née Gold)'s empathy. Presence of a nuclear power plant in Westbrook, fifty miles away, gives me nightmares. Bettina would love me to be politically active. I'll work (slowly) toward the political. Maybe I'll become an antinuclear activist. Bettina wasn't certain she wanted a child (me); Jacob forced the issue, she said. I can't imagine Jacob forcing.

Killer 69 is my most dangerous client. Dangerous to himself, dangerous to others. Travels with bodyguard. But I don't let him bring the bodyguard into the sessions. I'm trying to talk him out of his paranoid insistence on being accompanied by Bernard, fat bruiser. I'm trying to steer Killer 69's erotic fixation on me into therapeutically useful directions. I limit hands-on erotic work. He trades used vintage sports cars for a living.

Killer 69 Is Making Progress
A stranger whose arm he slugged on the street said to him, "That hurt my arm, when you slugged it." I told Killer 69 to repeat that statement aloud three times. To integrate Killer 69 into polite society *without compromising his radicalism* is our therapy's purpose.

Sheet, Draped over Killer 69's Buttocks
Killer 69 had a surprising island of insight this afternoon: as I reached my hands beneath the sheet, he said, "Abandon me." For Killer 69, the combination of abandonment and intrusion is aphrodisiac, and is his closest approximation to what pedestrian minds call "home."

Our Town Bears an Indeterminate, Pregnant Relation to Vaudevillian Pleasures
I write these reflections not to advance the cause of arts, letters, or science, but to remain alive (against contrary, seductive, entropic tide of self-annihilation).

DJ's Ass
Killer 69 told me in his session this morning: "I tricked for the first time with DJ." I pretended impassivity. I didn't tell Killer 69 that I'd had a similar encounter with DJ, a year ago, and that DJ had also told me, "You are exactly my type." I'd wanted him to specify *why I was his type.* He never did.

Sometimes I feel an eviscerating nostalgia for redheads who are cuter versions of me.

Killer 69's Ball-Sac
I am neither a quack nor a malcontent. Notice that my syntax is growing vortex-happy. I am qualified to treat post-traumatic stress

Wayne Koestenbaum

disorder, anxiety disorders, disruptive behavior disorders, communication disorders, mood disorders, depression disorders, and sexual and identity disorders. I will never send these meditations to the Centers for Disease Control or to the Orion Massage Academy in New Fayetteville. My eagerness to hold Killer 69's testicles gives me an adrenaline rush so powerful I'm nearly incapable of completing this sentence, or the next.

How Did Siegfried Kracauer Die?

One week without medication! I'm going cold turkey off my "tranquilizers." Don't be so inhibited. My parents wanted me to be charming. The purpose of writing is to stave off suicide; my sentences must remain cheerful, factual. To buck up, I should list my good deeds. I'm not a rapist. I give $200 per year to the Variety Springs Jewish Community Center. I don't call the police when I hear Benjamin Levi, downstairs, spanking one of his navvies. Does he rent them, or find them on the streets? How exactly did Pasolini die? Killer 69 suffers from Oppositional Defiant Disorder.

Sophie Tucker Played Valhalla Palace

Vaudeville took root in Variety Springs because no other town in the region (New Fayetteville, Sayreville, Standish, Valhalla Port, Freehold) would tolerate or house it. Only Variety Springs was spineless enough to accept vaudeville's imbecility. Variety Springs had no identity until vaudeville bestowed one on it. The major vaudeville house in town, Valhalla Palace, gave employment to a wide spectrum of social types, and girded the loins of Variety Springs as a boomtown. If Variety Springs ever had a boom, Valhalla Palace was its center. Sophie Tucker played Valhalla Palace. Fanny Brice played Valhalla Palace and haunted the nearby mineral baths. Valhalla Palace, with its pleasing Egyptian-Teutonic exterior, still exists, on Devereux Street, across from the statue of our town's founder, Alexey Devereux. For generations, admission to Valhalla Palace remained a nickel. Now Valhalla Palace is a convention center, but no conventions have seen fit to use the facilities. Valhalla Palace once showed first-run features; then it showed kung fu pictures, and porn; now Valhalla Palace hosts the occasional politician, revival meeting, or craft fair, but mostly remains dormant, waiting for a new function.

Happy Twentieth Anniversary of First Coitus

Twenty years ago, today: how glad I was to enter a vagina, finally—to experience its fortress, after years of propaganda and mystification. It's difficult to write on graph paper. Sounds of spanking downstairs. Last night I put my ear to the floor and heard Benjamin Levi babbling (on the phone?) about terrorism. Either he is planning some terrorist action, or he is having a phobic reaction to recent U.S. history. Benjamin Levi ignores my desirability. On Devereux Street I saw him wearing Birkenstocks and white socks. He has *not once* made an appointment with me for a massage. I began taking my medicine again last night, unfortunately, so I am once again *under the control of Dr. Pellegrino.* We'll call it a tranquilizer: a white pill, with a seam down its center, like an incised gut. Chalky taste. The pill gives me a sound sleep and no dreams. My parents don't approve of medications. They are old-fashioned talk therapists.

The Suicide of Isaac Gold

I was silent for an entire year as a child. During my silence, I plotted strategies for changing my personality and my curly red hair, resembling

Grandfather Isaac Gold's, whose death was a frequent dinner-table conversation subject—how to live as survivor of a vaudevillian suicide. I never knew exactly what vaudeville was—that mysterious art at which Isaac Gold had excelled, the art whose obsolescence provoked his suicide. Behind a bathroom door. Push open the door, try to push it open, can't push it open, because Isaac Gold's body, heavy with vaudeville's disappearance, lies behind it. His wife, Ludmilla Gold, née Kantrowitz, took the death in stride. If I end up killing myself, that's OK. What voice, raised to a certain pitch, doesn't approach suicide?

Marlon and Liz

As a youngster I met Marlon Brando. He had begun to get fat. He was sitting in a folding chair in the Poconos—a luxurious resort, where psychotherapists, intellectuals, and actors commingled. Across from him sat Elizabeth Taylor, though this fact was never proved to my satisfaction. They were rehearsing *The Glass Menagerie*—running through a scene, not embarrassed to be overheard. Brando's face seemed contorted in throes of thespian ecstasy. Soon afterward I saw on TV their live-broadcast version of *Glass Menagerie* (not preserved on tape, it vanished—a great lost performance, Brando playing Tom, Liz playing Laura, though both were too old for the roles); few sources mention their *Glass Menagerie,* which I had the good fortune to see in rehearsal in the Poconos, though Brando might have been rehearsing not with Liz herself but with Liz's stand-in, who looked like Annette Funicello.

Vaudeville Is Not Dead

Behaving like a lunatic won't undo Isaac Gold's suicide. His upper and lower lip weren't aligned, which gave him a shy demeanor, despite his bossiness. "Vaudeville is like Latin," he'd say, "a highly constructed language." "Do you mean that vaudeville is a dead language?" I'd respond. "Nonsense," he'd insist; "vaudeville is eternal." "Just like Latin," I'd say. We could go on like that for hours—useless stichomythia. He wanted me to revive vaudeville, and even though I said that "psychotherapy was today's vaudeville" (Bettina agreed), I disappointed him by not "going into" vaudeville, even if going into vaudeville was impossible because it was dead. Shortly before his 1984 suicide, the knowledge of vaudeville's death finally came home to him via a TV broadcast—archival footage of Sophie Tucker's funeral, 1966. He'd attended the ceremony, as had my mother, but he hadn't realized in 1966 that Sophie Tucker's passing was more than the death of the last of the Red Hot Mamas; it was the death of vaudeville, concentrated in one fat body's demise. For the eighteen years separating Sophie Tucker's decease and Isaac Gold's, he never watched one of her movies, even when *Thoroughbreds Don't Cry or Gay Love* showed up on the late show. He said, more than once, "It's tragic, that Sophie Tucker never made it as a major film star." "But Isaac," I'd say, "isn't vaudeville superior to cinema?" "Of course," he'd say, "but Sophie Tucker deserved film stardom." Sophie Tucker and my grandfather might have been lovers, though I have no proof; as Bettina put it, "Father kept vaudeville matters under wraps." Indeed, vaudeville specifics were not dinner conversation. "Keep vaudeville vague" was Isaac Gold's motto, and it became Bettina's, as well; vaudeville grandeur was a given, but my grandfather's significance—his place within vaudeville's cosmopolitan yet claustrophobic swirl—remains uncharted, like a vision of the Indies in 1489.

The Ego in Bits

"Do you know," Bettina Kracauer once said to me, "my revered

Melanie Klein died only six years before your grandfather's beloved Sophie Tucker? I'm not sure that Melanie Klein and Sophie Tucker met. Though Melanie Klein probably knew of Sophie Tucker's existence, it's unlikely that Sophie Tucker knew of Melanie Klein, though Klein's work on the psychoanalytic play technique might have had a trickle-down effect on Tucker's rendition of—or her self-perception while rendering—'You've Got to Make It Legal Mr. Siegel.' When Melanie Klein writes, in 1946, 'The various ways of splitting the ego and internal objects result in the feeling that the ego is in bits,' was she not mourning Sophie Tucker's underpaid labor at the German Village, on Broadway and Fortieth, in 1906, for a mere $15 a week?"

The "Tommy" Patch
Aeneas's pubic hair forms a flat, high, dark patch, kinky yet clean, organized yet extensive. It matches, in concentration, his face, and has the severity of *Last Year in Marienbad,* a Delphine Seyrig coldness and gravity. Aeneas's patch is black and smug; it ignores small people and strangers. Aeneas's patch: I call it "Tommy." I first saw "Tommy" in my treatment room. I prefer "Tommy"—that pubic patch of matte superiority—to Aeneas's penis.

In Baton Rouge and in Lisbon, the "Tommy" patch had admirers who could not match its immobility, its function as fence. *Don't trample me!* said his patch, in Baton Rouge, when it grew to its full breadth, but also in Lisbon, where it first germinated (he left Lisbon at age twelve, when his father died), and where it borrowed its airs, its bravura, its identity as shield of Achilles. In Lisbon the pubic-hair patch learned its barricade behavior, though in Baton Rouge it grew to full kingship; then, in Variety Springs, it could look back in complacent awe on its early accomplishments, and it could confidently predict another decade of sovereignty—for Aeneas is only thirty, and his patch will, until forty, be triumphant, at least in my biased eyes. I may be superior to Aeneas in intellect, but Aeneas's patch equalizes us by humbling or humiliating me, when I have the luxury to contemplate it, in the semidarkness of my treatment room. His "Tommy" patch can smite me when it pleases.

More on the "Tommy" Patch

It counterpoints his gaze. Aeneas's eyes see you, and his "Tommy" patch sees you. Also his mouth (third item) regards you. Mouth and eyes provide ironic supplement to "Tommy" patch. Aeneas can smile or smirk because he knows his "Tommy" patch immunizes him against your nitpicking. His patch, flat, never vibrates, rises, or assaults. When I see it, I am intrinsically without the tools to measure it. Observing it, I have no choice but to surrender, to live under its Book-of-Hours canopy, its Scrovegni-chapel tent. (I could never be this explicit in Dr. Pellegrino's presence.) When I first saw Aeneas's "Tommy" patch I knew I'd found the one object worthy of perpetual attention; I'd found the one zone that would never be kind to me, that would never have my interests at heart.

In Baton Rouge, Aeneas ate crab boil (so he told me) with his mother and his guy pals from school. After spilling crab boil on his white jeans, Aeneas dipped his restaurant napkin in ice water and wiped the stain off his pants at the crotch. The moistened stain, urine-like, gave voice to the confident yet speechless "Tommy" patch beneath, a "Tommy" patch that a girl or two had touched, before it became my property.

The Professor's Spanking Act

These notes are not escapist exercises, but calisthenics for the political work that will flog Variety Springs "within an inch of its life," as Bettina Kracauer used to say, describing Isaac Gold's "spanking" act, one of his vaudeville specialties, in which he, playing "The Professor," would spank a dilatory pupil, a girl in a tutu, who compulsively broke into hybrid jazz/ballet moves whenever Isaac ("The Professor") turned his back on the class and wrote mathematical formulae on the chalkboard. The culmination of the "spanking" act occurred when Isaac commanded his sidekick—victim of a *danseuse*—Tourette's, a coprolalia of the toe shoe—to stretch herself on Isaac's knee so he could theatrically wallop her, while a cymbal and tympani, in the orchestra pit, crashed and thumped in time with the Professor's hand strokes. At the end of the act, when Isaac once again turned his back, the dancer would reengage in her jazz/ballet spoof, this time mimicking the Professor. Her dancing replicated Isaac's characteristic patented waddle; though not corpulent, he shifted his weight from foot to foot as he walked, parodying an obese man's rocking perambulation. Had Isaac Gold once been fat? Or was he paying inverted homage to Sophie Tucker, his beau ideal, and also praising his late mother, Lotte Gold, stern and wide?

I come from a long line of sodomites—the Kracauers and the Golds. My erotic practices pale in comparison to their squalid behavior in clerestories and peanut galleries of vanished vaudeville houses.

My Slowness Stems from Sadism

Today my speech is slow. New patient: Hans, seventy years old, overweight, moles on his back. A Frankfurt art dealer, in town to sample healing waters. I am disgusted by no variety of erotic experience. Hans says he will fly to Bogotá tomorrow to visit his daughter, formerly a kidnapping victim, now a banker. As I massaged his back, grotesque but forgivable, Hans told me that his daughter never recovered; she "managed" her feelings, but she never fully "worked them through." I asked if Hans planned to work through *his* feelings. "No, just manage them," said Hans, cheerfully. His stubborn lack of insight appalls me— "a true child of Frankfurt," he proudly calls himself.

Bettina Kracauer's Andalusian Nouba

"Did I ever tell you about my friendship with Paul Bowles?" Bettina said, one night in the Poconos. We were, at table, our usual fivesome— Bettina and Jacob Kracauer, me, and Isaac and Ludmilla Gold.

Isaac said, "Bettina, I don't know if your son is old enough to hear the Paul Bowles story."

"Nonsense," said Ludmilla, "he's nearly a grown man. Look at him."

They all looked at me.

"Do I seem like a grown man?" I asked the assembled four.

"I'm not sure," said Bettina.

"It's definitely a matter of opinion," said Jacob.

"Maturity, like Latin," said Isaac Gold, "is complicated."

"Do you want to hear my Paul Bowles story?" said Bettina.

"We haven't figured out whether our son is mature enough to hear it," said Jacob.

"Let's ask him," said Ludmilla.

"I'll do it," said Bettina. "As his mother, I'm the logical candidate."

Everyone fell silent.

Bettina turned to me: "How mature do you feel, Siegfried?"

"I think the Paul Bowles story is too important to tell at dinner table, in a public restaurant," said Jacob.

The next morning, at breakfast, same table, same fivesome, I heard the simple story, not obscene. Bettina, prior to marriage, had gone to

Tangier for a psychotherapy conference; Paul Bowles had been keynote speaker. "His talk," Bettina said, "was anti-Freud, anti-psyche. Afterward, I accepted Paul's invitation to return to his apartment, where I heard, for the first time, a recording of Abdelkrim Rais's Moroccan-Andalusian orchestra playing an Andalusian *nouba*. As you know, Siegfried, there are different *noubas* for different times of the day. Whether Paul played me a morning, afternoon, or evening *nouba*, I don't remember, though I recall that Paul impressed on me the significance of the listener's state of mind, and how that same mood could be simulated afterward without rehearing the *nouba*. Once heard, the *nouba* became a permanent part of your physiology. If only I could sing for you, Siegfried, right here, in the Poconos, that Andalusian *nouba* I first heard in Paul's presence!"

Jacob Kracauer's Upper Lip Has an Opinion about the Creation Myth
My father's upper lip and lower lip have divergent theories about the origin of the species. His upper lip is full (Rita Hayworth) and venal (Mercedes McCambridge or Agnes Moorehead in the radio-play version of *Sorry, Wrong Number*). Are my father's eyes an adult raccoon's or a baby rabbit's? The many Jacob Kracauers coalesce into one scapegoated Green Hornet. Any sentence that describes him is like the long hallway in Cocteau's *Beauty and the Beast* (Bettina's favorite film). Down that paranoid corridor, the frightened beauty (played by Josette Day) wanders, confronted by animate candelabra, each intimating her failure to return home and care for her ailing father. This sentence, here, is the disobedient daughter's drugged refusal to return to the paternal cottage of penury and illness. Writing these words, I remain, ensorcelled and selfish, in the beast's moneyed domain. Too metaphorical!

The Painted Boy

Edmund White

I *have* written a few decent things recently. My yarn about the Wild West was good: solid. But no, not much else. Most of it blather. Now critics are saying I never knew what I was doing. That the good things—*The Red Badge,* "The Open Boat," "The Bride Comes to Yellow Sky," "The Blue Hotel"—were just happy hits. Damn them! I took six weeks to write "The Blue Hotel." I had such a strong feeling that the Swede felt fated to die, that he was shaking in fear in anticipation of his death that very day, though in reality he had nothing or no one to fear, and in the end he was the one who provoked the violence. Even in Cora's newspaper columns I could always put in a good word or two—something fresh and queer. Most writing is self-dictating: yard goods. I was the only one of my generation to add a beat here and steal a note there. Rubato, it's called in music; Huneker told me that.

I'd written forty pages of my boy-whore book, Garland read them over and then with all his Wisconsin gravity in that steel-cutting voice he said, "These are the best pages you've ever written and if you don't tear them up, every last word, you'll never have a career." He handed the pages back to me and asked, "No copies? This is the one and only version?"

"This is the one and only," I said.

"Then you must cast it into that fire," he said, for we were sitting in a luxurious hotel lobby on Mercer Street waiting for a friend to descend and a little fire was burning just a yard away from our boots.

I couldn't help feeling that Hamlin *envied* me my pages. He'd never written anything so raw and new, so *modern,* and urban. No, he has his rolling periods and his yarns about his father playing the defeated pioneer farmer in the Dakotas, but he couldn't have written my pages. No, Hamlin with his lips so white they looked as if he'd kissed a snowman, all the whiter because wreathed by his wispy pale brown beard and mustaches. His eyes sparkled with flint chips and he seemed so sure of himself. Of course, I was writing about an abomination though Elliott was just a kid, not a mildewed chump like Wilde— though you can find plenty of folks in England who knew him and would still defend him. We all hear them champion Wilde now, though no one stepped forward during the trial. Yeats was the only person who made sense when he talked about Wilde. Wilde's trial and the publication of *The Red Badge* occurred in the same year, 1895. But he represented an old Europe, vicious and stinking of putrefaction, whereas the *Badge* is a solid thing, trim and spare.

I threw my forty pages in the fire. It made me sick. A pearl worth more than all my tribe. And all through the lunch with its oysters and baron of beef I kept thinking the oysters were salty from my tears and the blood gathering in the silver serving dish—I thought that blood was my blood. I could barely eat and I couldn't follow the conversation with all its New York knowingness, reporter's shoptalk. Of course Hamlin hated my painted boy; he was even then scribbling his *Boy Life on the Prairie* in all its banal decency. Not that I'd ever dreamed of defending my little Elliott, but I knew his story was more poignant than scabrous.

God, I'm sounding absurd with my blood and tears and my resentment of old Ham. Hamlin was the one who gave me the fifteen dollars I'd needed to redeem the second half of *The Badge* from the typist. He was the one who had told me I was doing great things and got *Maggie* to William Dean Howells, and then Howells launched my career. Despite all the labels flying around in those days—I was supposed to be "an impressionist" and then there was Garland's "veritism" and Howells's "realism"—despite the commitment to the gritty truth, my truth, the truth about little Elliott, was too much for them to take on board. Hamlin had been roundly criticized for saying in one of his books that a conductor had stared at a female passenger "like a sex-maniac." That was enough to win him universal censure in America. No untoward deeds—just the word "sex-maniac," and next thing you know he was being compared to the sulfurous Zola himself. Oh, he's considered the devil's own disciple because his heroes sweat and do not wear socks and eat cold huckleberry pie. . . .

The only one who could cope with my Elliott was that mad, heavy-drinking, fast-talking, know-everything Jim Huneker. Jim would drink seventeen beers in an evening out and feel nothing. He'd teach piano to an all-Negro class at the conservatory off Seventeenth Street and then retire to his boardinghouse where he was in love with a married woman named Josephine.

Her husband, a Polish merchant, never touched her, so Huneker said. He'd just stare enraptured at her V-shaped corsage and succumb to a red-faced paroxysm of secret onanism. Huneker seduced the unhappy lady just by touching her, the first time a man had touched those perfect breasts. But he was a busy one—he once gave a dinner for all three of his ex-wives. He had a long, straight Roman nose he was so proud of that he liked to speak in profile, which could be disconcerting.

His very black crinkly hair sat on his white brow like a bad wig, but he made me pull on it once to prove to myself it was real.

Huneker was such a womanizer! I could write about him in a memoir, couldn't I? As a music critic he'd encouraged aspiring female singers to prejudice his reviews in their favor through what he called "horizontal methods." Huneker also had a quasiscientific interest in inversion. Usually he'd scorn it. He condemned *Leaves of Grass* as the "Bible of the third sex." Initially he was hostile to the eccentric, effeminate pianist Vladimir de Pachmann; he feared that Pachmann's silly shenanigans onstage might damage the reputation of serious musicians before the usual audience of American philistines. Pachmann would stop a concert to say to a woman in the front row, "Madam, you're beating your fan in two-thirds time and I'm playing in seven-eighths." Or, for no good reason, he'd interrupt his playing to pull his hoard of diamonds out of his pocket and sift them from one hand to another. Because of these hijinx Huneker called him "the Chopinzee," and they traded insults at Luchow's when they first met and poured steins of beer over each other's heads. But a year later they mellowed and Pachmann came to dinner and played for Huneker for five hours, till three in the morning.

Tchaikovsky also troubled Huneker for his indifference toward women. Huneker was particularly disturbed by the story that, seconds after Tchaikovsky met Saint-Saëns, the composer of *Samson and Delilah,* they were both in women's clothes dancing the tarantella. When Tchaikovsky died, Huneker said he was "the most interesting if not the greatest composer of his day"; Huneker also defended Wilde and said the English were silly to abhor him after they'd courted him for years.

I was with Huneker one wintry day walking up the Bowery. We'd just had lunch at the old Mouquin's down at Fulton Market and we were strolling along in one of those brisk winds that drive ice needles through your face even in the palisaded fastness of Manhattan. In spite of our sole meunière and red velvet banquette we were suffering from the elements. Sometimes weeks go by in New York and I scarcely notice if it's hot or cold, fair or cloudy—and then a stinky-hot day floats the reek of the tenements upstream or the gods decide to dump four feet of snow on the nation's busiest metropolis. And then the snow turns it into a creaking New England village.

The weak sunlight was filtering down through the rail slats of the overhead elevated tracks, and every few minutes another train rumbled slowly past above our heads like a heavy hand on the keyboard. Beside us, horses wearing blinkers were pulling carts down the center of our street between the El tracks. Their shaggy forms and pluming breath were scarcely visible through the blizzard of sideways snow. The dingy white awnings on every building were bulging above the sidewalks under the weight of snow. The poor prostitutes in their scanty clothes were tapping with their nails on the windowpanes trying to attract a bit of custom. One sad girl, all ribs and scrawny neck, huddled in a doorway and threw open her coat to show me her frozen wares. Huneker with his three plump wives and horizontal sopranos certainly couldn't bother even to sniff at these skinny desperadoes through his long Roman nose. We walked and walked until we decided we had had enough of the wind's icy tattooing of our faces. We were about to step into the Everett House on Fourth Avenue and Seventeenth Street to warm up.

Standing in the doorway was a slight youth with a thin face and dark violet eyes set close together and nearly crossed. He couldn't have been more than fifteen, but he already had circles under his eyes. He smiled and revealed small, bad teeth, each sculpted by decay into something individual. He stepped toward us and naturally we thought he was begging but then I saw his face was painted—carmined lips and kohled eyes (the dark circles I'd noticed were just mascara smudged by the snow).

The boy stumbled, and I caught his cold little hand in my bony paw. His eyes swam and floated up into his head; he fainted. Now I'm as frail as he was, but back then I was fit. I carried him into the Everett House.

He weighed so little that I wonder if he filled out his jacket and trousers with newspapers to keep warm or to appear less skinny. There was the faint smell of a cheap woman's perfume about him and, because of the way I was holding him, the stink of dirty, oily hair that had absorbed cigarette smoke the night before.

I was ashamed of myself for feeling embarrassed about carrying this queer little boy tart into a hotel of well-fed, loud-talking men. All of them were illuminated by Mister Edison's new hundred-bulb chandelier. The doorman took a step toward us, so agitated that the gold fringe of his epaulets was all atremble; he held up a white glove. Idiotically I said, "Don't worry, he's with me," and good old Huneker, who's a familiar face there, said, "Good God, man, the boy's fainted and we're going to get some hot soup down him. That's what he needs, hot soup. Order us some hot soup!" Huneker went on insisting on the soup as if it answered all questions about propriety.

There was a table free, but the headwaiter glanced at the manager —but he couldn't stop us. We headed right for the table, which was near Siberia close to the swinging kitchen doors. I placed my frail burden in a chair and, just to bluff my way out of being intimidated, I snapped my fingers and ordered some hot soup and a cup of tea. The headwaiter played with his huge menus like a fan dancer before he finally acquiesced and extended them to us. Slowly the businessmen at the other tables gave up gawking and returned to their conversations. Maybe that is why I was so sympathetic to Elliott, as I soon learned was his name. I'd had to carry him through a sea of disapproval.

Now that I looked at his painted face I feared I might vomit. Huneker was studying me and smiling almost satirically, as if he knew my discomfort might make a good story that very evening, when Josephine, she of the V-shaped corsage, held court. "Stephen pretends to be so worldly," I imagined he'd soon be saying, "but he is the son of a Methodist minister and a temperance worker mother and he *did* grow up in darkest New Jersey, and though he's fraternized with hordes of daughters of joy he'd never seen a little Ganymede butt-boy buggaree before and poor Stephen—you should've seen his face, he nearly vomited just as the headwaiter was confiding, 'The joint won't be served till five.'"

It sickened Elliott even to look at it, but I ordered him a plate of white meat of chicken, no skin and no sauce, as well as a dish of mashed potatoes, no butter. He was so weak I had to feed him myself.

"Are you ill, Elliott?" I asked him.

"Yes, sir."

"You don't need to 'sir' me. I'm Stevie."

Elliott's eyes swam up through milky seas of incomprehension—this man with the jaunty hat and scuffed shoes and big brown overcoat wanted to be called Stevie! Elliott whispered the name as if trying out a blasphemy.

"Tell me, Elliott—what's wrong with you? Do you think you have consumption?"

Elliott blinked, "Pardon?"

"Phthisis? Tuberculosis?"

More blinking.

Huneker butted in and said, "Good God, boy, bad lungs? Are you a lunger?"

Elliott (in a small voice): "I don't think so, sir."

Me: "Fever in the afternoon? Persistent cough? Sudden weight loss? Blood in the sputum?"

I laughed. "You can see I know all the symptoms. If you are in the incipient stage, you must live mostly outdoors, no matter what the season, eat at least five times a day, drink milk but not from tubercular cows—"

Huneker: "Are you mad? The boy is a beggar so of course he lives outdoors but not in nature but in this filthy metropolis! And he'd be lucky to eat a single meal a day.

Tell me, boy—"

Me: "His name is Elliott."

Huneker: "Far too grand a name for a street arab, I'd say. Tell me, Elliott, when did you eat last?"

Elliott: "Yesterday I had a cup of coffee and a biscuit."

Huneker (scorning him): "That a nice, generous *man* gave you, upon arising?"

Elliott (simply): "Yes."

After Huneker rushed off babbling about his usual cultural schedule, all Huysmans and Wagner, a silence settled over the boy and me. We were between shifts of waiters and diners and the windows were already dark though it was only 5:15 on a cold, rainy Thursday night in November. We breathed deep. The warmth of the hotel's luxurious heating had finally reached Elliott. He relaxed and let his coat fall open. He was wearing a girl's silk shirt, dirty pink ruffles under his blue-hued whiskerless chin.

He smiled and closed his coat again. We chitchatted about one thing and another and I told him a few new jokes and he laughed. He even tried to tell me a joke but it was pathetic, a little kid's joke. It was obvious that he'd been too weak even to talk but now, with some food in his stomach, he became voluble. He told me he hadn't spoken in his normal boy's voice for weeks and weeks. "Usually we're all shrieking and hissing like whores."

Me: "And saying what?"

He: "If you want to say someone is *like that* you say, at least *we* say, 'she'—and of course we really mean '*he*'—'she's *un peu* Marjorie.'"

I laughed so hard he didn't know whether to be pleased or offended, since laughing at someone's joke turned him into a performer, a figure of fun, and Elliott didn't see himself that way.

He said the perverse youngsters he knew called themselves Nancy Boys or Mary Anns. Automatically I pulled out my little black reporter's notebook and moved the elastic to one side and began to take notes. The boys would accost men at a big rowdy saloon on the Bowery they called Paresis Hall and ask, in shrill feminine voices, "Would you like a nice man, my love? I can be rough or I can be bitch. Want a *rollantino* up your bottom? Is that what you are, a brownie queen? Want me to brown you? Or do you want to be the man? Ooh la la, she thinks she's a man—well, she could die with the secret!"

As for his health, I divined from all the symptoms he was describing that he had syphilis and the next day I arranged for him to see a specialist and follow a cure (I had to borrow the money—fifty dollars, a minor fortune). I had to convince him that he needed to take care or he'd be dead by thirty. Though that threat frightened him no more than it did me. I expected to be dead by thirty or thirty-two—maybe that was why I was so fearless in battle. He seemed as weary of life as I was; we both imagined we'd been alive for a century already and we laughed over it.

I said, "Isn't it strange? How grown-ups are always talking about how life speeds by but it doesn't? In fact it just *lumbers* along so slowly." I realized that by referring to grown-ups I was turning myself into a big kid for his benefit.

He said, "Maybe time seems so slow to you because you look so young and people go on and on treating you in the same way."

I was astounded by this curiously mature observation—and chagrined by the first hint of flirtation. He was flirting with me.

I told him that I'd lost five brothers and sisters before I'd been born, which left me just eight. That made Elliott laugh, which he did behind his hand, as if he were ashamed of his smile.

"I'm the youngest of four, all brothers," he said. "My mama died when I was three—she and the baby both. We lived on a farm fifty miles beyond Utica. When I was just a little thing my Daddy started using me like I was a girl."

"He did?" I asked. I didn't want my startled question to scare him off his story. "Tell me more."

"And then my brothers—well, two of the three—joined in, especially when they'd all been drinking, jumping me not in front of each other but secretly in the barn after their chores or in the room I shared with my next older brother, the one who let me be. My daddy had been the county amateur boxing champion thirty years ago and he was still real rough. Almost anything could make him mad."

"Give me an example," I said.

"Well, if the bread box warn't closed proper and the outer slice had turned hard—don't you know, he'd start kicking furniture around. We didn't have two sticks stuck together because the two oldest boys took after him, and they'd flash out and swear something powerful and start kicking and throwing things. The only dishes we kept after Mama died were the tin ones and they were badly dented. Things sorta held together when Mama was around and we sat down to meals, at least to dinner at noon, and she made us boys go to church with her though Daddy would never go. Then when she died, we stopped seeing other folks except at school, but us kids missed two days out of three. Daddy could write enough to sign his name and saw he said no rhyme nor reason in book-larning for a field hand. I liked school and if I coulda went more regular I might've made a scholar, but Daddy liked us home, close to him, specially me since I fed the chickens and milked all four cows and tried to keep the house straight and a soup on the boil but Daddy always found fault with me, in particklar late at night when he'd been drinking and then he'd strap my bottom and use me like a girl and some days my ass, begging your pardon, hurt so much I couldn't sit still at school without crying. The teacher, Miss Stephens, thought something might be wrong, 'cause I had a black eye, sometime, or a split lip, and once she pushed my sleeve back and saw the burns where Daddy had played with me."

By this point we were walking up Broadway toward Thirtieth Street where I lived with five other male friends in a chaotic but amusing bear's den of bohemian camaraderie. I hoped none of them would see me with the painted boy. The rain was beginning to freeze and the pavement was treacherous. I steered Elliott into a hat shop and bought him a newspaper boy's cap, which he held in his hands and looked at so long that I had to order him to put it on.

The more Elliott talked the sadder I felt. His voice, which had at first been either embarrassed or hushed or suddenly strident with a whore's hard shriek, now had wandered back into something as flat as a farmer's fields. He was eager to tell me everything, and that I was taking notes, far from making him self-conscious, pleased him. He counted for something and his story as well. I sensed that he'd guessed his young life might make a good story but he hadn't told it yet. There was nothing rehearsed about his tale, but if he hesitated now he didn't pause from fear of shocking me but only because till now he'd never turned so many details into a plot. He had to convert all those separate instances and events into habits ("My Daddy *would* get drunk and beat me"). He had to supply motives ("He *never* had no way of holding his anger in") and paradoxes ("I guess I loved him, yeah, I guess I did and still do but I don't rightly know why").

He slipped on the ice at one point and he grabbed my arm but after another block I realized he was still clinging to me and walking as a woman would beside her man and I shook him off. As I did it I made a point of saying something especially friendly to him; I wanted him to recognize I was his friend but not his man. I felt he was a wonderful new source of information about the city and its lower depths, but I drew back with a powerful instinct toward health away from his frail, diseased frame. I couldn't rid myself of the idea that he wasn't just another boy but somehow a she-male, a member of the third sex, and that he'd never pitch a ball in the open field or with a lazy wave hail a friend fishing on the other shore. The whole sweet insouciance of a natural boy's mindless summer was irrevocably lost to him.

About the Contributors

Bruce Benderson is currently best known for his seventh book, a memoir called *The Romanian: Story of an Obsession* (2006). In 2004, Benderson won France's Prix de Flore for the translated version of this work. His monograph on the filmmaker James Bidgood was published in 1999, and his 1997 essay on urban culture, "Toward the New Degeneracy," was chosen by *Rolling Stone* magazine as one of the 100 most remarkable creative works of that year. "Mouth of the River" is taken from the forthcoming novel *Pacific Agony,* to be published in 2007 by Clear Cut Press in the United States, and also in France.

Mack Friedman is author of the novel *Setting the Lawn on Fire* (2005), winner of the first Edmund White Award for Debut Fiction from the Publishing Triangle. His first book, *Strapped for Cash: A History of American Hustler Culture* (2003), was a finalist for the Lambda Literary Award in GLBT Studies.

Robert Glück has written nine books of poetry and fiction. His latest—a book of stories—was entitled *Denny Smith* (2004). Other publications include the novels *Jack the Modernist* (1985) and *Margery Kempe* (1994), another book of stories, *Elements of a Coffee Service* (1983), and *Reader* (1989), a book of poems and short prose. Along with Camille Roy, Mary Burger, and Gail Scott, Glück edits *Narrativity,* a Web site on narrative theory. An anthology based on the Web site, *Biting the Error: Writers on Narrative,* was published in 2005. "Bisexual Pussy Boy" is taken from a forthcoming novel, *About Ed.*

Andrew Holleran is author of the novels *Dancer from the Dance* (1978), *Nights in Aruba* (1983), *The Beauty of Men* (1996), and *Grief* (2006). He has also published a short story collection, *In September, the Light Changes* (1999), and a book of essays, *Ground Zero* (1988).

Tennessee Jones has published a short story collection, *Deliver Me from Nowhere* (2005). He is also author of the long-running zine *Teenage Death Songs.*

Kevin Killian has written two novels, *Shy* (1989) and *Arctic Summer* (1997); a book of memoirs, *Bedrooms Have Windows* (1990); two books of stories, *Little Men* (1996) and *I Cry Like a Baby* (2001); as well as a collection of poems, *Argento Series* (2001). With Lewis Ellingham, he has written a biography of the poet Jack Spicer, *Poet Be Like God: Jack Spicer and the San Francisco Renaissance* (1998). Killian's latest book is *Selected Amazon Reviews* (2006). "Greensleeves" was first published in *Roughed Up: More Tales of Gay Men, Sex, and Power* (Alyson Books, 2003), edited by Simon Sheppard and M. Christian.

Wayne Koestenbaum has published one novel, *Moira Orfei in Aigues-Mortes* (2004), five books of poetry, and five books of nonfiction prose. His next book, *Hotel Theory,* will be published in 2007.

Shaun Levin's most recent book is a collection of stories, *A Year of Two Summers* (2005). He has also published a novella, *Seven Sweet Things* (2003), and is editor of *Chroma: A Queer Literary Journal.* "The Big Fry Up at the Crazy Horse Café" first appeared in *The Del Sol Review* (Winter 2006).

Michael Lowenthal is author of the novels *The Same Embrace* (1998), *Avoidance* (2002), and *Charity Girl* (2007). The recipient of fellowships from the Bread Loaf and Wesleyan writers' conferences, the Massachusetts Cultural Council, and the Hawthornden International Retreat for Writers, Lowenthal teaches creative writing at Boston College and in the low-residency MFA program at Lesley University. He also serves on the executive board of PEN New England. He can be reached via his Web site: www.michaellowenthal.com. "Marge" was first published in *Post Road*, no. 14 (Spring 2007).

Alistair McCartney has published one novel, *The End of the World Book* (2007).

David McConnell wrote the novel *The Firebrat* (2003). "Rivals" is taken from a forthcoming novel, *The Beads.*

James McCourt is author of three novels—*Mawrdew Czgowchwz* (1975), *Time Remaining* (1993), and *Delancey's Way* (2000)—and two story collections, *Kaye Wayfaring in "Avenged"* (1984) and *Wayfaring at Waverly in Silver Lake* (2002). His most recent publication is *Queer Street: The Rise and Fall of an American Culture, 1947–1985* (2004). McCourt has contributed to *The Yale Review, The New Yorker,* and *The Paris Review.* "Thermopylae" is taken from a forthcoming novel, *Now Voyagers,* due in late 2007 from Turtle Point Press.

Vestal McIntyre's first book is the story collection *You Are Not the One* (2005), published in the United States and the UK.

Ethan Mordden's fiction includes the "Buddies" cycle on life and love in gay Manhattan and a novel about Maria Callas, *The Venice Adriana* (1998). He has published both fiction and criticism in *The New Yorker,* and is currently researching a biography of Florenz Ziegfeld Jr.

Dale Peck has published three novels, *Martin and John* (1993), *The Law of Enclosures* (1996), and *Now It's Time to Say Goodbye* (1998); a nonfiction book about his father, *What We Lost* (2003); a collection of book reviews, *Hatchet Jobs* (2005); and a novel for children, *The Drift House: The First Voyage* (2005). "The Piers" is taken from his novel *The Garden of Lost and Found,* published by Carroll and Graf in 2007.

Patrick Ryan's first book was *Send Me* (2006). He is a recipient of a 2006 National Endowment for the Arts Grant for Fiction, and his young adult novel *Saints of Augustine* will come out in 2007.

John Weir is author of the novels *The Irreversible Decline of Eddie Socket* (1989) and *What I Did Wrong* (2006). "Neorealism at the Infiniplex" first appeared in the literary journal *Gulf Coast* (Winter/Spring 2006).

Edmund White has written some twenty books, including the autobiographical novels *A Boy's Own Story* (1982), *The Beautiful Room Is Empty* (1988), and *The Farewell Symphony* (1997). He won the National Book Critics' Circle Award for his 1993 biography of Jean Genet. White's most recent books are the novel *Fanny: A Fiction* (2003) and a memoir, *My Lives* (2006). "The Painted Boy" is excerpted from his novel *Hotel de Dream*, published in 2007 by Bloomsbury (UK) and Ecco/HarperCollins (USA).

About the Editor

Richard Canning has published *Gay Fiction Speaks: Conversations with Gay Novelists* (2001) and *Hear Us Out: Conversations with Gay Novelists* (2004), which won the 2005 Editors' Choice Lambda Literary Award. He is preparing an anthology of AIDS writing, *Vital Signs,* for publication by Carroll & Graf, and is coediting—with Dale Peck—a series of reissues of AIDS literary texts. He is also writing a short life of Oscar Wilde, as well as a long, critical life of the English novelist Ronald Firbank. Based in London, England, he teaches at the University of Sheffield, where he may be contacted.